Better Broken

Justine Iarann

Copyright © 2015 by Denise Harrison

Better Broken

All rights reserved. This book or any portion thereof may not be reproduced or used in any manner whatsoever without the express written permission of the author except for the use of brief quotations in a book review.

This book is a work of fiction. Any similarities to real people, living or dead, is purely coincidental. All characters and events in this work are figments of the author's imagination.

Cover Photography copyright © 2015 Magnus Hargis
Author may be contacted at: justineisallwrite@gmail.com

ISBN-13: 978-1514898833

ISBN-10: 1514898837

Published via
CreateSpace Independent Publishing Platform
An Amazon Company

Dedicated to all my family and friends who listened to me talk about my new imaginary friends for hours. They deserve credit for their long suffering endurance.

Yet, this dedication is also for those who are unfailingly dedicated to the safety and freedom of our great nation. Not just the soldiers, but their families as well, who bear the scars inside even if they look whole

Part One

Chapter One

At twenty three, Christine Everett, or Chrissie to her friends, starts work at a hospital in Virginia, completing clinical experience in order to finish up her Masters in Physical Therapy. Taller than average, with a curvy set of hips and chaotic strawberry blonde hair, she is hard to miss walking the halls.

On her first day at work she meets Suzie Ashford in the cafeteria, striking up a conversation about a book they are both reading. Less than a week later, they are best of friends, partners in crime, spending most shared days off getting into mischief all over the Eastern seaboard.

However, most of Chrissie's time outside of work is spent with Smoke, an unusually intelligent, uncommonly aware, big, black horse. Truth be told, she couldn't be happier, personally or professionally; everything in her life is just enough.

All sorts of folks, from elderly to athletes, find her open hearted and charming, including her current patient, Norma.

Better Broken

The older woman is talking excitedly about the cruise she and her husband are going on this coming summer, a celebration of their 30 years of marriage. Chrissie is trying very hard to follow the dear lady's non-stop chatter while stretching and flexing healing tissue around Norma's recent knee replacement.

"I don't see a ring on you, sweetheart." Norma interjects.

"No ma'am," Chrissie replies with a dazzling smile that lights up her aquamarine blue eyes. "But I am hoping one day to meet a Mr. Right like you have".

"Oh honey, I have no doubt, but men like my Russell are hard to come by. Don't lose hope while you are waiting."

"Norma, until that day, my horse will be plenty of company." Chrissie says with a wink.

During a lull between appointments Chrissie looks up from the bandage she is rewinding as another therapist walks in behind a new client. The man is in a wheelchair with a very obviously missing leg, unusual compared to the normal clientele. With his slightly fading tan, a dark high and tight haircut, and a nearly visible personal space bubble, he stands out even more from the typical baby boomer and athletic injury folks. Immediately, despite her brain screaming at her, Chrissie's hands itch to soothe the tension from the muscles he has obviously spent years acquiring.

"Pretty, isn't he?" Suzie quips, plopping all five foot four pixie of herself unceremoniously on to the table beside Chrissie.

A quick yes is all Chrissie can manage around her brain that has gone to mush under the influence of lust.

"Are we still on for drinks tonight?" she asks, hurrying to change the subject.

"Oh, you mean where I drink, and you keep me out of trouble, Saint Chrissie?"

The old barb has long since lost any sting so Chrissie rolls

Justine Iarann

her eyes and sticks her tongue out at her friend, who laughs. At that very moment she feels someone looking at her, turning slightly to catch the object of her vivid imagination watching them. A brief chink appears in the armor of his self-discipline when she meets his rich brown eyes and he barely lifts the corner of his mouth, expressing reluctant amusement at her childish behavior. Never one to waste a smile, Chrissie returns his tiny grin with a megawatt stunner. The door slams on his emotions, a curtain coming down between them as he turns his wheelchair toward his therapist who is setting up a weight rack.

Trying not to take it personally, she turns to Suzie, deciding a time and place for the nights adventure. It's going to be a mad rush to go to the barn and see her horse, then get presentable for the sort of club Suzie is planning on hunting at. It's not her scene, but Suzie never fails to show up at Chrissie's horse events if work doesn't get in the way. The least she can do is play designated driver on their rare night off together. It's just what you do for your best friend.

After Suzie leaves Chrissie pulls together an ice wrap and tens unit for her next client, an older gentlemen who reminds her very much of her grandfather, a cantankerous cattle rancher who recently passed away. She smiles wistfully at the memory of his callused hands demonstrating how to hold the reins of her first horse, showing her love the best way he knew how.

The back of her neck prickles with awareness, and she barely turns her head to catch the young man looking at her again. This time, his gaze is softer, the tiny grin he offers apologetic. She returns his regard with a nod of acknowledgement, waving goodbye as he rolls toward the door. He breaks eye contact, and her eyes are drawn to the sweat gathered on the back of his neck, where the urge to lick it away becomes overwhelming. The craving is quickly distracted by a burn scar that disappears under the collar of his shirt. Her fingers clench reflexively against the impulse to explore what she is guessing are war wounds. She shakes off the feeling and turns to her work.

The next day, at the same quiet break in the afternoon, in rolls the man she now knows is James Fletcher. After a nearly sleepless night, remembering the deep brown eyes gazing at her so intently, she had yielded to the temptation to peek at the scheduling roster.

This time, she is walking across the room to get some resistance bands for the client looking to regain mobility after a broken ankle has left her unstable, and unable to enjoy her own horses. While Chrissie is trying to stay focused it's hard not to feel him watching her stride by. Her cheeks pinken slightly, and she looks at him through her lashes to discover his grin is a bit more masculine, like he knows exactly what she imagines about his hands when she notices them rolling over the wheels of his chair. They are the hands of a working man, but with a limber quality she usually only sees in horsemen or musicians. Oh God, like her imagination needs more ammunition to work with? She shakes her head slightly to clear her thoughts, barely catching herself from tripping over a stability board left out on the floor.

Her patient is quiet, lost in her worries, even when Chrissie tries to bring up the horses they share a love for. They go through the motions, strengthening and limbering a joint nearly fused, and clearly painful. At the end, Chrissie settles at her feet, massaging the uninjured limb while the other sits wrapped in ice.

Working his way through a set of leg presses, James draws her eyes like a magnet. His face is impassive with concentration, and he uses his whole body, as though he can will his missing limb back in to being. It is amputated from just above the knee, and while he is wearing baggy sweats, it doesn't take much to imagine the rippling muscles beneath them.

Another stare redirects her attention- it's her client, looking intently at Chrissie's hands where they have stopped moving on her foot. As she begins to stammer an apology for being so unprofessional the woman pointedly looks toward James.

"If you are going to make a mistake that one would surely be worth making." the woman says, a glint of humor in her eyes.

Chrissie blushes, the heat of it burning her cheeks, then goes back to the business of healing.

By the time Chrissie punches the clock for lunch James is long gone. It leaves her unaccountably disappointed but she gathers up her bag to head to the atrium, hoping to find her favorite spot unoccupied. Humming a catchy top twenty tune under her breath, she hurries down the hall. In a few minutes she is tucked in the secluded corner, legs dangling over the arm of the chair, her back pressed to the wall. Daffodils are barely breaking through the soil outside the window and the sun feels glorious against her skin. Letting her eyes flutter closed, she heaves a deep breath, grateful for a moment's peace, particularly after her late night with Suzie.

Slightly elevated breathing breaks in to her reverie, coming from around the side of a huge potted tree. Before she can sit up, James Fletcher, the very source of her consternation, appears.

"Pardon me, ma'am," he says, the barest bourbon warm hint of the South in his voice "But you seem to have dropped your book."

With that he holds out the dog eared and well-worn paperback that had seen her through her awkward teenage years, and remains a true friend when she needs the escape. It has a fanciful white horse being ridden by a red haired girl on

Better Broken

its cover, certainly not a great first impression to give a guy you have a thing for.

"Thank you, I'm a bit scattered today, and I'd hate to lose an old friend." Cheeks flushed, she quickly sits upright to reach for the book.

Looking him fully in the eyes for the first time, a warm feeling like melting chocolate starts low in her belly. The rich brown holds a wealth of personality, but looking deeper shows a vulnerability that tugs at her heart. He rolls forward to meet her, setting the book in her hand, his index finger barely brushing the pulse at her wrist. That simple contact makes her skin go from warm to uncomfortably hot in an instant. As he withdraws a smile teases at the corners of his mouth, which she hopes is a mirror of her own regret. Then he reaches down beside his leg, lifting up a much abused novel of his own.

"I understand. Books have been my traveling companions over many miles, stateside and abroad. Unfriendly places felt a bit closer to home with them in my hand."

Then he smiles, truly smiles, and she is fascinated to watch it migrate from his full lips all the way to his depthless eyes. Chrissie isn't sure what threatens to overwhelm her more- that she wants to give him reason to smile that way more often, or that she has found a kindred spirit.

"Would you like to stay awhile? I usually don't share my quiet place with anyone, and there is room for one more. We can hang out with our old friends," she says, raising her book for emphasis. "Or we can make new friends."

He hesitates then frowns, his thick brows lowering. "I'd love to stay Christine, it's a lot nicer here, but I have to get back up to meet the prosthetics people."

Taken aback that he knows her name, her eyebrows climb toward her hairline. He smiles, tapping his left chest, and she looks down at her ID tag, laughing lightly.

"Part of the uniform, I never even notice it's there. Which I imagine you know all about as a soldier." His eyes widen, surprised at her insight. "You wear it on you even without the uniform." she says to smooth things over. "Since you are out of your military issued attire you are without your name tag, so I am at a disadvantage here."

He recovers in an instant, extending his hand to her. "Sergeant James Fletcher, ma'am. Army."

"Glad to meet you, Sgt. Fletcher, Chrissie Everett. Army brat." She sets her open palm in his, and the instant they touch a palpable shock shivers through her.

Turning her hand upward, he runs his thumb over her knuckles, seemingly without thought. She swallows hard around a spike of desire, eyelashes fluttering at his calloused touch. The instant he notices, he abruptly releases her, eyes darting sideways to avoid her gaze.

Disarming things with a lopsided smile, she brings her hand slowly back toward her body to make her regret clear. The awkward behavior that might be insulting to another doesn't faze her in the least. Instead, she wonders why he thinks it isn't okay to touch her. Having worked with her fair share of damaged horses she can see the hope, the need, but also the fearful doubt that colors it.

"Well, Sgt. Fletcher, maybe I'll see you up there. If not, I'm here nearly the same time every day I'm at work. Hopefully, we will get together with our old friends soon."

"I look forward to it Chrissie. And call me James- only my superiors call me Sgt. Fletcher." he says, a half-smile warming his eyes.

With that he wheels away, leaving Chrissie feeling like the sunshine won't keep her half as warm as James Fletcher could.

*****

Shaking his head, James rolls down the hall toward the

rehab unit. What an unlooked for slice of sunshine he has found, and he isn't talking about the light coming in the windows of her little haven. Chrissie is a gem, a treasure he can't have, will never enjoy. Her outward beauty, while striking enough to make him stare, is only a reflection of her genuine depth of heart. She deserves better, not just because of his missing limb, but because of the damage to his soul. That isn't going to stop him from warming himself in the light of her generous smile, and the heat her laughter starts in his groin.

Lord, what he wouldn't give to be whole enough to pursue her, to make her his. To trace her high cheekbones and tip those decadently full lips up for a kiss. It would be hotter than a Texas summer to hold on to the dip of her waist, to fill his hands with her full hips. The thought alone makes his palms tingle with the urge to touch her.

What a wonder it is, to feel anything for a woman again. He worried more had been damaged than his leg these last couple months, particularly after his long time fiancée had broken things off because he couldn't rise to the occasion for her. He had been pretty understanding- who wants a broken man? She had started getting pretty ugly with the words before it was all over, insulting his manhood, questioning his honor, and generally being a bitch.

Actually, maybe bitch is the wrong word… he'd known plenty of wonderful female dogs from years with his dads hunting guide service. Yes, calling her a bitch would be disparaging to those fine, devoted hunting dogs. Things had gotten pretty dark for a while as he resisted the urge to hurt her or himself. In his heart he didn't want her hurt, he was just so tired of hurting alone. The day he came home and found her stuff gone had been a relief.

Now, here in Richmond for some extra rehab, and to be fitted for his first prosthesis, there is a lot of dread involved.

Justine Iarann

Will it even work for him- will he get a life back? He had filled the days with wheelchair basketball with the local veterans group or exercising dogs for the humane society near his apartment in Georgia. Yet, nothing could compare to getting around on his own two legs, even if one of them is artificial.

When he reaches the rehab unit a sweet faced older woman is holding the door open for him. As he rolls in she thanks him for his service, and he sincerely thanks her in return- for the first time since the IED hit his unit, killing two of his friends and leaving him damaged, he might have something to be grateful to be alive for.

Chapter Two

Days pass without James crossing the threshold of the unit, leaving Chrissie anxious. Just as anticipation is driving her to peek at the schedule again she feels the wholly welcome sensation of his gaze on her back. Standing beside a client working diligently on the recumbent bike, she turns ever so slightly, and finds herself looking much further up than expected. He is on crutches, and while his expression is one of disgust, she smiles her approval.

Professionally speaking, he needs to be strengthening his remaining leg- personally, she couldn't be more pleased to see how much taller he is than her, cliché or no. He pointedly looks down at his crutches and grimaces a little, then shrugs before swinging over to the platform table. Today is a little different, as he sits down to remove the bandages from his residual limb, his therapist demonstrating desensitizing exercises to ready him for the prosthesis. Chrissie looks away, not wanting to invade his privacy, though mainly it is to return her energy to her own patient. Truth be told, she is wishing far too much that the hands helping him were hers.

When her lunch break finally arrives she heads directly for her sunny haven, fairly humming with happiness. It is wonderful to watch him make progress, and soon he will regain the independence she can tell he fiercely misses.

A smile splits her face when she rounds the corner to find James sitting in the sunlight. He looks up at her footsteps, pushing himself into stand to greet her, ruefully waving at his remaining leg.

"I'd step forward to say hello, but you have the advantage on me."

Laughing gently at his self-deprecation, she steps forward to close the distance. She wants to move closer, but uses what will power she has to control the eagerness that wells up whenever he is near.

"I'd say you still have a fair shot at catching me if you'd use the tools at your disposal." she says, looking pointedly at the crutches half hidden behind the potted tree.

"If you wanted to run, I wouldn't stop you." he replies, darkness lacing his words like arsenic in whiskey.

Rather than dwell on the crippling doubt he has laid bare she touches the tense arm he supporting himself with, stepping closer, and willing his shuttered eyes to hers.

"No running, Sgt. Fletcher. At least not until I'm sure you'll chase me."

His brows arch with surprise, eyes reflecting a bit of wolfish hunger as he flashes one of his frequent half grins.

"I'm pretty sure you'd be worth the effort, Chrissie."

"Thank you kindly." she quips, before quickly stepping over to her own chair. It is dangerous being so close, with his soap and fresh loam scent washing over her.

Kicking off her sneakers, she tucks her feet under her to sit before reaching in her bag for a bottle of tea and a sandwich. Waiting for him to resume his own perch, she watches the muscles ripple in his forearms as he lowers himself, her fingers tingling at the remembered texture of the hair that dusts them.

"Are you hungry?" she asks after swallowing down her own desires. "I have plenty to share."

Maybe it is her imagination, but the wolf returns to his gaze, like he isn't thinking about the sandwich at all. The moment ends quickly, though not before her nipples pucker to the point of ache, leaving her breathing slowly through her nose, trying to settle her over-eager libido.

"I'd hate to deprive you, Chrissie, though I thank you for the offer."

"Oh, no, I'd be happy to break bread with you." She tempts him, opening the sandwich container to let the smell of her almost famous chicken salad fill the air. Momma didn't raise a fool, and rule one was that the fastest route to a man's heart is through food. Especially an Army man.

Watching his lips quirk as he considers the offer is as entertaining as the moment he caves to the temptation. Handing over the larger half of the sandwich, she sits back to observe him. He tries to contain his enthusiasm, employing a masterful level of self-control, consuming everything with polite bites. Chrissie isn't fooled. By her guess, it has been a while since he has eaten homemade. She sets a bottle of water beside him, then settles in to enjoy her own half, which she is fairly sure is one of her best efforts since her Momma had shared the recipe six years ago.

*****

As he chews the hearty sandwich James contemplates the woman across from him- her freckled face is peach kissed even in the blazing light of the atrium, and her plump lips fascinate him as she works through her own lunch. Each downward sweep of her heavy lashes leaves him eagerly looking forward to the next moment their eyes meet. If he is to guess, she had made the sandwich herself, and while that is a wonderful treat, what is so amazing is that he can feel the care she had put in to it. Maybe especially for him. She is a miracle, and he is pretty damn sure he doesn't deserve it at all.

At every turn, she broadsides him with her candor and open heart, leaving him flooded with warmth. It is an alien feeling after so long with his own darkness.

"So, Miss Everett, how is your day going?" he asks, after a swallow of water to wash down the last bite of sandwich.

She finishes chewing her bite before answering.

"Actually, it's Chrissie to you, sir. And my day is going exceptionally well. I thank you for the company that is making it so very pleasurable."

Pleasurable. Oh, he wants to make things very pleasurable for her alright, but despite the seclusion of their retreat, so many people are only foot steps away. He takes another gulp of water to cover his delay in conversation.

"Then, Chrissie, I thank you to remember to call me James. No Sgt. Fletcher for you."

She laughs softly at his rebuff, smile lines popping up around her eyes.

"Ah, I see how it is. Turnabout is fair play. I shall remember the rules of engagement in the future, James."

Oh, and witty too. He is doomed.

"Any plans you are looking forward to after work?"

"Ah, yes, I have a riding lesson with the sadist also known as my dressage instructor." A wide smile lights her face. "Luckily, it means an hour with my favorite guy."

"Oh, well, that's nice." is the best he can manage without choking on the words. She is taken. Son of a bitch.

Again, her laughter shoots straight through the darkness he lives in, and wraps itself around his heart.

"Oh no, James. I mean with my horse, Smoke. He has

Better Broken

been the only man in my life for well over a year, and the first in my heart since I was 17."

The fist clenched on the arm of the chair relaxes as he processes the information. Not taken, though not easy either, by the way she speaks about her lack of boyfriend. Casually, like it doesn't bother her at all. He wants it to bother her- he wants to get as far under her skin as she already is under his.

"Well, I had a filly of my own when I was a boy working for my father. I haven't thought of her in years, but I know how dear she was to me then." He smiles wistfully, wondering if his father still has the big red walker he had called Sweet Pea.

"Now you are going to tell me you play the piano." she says, eyes bright with amusement.

"Hmmm. I hate to disappoint you, but no piano." he replies, confusion tugging his brows lower.

"Oh good, I was beginning to believe you were too perfect to be true." Those damnably blue eyes catch the light exquisitely.

"Ah, no, not perfect. Truth is much stranger than fiction, and I am too flawed to claim any title other than damaged." he answers with an almost resigned tone. She looks at him, half softness and half tough, ready to redirect him, but he beats her to the punch line. "I do, however, play the guitar."

His deadpan delivery shocks sunny, open mouthed laughter from her while she clutches at her heart as if wounded.

"Touché, James Fletcher." she answers, once she regains her breath.

With the worst timing, possible only in moments like this, her watch beeps loudly, breaking the moment in to pieces he wishes he could gather up and hoard like treasure.

"The voice of reason rudely intrudes, James." She sighs earnestly. "As much as I would love to spend the afternoon trading words with you, I have clients who hold me to a higher standard."

Gathering her things to leave, he takes the moments available to study her, memorizing the curve of her neck, and the gentle strength in her hands. He envies the lucky souls she is going back to, but he also understands her call to duty. Her conviction to her cause is as admirable to him as the bow of her mobile lips.

"Hope to see you again soon, Chrissie." he says, standing to see her off.

"Sooner rather than later, I hope." she replies, taking his hand briefly. He entertains the notion of lifting her hand to his lips, but lets the moment pass, not wanting to risk overwhelming her. Her fingers slip from his grasp, and he watches her walk away, thinking that the only thing saving him from chasing her is the damned crutches.

*****

The next day, and the one after, they share time in that sunny slice of heaven. She brings sandwiches to share, and he takes it in kind to bring cookies for dessert. They discuss books and dogs, travels and family, or lack thereof.

He learns she was mostly been raised by her mother, as her father had been a career Army officer, more interested in climbing the ladder of success and politics than in his own family. They divorced when Chrissie was 10, and she had finished childhood on her grandfather's ranch in Colorado, where her intense love of horses had been nurtured.

She listens to him talk about growing up in Texas hill country with his father, after his mother died of breast cancer. He is inordinately fond of barbecue, and hunting dogs, with a serious education in firearms. Between his need to escape the lonely life with his father, and his familiarity with guns, he decided the Army was his best road out of town. She never fishes for information about his injury, or where he had sustained it. He remains gentlemanly and cordial in all ways, and those stolen hours become his one real joy.

On the third day, as they are debating the merits of buying books versus borrowing them from the library, the sound of a hurried approach makes James alert, eyes widening as an interloper enters their sanctuary.

"Chrissie Everett, are you hiding from me?" A tiny fairy of a woman strides around the corner like an Amazon. She doesn't even notice James, she is so focused on her prey. "We have plans tonight, like it or not."

James coughs pointedly, once his heartrate lowers, and she pivots on her four inch heels to fix him with a mildly astonished glare. The wind goes right out of her sails as she looks him over, then back at Chrissie.

"Okay, good excuse. But tonight, you and I, we talk!"

With that, she marches right back out the way she came, taking a good bit of air with her.

"So sorry, James, Suzie is a force of nature." Chrissie apologizes, a flush dusting her cheeks.

"You don't say," he says with a grin, despite the edge of panic still worrying at him. "She's quite a sight to behold."

Something hard flashes in her eyes then, something borderline violent, but rather than worrying him it gives him hope to think it could be jealousy.

"She reminds me a lot of my sister, Jenn."

Her instant smile confirms his suspicions, and he has to restrain himself from cheering as she turns conversation back to the safety of books. Hope settles in his chest like a flighty bird- one wrong move might startle it away, but if he stays very still, perhaps it will linger.

As they near the end of their hour, he leans forward, catching her eyes. She angles toward him, mirroring his posture, waiting for whatever he wants to say.

"So, tomorrow, I am getting my first prosthetic." It's hard

to squeeze the words around the tightness in his chest.

"Good for you." Her luminous smile encourages him.

"The thing is, the appointment is scheduled for the end of the day," He fidgets with the seam of his pants before continuing. "And I'd like you to come. I know you aren't my therapist, so you don't have to, but I'd like a friend to be there."

"Don't you have any family or buddies nearby you'd like to come support you?" she squeaks out after a moment, eyes wide.

"No, actually, I don't," A self-depreciating grin cracks the tightness of his face. "But even if I did, I don't think I'd want to share this with anyone else but you."

Moisture wells in her eyes as she gazes at him with something like wonder.

"I'll be there." she answers. "With bells on, if you like."

"I think we can do without the bells, but I'm glad you'll be there." he laughs, ready to look forward instead of lingering in the past.

*****

That night, as the two women sit on the floor of Suzie's apartment with a bottle of wine and an open pizza box on the table between them, Suzie starts the interrogation.

"Are you CRAZY?"

"Seriously? Says she who tried dating a prison inmate online once?" Chrissie says with a roll of her eyes.

"Hey, I was lonely, and there were far too many tequila shots that preceded that experiment." Suzie argues heatedly. "You, on the other hand, are never more than mildly buzzed, therefor have NO excuse."

Suzie's cat, Oscar, strolls up to beg a piece of sardine off Suzie's half of the pizza, which she hands him absentmindedly.

"I don't think I need to defend myself. I've been very

circumspect in every way. We just talk, Suzie."

"I'm not questioning your professionalism, my friend. Only your sanity. He is a soldier returning from war, which alone is enough to throw up red flags. That man is trouble in spades." A frustrated huff blows Suzie's bangs back off her forehead.

"You are a counselor, I would think you more than anyone would understand how much he needs a friend." Chrissie rebuffs with a scowl.

"Oh sure. Friends." Suzie scoffs, rolling her eyes. "I've seen you looking at him. You may enjoy being his friend, but you would love nothing more than to ride him at a gallop. Tell me I'm lying?"

Chrissie flushes uncomfortably scarlet, not necessarily at Suzie's crude manner, but that she has been caught out.

"Look, Strawberry Tall-cake, you are too honest to deny it. And I've got news for you. The heat in that man's eyes should have scalded your panties off a week ago."

Now, Chrissie has to gulp for breath around the tight hope gripping her heart.

"Are you sure, Suz?" The question comes out as a broken stammer. "I couldn't bear to be wrong about this."

"I knew it!" Suzie crows triumphantly, bouncing in place. "I won't tell you that I think what you are signing up for is all wine and roses. Luckily, you are more of a daisies and beer girl anyway. I won't even talk about his injury, you are better equipped than I am to know the realities of it. Just be careful. Most soldiers come back far more scarred on the inside than on the outside and those wounds take a lot longer to heal."

"I know. Sometimes, for a moment, you can see them in his eyes, still bleeding out and hurting." Chrissie answers, her whole body stilling at the memory.

Suzie hugs her best girlfriend tightly, for once out of words.

Chapter Three

As clients begin to filter out for the afternoon, James swings in on his hated crutches, looking around for the telltale blaze of Chrissie's hair. She's stacking hand weights in the corner and before he can move, she turns to catch his eyes like she can feel his gaze. The miracle of her ready smile steadies the pulse moving sluggishly through his veins.

He meets her at the raised padded table in the middle of the room, and they sit down, much closer together than their separate chairs usually keep them. The sweet clover and honey scent of her washes over him for the first time, and he closes his eyes briefly to drink it in.

"Are you okay, James?" she asks, concern evident in her voice, fingers landing feather light on his thigh.

His eyes snap open, more okay than he has been in a coon's age. Then he notices she is touching his leg, his incomplete leg, not clinically, not even aware that she is doing it. She is touching him, and it's like a fire burning through his body, leaving a cleansed trail behind it. Leaning forward, he watches her lips part, waiting for his kiss.

"Mr. Fletcher, glad to see you here early." Marti, his therapist, strides in, eyes fixated on her clipboard.

Chrissie rears back like she has been slapped, panic raw in her eyes. He touches her hand briefly where it rests on the table, then withdraws. There is no way he wants to compromise Chrissie's work environment, and he will have to be doubly careful to protect her from now on.

A short, eager gentleman walks in moments later, with the object of all James's anxiety tucked under his arm.

"Fletch, you ready to get this show on the road?" he says with a huge grin.

"Hey Spence, as long as it's better looking than you, I'm ready to go." James volleys back.

Spencer Chase is a coincidence of good fortune in James opinion. They had attended basic together many years ago when Spence had been injured during a live fire exercise. They had kept in contact over the years, and he is the whole reason James is in Richmond for his prosthesis rather than back at Walter Reed. The instant he had walked into James treatment room for the initial consultation they had fallen right back in to the patterns of their old friendship, including the trading of insults.

"Well, she isn't as pretty as she could be yet, but it's a step in the right direction." Spencer quips, as James scoffs at the horribly inappropriate pun.

"Don't quit the day job, Spence. Your comedy routine is in as poor taste as it ever was." Chrissie is grinning at their exchange of banter, steadying him by her presence alone.

His therapist sits down on a low stool, helping to remove his usual leg cover, then shows him how to slide on the new liner to protect the sensitive skin. Spence kneels down to put the socket of the artificial limb in to James grasp, demonstrating the seal that will allow it to secure.

"You ready for the last suit you are ever going to wear, Agent J?"

James snorts derisively at the movie quote, and Chrissie stifles a giggle. Then without any ceremony or fanfare, Spencer helps him slide the apparatus on. They lock the seal and Spencer steps back.

"How does it feel, Mr. Fletcher?" Marti asks, all business.

"Fine, I guess. I don't know how it's supposed to feel." The woman never looks high enough to see his raised eyebrow at her short manner. From the corner of his eye he sees Chrissie hide a tiny smile behind her hand. My God, how much worse this all would have been without her sunshine to push back the dark words that could have come so easily.

"She means is it pinching or hurting anywhere." Spence says, filling in admirably.

"No, not a bit. But I'm not doing anything yet."

"We will get to that in a moment, Mr. Fletcher. First thing is first." Marti directs him through a series of exercises meant to accustom him to the additional weight of the aluminum and carbon fiber limb, then affixes a gait belt around his waist. Chrissie steps further back to watch, the professional in her absorbing everything even as the woman he admires is cheering him on.

At last, Spence steps up to offer him a hand, and while James would usually refuse the help, it feels appropriate for a brother in arms to draw him forward into this new chapter of life. He wobbles for a second before spreading his legs further apart to find his balance, Marti's hands secure on the belt to steady him. Spence shows him how the new joint works, and in seconds James makes his first step, using a walker for balance. The therapist helps him engage the muscles that draw his prosthetic forward, then he is walking another step. It is a strange sensation, as the residual limb bears weight and pressure, but despite the discomfort, the hope in his chest begins to make itself at home. The grimace that accompanied so many of his sessions with Marti fades away, and a smile takes its place.

He looks up at Chrissie who is trying to maintain professional distance, but she doesn't bother to hide the tears of happiness making her eyes glisten. He cannot cross the room to take her hand like he wants to- despite that, he locks his eyes on hers and takes a few symbolic steps toward her. Toward his future.

*****

The hallways of the hospital are quiet in the early evening, giving James and Chrissie time to enjoy each other's company. They hadn't seen each other since his appointment two nights ago and had felt the lack of that precious time.

Lost in thought, happy to amble alongside him, Chrissie is running circles in her mind. He has taken a crucial step toward recovery, but being invited along on the journey has opened her own eyes. She had yet to pick a subject for her thesis, yet now, she has a direction to go. Just as her thoughts start to circle again, she remembers their near miss kiss that they hadn't yet had the privacy to attempt again and stumbles, mentally and physically. He falters, and shoots her a look of concern, but she smiles reassuringly.

"So, may I walk you out to your car?" His tone is light, but still feels heavy with import.

"Sure." Anticipation thickens something low in her gut. "As long as you are alright. It's not a short trip to staff parking."

"I haven't been able to walk on my own in months, Chrissie. I can assure you that I won't be looking to sit anytime soon."

Knowing his will power can carry the occasion, she continues walking. The sun is setting, brightening colors and casting long shadows through the windows. A frown shows his irritation at the slow speed, and the use of a cane, but she is content to keep pace.

Moving slowly in comparison to a couple days before, James doesn't miss the crutches one bit. Sure, every hallway takes much longer to travel, but he finds peace in her presence. Every stride is a victory, and every heart beat is a bit stronger knowing she wants his company. The echoing warmth of her hand still lingers on his leg, comforting and exhilarating in the same instant.

Before very long, they pass through the double doors that lead outside, surrounded by the rapidly chilling air of early spring. The silent companionship between them is soothing, and he wishes he felt stable enough to reach for her hand. She leads him down a row of cars to a beat up green Subaru decorated with several horse related bumper stickers.

"I should have guessed this one was yours." he teases.

"I have no idea what you are talking about." Her deadpan denial is completely ruined by the threat of a grin on the corner of her mouth.

He laughs, wobbling a little, and she drops her bag reflexively, steadying him with her hands on his hips.

"Are you okay, James?" she says, concern plain in her voice, but he is too fascinated by the teeth worrying her upper lip to step away.

"I am far more than okay." he rumbles, the shadows he holds a tight leash on prowling restlessly. "The question is, are you okay?"

A shiver works its way over her skin, and before he can worry that she is afraid, she nods. Words may have escaped her, but her eyes give him the truth.

Her pulse gallops wildly as he gently tucks a wayward curl behind her ear. When he cradles the base of her skull Chrissie forgets to breathe, watching him lean in.

"Such a gift." he whispers, feathering a kiss onto her forehead.

Warmth spreads through her, like the petals of a flower opening to the sun at the touch of his lips. He straightens then, as if to move away, but she can't bear to let him go. Using her advantage, she slowly pulls him closer with the hands still resting on his hips.

He drops his cane, throwing his hands up on to the roof of her car, afraid fall on her, but she draws him in like a gravity field.

"I'm not done with you yet, Sgt. Fletcher." she breathes, eyes locked boldly on his as he comes fully to rest against her. What had been warm heat now turns to a bonfire, and she could blow away like an ember in the wind without his weight anchoring her.

"Chrissie, what did we say about name calling?" He contrives a strained smile, darkness trying to wrestle for control. He cannot trust himself and he cannot bear to harm her- she doesn't know how dangerous he can be. The temptation of her would be easy to yield to, but the risk is too great.

Flexing his arms to push away, she surprises him, raising up on her toes, pressing her lips to his. The soft contact tilts his whole world on its axis. Gentle exploration along his bottom lip spreads an incandescent glow through every limb. As he stands awestruck, her fingers stray, tracing the thin grey fabric of his Army t-shirt, dancing up the ladder of muscles leading toward his ribcage.

Like a drowning swimmer, he gasps, and grabs for a thread of sanity, concern for her allowing him to break away. He moves as far as his braced arm permits and she drops her eyes, wrapping her arms around herself. It takes a moment to realize that she is hurt by his withdrawal, and he curses his own idiocy.

Slowly, he wraps his hand around the back of her neck, urging her to lift her eyes with a soft stroke of his thumb under her rigid jaw. She yields reluctantly, the glistening tell tale of unshed tears hanging defiantly in her lashes.

"Oh no, lady, this won't do at all." he says, voice deepening with sincere regret. Careful not to press himself back into the welcoming softness of her, he brushes their lips together. She sighs against his mouth and tilts her face up, encouraging him to taste. One of her hands lifts to his shoulder, then comes up to rest in the close cropped darkness of his hair. He does not press the advantage, slowly tracing her lush mouth, lingering on the rich vanilla spice of her tender kiss.

Before it becomes too much to control, he lifts away slightly to draw her into a hug. She settles in his embrace, arms wrapped around his torso, like she has always been there. With her in his arms, he feels strong, whole and complete. He squeezes a bit tighter, feeling her lips press a kiss to his chest just over his heart.

"Sweetheart, don't take this the wrong way, but you keep this up, and you are going to break me." he says, leaning down to chuckle in her ear.

She shivers lightly as the vibration moves through her, then leans back to study his expression before replying.

"Sometimes, just sometimes, things need breaking so we can build them back up." His eyes tighten defensively, but before he can close the door on his emotions, she sneaks him a grin. "In your case, however, maybe I had best run a bit more until I catch you."

Her playful smile stitches closed another wound in his heart, and he hugs her once more before taking a wobbly step back. Wordlessly, she hands him the cane, and he leans against it as she gathers her bag.

"I should go." she says, half statement, half question.

"Probably." he affirms. "I'll see you tomorrow, right?"

"Yes. Though I doubt I will get much sleep between now and then, James."

Quickly rummaging through her work bag, she pulls out a pen and notepad. Leaning against the hood of her car, she scribbles something down, then holds the paper out with a twinkle in her eyes.

"I'm entrusting you with classified material, Sgt. Fletcher. Can you be relied upon to make use of this information in the normal course of your duties?"

He looks down at what appears to be her phone number and grins.

"Yes, ma'am." he replies briskly, making a fair effort at drawing himself to attention.

"Then carry on soldier." Gifting him with a quick kiss on the cheek she hands him the note.

A minute later, she is putting her car in reverse, then pulling away. A big grin is spreading across his face despite the dawning realization that he is parked on the opposite side of the hospital from here. Well, he needs the practice of being on his own two feet, doesn't he?

Justine Iarann

Chapter Four

The next morning Chrissie arrives to work early, wrapped possessively around an extra strong chai tea, praying the caffeine will do its job quickly. Sleep had been extra elusive in between dreams of the complex man making himself at home in her heart.

"Miss Everett," calls the office manager as Chrissie walks by. "I need to speak to you."

Anxiety rises at the change in routine as she hurries toward the desk. Max is a bit high strung, though generally kind, and keeps the clinic running ship shape, so this is very unusual. Not even looking up from the scheduling papers in hand, he leans against the counter, scribbling furiously.

"Marti Clark called in sick this morning, viral flu. I'm trying to rearrange her schedule, and need you to fill a block or two for me."

"Sure, Max, anything for you." she says with a charming smile, relief making her muscles lax.

Better Broken

He waves her off, directing her to come back in fifteen to get the amended schedule, then disappears into his office with a phone already pressed to his ear.

Jetting down the hall to drop off her things in the lounge, Chrissie then settles on the floor of the therapy room for a round of yoga stretches. It's a daily time to center herself, this morning being no exception, as her head calms and her heartrate begins to rise. The sun clears the neighboring hospital wing as she finishes, and she bows her head in gratitude for the baptism. Sunshine lights over the skin that James's hand had rested upon last night, and she feels his touch all over again.

Shaking away the feelings as her watch beeps the hour, she turns down the hall to catch up with Max. He is on the phone still, but waves a stack of files at her with a sheet of paper attached to the top. She doesn't stick around, grabbing the files and heading for the staff table to discover what she's in for. The top two are no surprise, clients already on her roster. The third is a recovering stroke victim with copious notes regarding course of treatment.

At the fourth, Chrissie comes to a screeching halt as she reads 'Fletcher, James Adam' on the top of the file. While she does want to work with him, now that she has decided on a specialization, the night before colors everything between them. Marti had again left a rigorous treatment plan for gait training, but the end of the session recommended stretching and massage. Which means getting her hands on the ridiculously tempting man. Heaven help her, sometimes getting what you want doesn't work out quite the way you planned.

Every session of the morning goes by smoothly, though the time moves too slowly. Or too fast. Either way, her pulse is ratcheting up with every passing minute, like a clock wound too tightly. As she finishes the appointment before his, her

Justine Iarann

thoughts are pinging a mile a minute, mostly to do with James's eyes scalding her all the way down to her toes. Amazingly, no one notices the flush growing on her skin. Finally, it is time.

File in hand, she walks to the door of the waiting room, opening it wide to call his name. His back is to her, and he almost bobbles, trying to turn while still rising at the sound of her voice saying his name. Recovering admirably, he walks carefully to the door, eyes wide with a million questions he can't ask. She tries to relieve some of the curiosity with her opening conversation.

"Good morning! Marti Clark was unable to come in to the clinic today, and I am filling in for a couple of her clients. My name is Christine Everett. How are you feeling today?"

The tension in his face lessens with her explanation. "I'm feeling pretty well, though sore from the unaccustomed activity."

Knowing the unaccustomed activity was on her behalf, she blushes lightly, but retains a professional manner.

"Today, we are going to focus on fluid movement and balance, so we shouldn't wear you out too much." she reassures him.

They move through some pre-work stretching, a slight touch to the back or shoulder guiding him in to correct form. The treadmill is also fairly painless, though her breast brushes against his arm as she changes the settings, leaving her skin warm all over. She doesn't look up, afraid one glance will burn her to the ground. He proves an apt pupil, muscle memory helping him adjust to her suggestions with military precision as she tweaks his strides.

Stability work leaves him a little frustrated, will alone unable to keep him steady as she challenges his center of gravity. While he uses the parallel bars to steady himself, she tosses him a small medicine ball, and by the third bobble a tic

Better Broken

appears in his jaw.

"Do you need a break?" she asks, keeping her tone carefully neutral.

"No." He snarls reflexively before catching himself, his whole body softening as he looks up. "Sorry."

"Don't apologize, it's my job to push you, and I've heard worse." she says, deliberately offering him a challenging grin. "Use the tools you have until you don't need them anymore. Now, do you think you've got another twenty in you?"

"Yes ma'am." he answers, adeptly tossing the ball back, a tiny smile threatening his stoic bearing.

Despite a few more unsteady moments he finishes the exercise with several solid catches, and she puts the ball away with a satisfied smile. Then comes the real heat test.

"James, if you will head back to table three, we will finish up with some more stretching and a bit of relaxation work."

Now his head snaps up, rising tension tightening his spine one vertebrae at a time as she follows him back to the open cubicle. He sits on the table, hands clenched around the edge like any movement could shatter him into pieces.

"Are there any places in particular that you are experiencing discomfort?" she asks, eyes fixed pointedly on her notepad.

His groin aches excruciatingly in response to her words, but he keeps himself in check.

"Well, the left lower back and hip is pretty tight. In fact, my whole back is a little sore."

Unsurprised, she nods, scribbling a few notes on his file. "I don't doubt it. Your posture is changed by the addition of the prosthesis and it will take time to adjust to the new way of standing, walking. If you would lay face down on the table, we can see about easing things for you."

Chrissie will not meet his eyes, so he turns to assume the prescribed position. She washes her hands before turning back to him, fingers quivering with nervousness, and he finally catches her eye.

"You don't have to do this." he whispers, trying to ease her distress.

"The hell I don't." she growls quietly, her shoulders straightening with resolve, eyes flashing as she moves to his side. She pulls his shirt up very professionally, but the instant her palms touch his back he is terribly glad to be lying face down. Her whole hand strokes over his skin, immediately raising goose bumps, adding texture to an area already marked with scars. Moving over the area slowly, as if hunting for something, her palm follows the contour of his spine. In a moment, her nimble fingers find the knots that are causing him issues, and then he is not only turned on- he is grateful beyond belief that her caring touch is soothing the very real pain marring his mood. Under her ministrations he begins to relax, soaking in the warmth and skill in her hands.

Working her way slowly over the firm muscles in his shoulders, pouring feelings she can't find words for yet into each touch, Chrissie takes her time with each spot until the stiffness abates. Her fingers yearn to trace the puckered scars along his torso, but she clings to her professionalism with fierce determination. However, nothing can stop the tightness gathering in her throat, thinking of how easily she would never have met him, heat snuffed out before she knew it existed. When her watch beeps the hour she dashes away a tear before pulling his shirt down. Soft with affection for him, yet brimming with defiance, she meets his eyes as he sits up. He had needed her attentions, his body straining to cope with the changes forced on it.

"Thank you, Miss Everett." Sincerity bleeds through his voice, soothing her agitation. "I'll be happy to report to Marti that you were an excellent stand in. I feel much better."

Posture softening, Chrissie shakes his hand, and he folds

his fingers around hers. Looking quickly over his shoulder to assess the room, he risks lifting her knuckles for a quick kiss, hidden from the people behind him. She rewards him with a blush, brushing her other hand against his cheek before turning to lead him out of the unit.

James isn't in their spot at lunch, and she begins to fear she overstepped the physical boundaries he is comfortable with. Anxiety rides her through the afternoon sessions despite every effort to shake it off. Toward the end, she gets angry with herself for letting this consume her so much, and manages a productive end to the very long day. Checking her phone as soon as she clocks out, she is disappointed to see no missed calls or messages. Her strides grow quick, impatient, as she nears her vehicle, and Chrissie is near tears by the time she wrenches open the door. Dabbing at her eyes with her coat sleeve she sees a note tucked under her windshield wiper. An unfamiliar number is scrawled beneath an arrow drawn beside a looping J, the sight drying her tears immediately.

Shooting James a quick text before pulling out of the lot she tells him to expect a call when she gets home. Once at her apartment she puts leftover Indian food in the microwave to heat while she changes into her Mickey Mouse pajamas. Only then does she settle on the couch to call him. It rings three times, her heart pounding louder with each tone.

"Good evening, lady." His voice is thick, gruff with sleep, but it feels like a caress just the same.

"Did I wake you?" Hope and anxiety combine, leaving her fidgeting with the hem of her shirt.

"Yes, you did, which is why I missed your text. Sorry for missing lunch, but after our session I was exhausted. Came back to the hotel and passed out."

"That's not unusual." she says, slipping easily into professional mode. "Massage often releases built up lactic acid in the muscle tissue. When that happens, we can get very tired while the body flushes it out. Have you been drinking lots of water?"

"Yes, Doc, I have been a very good patient today." he replies with a little tease in his voice, laughing when she growls at him. "You are getting home awfully late. Was everything okay at the clinic?"

"Yes, but I had the additional work load with Marti being out." A tired sigh escapes as she slides deeper into the embrace of the sofa.

"I apologize for adding to your troubles."

"James, you made this whole day bearable. I missed seeing you at lunch, but I am so glad to hear your voice tonight. I was worried I had over stepped myself."

"Chrissie, I could not be more grateful for you today." His voice deepens an octave, her skin prickling in response. "Not just because I enjoyed you touching me, but because you did more good than my regular 'nurse ratchet' ever has. You have a gift."

"Thank you." Grateful to be recognized for her craft and as a woman, the praise warms her all over. "I wasn't sure you would let me touch you after last night's confusion."

"I wasn't confused, sweetheart." he says, voice grown careful and soft. "I was trying to protect you."

"James, I can assure you, I did not want you to rescue me." she states boldly, grateful for the distance between them. This feels so raw that looking in his eyes might take away her bravery. "I'd have happily burned alive in those moments with you."

He groans and the sheets rustle as he shifts, her imagination painting vivid pictures of him in bed that leave her pressing her thighs together.

"Good Lord, woman, you really are going to be the death of me." But he says it with a little humor, so she smiles at the tiny victory.

"Now, Sgt. Fletcher, would you like to explain why you didn't call rather than leaving notes for me to find?" she queries.

His casual laugh lightens her heart. "Would you believe, I left your number in my pants pocket yesterday, and it went in the wash? I hoped I would be the only guy leaving you messages, and that wind wouldn't whisk it away."

"What was with the arrow?"

"That is an old hold over from my early days in the Army. The guys called me Fletch, like the feathers on an arrow, so it became part of my signature. If anyone found it, I didn't want them to know a client was leaving you love notes."

Her heart stutters a little at the choice of words, but she tries not to make a big deal over what is just an expression.

"You can leave me love notes any time you like, James." she offers cavalierly.

"I bet you say that to all the guys." His chuckle comes off tense and dark, with a hint of jealousy.

"No, never before. And I am beginning to suspect never to another." she says with strained honesty, hoping he will understand. Nothing but silence fills the other end of the line, so quiet she can't even hear him breathe. "James, are you okay?"

He laughs abruptly, then softly replies. "I'm beginning to suspect you will be asking me that for the rest of my life."

Chrissie sighs in relief, and hears him echo her. "Gladly."

"Chrissie, I'd best get off the phone before I make a complete fool of myself. Will I see you tomorrow?"

Thinking of her plans with Smoke, she grimaces. "No, I won't be at the hospital tomorrow. I am committed to the other man in my life."

"Well, dammit." The frustration in his voice mimics her feelings exactly. "How about the evening? Would you like to have dinner with me?"

Grinning like an idiot, Chrissie is grateful he can't see her foolish expression. "Certainly. Call me tomorrow afternoon, and we can make arrangements."

"Sounds good. Sleep well, Sunshine."

"Same to you, James." she says, voice heavy with unspoken feeling, then hangs up the phone.

Now, how the heck is she supposed to sleep?

*****

James tries to sleep again, and is fairly successful until he falls into surreal nightmares of the day he lost his leg. The stinging grit of sand in every wound, despite the screaming pain racing up from the place his leg used to be. Blood, boiling hot on his skin, not only his blood but that of his friend, his battle brother, who now lay still beside him, the life in his eyes gone. He can't hear anything past the ringing in his ears, not even his own voice as he screams for help. It is mere moments before the medic reaches him, but the panic rises regardless, and he fights against the man trying to save his life.

At that moment, he shoots straight up in bed, sweating and struggling to breathe his way out of the clutches of the dream. His leg aches with remembered pain, and he rubs reflexively at his thigh, startling when his fingers move downward and encounter only air. Grief wells up, a familiar enemy, tears burning his eyes as he fights it back. Clutching the sheet to keep himself from flying apart, he gulps down a glass of water, desperate to reconnect with the real world.

It takes a few minutes before he is able to lay back and stare at the ceiling, wishing desperately that he could reach for Chrissie. The only time he feels grounded anymore is when she is there, sharing her light with him. Perhaps he does want to lose himself in the softness of her body, but what he truly needs is the salve she spreads on his soul.

Chapter Five

Morning breaks cotton candy pink and blue as Chrissie auto pilots down the familiar road toward the barn. She had tossed and turned through the night, completely unlike her normal behavior. Usually, she falls straight asleep and doesn't wake until the alarm goes off. Lately, she tangles in her blankets after fitful, surreal nightmares, but mostly she wakes with a moan, the image of James's head bent to suckle her breast burned in to her brain. Even now, the remembered ache puckers her nipples, pressing them sharply to the thick fabric of her sports bra. She squirms in her seat, hands gripping the steering wheel tightly, needing something to control.

With gratitude, she spots the gate marking her turn and steers her car down the well-tended gravel road. Black four rail fencing stretches in to the distance, framing green fields as horses dot the landscape with random color. She rolls down the window to catch the scents that never fail to soothe her, damp earth and mown grass fresh in the air. Horses have been her refuge all her life, and she prays today will be the same.

As she approaches the barn her big black horse walks out of his stall to watch her park, moving the length of his run to be sure he has her attention. He whinny's a special greeting as she steps out, then ducks back inside to meet her at his door. The quiet peace and precision of the barn centers her, the worn wood of Smoke's stall door pressing familiar patterns in to her fingertips, grounding her firmly in the present.

Drawing open the door, the other hand immediately reaches to pet Smoke's much beloved face, tracing the complicated whorl of hair in the middle of his forehead. She kisses his silken nose and runs scritches down his neck while he reciprocates with lip wiggles at her cheek, making her giggle.

Though his ebony coat is clean, she still observes the ritual of grooming before tossing his tack on with practiced ease. When she climbs in the saddle Smoke turns to take the peppermint she always offers, then they walk toward the dressage arena on a long rein. His rhythmic stride rolls her hips, loosening her body a muscle fiber at a time. Everything feels right as they begin their warm up, stretching and flowing until every movement blends seamlessly in to the next.

It's not until Chrissie takes up the reins to begin real work that things begin to head south. It starts with some tense and bouncy strides in the trot, like the normally willing black giant is complaining about something. A wrinkle forms between Chrissie's brows, and she concentrates extra hard on the next movement, timing her leg and rein perfectly. Despite that, the big guy is fed up, throwing a very small buck to express his displeasure. Something is wrong, she can tell, though they repeat the movement so his misbehavior is not rewarded.

Afterward, she asks for a walk- he halts completely and looks back at her with one eye. Fidgeting under the intense

Better Broken

scrutiny, she knows her head and her heart are not really in the game. Smoke has never ever let her be anything other than genuine, and there is no point in trying to fake it.

"Okay buddy, I get it. I'm a mess, and you don't deserve to have to carry that around. How about a nice trail ride?"

Once headed down the driveway toward the tree line he begins to relax, ears forward, walking powerfully. Chrissie fights with a large dose of guilt- learning to leave her troubles behind every time she stepped in the saddle had been her first lesson in horsemanship. James is having an even greater effect on her than her sleep.

She tries to dismiss James from her thoughts as Smoke carries her over a hill and across the creek, but he is never very far from her heart. He would love watching the deer bound down the trail ahead, or the way the birds break cover and wheel together toward the next hedgerow. How wonderful it would be, to share this precious sanctuary with him. To give the gift of peace, because horses never care if you are a little broken as long as you come to them honestly.

These thoughts circle around in her busy brain until they crest the hill into the big meadow at the back of the farm- Smoke puts a little more swing into his steps, ears flicking sharply forward and back again, waiting for her to ask him to run. So she raises up in the saddle and closes her legs- the moment he begins to gallop every single trouble and each tiny worry falls away. There is only the air rushing over her face and the thundering sound of his big feet pounding out the rhythm of her heart against the rich dirt beneath them. She gives him the reins, and urges him on with her voice, not asking him to slow until his energy begins to fade. Her hand strokes over his glossy neck in gratitude, thankful to have her heart uncluttered and her spirits raised from that bit of freedom they shared.

The rest of their ride is quiet, skirting the edge of a cattle pasture then dropping back down the hillside toward the barn. She waves absently at some riders in the distance as thoughts of James work their way back in, but now the thoughts are clearer, more focused.

She loves him, as fiercely as she loves the horses and her work. It burns through her veins, not just because she thrills to his touch, but because she wants more of his heart. That great big heart that he is keeping in the darkness, not allowing it to venture too closely to the light. She loves his laughter, rare and precious, and his stone hard determination, his likeminded affection for books, and the way he can focus his will wholly on whatever is before him. How she prays that he cares for her even half as much as she feels for him.

Smoke stops of his own accord when they arrive at the barn, and it is time for Chrissie to climb down. She vaults softly to the ground, and immediately loosens the girth before leading her faithful friend into the cool shadows of the stable. After grooming him in thanks, she returns him to his stall, but rather than turning toward his breakfast he looks at her with both eyes, then drops his nose to rest over her heart. Perhaps it is only coincidence, but Chrissie has known him far too long not to recognize when he is being deliberate. Her head falls forward to brush a gentle kiss onto his face.

"Thanks for understanding, big guy. Maybe, if we are lucky, he will come with me sometime soon. I think you might like him."

Smoke bumps her gently with his muzzle, then turns away. She scoops up his equipment, ducking into the tack room where she cleans and conditions the leather. As she puts the saddle away a sheet covered bundle catches her curiosity. Lifting the corner reveals a beautiful russet leather harness, burnished brass shining even in the low light. It recalls a memory of her grandfather, teaching Smoke to pull a cart even before he was old enough to carry a rider, and the idea

Better Broken

of how to share her horse with James begins to form. Of course! She can drive them down the trails, if he's interested, but being back in nature could work more good than a hundred hours of therapy ever would.

Heading toward her car she stops briefly to slip Smoke another mint, then climbs behind the wheel. Before she can put the vehicle in drive the flashing light of her cell alerts her to a waiting text.

'Hey Sunshine. Hope you are having a great morning. Decided I should ask you where we should have dinner. I don't know any decent places around here. And I need to know where to pick you up.'

Chrissie texts back. 'I know just the place. I'm at 401 Poplar Ave #109, see you around six. Morning was great, but would have been better with you. :-)'

Simple happiness infuses her whole being as she heads back down the driveway, eager to see him despite the hours still separating them.

*****

Pulling in to the apartment complex shortly before the scheduled time, James finds a parking spot on the outskirts of the lot. Sure, he could use the handicapped tag, but it chafes him to need it, and frankly, he is feeling pretty good right now. In fact, he hopes the walk will calm the nerves that are eating him alive from the inside.

He slides off the seat of his truck, and grabs hold of the cane that he now loathes almost as much as the crutches. Soon he hopes to be able to do without, but for now it is a necessary tool. After a few minutes of hunting for apartment numbers he stands before her door, hesitating before knocking. The afternoon had grown overcast and chilly, but despite the cool weather, he still has to wipe the sweat off his palms. He is no coward by any stretch, but he is genuinely afraid to take this next step toward a reality with her. The closer he allows himself, the bigger the risk that he will hurt her, or worse, that she will find the damage in him to be more than she can endure.

Shaking off the thoughts clouding his head, he knocks briskly on the door. Her footsteps are quick, as though she is as eager to see him as he is to see her. When the door opens he has to swallow down his heart as it leaps in to his throat. For the first time, she has her hair loose, curling with flaming abandon to frame her face. Casually dressed in a pair of jeans that hug her generous hips, they reveal far more than the work attire he normally sees her in. Her slightly oversized sweater is a bright blue, which lights her eyes from within. Her bare feet are unexpected though, as is the smell of barbeque wafting from inside.

"Come on in." she says, stepping back so he can move past her.

Clearing his throat, he lifts a single sunflower up in his free hand. The smile she favors him with is bright enough to make the cloudy evening appear luminescent as she draws him inside with her fingers circled around his wrist. He lets himself be led, fingers numb with excitement, thrilling when she winds an arm around him. Her eyes never leave his as she lifts the flower up, brushing the petals against her freckled nose.

"James, you didn't have to, you know." Her whole face shines with pleasure over the tiny gesture.

"I know, but as soon as I saw it, I wanted you to have it." he says gruffly, trying not to think too hard about the soft coral of her lips as she speaks. "So, are you about ready to go?"

"Actually, I brought dinner here. Is that okay?" she asks, her eyes uncertain.

He can't help it, his voice deepening as he reassures her. "Chrissie, stop worrying about if I am okay. I'm okay every moment I am with you."

A pretty blush migrates up from the low scoop collar of her sweater until her cheek shows a warm pink, and he pulls her close. There is no hesitation in her, lifting her lips up for him, and he obliges with a gentle kiss. Heat builds quickly and she makes the first move to step back, as if afraid to chase him off. He rubs his cheek against hers before letting her go, touched at her thoughtfulness, but missing her immediately.

She walks toward the tiny kitchen, hips swaying alluringly in the fitted denim, red gold hair cascading down to middle of her back like a fiery waterfall. It is impossible to ignore the rush of blood to his groin, and he licks his lips, tasting the vanilla chap stick that had flavored their kiss. No makeup, no artifice, just natural beauty and charm making him hard, leaving him stunned.

In fair danger of imploding from the heat, Chrissie buries her nose in the flower again. Seeing him on her doorstep in jeans and a polo had been a visual treat, considering she has only ever seen him in workout clothing. The pale blue of his shirt makes his brown eyes appear an even deeper shade of chocolate than usual, and the clean scent of him is making her head swim. It is a strategic retreat as she heads to the kitchen to put his impossibly sweet gift in a jar of water, else she might yield to the temptation to ravage him where he stands. The blush that rises on her cheeks at the thought feels hot enough to raise blisters.

"Make yourself comfortable." she calls over her shoulder, busying herself with the plates and silverware while the color on her face fades.

Making a brief circuit of the room, he notes the over full bookshelves, which hold not only books, but photos. One appears to be of her with her mother standing at the summit of a mountain. The rest are of her horse, a big black beast whose size is belied by the softness around his eyes in every photo with her in it. James instantly feels a kinship, knowing how she softens his own heart so easily with a simple smile.

The couch looks safe, so he lowers himself carefully, grateful that it is firm enough to support his slightly wobbly decent. His eyes track her as she fusses, putting their plates next to each other at the small round table rather than across from each other. Close enough to touch each other, he notices, and marvels again that she wants to be close to him at all. She beckons him to the table, and he shoots to his feet like an over eager dog, forgetting his physical shortcomings. Yet, she is immediately there, her hand on his elbow to steady him. The instant he is sure of his balance she slides her hand down to his as if it was her original intent, never drawing attention to the weakness that strains his patience.

The table is arrayed with so much food he isn't sure where to look first. There is brisket and pulled pork, with a plate of ribs beside it, a bowl of potato salad and another of coleslaw sitting next to a pile of bread.

"How many people are you feeding tonight?" he marvels, fascinated by the quick return of color to her cheeks.

"Well, I didn't know what you liked, so I brought home a little bit of everything. It makes good leftovers for lunch this coming work week, so there is no pressure if you don't like something."

He chuckles but agrees, pulling out one of the tall backed chairs for her. When she hesitates he takes her hand and draws her forward. Yielding graciously, she sits, and he drops a quick kiss on the top of her head before pulling out his own seat. Before picking up anything for herself she offers him a scoop of the potato salad.

"This is the only thing I made myself, the rest I picked up at Rufus Waite's place here in town. I don't like his white potato salad, he doesn't make it with mustard and hard boiled eggs like I do."

Better Broken

He smiles, not only at her thoughtfulness, but also because she speaks what is on her mind, and makes no apologies for it. Sure, she is tactful, but she is never anything less than genuine. They dish their plates in silence and she puts a little of everything on her plate, not just a bird sized portion of food. Another thing to admire- he hates it when women starve themselves to look like rail thin super models.

At the first bite of brisket, a favorite from his youth, he groans as the tender meat falls apart in his mouth. She grins with satisfaction, then bites into a sauce covered rib, licking the extra off her lips with enjoyment. He nearly drops his fork when her tongue darts out to catch the sauce also dripping off her fingers- part of him chafes to satisfy a very different hunger than they are currently tending to. Regardless, he forces himself to take a bite of the potato salad and is not disappointed in the slightest. The smooth texture and vinegary bite are the perfect complement to the rich, smoky flavor of the meat, and he lifts a second forkful toward her in salute.

"As good as my Momma's ever was, and that is high praise, I assure you."

She says nothing, but smiles widely, glad he is enjoying himself. In fact, watching him eat is feeding a part of her soul, sustaining her better than the food she is consuming.

They finish their meal mostly in silence, and when he sits back from the table James finds himself uncomfortably full.

"Wow, Chrissie that was great. A girl who knows good barbeque is very rare outside of the South."

"I'm so glad you enjoyed it- Rufus always does a good job. You'll have to go down and visit with him sometime. He is a character without compare and I know he'd love to talk to a fellow Texan." she answers, leaning forward with her chin on her hand.

He leans forward too, tempted when her lips part

expectantly, but instead he lifts his napkin to touch the side of her mouth.

"You missed a spot." he says teasingly.

Eyes flashing, her tongue darts out to lick the spot he is touching- moist heat brushes lightly over the barest bit of his fingers, and he has to clench the opposite hand until the knuckles pop to maintain his precious control. They both sit back from each other at the same moment, and she rises to gather plates, retreating to the relative safety of the kitchen.

"How about a walk?" he asks, trying to turn his thoughts back to something neutral. Trying not to imagine that pink tongue touching other parts of his anatomy.

"Sure! Do you have a jacket? It's getting cool outside, and they said it might rain."

As if her words invited it, the quiet of her apartment is suddenly broken with a distant rumble of thunder and the tinny hint of rain drops on the living room window.

"So much for that." Her easy laughter eases the frown that had risen at being thwarted. "Do you feel like watching a movie?"

"I suppose that'll do." he concedes.

"Go peruse the pathetic selection available while I finish cleaning up." she says over her shoulder from her spot at the sink.

Standing up stiffly, he wishes they could walk. The big meal is making him sleepy, and he doesn't want to cut short this precious time together. Settling for the short stroll to the TV and a few stretches to get the blood moving, he scans over what truly is a paltry DVD collection. Yet, it is by no means pathetic, holding not just the usual chick flicks, but a couple outright comedies, a few fantasy action and a Shakespeare adaptation. As he nears the end, he spots a larger DVD case marked with the name of his favorite childhood show. It's an old black and white, often rerun series about life

Better Broken

in a small town with a comic and heartwarming cast of characters. Finding it on her shelf is as welcome a surprise to him as the ongoing miracle she is working on his heart. He grabs hold of the case and loads the first disc in the player, navigating the remote control with ease, then turns back to the couch. She is already there, feet tucked under her, and she smiles broadly as the opening credits begin to roll.

"Really? I thought I was the only sap in the world who still watches these." she teases.

"I'm trusting you with classified information." he says, echoing her words from a couple nights before, his smile mirroring hers. "If the guys in my unit ever found out, I'd be razzed for the rest of my life." Cautiously, he sits on the edge of the cushions and uses his arms to move back in to a more comfortable position.

"Your secret is safe with me, Barney Fife." she says with a laugh and a wink.

Chuckling at her reference to the show, he leans back to watch the dark haired man on the screen walking down the road with his son. A faint ghost of a fantasy hits him like a hard blow to the solar plexus, the possibility of someday taking his own red headed son fishing. Eyes darting to Chrissie's flame haired beauty, his heart opens a little more at the thought of her carrying his children, leaving him aware that his feelings have progressed far beyond trivial lust.

A sharp crack of lightning from the storm outside startles him, panic thickening his throat even though he knows they are safe. Chrissie looks over at just that moment, part of him latching on to those tranquil blue eyes like a lifeline.

"Would you be willing to come over here and keep me company?" he asks, forming the words carefully around the adrenaline muddying his senses.

Wordlessly, she slides over the cushions to fit herself under the arm he has laid along the back of the couch,

Justine Iarann

pillowing her head on his chest. Though afraid the power of her touch will prove be overwhelming his heart rate slows to a comfortable pace as her hand rests on the denim covering the fittings of his prosthesis. Right here, with her beside him, it's like home is supposed to feel.

His hand settles on her shoulder as his eyes return to the scenes playing out on the TV, distracting himself with the silky feel of her hair sliding through his fingers. Gradually, the sharp edge of fear slides away from his throat, letting him regain equilibrium. They both laugh at the good hearted, but bumbling antics of the sheriff's deputy, and time passes in a contented haze.

At one point, Chrissie notices his breathing has slowed, and she finds his eyes closed, head tipped on to the sofa back. Glad to see him rest, she settles more comfortably against his side, wrapping her free arm around his torso and hooking a finger in his pocket to keep it in place. Half way through the next show, she too drifts to sleep, sheltered in the welcome strength of his arm.

James drifts awake near one AM, dreaming of supple skin under the fingers of his left hand. He strokes over it softly, wishing it were real, then startles as the pleasant weight against him shifts. Eyes still full of sleep, he studies her in the dim light from the TV, head pillowed on his lap, cheek pressed to the small expanse of his thigh that is not covered in hardened plastic. The only thing separating the warmth of her skin from his is the thin washed denim he wears.

He lets the hand at her waist drift lazily over the creamy skin exposed by her sweater, and she shifts again with a slight sound, almost a purr. Unable to resist her allure, he draws up to move her hair back from the shell of her ear, tracing the curve of pearlescent skin down to her jaw. Now she truly stirs, turning her cheek in to his palm, eyes seeking his.

"James," she whispers softly, careful not to break the

tender mood. "I haven't slept like that since before we met. Thank you."

Her eyes are nearly midnight blue, showing a vulnerable need that calls to him far more than any words.

"Chrissie, I haven't slept that quietly in years. It's me that should be thanking you."

Using the strength of his arms, he draws her up over his lap sideways, most of her weight born up on his complete leg. Trepidation eats at him, bringing her so close, but the need is finally greater than the fear. The faith in her eyes frightens him as much as the very real possibility that he could hurt her. Tenderly, he leans in for a kiss, and the instant they touch he is washed in slow burning fire, lost in the feel of her.

Winding her hands behind his head, Chrissie pulls him closer, angling until her breasts press against the muscled breadth of his chest. It's impossible for him not to feel her nipples harden at the friction.

When Chrissie sighs against his mouth he presses between her lips, stroking his tongue briefly against hers, reveling in the silken touch. Her response incinerates any tenderness in him as she returns the kiss with a tiny growl of blatant hunger. James pulls at her with both hands now, ravenous for the light she is setting off along every nerve ending.

Drawing his hand back to the skin along her waist, she shows him what she needs, and he follows her lead willingly. Painting a blaze along her ribs with the palm of his hand, his fingertips touch the tender skin beneath her bra, stroking his thumb back and forth just under the lacy edge. Gasping for air at the intensity of sensation, she breaks their kiss, leaning against his shoulder and panting weakly.

"Are you okay, Chrissie?" he says, half playful, half serious.

Recognizing the echo of an earlier conversations, she laughs softly.

"More than okay, James. The question is, are you okay?"

Justine Iarann

She is giving him an out and frankly, he should take it. Yet, she feels so good he can't bear to let her go. He answers by raising his hand a bit more to cup her breast, gratified by the shiver that moves over her skin.

Shifting restlessly, she groans in frustration, and he lets her go, afraid he may have over assumed his welcome. Then she is turning, straddling his lap, her heat so close it unravels him even more. As she leans in to capture his lips, he reaches under her sweater to hook his thumbs in the waist of her jeans, tugging her forward until her hips are flush against his. Any thought of restrain goes up in flaming wash of glory as she rocks forward over the firm evidence of his lust.

Frantically torn between need and panic, he goes still, both hands splaying over her back as he draws in a ragged breath. She waits him out, unmoving except for her lips, which are planting gentle kisses over the top of his head as it rests against her chest.

"James, it's okay. It's more than okay. I trust you."

The words take a few seconds to sink in through the tension, but slowly he relaxes under her, resting his ear over her heart. Its strong beat echoes through him until he finds peace in the midst of the chaos, an anchor in the storm that he will always live within. She leans back, smiling as she lifts the hem of her sweater, drawing it over her head. He doesn't see where she drops it, transfixed by her full breasts, the pale flesh framed exquisitely by a dark blue bra trimmed in lace. His eyes rove down to where her hips swell into the waist of her jeans, and he sets his hands back along her ribcage. Slowly, he pulls her closer, setting a speed that tests both of their patience, but she follows his lead.

It takes forever for his lips to settle on the now cool skin of her chest, but in less than a second the fire to springs back to life. Kissing a trail toward one breast, he swipes his tongue along the laced edge of her bra, and she falls back, trusting the strength of his hands.

He holds her still for the slow migration to her other breast, concentrating on the salted honey taste of her satin skin. When he reaches the other edge of lace he splays a hand across her back to undo the hooks keeping her concealed.

A shrug of her shoulders eases the straps down and he uses his teeth to pull the fabric away. Both nipples pebble hard at the exposure to air, but the feeling barely registers when he bends his head to her breast just like in her dreams. Hot breath brings her a step closer to ruin, and when his lips close over her nipple she breaks apart a little more, drowning in sensation. He pulls her closer as she shudders in his arms, then rocks his hips against her. It takes her a minute to regain any control over herself as he reaches into her hair and tilts her neck to his lips, working his way slowly toward her mouth.

After they softly kiss, she moves back enough to say "Who is going to break who, James?"

"I think, in the end, it's going to break us both, darlin'." he replies, pressing his forehead to hers, and gazing earnestly into her eyes. "But maybe not tonight."

Sighing deeply, she settles against him until their heart rates slow, but she goes with a bit of fight, her fingers drawing circles along the unbuttoned neckline of his shirt.

"That's cheating, Chrissie." he chuckles, dropping a kiss on her bare shoulder.

"All is fair in love and war, Sgt. Fletcher." she says seriously.

"So it is, my dear, so it is." he replies, reading the truth in her eyes before drawing her in for a hug.

Almost desperately, she squeezes him back, then relaxes, now running kisses along the column of his neck. He holds her close, mentally reciting the list of gear he usually carried in the field, anything to take his mind off the tenderness of her touch.

With a heavy sigh that tugs at his heart, she sits up in his arms. When she moves to put her bra back on he leans forward to run his tongue over her nipple, and she gasps, startled.

"Something to remember me by." he says with a playful grin, though a sharper need had prompted the tease.

She responds in kind, slowly grinding her hips against his still firm erection, and he shudders.

"Turnabout is fair play." she growls.

Saucily, she tosses her bra on to a nearby chair, then stands. He smiles appreciatively at the display, her peaked nipples pressing against the fabric of her sweater when she drags it back on. Then he shifts forward, his cock rubbing uncomfortably against his zipper, tearing a groan from his lips. Chrissie looks over with concern, but when she deduces the source of his discomfort, she smiles like the cat who ate the canary.

Walking to TV to shut it down, she gives him time to pull himself together. Amazingly, his damaged leg feels fine, though his intact leg burns fiercely as the blood returns to his foot. He rolls the ankle around, waiting for the pins and needles to pass, then braces against the arm of the couch to stand, cane close at hand. Walking carefully up behind her, he wraps an arm around her waist, and draws her against him.

"Thank you, love." he whispers into her hair, and she melts into him, wrapping her arm over his and squeezing tightly.

"Anytime, dear heart." she responds. "Now you had best go before I do something you might regret in the morning."

"Never regret, not ever, sweetheart. It's just something this important I want to take my time with."

As she turns in his arm, then stands on her toes to share a kiss with him, her eyes are glistening again.

Better Broken

"Then I guess it's my turn to say thank you." she says, before stepping away toward the door. "I won't be at work tomorrow, I have plans with Suzie. Will you call me?"

"Absolutely." he affirms. A cold breeze finds its way in when she opens the door, making them both shiver. He gives her one last hug, and a brief kiss, then walks as quickly as he can out the door.

"Go get warm, and sleep well." he tosses over his shoulder.

"Good night." she says, and the door closes, leaving him standing in the mediocre light of a nearby street light.

Chilled, he limps hurriedly to his truck and slides clumsily on to the seat, slamming the door behind him in haste. The engine rumbles to life, and before the heater even kicks in he is driving away. Everything in him is screaming that he is going the wrong direction.

Justine Iarann

Chapter Six

In the morning, James barely makes it to his physical therapy appointment on time. The whole experience has lost its shine, comparing the caring Chrissie puts in her work to the very clinical manner of his regular therapist. Marti treats him like a science experiment under a microscope, everything cataloged and filed, with little to encourage him. Yet, he goes through the motions with utter concentration, prepared to push himself back toward some sense of normality. There is still the question of returning to active duty or bowing out, but he fully intends to stretch the limits of his body. Everything feels doable with Chrissie in his life, and he is eager to see where their journey will lead. At the end of the hour Marti leaves him with a new set of exercises to do on his own, and he heads back to his truck. Outside, the trees are beginning to display some faint green, and the sky shows clear, clean after last night's rain.

On the way back to the hotel his cell phone begins to ring.

Better Broken

Eagerly, he accepts the call, putting it on speaker.

"Hey Sunshine." he says with undisguised warmth.

"James?" says his sister, her tone confused.

"Aw, Jenn, sorry. I was expecting someone else."

"Clearly." Her response has a humorous edge, but there is stress in her voice. "I wish I were calling to get the skinny on the new woman, but it's actually about Dad."

"Jenn, you know I don't want to talk to him." Just like that, his mood darkens like an incoming storm.

"No, actually, you can't talk to him." she chokes out, and James's heart bottoms out at the pain in her voice. "I'm on my way to Medina right now. He is in the hospital."

"What happened?"

"I don't know yet, only that Charlie Townsend next door went over to chat, and found Dad unconscious on the floor of the kitchen. The doctors are doing tests, and I should know more soon."

"Stubborn old bastard." he grumbles, navigating around a slow moving Buick.

"Like you have room to talk, big brother? How long has it been since you've spoken to each other?"

"That's a whole other kettle of fish, Jenn. Let it alone. In the meantime, do you need anything from me?"

"I may be asking you to come down to help, if things are bad enough to keep him in the hospital. The dogs and horses will need taking care of. Charlie said he could handle it for a couple days, but then he is in the field for a week. I wanted you to have fair warning, since I know you are involved with all your doctor appointments."

James rubs distractedly at the stubble he hadn't yet shaved, his heart now aching for a much more urgent reason.

"Alright, keep me updated. I'll have to wind some things up here, but I could leave as soon as tomorrow."

"Thanks, Jamesy, you are a life saver. I'll call you later."

Justine Iarann

They say goodbye, and Jenn hangs up, leaving James at a loss. If he has to go away, how will he make things right with Chrissie? And perhaps even more tellingly, what the hell is he going to do without her?

*****

About the same time James is dealing with his troubles, Chrissie walks in to the yoga studio Suzie works at part time. She kicks off her shoes by the front desk as Suzie breezes past, and Chrissie falls in behind her. The women in the class offer greetings while Suzie gets her own mat unrolled at the front of the room, and turns on a little light instrumental music. Putting on her 'counselor voice', a warm and personal tone, Suzie directs the group in breathing exercises to begin the hour of yoga.

It is a simple thing, to follow along with the familiar routine, limbering muscles until the blood is flowing cleanly through her body. The breathing exercises alone center her, leaving her ready to take on whatever comes next. As she settles in to her own heart, seeing everything clearly, what appears is not herself. It is James, her love for him reflecting in his eyes. The image brings a tear to her eye, and she inhales fully, accepting that her heart is no longer hers. Several times over the hour her concentration is broken thinking of him, and she wonders if there is any part of her that will remain untouched by him.

When class is over the two best friends settle into oversized arm chairs at the next door tea shop, and Suzie turns to her.

"Chrissie, I gather you are a little distracted today." she says, softening the chastisement with a puckish grin.

Chrissie laughs at the vast understatement. "I don't think there will be a moment of my life that I won't be distracted by that man, ever again."

Suzie starts a little in her seat to see the love shining in her dear friends eyes. This sort of love is like the holy grail- you could spend your whole life searching without ever finding it.

"I gather Operation: Soldier is going well then?" she asks, pressing for details.

"You know I don't kiss and tell, Suz. I can say that while the road may be rocky, I think we will navigate it just fine together." Chrissie says, feeling the truth in her bones.

"He is, um, okay?" Suzie queries. "You know, I mean, okay, okay?"

"You letch!" Chrissie laughs at the curiosity and discomfort warring in her friend's expression. "Yes, I can affirm that he is 'okay'. If I had to hazard a guess, I'd say he is far better than okay."

"You don't know yet?" Suzie squeaks, pausing her line of questioning as their respective pots of tea arrive. Fragrant steam lifts from the spouts, the scent a comfort to them both. As dissimilar as they may be in personality, there is so much they both love the same. After the server walks away, Suzie continues.

"My friend, I don't know how you have managed to resist showing up at his door naked yet. You know I have done worse than that for lesser men."

Chrissie smiles softly at the mild self-deprecation, wondering when her friend will stop chasing the wrong men. She is a gorgeous woman with a soul facetted like a priceless jewel- sure, there are flaws, but in Suzie's case, it makes her shine even brighter.

"Suzie, sometimes the best things in life need to be waited for. As hot as the sparks are on this fire, I don't doubt that the end result will be anything less than an inferno."

"I think I'd be throwing more fuel on it, were I you." Suzie scoffs. "But I'm not, and I'm okay with that. You know me, all or nothing."

Nodding an agreement Chrissie turns to her tea, going

silent for the first few sips of dark perfume. As she looks in to the cup, sweetened only with sugar, no milk to cloud the color, she sees James's eyes. Her sigh catches Suzie's attention.

"Wow, you have it bad!"

"Actually, I have it very, very good." Chrissie responds with a silly grin.

"You love him, don't you?" Suzie asks gently.

"Yes, I do." she says, emboldened by hearing the words aloud. "I, Chrissie Everett, am in love with James Fletcher."

The bravery in her words is belied by the stretch of quiet at the end. Suzie lets her steep in her own declaration for a few seconds.

"If he hurts you, I swear to heaven I will chop off his other leg." Suzie says in vicious defense of her friend's tender heart.

Chrissie is taken aback at her fierce tone. "You would do no such thing, Suzie Ashford. He is a hero who nearly paid the ultimate price for our freedom, and you owe him your respect for that, if nothing else!"

"Well, okay, I suppose I'd just have to key his car or something." Suzie growls as she leans back in her chair. "Still, he better not hurt you."

"I know, deep in my heart, that if he does, it will totally be worth it." Chrissie half whispers, praying she never has to find out if that is true.

Later in the afternoon, Chrissie is curled around a book, leaning heavily into the corner of the sofa she had occupied with James. She has re-read the same page several times, absently running her hand over the back of the couch where his head had rested while they slept. What a love sick sap she is, but she can't really be mad at herself for it. No shining white prince fantasies are running around in her head, maybe more of a knight in battered armor. Sure, she is frustrated to no end by his need to protect her from himself, but she understands it. He simply values her well-being more than he does his own, a welcome change from the men in her past. Which means she wants to be there when he is beaten up by his own darkness, stepping in beside him to fight it back.

A knock on the door startles her, book dropping from nervous fingers as she rises from the sofa. The peephole reveals James on her front step, and she vainly attempts to straighten her disheveled hair. Still in her yoga pants and a ratty t-shirt, her appearance is not very flattering, but it would be rude to keep him waiting. She swings the door wide for him to come in, hoping he won't find the get up unappealing.

His response is far different than she feared, and it takes considerable will power not to drag her to him for a thorough mussing. The workout pants trace every line of her delectable hips and leave little to imagination, his hands itching to explore her softness. He settles for a gentlemanly kiss on the hand, letting his eyes do the roving.

A blush rises up her neck at his proprietary gaze. Apparently, he still likes what he sees.

They settle on the sofa, and while she doesn't cuddle close, she sits right beside him, turning sideways to catch his gaze.

"I wasn't expecting company, James, but I am glad you came. You've been on my mind all day."

The smile he tries to reply with stops short of his eyes. A little wrinkle starts between her eyebrows, and he leans forward to kiss it away. Letting him smooth it, she then tips up to catch his lips, concern keeping the kiss brief; as she pulls back, he exhales forcefully.

"Life has gotten complicated." he groans, not wanting to dim the soft mood, but needing to lift the weight settled on his chest. "My sister called today."

Waiting on him to elaborate, she curls her hand around his where it rests on her thigh.

"My father is in the hospital." The heaviness in his voice is not lost on her. "Jenn said he is conscious now, and after some testing, they discovered cirrhosis of the liver."

"And you need to go." she says quietly, surely.

"I think I do. The old man and I haven't spoken since before I left for the Middle East. The words exchanged were heated. I don't know if I will go see him, Jenn is at the hospital while they get things under control. But someone needs to go take care of the kennel and horses while he is there."

Running her free hand up his shoulder to where it meets his neck, she begins to massage the tension he carries, showing no hesitation at the scar tissue beneath her fingers. James sighs deeply, bowing his head under her healing touch, and briefly gives up the stress that he is bearing.

"This is a mess, Chrissie. An absolute mess."

"James, it's okay. I'm not going anywhere." she says, her voice soft. "Do you trust me?"

"Of course. Always." he answers, looking up in confusion.

"Then come in here and let me work on you for a while." she says, tugging gently at his hand as she gets up.

Steadier than the night before, he rises and lets her guide him to the bedroom. The dim sanctuary has little light coming through the curtains, bed covered in an elaborate quilt and her workout bag still sitting on the edge. She releases him and he realizes that he has walked without the cane- again, the ways she heals him are astounding. After pulling back the blanket she tosses her bag on a chair in the corner.

"Alright, soldier, I need you to strip. Everything but your skivvies." Her smile is encouraging, and maybe a little challenging, much like the other day at therapy.

Seeing her bet, he raises the hem of his shirt, her breath catching as he reveals the rippling abdomen she has thus far

Better Broken

only explored through his clothes. He isn't deeply cut like a body builder, but every muscle is defined by years of honing himself in to a warrior, strong and capable. His body serves a purpose, not like obsessive gym gorillas who cannot reach their own toes.

Struck still as she steps forward, James sighs at the soft kiss she plants on his collar bone. Then she walks him backward, giving him time to choose his steps, keeping his balance with her hands on his hips. The bed bumps against the back of his knee and he reaches between them to undo the button on his jeans. Her pupils go wide at the rapid hiss of the zipper, then he pushes them over his hips, revealing a pair of dark boxers. Sitting down on the edge of the mattress, he is fascinated at her nimble fingers as she draws the pants down and presses the button that releases the seal on his prosthesis. Drawing off the shoe on his intact foot, she slips the pants off entirely along with his artificial leg. He sucks in a breath as she pulls down the cuff covering his residual limb, his skin so sensitized to her that he feels each fingertip. The feather light kiss she lays on top of the scarred thigh nearly stops his heart. Her eyes are dark blue when she looks up.

"I'm glad you don't feel like running from me anymore, Sgt. Fletcher."

No, now he is running toward her, running back to the light that has been gone so long from his life.

"James, if you will lay face down for me, I'll see what I can do to make you comfortable."

The blood rushing to his groin will make this uncomfortable regardless, but he remembers her soothing touch from before. So he stretches out across the cool sheets and feels her draw off his remaining sock, laying him nearly bare before her. The bed shifts as she crawls to his side, resting there on her knees, then her hands deliver a firm stroke from the small of his back all the way up between his shoulders. He releases a pent up breath and focuses on her touch, the warm caring she is spreading over him.

Occasionally, he feels her linger on a scar, tracing the lines of each divot and pucker. Sometimes, he can't even feel the touch, nerves too damaged to allow it, but he knows because he doesn't feel her anywhere else. What he can feel, even as she traces the patch of numb flesh along his side, is the love.

It isn't long until he notices that she is inhaling and exhaling purposefully, and then he finds himself matching the deliberate breaths. Soon, he is drifting in a fully relaxed haze, then she shifts position to sit astride his hips, slowly lowering her weight. His hips stretch under the traction, then pop as his lower back settles into correct position.

Turning his face into the bed, he groans at the release of tension, then follows it with gasp as she finds the first knot along his left side, rolling over it with firm strokes until it slowly gives itself up. She works through several more places and his hands move back to her knees, caressing the tops of her thighs through the thin fabric of her pants.

She leans down the length of him, her body molding against his back. "You had best stop that if you want me to finish what I'm doing." she whispers, words hot on his neck.

Turning his head to one side, he smiles and leaves his hands resting where they are.

Time slows to a precious crawl as she works through the stiffness, moving up to straddle his waist and working over his neck with the same thorough rhythm she had used before. Then his skin grows goose bumps as she starts in on his scalp, sliding her fingers around the top of his ears and back to the spot where his skull joins his spine. It is a strange blend of invigorating and peaceful that leaves him clearly aware of every place her body is making contact with his. After a few minutes, she moves off of him and lays down, pillowing her head on her hands as she waits for him to open his eyes.

Most of the stress he had carried in the door is gone, and he smiles at her pleased expression.

"Wow, Sunshine. Just wow."

"You know, I've been wanting to do that from the very first day I saw you." she answers with her own smile.

"And here I've been wasting time." he teases. "You are awfully good."

"I put myself through college as a massage therapist, so I've had lots of practice."

A little flash in his eyes betrays his jealousy at all the other men she had soothed.

"Of course, none of my clients received the experience you did. I don't climb on to just anybody." she says with a wink.

"No?"

"No," she says seriously, "only you."

He grunts in satisfaction, a very male noise, and she giggles, then begins to laugh at his affronted expression.

"Oh really?" he says sternly, reaching over to tickle his fingers over her ribs, which makes her squeal and pull away. He laughs at her piqued attitude and is rewarded with a bright smile. Slowly, she settles back down on her stomach, and he turns toward her, pulling a pillow under his head for support.

"So, when are you heading out?" she asks, expression now serious.

"Tomorrow." he answers with a frown.

"Ah, so we only have tonight left." The sadness in her eyes swallows his original worry that she would be mad, leaving an ache of regret in its place. "In that case, will you stay with me tonight? I don't know when I'll sleep well again, once you go."

The offer surprises him, and though he doesn't like hurting her it soothes his heart to know she is not going to enjoy the time apart either.

"Sure. How about we order in and we can finish the DVD we didn't watch last night?"

"Sounds perfect." But rather than rising, she rolls to her side and scoots closer.

The intimacy of lying face to face is achingly honest, watching emotions swirling through her eyes. After a few moments, he unfolds the arm under his head and invites her closer. All warmth and softness, she comes, until her head is resting on his bicep and her arm circles his waist. The light swell of her stomach is a welcoming softness for his burgeoning erection, and her nipples rub against his chest as they breathe. He splays his free hand over the small of her back, then down over her full hip, coming to rest on the swell of her backside. She sighs against his skin, and follows it with a brush of lips.

To stay right here, forever, would be an unbelievable bliss. Wishing he could say to hell with his father, he brushes a kiss to Chrissie's forehead. A few moments later, the fingers dancing through the hair on his chest grow still, and her breathing slows. She is asleep, and he finds he could care less about dinner, just having her in his arms. A minute more has him matching breaths again, then he drifts off to join her in sleep.

When dawn wakes him the sun is beginning to blaze around the edges of the heavy curtains. James is on his back and Chrissie is now curled away from him. The covers are pulled over them, meaning she must have woken at some point in the night. He, on the other hand, had slept the night through, almost nine hours. It's a sleep he hasn't known since boyhood and he knows it for the treasure that it is. Rolling on his side, he pulls her close, and she responds instantly, arching her hips in welcome. No longer in her workout clothes but a pair of cotton flannel shorts and a Mickey Mouse t-shirt, it gives his hands easy access to her rib cage.

Better Broken

He slides his hand up to tease her nipple. Groaning in response, she pulls his head down to her neck where he plants kisses along the soft skin. Now she slides along the length of him, her generous buttocks stroking his thickening cock, letting him know he is welcome to all of her. Squeezing his eyes shut, he grows still, struggling with too much feeling.

Wanting so badly to follow his lead, wanting him to stay a little longer, Chrissie also freezes. James knows his weakness is not hers and refuses to leave her wanting this morning, so he spreads his palm flat over her stomach, slowly sliding his hand beneath the waist line of her shorts. Her breath hitches as his calluses brush her hip bone and his fingers invade the soft curls near her vagina, finding a welcome in the moist heat there. He can't help but groan, grinding his erection between them to discover her so wet and needy.

It dawns on Chrissie what he intends and she turns in his arms, unwilling to let him satisfy her if she can't give him the same release.

"James," Urgency makes her voice crack. "James, listen to me."

He nearly doesn't hear her around the blood thundering in his ears, but her hands on his face prompt him to focus.

"As much I want you, I can't let you do this." she whispers brokenly, tears threatening in her eyes, now vivid cerulean blue in the growing sunlight. "I refuse to be broken alone. The first time, we will break apart together, or not at all."

Her conviction reaches him like nothing else possibly could have, and recognizing the strength of it, he pulls her close for a tender kiss. She can taste the remorse in it, and tries to soothe it away.

"It's always more than okay, James. Always." she whispers, her lips still touching his. Then she kisses him fiercely, nearly climbing into his skin she holds him so tightly. The hunger washes away his regrets, and he sighs deeply when she pulls away for a breath.

"You know something, Chrissie Everett, I think I may not survive loving you, but I sure am going to give it my best shot."

The tears that threatened earlier now fall, and he wipes them away with his thumbs.

"Well, I absolutely forbid you to do anything that would prevent me from loving you right back, you idiot." she answers, joy lighting her soul so brightly it dims the sun.

His eyes flash, this time with a tiny glimmer of light, and he smiles at her teasing endearment. Their lips meet again, almost reverent, worshiping each other softly until her alarm clock goes off.

"I have to get ready for work, my heart." she says, tipping her forehead on to his with disappointment. "Duty calls for both of us."

Releasing her with a groan, he rolls over on to his back then to a sitting position while she climbs off the other side of the bed.

"I'm going to hop in the shower really fast, can you wait until I am done to say goodbye?"

Lust chokes his words at the thought of her naked and wet in the shower, but he manages a nod in reply. It doesn't help that her hips tease him with a sassy sway as she walks in the bathroom and closes the door.

Finding his pants right beside the bed he begins the process of dressing, first rolling the gel sleeve on his residual limb, then sliding on the socket. He stands, body weight forcing extra air from the seal, and then slides his pants on. It is complicated by his erection, an involuntary smile starting that the most difficult part of his morning routine is not the prosthetic for a change. It takes some adjustment so that he isn't rubbing too much, then he reaches for the rest of his clothing.

Better Broken

Fifteen minutes pass, and he tries to occupy the time, heading to the kitchen to see if she has a coffee pot. He finds it already plugged in but can't locate the coffee anywhere. She walks in as he is rifling through cabinets, wrapping her arms around him from behind and tucking her hands in the front pockets of his jeans, dangerously close to his softening member.

"May I help you find something, Sgt. Fletcher?" she teases, delivering a love nip to his shoulder blade. He growls as his cock leaps in response, wishing he felt stable enough to turn around and grab ahold of her.

"Coffee, Miss Everett. And soon, I hope." he answers gruffly.

"Really, didn't you get enough sleep last night?" she says, moving away to pull a canister out from behind the toaster. "Because I feel amazing."

"You look amazing." he says, stepping the short distance across her tiny kitchen to press her up against the counter. "Almost good enough to eat." he grinds out, leaning down to return her love bite, right along the unbuttoned neck line of the polo shirt she wears for work. Her hands come up to his head immediately, encouraging him to linger awhile, but he steps back with a teasing grin. "Coffee first."

"You drive a hard bargain, my dear, but I shall comply. I need more kissing before you go."

The heartache in her voice immediately makes him regret the tease, but she doses the coffee maker, setting it to percolate. Then she is walking back to his arms, and he holds them open in welcome, glad he can finally stand completely without the support of the cane. They hold each other as the coffee drips slowly into the pot, until she puts her lips over his heart again, a gesture he is going to miss while they are apart.

"I love it when you do that."

"Good, because I love doing it." she whispers, pressing several more around the same spot.

Tightening his arms around her, he tangles a hand in her braid, tipping her lips up. He kisses her with excruciating thoroughness until she is all he can taste, vanilla and cinnamon, the flavors warm against his tongue.

"On second thought, no coffee, Chrissie. You are the only thing I want to taste when I leave."

Raising up on her toes, she kisses him so deeply he is sure she can see clear through him. The darkness cracks around his heart, letting her light shine through on to every wound, cleansed with the breath they share, and the tears that run from her face on to his. He tastes them on her lips, the bitterness a sharp counterpoint to her sweetness. When they break apart, his heart is now clean enough to offer up to her fully.

"Sunshine, I'm going to miss you," he says earnestly. "And I want you to know I love you."

"I love you too, my dear." she answers without pause. "I will miss you every moment, and I'll be here waiting when you come back."

Not wanting to make her late, he lets her go and she pours the entire pot of fresh coffee down the sink, a symbol of her desire to take his taste with her as well. They share a smile, and he takes her hand as they step out the door, walking her to her car. Their goodbye kiss is brief, but no less heartfelt, as she pulls him into her with her fist wrapped in his shirt.

"Drive safe, James. And come back soon. I'm not done with you yet." she reminds him, a flash of their first kiss blazing across his memory.

"I'll be as quick as I can, Sunshine. It's a dark world out there without you."

James watches Chrissie pull safely out of the parking lot then climbs in his old grey Ford pickup next to the duffel

Better Broken

sitting on the seat. He drops a text to his sister, letting her know he is on his way, then bends his head over the steering wheel in a quick prayer to return soon. The darkness within had only just been broken, and it had been his enemy for too many long nights to presume it would be vanquished so easily. Her light is the only weapon he had found that drove it back.

Justine Iarann

Chapter Seven

The drive to Texas is excruciatingly long. Chrissie and he talk every night as she drives home from work or the barn, but he misses her so fiercely it aches. Day one is tough, sitting still for so long and knowing that he is close enough to turn around to head back to her arms. Yet, it's bearable for all that, with beautiful weather and amazing scenery. Day two, it is warm enough to wear shorts, which simplifies taking off his prosthesis while he drives. The back of his thigh is sore from wearing it against the seat the day before, but by days end he enters the hotel on his loathed crutches, the limb too sore to bear walking on. After a night of compression bandaging and ice, it is moderately tolerable for the half day drive to reach Medina, and hopefully for the chores that await him. Charlie had left town last night, which means all the critters have to be tended as soon as James arrives.

Cresting the hill overlooking the ranch, he is pleased to note that some things hadn't changed- the place is still

Better Broken

spotless, low white buildings freshly painted, weeds cut back and fences strung tight. Despite his father's rapid sink in to alcoholism after the death of James's mother, he still managed to maintain the jewel that is Dog Tired Ranch.

Heading straight to the kennels he is rewarded with the immediate rise in noise as every dog runs outside to sing him a welcome. It is a sound he had missed, regardless of the fact that their volume alone is making his ears ring. The scent hounds have a distinct bell like tone which offsets the higher pitched, needy voices of the bird dogs, so frantic for attention.

As he climbs out of the truck and slides into his limb, he is accosted by four barn cats winding around his feet, irrespective of which is real or artificial. Knowing he could likely trip over them, and not wanting to risk a fall, he grabs his cane before heading to the kennel. The cats all stop at the door with their ears flattened, unwilling to enter the cacophony inside, their patent disgust teasing a weary laugh from him.

Just to the right, once inside, is the feed room. He steps in, eyes falling on the meticulously written board with each dogs rations listed, and then on to the feed cart, already loaded with filled bowls. He is going to owe Charlie a beer when the man gets back, for saving him the trouble. It is the work of moments to roll the cart down the aisle, pushing bowls under kennel doors, until the frenzied chorus is silenced with the business of eating. When he comes to the end, he notices one dog alone in the nursery area, her voice rising back up in pitch as she recognizes him. It is Lucy, a Plott Hound born shortly before he left, that he had bottle nursed when she was the runt of her litter. He opens the door and she slowly leans against his intact leg, as though she understands his instability. Stroking her silky brindle ears, he gusts out a sigh of relief, her welcome easing his fatigue.

Justine Iarann

"Good girl, Luce." he tells her, leaning down a little to gently slap the side of her sturdy ribcage with affection, careful of her heavy belly. Her tail beats a happy rhythm as she gazes up at him, her tongue lolling out in joy. It is hard to leave her, but there are horses still to check on.

The walk down to the barn is a little more challenging, with the slope of the hill and some loose gravel to contend with. He manages it with few bobbles, walking in the open door of the airy barn to find it empty of horses. It is quiet and peaceful, except for the cats who are demanding their own food, so he tosses his feline entourage some kitty kibble and walks back outside. Around the south side, lounging about a large round bale of hay, is a small herd of lanky and content horses. Satisfied, he tops off the water trough, then heads back to the truck.

Another quarter mile drive takes him to the house, a white ranch style with a deep porch, shaded in a grove of live oak. His childhood memories make it easy to imagine his mother waiting in the kitchen, a short white apron on over her boots and jeans, making pancakes after Saturday chores are done. But she had been gone more than a decade, and the shadow over the house is palpable.

As he pulls around the back of the house to park he finds a car already in the drive, the back door standing wide open behind the screen. He would have been concerned, if this were anywhere else but middle of nowhere, Texas.

"Hello, anyone here?" He is rewarded with a familiar feminine voice from the laundry room.

Charlie Townsend's wife, Carol, is starting a load of sheets, her hands moving steadily on the knobs of the old washer. The short, huggable woman was his mother's best friend in this tiny town, and had taken it upon herself after his mother died to take care of them. Jenn in particular had enjoyed her motherly affection, but even James had sometimes needed

Better Broken

her support and guidance.

"Jenn told me you were coming, and I wanted you to have a fresh bed to lie in. I put some groceries in the ice box too." she says, as she straightens up and opens her arms for the requisite hug. He is instantly folded into her embrace, surrounded by a scent of lemon soap and sage that had always soothed him.

"Good to see you, Aunt Carol." he rumbles against the top of her head, the short silvery strands tickling his nose.

"Good to see you too, my boy." She chuckles and lets him go. "We weren't sure you'd be making it home."

Her gaze is pointedly directed at his missing limb, then back to his face, and he grimaces in response.

"Yeah, there were some times I wasn't sure either."

Nodding her acknowledgement, she moves on, grabbing hold of the laundry hamper before traveling down the hall to his old room. Caught her wake, James is struck still as he clears the door, feeling like he stepped out of a time machine. Nothing had changed at all, from the old duvet on the bed, to the letterman jacket draped over the desk chair- he runs a hand over the sleeve, the leather dry and flakey with age, and a film of dust coating his fingertips when he pulls away. The tall dresser is still littered with trophies from baseball and pictures from high school, nostalgia an unexpected result as he studies the once familiar faces.

"I have to do a few more things before you are all set, so go grab some food and have a sit while I finish up." Carol directs.

He manages a yes ma'am before she starts shooing him with a broom, so he leaves, knowing even if he had offered to help, she wouldn't have allowed him- it is just her way. Instead, he retrieves his duffel from the truck, dropping it on a kitchen chair before grabbing a cold chicken leg and a glass of sweet tea. In the living room, he looks dubiously at the low slung old couch before lowering carefully on to the dated floral fabric. There is a leather recliner that would serve him better, but years of conditioning as a boy keeps him from sitting in his father's chair.

A warm, easy breeze moves the lace curtains his mother had hung when he was eight. There is a large photo of the whole family, smiling and complete when he was ten, hanging near the hall. The crochet afghan on the sofa she had made when she lay in bed after a tough round of chemo. The watercolor landscape over the old brick mantle she had done after her hair had fallen out, her scribbled signature shoved in the corner of the frame like an afterthought. On the table beside his father's chair winks the tiny diamond of Jamie Fletcher's wedding ring, right next to an half empty glass of whiskey. All these years later, he finally understands that his own father had drown his darkness in a bottle after he had lost his guiding light.

At that moment, his phone beeps, and he fishes it from his pocket to read Chrissie's message. It's a photo of the chair he usually occupies during their lunches, simply captioned 'I miss you'.

A heavy sigh gusts from him and he takes a drink of the tea to wash down the lump forming in his throat, closing his eyes on all the past and present heartaches. Carol walks back down the hall shortly after he manages to pull himself together.

"James, you have yourself a lie down and after you finish chores tonight, you drive over and have supper. Charlie not being home will give me the bother of leftovers if you don't come eat."

Her tone brooks no argument, so he simply agrees. She is out the back door, car moving down the driveway before he can get up off the sofa. It doesn't take long to strip down and slide under the fresh sheets now on his bed. He manages a quick text back to Chrissie before exhaustion drags him under wholesale.

'Miss you too, Sunshine. Safely here. I'll call tonight.'

Then he dozes off, almost able to feel Chrissie's touch in the breeze blowing through the window, caressing him with the sun that lay across his shoulder.

*****

Being a mess is a foreign feeling for Chrissie. Twice, she'd nearly been late to the clinic, sliding in by a hair. She can't get enough sleep, which means she also can't get enough caffeine. Sometimes, she drifts to sleep curled around the pillow James had slept on, but then wakes after a few hours, reaching for him. Yes, she is managing, still getting her job done with excellent reviews, still following her schedule, only never quite in the groove.

Smoke is being very kind, letting her be a sloppy rider without qualm, covering her mistakes. Suzie tries dragging her out to a party, going to movies, taking her shopping. Nothing comes together, everything is slightly out of reach, to the point that she is angry with herself. As a fully functional adult, happily in love, with a great career, the world should be her oyster- so why can't she find the damned pearl?

Unable to bear looking at the chair across from her, she avoids the sunny alcove that now feels so very empty. Books are little solace, and she doesn't have the patience for TV. Whenever she is ready to scream at her lack of control, she remembers some of her clients, who truly have no control, and she pulls herself together.

When James calls her that night she scrambles to reach the phone, in the middle of brushing her teeth to get ready for bed.

"Hey Sunshine, how are you tonight?"

"I'm doing alright." she lies, hearing how tired his voice is. "How are you doing, being home?"

"Truth be told, it's not home anymore. Home is in your arms."

Her eyes water unbearably at the declaration.

"Same here, James. Which means things actually suck for me right now."

"Ah, I thought maybe you were fibbing." he teases, the smile in his voice easing her aching heart.

"Enough about me, then. Tell me how you are doing?"

"Well, I've re-discovered some old friends. One of the dogs I bottle fed as a pup is still here. My father would be horrified to know she is in the house with me tonight, but I couldn't bear to leave her. My old mare is still here- she must be twenty now, but she looks great and clearly remembers me, judging by the nibbling I received."

"Old friends are the best." Laughter bubbles up at the mental picture of his boyhood horse using him as a dishrag.

"So are new ones, Miss Everett." he replies, his voice deep with the memory of their first conversation.

"So they are, Sgt. Fletcher." Chrissie says, her own voice growing quiet.

"You sound tired, Chrissie. How are you, really?"

The groan she utters isn't very lady like, but it certainly conveys a good deal more than words would have.

"James, I am a walking disaster zone. I haven't slept a full night since you left, and it's throwing everything off."

"I'm really sorry, Sunshine. I've had insomnia for so long, it's normal for me. The nights with you have been the best sleep of my life."

"How do you cope?" she asks seriously. "I'm completely at a loss."

"Well, I used to go running." The clipped delivery betrays his impatience.

"And you will again, stubborn man. Give yourself time to walk first!" she rebuts, her professional edge surpassing any lover like sympathy for a moment.

He chuckles at her stern tone. "Also, for the insomnia, I still work out hard in the afternoons. You said you were taking yoga on your days off, maybe it would help to do more classes?"

"Well, I can probably do that." she acquiesces. "Or are you just trying to get me more limber for when you get back?"

The tease makes him laugh and she loves the sound, even over the miles.

"Hey, whatever side effects it has, that certainly isn't a bad one!"

They talk for a while longer, about inconsequential things that somehow matter when you are desperate to stay on the phone, but it isn't long before she is yawning.

"Chrissie, you need to get to sleep. Morning is going to come much sooner for you than me." he scolds fondly.

She can't argue with him, as much as she wishes she could. So she says her goodnights, ending with an I love you, thrilled as always to hear him say he loves her too. After they hang up, she stares at the ceiling, exhausted and almost to the point of tears. He may call her his sunshine, but truthfully, what is light without the darkness to compare it to?

Justine Iarann

Chapter Eight

It takes a week for James to settle in, to feel strong enough to exercise the dogs. At first he takes single dogs out, then couples and sets as he becomes more stable. Sure, it is only up and down the driveway, but it is better than staying in their kennels. Certainly, it is effective therapy, giving him time to learn his prosthesis and its limits. Lucy comes to live in his room for the time being, happily ensconced on a pile of old sleeping bags from the barn.

    His father isn't getting any better, but he also isn't getting worse, and is starting to make noises about coming home. Jenn is trying her hardest to get James to come see their dad before that happens, and while he fights it tooth and nail, he sees the logic. Best to do any squabbling on more neutral ground, rather than at the house which holds so many past words of anger. If he needs to stay for the dogs and horses, he will, but it would be much easier if the two of them aren't at each other's throats.

Better Broken

So, after a long evening talking to Chrissie about the problem, he resolves to go have it out with the old man the next morning. The drive in to Kerrville isn't very long, but dread makes it more exhausting than the drive from Virginia had been. Jenn meets him in the lobby with a wobbly smile- she had been the only family that had come to see him when he had been in Walter Reed, the only one he had trusted close when he was hurting so badly.

"Hey sis." he says, gathering her in for a hug. Her head hits him at chest level, just as his mother's would have. Jenn squeezes him tightly, and he tries to convey a world of feeling in the hug he returns. Time and distance will never change the love he feels for his little sister, nor the urge to protect her. Too many years covering for a father who was hidden in the depths of a bottle had left their mark on them both.

Conversation is brief, since they had spoken in depth last night, and she leads him down the halls to his father's room. It is a shock to see his father in the hospital bed, his body spare with illness and the lifelong tan fading in the fluorescent light. Jenn squeezes his hand in the silence as the two men size each other up. Aside from the illness, looking at his father is like looking toward his future; some difference in hair color is all that separates them, his father's being lighter than James's near black, which James came by from his mother.

"Boy." is all his father says, nodding his head. "Jenny, you go get some coffee or somethin'."

Grateful for the look of concern she gives him before walking out, James answers his father in kind with a tip of his head. "Sir."

"Come on in and sit." Jeff Fletcher says gruffly, waving a hand at a chair. "Tell me about the dogs."

It is disconcerting to have his father treating him so politely, not to mention the flashbacks James is having to his own lengthy stay in a hospital bed. The antiseptic smell of the room alone is enough to incite a low hum of panic, but he takes the offer, trying to remain civil. Trying not to remember the long, sweaty nights coming to terms with the pain in his ravaged body and soul. It is easy to talk about the dogs, a subject they had always agreed on, and a common ground he knows will never change. They both make eye contact, taking measure of each other as they speak.

"I've got one of those ATVs in the barn, under a tarp. You could probably figure it out pretty quick, if you wanted to take the hounds on a long run."

A bit taken aback at the old man's thoughtfulness for his current condition, James knows the bigger motivator is keeping his precious pack in hunting shape. Hog season starts soon.

"Thank you, sir. I'll keep that in mind. It would be better than walking as I am not up to speed yet." he concedes.

"And you should take out a couple of the younger gun dogs for some work in the brush. You remember where the key for the gun cabinet is?"

"I'll never forget, sir. Thank you."

Finally, polite platitudes and neutral ground extinguished, they come down to brass tacks.

"Boy, I wanted to say somethin', in case this trouble with my liver heads south fast." His father's deep Texan drawl thickens with emotion. "I ain't sorry for a damn thing that passed between us. But I know your Momma, she'd beat me with a skillet if I made it to heaven without makin' things right."

James holds his father's gaze and waits, afraid if he speaks this will all go to hell in the proverbial hand basket.

"I'm proud to see the man you have grown in to, strong as hell, I can see it in your spine. The Army did you some good, but you wouldn't have been that tough to start with if it hadn't been for the bull I put you through. I didn't know how to do any different than my own daddy did to me, once your Momma passed."

Shocked by the admission, it twists James's gut to see his father's eyes gather unshed tears. Not this man, this tough, hard boiled bastard who had driven him away. He clings to his anger, refusing to soften.

"I kept pushin' you away, and pushin' you away. Jenny keeps sayin' it's because we are too damn alike, and I am gettin' to think she might be right."

If not for the discipline of expression he had been schooled in since joining the Army, James might have resembled a large mouth bass at his father's words. As it is, he keeps his face impassive, only a tic in his jaw giving away the depth of his emotions.

"Sir, I can't imagine this is going to surprise you much, but I'm going to be angry with you a bit longer." James says, gruffly. Then his voice softens as he thinks of Chrissie's warm influence. "I think though, maybe I could be ready to start working on some forgiveness."

Apparently, his expression is more transparent than he thought, because his father's next words say it all.

"I see that maybe you've found your own light, have you, my boy?"

Not quite ready to let everything slide, James tightens his resolve and his jaw, briefly answering. "Yes, Sir."

"Good for you, son. Don't you let that go, for nothin'." his father says with conviction, twisting his weathered hands in to his blankets over the top of his distended belly. "Irreplaceable treasure, your Mother, and I miss her every God damned day."

"Yeah, that I can understand." James says with a huff of frustrated breath, and then unbends enough for a sympathetic grimace. "Every God damned hour."

Justine Iarann

His dad nods emphatically in response, then returns conversation to the dogs, trying for neutrality until Jenn comes back.

"I imagine you have the brindle bitch in the house." Jeff barks, eyebrows drawing downward.

James keeps his face carefully composed. "I have no idea what you mean, Sir." The deepening smile lines around his father's eyes show he knows the truth.

"I'll be home soon, once I argue these hell bent panic mongers in to lettin' me go. In the meantime, if she whelps, don't you over handle those pups. Her last batch went for a pretty penny, and I don't want them coddled."

"Yes, Sir. I mean, no, Sir." James replies, unable to resist a very small grin back at his father.

Jeff Fletcher is the king of over handling puppies, and has no room to talk. He remembers his father bringing litters to the house, letting them boil through the kitchen with reckless abandon, and his mother chasing them back out laughing. The man is a good father figure- only not so much good with hot headed teenage boys that are far too much like him for comfort. If his father is a mirror of James's future, he can imagine his Dad sees an echo of his past.

While it is nice to have the truce flag waved between them, James is glad when Jenn returns. She approaches cautiously at first, as if looking to see if any blood has been shed. The smile she lays on them both is relieved to say the least.

"Well, Sir, I imagine I need to get back for the afternoon chores. Jenn will give you my number, if you think of anything that needs doing, until they let you out of here." He rises from his chair, carefully straightening his stiff limbs before offering an open hand to his father. "Jenn, you call me later if they give y'all any updates."

"It was good to see you, son." his father says roughly, clasping his hand with reserved enthusiasm, seemingly relieved at the proffered olive branch.

With that, James makes his exit, and despite the limp he carries his footsteps on the way out the door are so much lighter.

*****

Chrissie and Suzie are out mid-week to celebrate- earlier that day, Chrissie received an excellent job offer upon graduation, back in her home state of Colorado. It isn't even very far from her mother, so she should be overjoyed. Though it is all she had prayed for, her heart simply isn't in the rejoicing mood, no matter how Suzie tries to entice her. Currently, they are sitting in an ice cream shop sharing a banana split- or rather, Suzie is eating while Chrissie is just stirring it around.

"Alright, that's it! I am revoking your ice cream privileges for abuse to delicious concoctions!" Suzie exclaims, pulling the dish away from Chrissie to save it from its sticky fate.

Chrissie barely rolls her eyes and sets her spoon down in defeat. This should be the best day ever, she should have already called her mother to share the news. Yet, all she can think about is James.

"Suz, I don't know how this could possibly work." She slumps in her chair with a heavy sigh. "I'm going to be leaving and then what about James?"

"It's simple. It will work, or it won't." Suzie scoffs, Chrissie's heart aching at the callus words. "But you aren't getting anywhere sitting here stewing in chocolate sauce and whipped cream. You'll have to lob the ball in to his court, and see where it lands."

"But what if it doesn't work?" Strain makes her voice low. "How can I let this job go? I know they made noises about keeping me here at Adventist, but his Army life had him in Georgia, and now he's in Texas for who knows how long?"

"Oh no, Saint Chrissie, there will be no martyring yourself

for the sake of a man, I forbid it." Suzie practically growls at her. "You follow your own star. If he loves you, he'll find a way. Or rather, you'll both find a way. Now, since you are going to be hung up on this until you talk to that ridiculous man, I want you to go home and call him. And stop beating up innocent ice cream." she finishes, pulling the remains of the banana split within the circle of her arms as if to protect it.

Her friend's ridiculousness prompts a smile, but there is wisdom in her words. She will not be able to think straight until she tells James what is on her heart. So she gives Suzie a quick hug and makes her exit, pulling on a coat against the chill in the night air.

When she reaches home, she goes straight in to sit on the corner of the couch that makes her feel closest to James, as though he is there for her to lean against. The phone call goes directly to voicemail, so she hangs up and sends a text.

'Big news, call me as soon as you have a quiet minute.'

A long shower proves an adequate distraction while she waits, taking extra care with her wild curls. She even does some light yoga, having started more classes during the week to keep her centered and on track. It is helping a little, at least getting her enough rest to achieve her days without being scatterbrained. She curls back up on the sofa and contemplates putting in the DVD they watched together, hoping it would help the time pass. When she gives up and heads to bed, her phone rings at last.

"James, I was just climbing into bed."

"Hey Sunshine," he says in greeting. "I can let you go, if you're tired."

"No, I am fine." she says, trying to put a smile in her voice. "Actually, I doubt I could sleep with such big news to share! Where were you earlier?"

"I took a pack of the hounds out for some work in the

Better Broken

hills and didn't have any signal, so I just got your message. What's the big news?"

"Well," Worry puts hesitation in her words. "I received a job offer for this fall."

"Wow! Well done, and I know well deserved. Must be that stellar recommendation I gave Marti, for Adventist to want to keep you." he teases.

Chrissie is partly frustrated as well as a little proud when she answers. "Adventist made some noise about it, but this is actually back in Colorado, not too far from my Mom. It's an incredible offer, considering my level of experience, and I have always meant to go back there." she finishes in a rush, trying to get it all out at once.

Worry thickens her throat when James is silent for a moment, but he answers as she opens her mouth to ask if he is okay.

"That's great, Sunshine. A really amazing opportunity. I'm so proud of you!"

"Are you sure it's alright?" Nerves leave her chewing on the corner of her thumbnail. "I mean, I can fly out and see you every couple of weeks. Or I could wait out Adventist? I could even apply in Texas if you want to stay there."

"No, no, Chrissie, don't you dare let this go. I mean, this is what you dreamed of, and I don't want you giving anything up on account of me. I don't even know what I am doing with my life yet, now that I am getting back on my feet. Literally."

"Thank you, love." Relieved to hear the bit of humor in his voice at the end, she flops back into the pillows. "But the thing is, I dream of you too. I don't know how I'll be able to be apart from you so much. I don't think it's fair."

"Hey, I may decide to finish up my enlistment, if they will clear me medically. That probably means being deployed, which wouldn't be very fair to you either. You chase your dreams as fast and as far as they will take you, and we will find a way to be together. I love you too much to stand in the way of what makes you happy."

"James, you are what makes me happy too." she says quietly.

"Sunshine, you have no idea how much I wish I were there to hug you tight. We will make everything work in the end, I promise."

"I'll hold you to that, Sgt. Fletcher." Genuine happiness coloring her words, she curls up against the headboard. "You have said what a gift I am to you, but you have to know I can't imagine my life without you in it now. I love you."

"I love you too, Sunshine. Always."

They hang up shortly, Chrissie able to slip off in to a fairly peaceful night of sleep. Her dreams are filled with James, the two of them walking together in the pine forests of Colorado.

*****

Sleep is much more elusive for James. He hadn't been honest with Chrissie, torn between his desire for her happiness and his need for her in his life. How could they possibly make this happen? Spence hooked him up with a great prosthetist in San Antonio, and he had started regular physical training again, so it won't be long before he is able to decide what to do with his life.

He has a few conversations under his belt with his commanding officers regarding return to duty. While they haven't come to a decision yet, he worries he won't be able to hack it. Not for physical reasons, as he is getting stronger every day now, but because of nightmares that are getting worse the longer he's without Chrissie. It's an insurmountable hurdle to overcome, seeing his dead friends almost every night when he sleeps, still bathed in blood and laced with survivor's guilt. He's exchanged emails with his buddies still in the big sandbox of the Middle East, and they are happy for

Better Broken

him, he just isn't sure he can face them yet. Or ever. Maybe that is the coward's way, but time will tell.

Now, he could follow in Chrissie's wake, but what kind of life would that be for her? To spend her day healing people, and then have to come home to hold him together too? That isn't fair, and he can't ask that of her, no matter how much he needs her. She deserves so much better than he can offer, life with a cripple. He has no illusions as to what that means, wheelchairs and other mobility devices cluttering up a home. As much as he had fantasized about their having children, how can he ask her to raise them with a man who will never be whole? Over and over, he runs circles in his mind, until his heart is a whirling maelstrom of doubt.

Finally, he climbs out of bed and heads to the front porch to stare down the road, wishing he could run, truly run. Maybe he can't outstrip this problem, but he could lose it for a while in sweat and effort. Instead, he sits on the steps, Lucy's claws ticking on the old hardwood to come join him. He wraps his arm around her as she slides her head under his arm and whines, offering him a wet kiss to his cheek. Or maybe she is licking off the tears running down his face.

Justine Iarann

Chapter Nine

The next day the situation is no clearer, but he chooses a couple of the young gun dogs to go out for refinement training on their mouth softness and sending skills. He takes his old rifle from the gun cabinet, a familiar comforting weight, to be sure the dogs are properly conditioned to the sound, and for safety. The local wild hogs are very territorial if provoked, and it is best to be caught prepared. Both dogs are hungry for a run, bounding around and bumping into each other as he fires up the ATV, and it makes him wish he felt like smiling.

    A mile later and the lean dogs are trotting along quiet, so he pulls over in to a good clearing, stopping to appreciate the sweeping expanse of hills before him. In the distance a faint bluish tint heralds the coming of the bluebonnets, mid-morning sun soothing on his shoulders. Both dogs, Bud and Shane, are eager when he pulls out the bumper to practice retrieves with. It takes a few minutes to get the youngsters focused enough to send individually without them tangling together. He works the whistle to direct them in the brush as though it had never left his lips, and it feels great to be good at something again. He doesn't work them long, only until they are getting consistent and then stops- they will give a better effort later if he quits before they are too tired. Leaning against the ATV, he bends over easily to take the retrieving dummy and strokes the dogs for good behavior, finally smiling at their eagerness.

He sets the dogs down one more time and pulls out the rifle to fire it off when a hog breaks cover at twenty yards, crashing in the low brush lining a gully. Shane, the year old shorthair, doesn't even hear him say whoa or pay any attention to the whistle, just sets off after the pig. James is already lifting the rifle to his shoulder, eye finding the scope with practiced ease, still whistling to get the young dog to turn back. Shane moves up harmlessly enough, simply curious, but the sow must have her brood nearby, and she turns to confront him rather than running like normal. Being naive at best, Shane steps closer for a good sniff and the sow whips out fast to grab a front paw, biting down. The squeal of pain from the dog is instantaneous, as is the report of the rifle James holds. The sow makes it ten feet before collapsing in the scrub, a cloud of red dust rising to mark the spot. James himself is practically frozen, rifle still to his shoulder, but hands gone numb, heart beating frantically with the panic that swoops over him.

He could have stood there for God knows how long, trying to see through the darkness that threatens his vision, if not for Shane's very real cries of distress. Not trusting his legs, he drives the ATV over, and finds the dog holding up a clearly fractured limb, blood dripping into the dirt. Automatically, James grabs the first aid kit to tend the distressed dog while the other hound stands back, whining with anxiety. When he gets close enough to grab the big dog his fingers are sure of his actions, but inside he is a hurricane, consumed in memories of blood and dust in a whole other country. Once the wound is splinted sufficiently, it is easy to lift the dog up on the ATV, adrenaline and training seeing him through the moment, but on the long trip back to the kennels, he begins to shake.

By the time they reach his truck and he puts Bud away, Shane has begun to shake as well, bandage bled through. On the way to the vet the smell of blood is overwhelming in the close confines of the truck- even with the windows open, bile rises in his throat, and James clutches the steering wheel, desperate to get level. Yet, every time he blinks his eyes he is back to the ear ringing fear of the day he lost his leg.

He walks in the clinic and asks for help, barely able to trust his legs to carry him, let alone the big shorthair. The techs are fast and strong, reassuringly efficient, now reminding him of the medics who had saved his life. He can't blame Shane for struggling when they unwrap the bandage, and nearly weeps when the dog snaps at the girl holding him. Remembering the panic laced punch he had thrown at the medics trying to keep him alive makes his breath come even shorter. As they muzzle the dog James excuses himself and goes back out to the truck to lean on the steering wheel, choking back sobs, tears falling down his face without rational thought.

When he can breathe again, the tears drying up, he calls his father first to let him know what has happened. Thankfully, the old man has dealt with hundreds of hog injured dogs in his career, and takes it in stride. If he hears any shake in James, he says nothing, for which James is both grateful and sorry.

A vet tech comes out to give him the update right before he dials Chrissie, so he closes his phone. The break is clean, but will need surgery to pin together the two broken bones.

James doesn't have to call his father to know that they will do whatever is needed to fix him; dogs are family, and you don't quit on family. He gives the go ahead for the procedure, and they let him know he can probably take Shane home the next day if everything goes right.

The drive back to the ranch is a blur, and he actually misses the turn for the driveway in his haze, having to loop back. Nothing stops him from evening chores though- a lifetime of taking care of the dogs first is ingrained in the fiber of his soul. Past that, all he can manage is taking off his boots and falling on to the sofa, so exhausted he can barely feel his own face. The oblivion that swallows him is a welcome relief, though the darkness that comes with it threatens to swallow his soul.

*****

Cheerful and energetic with all the hope she feels for the future, Chrissie skates through the day with her usual aplomb. Faith is a beautiful gift and she is determined to cherish it entirely. With a happy heart she calls James on the way home, leaving a message to let him know she is looking forward to talking with him.

Hours later, after dozing off on the sofa, she wakes in a spike of panic, her heart racing fiercely, and she begins to worry. He never fails to call her back, and it is already two AM. What if something has gone wrong? Does anyone even know to call her? On the other hand, she doesn't want to call him in the middle of the night. What if he had just fallen asleep? It would disturb the precious little rest he ever gets, and that simply wouldn't be fair. He has been so happy with his work, feeling capable and strong again, even able to sleep a little longer at night. No, she can wait. She will always wait.

So she tucks herself into bed, wrapping around the pillow he had slept on, drawing in the faint hint of clean earth that he left behind. It is all she has, she realizes. There are no photos, no other ways to mark his presence in her life except for the space he occupies in her heart. And while part of her argues that it is irrational, Chrissie can't help the tears that fall on his pillow as she tries to go back to sleep.

Chapter Ten

Feeling completely hung over and wrung out, James wakes late. After a scalding hot shower he manages morning chores, at least the feeding and cleaning. There are messages on the phone, not just from Chrissie, but from Jenn, his Dad and Aunt Carol as well. Unable to decide who to call first, he sits on the front porch with Lucy again, stroking her ears repetitively.

According to Jenn's message their father is being discharged today, and they will be rolling into the ranch by afternoon. His Dad wants an update on the injured dog, Aunt Carol is threatening to send Charlie over if James doesn't call back soon. Chrissie, his darling Sunshine, only called to touch base before their normal evening chat.

Chrissie. His greatest gift. The one he isn't worthy of. The one who deserves so much better than the shell shocked coward he is becoming. Sure, she has no problem with his physical injuries, but they are a vague shadow compared to the darkness that is eating him alive. He couldn't live with dragging her down from the heights she has worked so hard to reach, but he also doesn't know how to live without her. He loves her so very much, not because she loves him, not even because she brings him peace. He loves her laughter, how real she is, how very genuine, authentic and unapologetic she is about her whole life. The fact that she loves with such complete faith and devotion. They only have a couple weeks between them, but she is so entwined in his heart. He can't risk shutting that light away in the darkness, dimming the brightness she shares with so many. He can't gamble that his broken will not become her broken.

The futility of it all leaves him rubbing the stubble on his jaw, just to do something, to feel something. He needs her, but he needs her to be okay even more, and he can't be that for her. Which leaves a bleak road ahead, without her to light the way. The only joy will be knowing she is free of this wretched midnight that lives in his heart.

He calls her back that afternoon while he knows she is working, leaving her a message, telling her a lie, that everything is fine. Then he leaves to pick up Shane from the vet, trying to beat his father home. It still feels like he is moving in a fog, but if he keeps moving, one step in front of the other, he might come out the other side.

*****

Relief floods Chrissie at the sound of James on her voicemail. Her footsteps are lighter, and even Max, the jaded office manager, unbends enough to smile at her humming a cheery song as she passes his office. Her afternoon is devoted to Smoke, with a hearty grooming session to begin the spring shedding season in earnest. She takes him to one of the grassy paddocks to do the brushing, letting the clumps of hair drift in the breeze where birds can use it to line their nests. Smoke is even more mellow than normal, and the sun is shining kindly on them, so Chrissie lays down in the grass and stares at the clouds blowing by.

When James comes back, she is going to invite him out to meet the 'other man' in her life, and to share some of this tranquility. He needs it far more than any other person she has ever met, and it isn't just because she loves him that she feels that way. It calls to her, an urge to share the strength horses give, the patience they offer, and the honesty they value above all. Maybe someday she can share it with more than James. Surely there are other men and women that have been hurt, who feel broken, feel that maybe they aren't capable of achieving dreams anymore. Wounded souls that need the wordless acceptance of a horse so they can begin healing.

Tonight, she will discuss this with James- maybe he will know the right people to talk to. Or maybe she will listen to him talk, his faint accent soothing her like the taste of warm pecan pie always does. She pictures his hands stroking kindly over the dogs he loves, fingers strong and sure. It's easy to imagine standing on a front porch, watching him walk up the drive with a few hounds dancing around him. Then someday, their child clinging tightly to his hand, the same thumb that drew warmth over her skin now lovingly sweeping over the little fingers he holds.

Smoke choses that very moment to return from the trough, his lips dripping water all over her with an expression of amusement, if you wanted to give a horse human emotions. Chrissie can't help but laugh after she stops sputtering.

"You ridiculous animal! Do you think I needed a cold shower?" She laughs twice as hard when Smoke nods his head emphatically, a party trick she had taught him when he was a colt. Sometimes, even without a cue, if she asks a question with the right inflection, he nods or shakes his head,

Justine Iarann

hoping to get a cookie for being cute. Being all out of cookies, she scratches his neck, then leads him back to the barn.

Later at home, she waits patiently for James's call, making herself busy by starting work on her thesis. As it comes close to bedtime, she begins to worry again, growling with frustration when her pen stops working, or pacing another useless lap around the small apartment. Finally, she can't bear it anymore, settling on the end of the bed to dial his number.

"James," she says with relief when he answers. "I was starting to worry. Hope I didn't bother you."

"Hey Sunshine. Actually, we are trying to get Dad settled in here at the house. We just got him in here after he insisted on going to the kennel first."

The little bit of humor in his voice is reassuring, but something undefinable sets her on edge. "Are you okay, my dear? You sound tired."

"It's nothing, Chrissie. A long day yesterday with an injured dog, and now Dad is here so everything is going to change again."

It isn't her imagination. There is a shadow, a defensive feel to his words, like he is hiding something.

"Well, you know you can call me anytime, if you need to talk. I think you know by now you can trust me with you." she says, making sure he can clearly hear her smile and the affection she is trying to share. "I wish I were there to help lighten the load some."

"I wish you were too, Sunshine."

There is some noise in the background, then someone calling James by name.

"Chrissie, I have to go. Jenn needs me to wrangle Dad in to sleeping in his bed, rather than the armchair. I love you."

Following his lead as always, she lets him bow out and they say their goodnights. Chrissie is at a loss as to what is wrong, and tries to shake the feeling that James is being dishonest, a first. It is difficult at best to lay down and try to sleep.

What she doesn't know is when she hangs up, James sits staring at the phone for a long time, thinking that while he can certainly trust her with all of him, he doesn't trust himself with her.

*****

A week later, Chrissie is not just hurt, but terribly angry as well. He had blown off their evening calls several times, always with good excuses that make her feel like a heel. It is always something- dinner with family, the lame dog wreaking havoc in the house, a broken down truck. It isn't that those things aren't important- they are the business of living that everyone faces. This, however, feels very deliberate, and it is time to make her misgivings know.

When he answers the phone that night he doesn't call her Sunshine, and it tears at her to miss that word so much. He is distracted and unfocused until she confronts him.

"James, what is wrong? And don't lie to me. Don't insult me that way." she says, trying so hard to keep her tone kind and soft.

The silence on the other end of the line is heavy, like a storm about to break, and his deep sigh slices into her heart.

"I can't Chrissie. I just can't. I can't tell you now, maybe not ever. In fact, I can't do this to you at all."

She is dumbstruck, unwilling to give him an answer that he could take for agreement, or argument, not wanting to concede this either. In her silence, he continues to speak.

"I am broken." he begins, and she tries to interrupt, to tell him how strong and resilient he is, but he speaks over her. "I am broken, I always will be. And I can't make you take that on. You deserve better and I want you to have better than being saddled with a cripple."

As soon as he pauses for a breath, she leaps in. "James, don't you ever think that about yourself! You are a beautiful soul, a fabulous human being, and the man I love! Together, we can overcome anything, absolutely anything."

His voice is choked when he answers her, and she struggles to breathe around the pain in her chest. "No, Chrissie, YOU can overcome anything. Anything except me. Goodbye, Sunshine."

The line goes dead, and in that moment so does a piece of Chrissie's heart.

*****

It's nice to think that life would stop while two lovers lay in their respective beds, unable to sleep around the gulping sobs that rack them both. It would be even better to assure ourselves that Chrissie's continued attempts to contact James are finally received. Maybe the scathing message that Suzie leaves on his phone about how he deserves to rot because of how broken Chrissie is, that he is an ass of monumental proportions- maybe that finally reaches him. Yet James can't argue a word of what Suzie says, since that is what he believes of himself. His father tries to convince him of his idiocy, angry words once again echoing in the house, and James moves himself in to the barn loft to escape the pity and disappointment in his father eyes.

Jenn returns to her job in Dallas, leaving him alone to make sure the old man takes his pills and does as the doctor says. It makes a good distraction from the darkness growing in his chest. Only the dogs can soothe him, so he sleeps with Lucy by his bed until her puppies arrive. Then he brings in Shane, the young dog still recovering from his broken leg. He considers trying to ride his old mare, but the mere idea brings up thoughts of Chrissie so he decides against it. One day runs in to the next, busy prepping dogs for the guides who are helping his dad through the hunting seasons. Trying not to

Better Broken

wake up with tears soaking his pillow from dreams of Chrissie or nightmares of blood and sand.

    Chrissie maintains her work and school life through force of will alone, though anyone who knows her can see a little distance in her manner, not getting too close to the patients. Suzie tries desperately to distract her- the weekend after Chrissie graduates with her Masters they fly out to Colorado to see Chrissie's mom, Catherine, and go apartment hunting. They have a good deal of fun, with Chrissie showing her friend all the places that she loved during her childhood. The hospital that is hiring her throws a little welcome party, and she puts on the best face she can, trying to find some joy despite the heart ache. Only Suzie and Smoke really know what is going on, letting her cling to them when she breaks down. Shoring her up when she is sure she can't stand another minute on her own two feet without James in her life. Because no matter how much it hurts, whenever she closes her eyes, she still sees him in her heart.

Justine Iarann

Part Two

Chapter Eleven

Winter in Colorado, there really is nothing more amazingly spectacular. The pristine snow thick on the pines makes the world new, interspersed with sunny days warm enough to do without a jacket. It is one of those sunny days where snow lingers on the shadowed side of things that finds Chrissie out running, letting the slap of the trail against her feet drop her into a thoughtless haze. She had taken up running after the move, something that leaves her exhausted enough to sleep. The yoga does her no good, as it makes her miss Suzie, and gives too much time for internal reflection. Running is enough to keep her from studying the dark spot in her heart. Sometimes, she still misses James, yet the tears are becoming less frequent, no longer leaving her breathless with hurt. All she hopes for is that wherever he is, he is well. It is the best she can manage.

Coming down the hill toward the trailhead she drops to a walk, drawing in deep gulps of the cold air to slow her heartrate. Mornings like this recharge her, leave her ready to face the work week, able to pour herself in to her client's needs. It is easy to get lost in work again, dealing mostly with amputees and folks with other limb limitations after accidents. Occasionally, a new person with a missing leg comes in, and her heart clenches at James memory- even that, she uses, rolling up the energy of her emotions into a smile for the client.

Sweat cools on her skin as she slides into the truck, rubbing her arms against an oncoming chill. The new to her vehicle starts right up, heater blasting warm air in less than a minute. The Subaru had lasted through the trip from Virginia before having major mechanical problems, and the truck is better anyway, for traveling around with Smoke. They are spending hours on the trails every week, and attending as many dressage shows as possible, all activities to distract from the ache that she is trying to ignore.

Once, in the midst of a terrible day, with her temper on far too short a fuse, Smoke actually bucked her off, a first for them. Sure, she had fallen off him before, accidents happen. The shock of him deliberately unloading her had left her sitting on her butt in the middle of the arena, so close to tears that she nearly embarrassed herself in front of everyone at their new barn. He walked back to her after the fall, his muzzle touching her cheek, and she utterly deflates, unable to remain upset. After checking him thoroughly for any physical discomfort, she concludes that the discomfort he objected to was her.

It had taken a few late night talks with Suzie to work through the anger, to discover that the root of it was James taking away her choice in the matter. He hadn't even asked what she wanted, just did what he thought was best. And it simply wasn't fair. Sure, life isn't fair, and many day to day choices are taken out of her hands, but he hadn't even considered her thoughts. He had discounted her strength, trying to protect her, and while the gesture was unselfish, the way he did it was selfish in the extreme.

As she drives back down the mountain to her tiny apartment the sky is so bright a blue she can't help smiling, and then an upbeat country song comes on the radio. For the first time in months she sings along, and while she doesn't know all the words it doesn't matter at all.

*****

Spring arrives, and while daffodils breaking the soil sometimes gives her a quick pang, Chrissie is healing and busy building her life. She calls Suzie at least once a week, missing her best friend terribly, but they make plans to get together in the summer. Chrissie's mom, Catherine, a bright and lovely soul who is heavily involved in the arts and volunteer communities, makes sure they have dinner together frequently. She has always been an anchor for Chrissie, and in this case, is instrumental in the rebuilding of her heart. Sometimes, they go to gallery openings, or shopping in the eclectic town of Boulder. Once, they visit a hot springs spa- it helps recharge Chrissie's soul, being surrounded by the glory of the mountains and her mother's love.

A week later, Colorado decides to have a mood swing, dumping a foot of snow overnight after a stretch of fabulous weather. Chrissie is running late, having been stuck behind an accident on the highway. The day doesn't get much better trying to play catch up, and she barely has time to run down to the coffee shop for a chai and pastry during her abbreviated lunch break. In fact, she is jogging down the hallway, trying to get back up to the rehab unit before her afternoon sessions begin, thinking of an older gentleman who lost his leg to diabetes. She never sees it coming, rounding a corner at full tilt, and crashing straight in to a warm body.

It knocks her off her feet, the impact is so unexpected, and it takes every ounce of self-control she has not to swear profusely. She looks up at the victim of her lack of attention, seeing what is left of her chai splashed all over the white shirt and striped silk tie of a doctor. As her eyes continue upward she finds a handsome, broad shouldered man gazing back at her, his thick brown hair swept carelessly to one side, bright blue eyes flaring open with shock. Scrambling to her feet, Chrissie barely squeaks out an apology before making a fast exit down the hall, leaving the guy completely flat footed. Her brain is whirling in panic, otherwise she would have at least offered him one of the napkins that are scattered all over the floor.

Once her heart rate returns to normal she manages her afternoon appointments, all inpatient folks recovering from surgery. Afterward, she walks in to the shared space all the therapists use as an office, shocked to see an envelope with her name on it sitting by her bag. Inside is a silly card with a puppy skidding across hardwood and the words 'My apologies' scrawled messily across the inside. It is signed Dr. Mason. Chrissie goes out to the unit desk to ask Abigail, one of the duty nurses, if she knows who he is.

"Dr. Mason? Dr. Thomas Mason? Most eligible bachelor in hospital history, and object of every single girl's fantasies?" Abigail is agog at her question. "He is a rising star in orthopedic surgery, and here in the unit pretty frequently. I'm surprised you haven't run into him."

Chrissie laughs at the pun Abigail doesn't even know she made before heading back to the office to do paperwork. A smile lingers on her lips as she stares at the card now propped against her bag. It is terribly considerate of him to not be angry about ruining his shirt. Hopefully, she will see him soon to thank him for his kindness.

*****

A week later finds Chrissie working with a lady who

fractured her wrist, exploring range of motion to get her back to playing piano as quickly as possible. She pays no attention to anything but her client until she notices the woman looking up with a bright smile.

"Dr. Mason," the woman says, the grin expanding impossibly. "How kind of you to check on me!"

Chrissie turns to see him offer the woman a heart stopping smile. "Lydia, how are things coming along?"

"Oh, Miss Everett here thinks it won't be very long at all before I can return to the stage!"

"Excellent! I will be sure to let Mother and Father know. They have been in despair about the man who took your place for the winter season, simply not the same without you." he says, his voice a pleasant burr of practiced charm.

His easy flattery makes the woman simper, and he turns to catch Chrissie smiling at the display. "Miss Everett, a private word regarding our star?"

Lydia shoo's at Chrissie with her good hand, beaming with pleasure at the attention she is gathering from the other people in the room. Chrissie steps toward him, and he takes her elbow to walk her around the corner. The gesture vaguely irritates her, but at the same time she is relieved to find no anger in his manner after their collision.

"How may I help you, Doctor?" Turning to face him when he releases her, she crosses her arms.

"Actually, Miss Everett, you could allow me to replace the drink that I wore back to my office in such ignominy." His rakish grin brings to mind a soap opera star her mother used to watch. "It's the least you could do in view of the very expensive tie that was ruined."

"I am so sorry, Doctor Mason. I was not myself that day and should have stayed long enough to make a proper apology." she answers, heat creeping up her cheeks.

Brushing it off, he then asks her to join him after his shift

Better Broken

at a nearby cafe. Chrissie considers the offer and accepts, despite her previous commitment to Smoke. After all, she owes him this much at least.

That afternoon, Chrissie sits in the cafe over a half hour, waiting for him to show. Unsurprised to be stood up, she goes to see Smoke for a while, his company being infinitely preferable to a stuffy doctors any day.

What does surprise her is walking in the next day to find a white carry out cup full of hot chai with another 'My apologies' scrolled across it and a croissant waiting at her desk. The thoughtful gesture is more than she expects from such a confirmed player. After the days shift she walks out to the employee lot to find him waiting on a bench.

He stands the instant he sees her, smiling like a fashion model, the surety of his gaze making her uncomfortable. But she returns the warm handshake he offers, his fingers lingering a bit longer than a common clasp warrants.

"So, how about that coffee?" he asks, confident in her answer.

"Thank you, but no, Dr. Mason." She begins to walk away, leaving him nonplussed. "I appreciate the gesture, but must maintain a professional relationship with everyone here."

Like an overzealous puppy he shadows her footsteps, so she slows, then turns to face him.

"Miss Everett, please, let me take you out. We won't be long, and my honor demands it after standing you up. I had an emergency surgery." he says with another suave grin.

Involuntarily, she smiles at his boyish enthusiasm, softening to the easy charm.

"Where should we meet, then?"

"Actually, we could go now. I'll take you out to dinner, and then bring you back here to your vehicle."

"Doctor Mason, I am fresh off my shift, and certainly not dressed for dinner." Shaking her head to reinforce the

Justine Iarann

statement, she tries to firm her resolve.

"Then when would you like to go?" He fidgets in place like an eager colt, which is ridiculously appealing considering his reputation as a ladies man.

"If you would like to meet later, I can certainly go home and get ready. Or we could go to Molly's Diner now."

He visibly balks at the idea of such a low rent district hangout, usually filled with hospital personnel. The gossip chain is blisteringly fast among the staff, and not a complication he would appreciate in the least.

"Alright, Miss Everett, I will see your offer and raise you one. How about I pick you up at your place at seven, for dinner at Jonesy's." he says, making a statement out of the question with a surety that is almost soothing even as it chafes.

"Attire?"

"Classy casual, nothing more."

Accepting his invite, she bows out quickly after giving her address, hurrying home to get ready. Chrissie stews a while over what to wear because she doesn't want to overdo and give the wrong impression. As a handsome, self-assured, successful man, he is used to getting what he wants and she doesn't want him to think he can have her easily. She decides on a teal cardigan, dark jeans and flats- warm enough for the cool of a spring evening, not revealing but certainly flattering.

Right on time, he knocks at her door, wearing a dark sweater over another collared shirt, but unbent enough to wear jeans. It is enough to convince Chrissie she has picked the right outfit, which his pale eyes rove over appreciatively.

"Lovely, Miss Everett," he says, bowing slightly over the hand she extends to him. "Or may I call you Christine?"

"I could allow it, Dr. Mason, if I may call you Thomas." Being the sole focus of his intent makes her restless, and she shifts her weight from one foot to the other just to move.

"Of course, Christine. Shall we?"

A sleek luxury car waits at the curb, and he hands her in as if she is something special, warming her to his cocky attitude. The proof that it is warranted is beginning to show through, much deeper than a surface coating of polish.

They talk little, only vague pleasantries as he navigates the downtown evening traffic and slides in to a valet parking lane. Once they are inside the funky eatery, seated across from each other, he turns his considerable attentions completely on her.

"So, Miss Everett, while I am used to women falling at my feet, it's usually not quite so literally." A smile glimmers in his eyes as much as on his lips, amused at his own wit.

Chrissie can't help the light flush that runs up her skin, and he smiles even wider at her color.

"About that, Dr. Mason, I want to apologize. I was absolutely careless, and I remain very sorry for ruining your shirt."

"Truly, Christine, it was nothing. Shirts are a dime a dozen, but women like you are priceless." An indulgent chuckle finishes his statement.

Her cheeks burn at the pretty words, even if she isn't sure how genuine they are. She covers any discomfort by looking over the menu, discovering it all sounds pretty edible despite her worries that he would drag her out someplace ridiculously expensive and overdone. Sure, it's trendy, and the blend of adult alternative and blues music playing in the background is a little different than her normal scene, but it reminds her of nights out with Suzie in Virginia. When she smiles at the memory he looks pleased, even if he doesn't know why she is smiling.

"Anything you suggest, Thomas?" she inquires, hoping to make some conversation.

"I really enjoy the mussels, and I often have the steak. I've never eaten a bad thing off this menu, and it's a fairly regular stop for me. What were you thinking of having?"

Chrissie contemplates behaving more elegantly, but decides to be honest about herself. "Truthfully, I've never had mussels. The burgers sound good."

He is taken aback by her admission, and insists they order mussels as an appetizer. The earthy, briny flavor is a pleasant surprise, enhanced by a little white wine. She still orders a burger and laughs at the wrinkle that forms over his nose, lending humanity to his otherwise flawless face.

"Is my fare a little low class for you, Dr. Mason?" she teases.

His face immediately clears. "No, Miss Everett, only surprised that with all the other options available, you choose a cheeseburger."

"Ah, I see. Well, I am a girl with simple tastes."

"Yet, you have a sense of adventure about you. A burger is so mundane, even if I am sure it will be done perfectly."

"Dr. Mason, we are here because your honor demanded it. You have already replaced the chai that you wore so thoroughly. So why should it matter what I order?"

"Because I am trying to impress you, Christine. It is very hard to impress a woman who is happy with ground beef when she could have had duck comfit." The seriousness in his eyes makes her shift in her seat.

"Dr. Mason, I could no more fly in your circle than you could be happy in mine." She chuckles to lighten the weight his words place on her heart. "Why would you want to impress a girl like me?"

"Christine, you are not a girl, you are all woman." he says, bridging the space between them by placing his hand over hers. "I hate to sound trite or cliché, but I believe fate brought us together in that hall. I don't know why, or to what purpose, but I can't stop thinking about you."

Better Broken

She wants to retreat from his admission, to pull her hand back in to her lap and look away. Or even to flee entirely. Yet, she manages to stay, meeting his gaze with echoing seriousness.

"Thank you for the pretty compliment, Thomas, but fair words alone will not win fair lady. I'm flattered to be invited out, but I am not sure we should spend time together. It simply wouldn't be professional, and I value my career far too much."

"See, already something we have in common. I am on the fast track for success in my department and have big plans for the future. I'm sure you too chase your goals with single mindedness." he says, jumping on that tenuous link to keep them together. "Let's enjoy dinner, and see where we are then." he finishes as the waiter approaches with their plates, letting go of her hand.

It's hard not to concede his point as she works on her food. It's not that she doesn't enjoy going nice places or having finer things, it's simply that they are not a priority. While he clearly puts finer things as a priority, he can also unbend enough for places a little more funky, food a little more common. The spirit of fun he has is contagious.

So, she gives him the evening to charm her with witty repartee, and smiles that would melt the hearts of lesser souls. Her lips mirror his smiles as he makes jokes and plays a bit of the fool. At one point he takes her hand again, and she finds herself allowing it. Maybe her judgment was too harsh in the beginning? Maybe he is a decent man who just happens to have never been told no much.

As they leave the restaurant and he waves for the valet attendant, he still holds her hand. Surprisingly, it is easy to be in his company, to have his deft fingers drawing a circle of warmth on the pulse point of her wrist. When they pull up to her apartment building, he kills the engine and opens her door to walk her up. As they stand on the threshold she turns to thank him for the evening, surprised when he pulls her to him. Breath hitches in her throat at his hungry look, and she is shocked at the excitement racing through her as his lips descend. His kiss is soft, but there is an edge of need in the tension of his hands at her waist. Not wanting to encourage him, she turns away to draw a breath, resting her forehead on his muscular chest.

"I'm sorry, Christine, that was much too bold of me." The words rumble out of his chest, a hand softly stroking her back.

"Perhaps it was more than I was expecting, but I cannot say I did not enjoy it." she says with a smile, leaning away. The shadows of regret in his eyes clears at her words, the confident surgeon moving back in to control. "Perhaps, at some point, we can try it again. Just not tonight. We both have work tomorrow."

A little chagrined to be reminded of his responsibilities, he accepts the wisdom of her words. With a quick peck on her cheek, he then jogs back to his car, waving a farewell before speeding off. Chrissie draws a deep breath and looks up at the night sky, thinking of a very different kiss she once enjoyed on a spring evening; how it had lit her on fire and she would have happily gone up in flames. Shaking her head, she steps inside the quiet of her tiny apartment, alone, and finally beginning to be okay with it.

*****

It is hard not to be charmed by the good doctor over the next few days, as he leaves her texts and notes on her desk. One day, a small but exquisite bouquet of pink roses arrives at the rehab unit with her name on it. They cause quite a stir as the card does not have a signature, simply inscribed 'Because they remind me of the blush on your cheeks'. Her co-workers tease mercilessly about her secret admirer, and the

Better Broken

very blush the card speaks of spends most of the day on her face.

Chrissie keeps putting him off, mainly to prepare for a horse show on the weekend- there is so much to do before Smoke and she are ready. They are moving up a level at this competition, and it is nerve wracking in the extreme. Every night is filled with grooming, tack cleaning, and boot polishing, then working on movements from the dressage test. Thomas offers to help, but she isn't ready to share her safe haven with him yet. Frankly, she wonders how a well to do playboy possibly thinks he can help, though she does chastise herself for assuming he will only get in the way.

The weekend arrives, and she loads up Smoke in the wee hours of the morning for the drive to the show grounds. His braids are tight along his neck, and his coat shines variegated shades of ebony in the sunlight when she unloads him. Completely focused on her horse, she stretches and massages a few of his more tense spots, meticulously making sure every piece of his tack is properly adjusted. He bumps her gently with his nose as she puts on his bridle, so she stops a moment and hugs on his face.

"I love you, big man. How about we go show them what we are made of?" she whispers near his ear, startled into a laugh when he pulls back to nod at her enthusiastically.

She slips him a peppermint and then turns to pull on her show coat. Moments later, she is in the saddle and on her way to the arena where they have to jockey for space to warm up. It takes very little to get mentally and physically in tune with each other, so Chrissie rewards them both by parking under a shade tree to wait their turn. Once the ring steward waves them in, everything melts away for Chrissie, barely seeing the beautiful landscape or the other riders waiting. Each moment of the test is a muscle and mind symphony of movement, one supple bend leading in to a powerful trot, then a whisper of leg to ask for the canter. When they reach the final halt to deliver a salute, both horse and rider give a big exhale of contentment, having left the very best they can do laying on the dirt of the arena. Now, hopefully the judges will recognize it as well.

The polite applause that accompanies their exit is wonderful, but the unexpectedly enthusiastic clapping is a big surprise that makes Chrissie turn in her saddle. To her embarrassment and pleasure, it is Thomas, standing on his feet like he is cheering at the World Series.

She waves at him and smiles, but keeps Smoke walking all the way to the trailer, needing a few moments to collect herself after the high of being so connected to her horse. Smoke simply basks in the afterglow, eyes half closed in the warm sunshine as they make their way down the busy lanes of the show grounds. When she vaults off his back and immediately loosens the girth he chuffs a big sigh, exploring the bare skin of her wrist with his lips as she rubs his ears. Pulling off his bridle, she keeps rubbing him, telling him what a good boy he is with every word and gesture. By the time Thomas finds them the big black horse is standing hipshot and relaxed with a full bag of hay and a bucket of water while Chrissie sucks down an entire bottle of ice tea.

Hot, sweaty and flushed as he walks up, she is justifiably shocked when he pulls her off her feet and swings her around, whooping with excitement.

"Christine, that was amazing!" he crows as he sets her down. "I've never seen anything like it!"

Stands there in the circle of his arms, a hand pressed to his chest, she is still a little giddy when he leans down and kisses her. It might have crossed her mind to object if she wasn't already emotionally high from her ride, but in the moment, it is easy to kiss him back, wrapping her arms around his neck. It isn't until he presses his suit, trying to deepen the kiss that she begins to push away, and he gently sets her back on her feet, giving her space. Moving away to put things back in the trailer for the trip home, she manages to regain her composure. When she finally turns around he stands with his hands in the pockets of his slacks, looking slightly sheepish, but still a little proud. She's beginning to suspect it is an air he always wears, unconsciously.

"Thomas, I am so sorry. I didn't mean to lead you on that way." She brushes back the hairs escaping her French braid, a little bit of pink creeping up her neck.

He steps forward to take the hand she raised, pulling it against the solid feel of his chest.

"Actually, Christine, once again, I insist the fault is mine. You simply felt so good in my arms I couldn't resist the temptation. I hope you will forgive me."

Standing so close, with the puppy dog eyes he is giving her and the attention he is paying, she can't resist him.

"Of course, Thomas, of course." she says, her eyes soft on his. "I appreciate that you came today. That support means so much to me. I think I need to move slowly with you. It's all very overwhelming."

He chuckles, the sound all red blooded male. "Thank you. I shall endeavor to behave myself better around you, but you are very tempting."

The compliment prompts another blush, but she turns away to introduce him to her horse.

"Thomas, this is my partner, Smoke." She steps close to her horse, stroking the muscles rippling his shoulder to get his attention. The gelding brings his head around to look at the man, focusing on Thomas only momentarily before returning to his hay. He accepts Thomas giving him a pat much the same way he accepts a butterfly landing on him, mostly ignoring the gesture while remaining fully aware of the touch. A wrinkle appears between Chrissie's eyes. "I apologize, he is usually much more social."

"It's alright, Christine. I'd bet he is jealous to have to your attention on someone else." Another tolerant chuckle pricks at her conscience. "I can't blame him."

Acquiescing the possibility, she asks him to accompany her to the show office to get her scores. As they walk he takes her hand again, and she finds herself comfortable with the gesture, even managing a smile as he talks about his day.

The test sheet reveals good marks with one really notable comment from the judge about great harmony between horse and rider. It only garners them a third place, but Chrissie couldn't be more pleased. Thomas, however, complains she should have won, no one else was as great as they were, and maybe she should talk to someone about it. She soothes his pique without trying to explain the scoring system too much, knowing his objections are really for her benefit.

She agrees to meet him for dinner again, despite the long drive ahead, but only if she can pick where, which he agrees to easily.

Luckily, there is very little traffic on the road home, so she quickly has Smoke back in his stall after a good grooming to reward his efforts. Looking forward to spending the evening with Thomas, she rushes back home for a much needed shower; it is a relief to have someone on her side here in Colorado, aside from her mother. And, while she is being honest, it is exhilarating to have such a handsome man be attracted to her. She texts him as she is getting ready, telling him to meet her at a specific street corner in Boulder, with no other directions. His reaction to her surprise will certainly be telling.

Arriving early, as is her habit, she begins to get impatient when he is late, fussing with the ties on her sundress as she scans the crowds. Just as she is leaning toward irritated she spots him threading his way through the weekend throng, the sleeves of his oxford shirt rolled up to reveal toned arms, and well fitted khakis over a pair of loafers. It's more casual than she had been expecting, not because she is dressed any fancier, but because he is so formal all the time. His smile broadens when he spots her, and a couple women nearby admire him as he walks past, which makes her smile back just as widely. He can't help being appealing, it is as much a part of his outfit as the ever present button down shirt.

As he closes the distance a flush creeps over her skin because he has eyes only for her. It is amazing how powerful that undivided focus makes her feel, like she truly can accomplish anything, simply because that is how he sees things. His surety is a balm for her heart, softening her to him as she recognizes it for the gift it is. When he reaches for her hand, she reaches for him too, surprise registering on his face at the gesture.

"Christine, you look lovely this evening." he says with genuine appreciation, eyes traveling casually over her as he tucks her hand in to the crook of his elbow.

"Thank you, Thomas. You look quite handsome and relaxed as well." Chrissie bumps against him companionably as she guides them a few blocks down the street.

"Where are we off to enjoy dinner?"

"Right here."

Their destination is an unmistakably pink food truck with a line about twenty people long, all of them chatting amicably in the lowering light.

Clearing his throat, he looks over at her a little sheepishly. "Really? I can't say as this has ever been on my list of things to do, but if you are sure."

"No, Thomas, I'm not sure at all. It's an adventure." she says, daring him with her eyes. He doesn't disappoint, and steps in to the line, unable to back down from a challenge.

Thirty minutes later, after some quiet conversation, they

are sitting down on a park bench with paper plates covered in tacos. She actually laughs as he hesitates to eat, lifting up her own taco el pastor for a big bite. Like spicy sunshine, the flavor of pork and pineapple rolls across her taste buds, eliciting a groan of pure, unadulterated satisfaction. As she chews Thomas takes a tentative bite, and then he too is reduced to animal noises of contentment. Their meal disappears quickly, and she proposes a walk to let their food settle. Hand in hand, he lets her drag him along the Pearl Street Mall, stopping to look in windows and to watch street performers busking for tips.

After a while their footsteps slow, and he asks to walk her back to her car. When they reach the shadowed lot, he turns her into his arms and bends down- Chrissie doesn't push back this time, simply lifts her face up to meet him. She can feel the smile on his lips as they touch hers, and a little drunk on the feeling of being wanted she lets him press closer, opening her lips under his. The kiss is thorough, careful, each moment drawn out, stroking his tongue over hers like he can't get enough, fading her wits at the edges. It goes on forever as her arms slowly wind up around his neck, and her fingers clench in his thick hair, which feels foreign for a moment. But he keeps tasting her so carefully she can't stop. When he finally pulls back for a breath, he groans.

"Christine, you've lit me on fire, baby."

As her mind clears, she takes a few deep breaths and shakes her head, still wrapped in his arms. "I can't believe this is happening, Thomas. I don't know how this could possibly work."

He chuckles at her insecurity, which chafes, but his smile is oh so sure.

"Baby, it's easy. We take it a day at a time, and every day I will remind you exactly how great things can be between us. Some days, I'll be stuck at work, but I can promise you I would much rather be kissing your luscious lips."

Taking possession of her mouth again, he kisses her as if he is trying to draw her inside of him, running his hands down to her hips to pull their bodies flush. It is comforting to have the evidence of his attraction pressed between them, to know she is so desirable, but a rational part of her is hanging on for dear life. Kicking and screaming, it demands she pay attention to exactly where this is going and how fast. Finally, she listens, carefully disengaging from his addictive embrace.

When she stands fully on her own feet and his hands are back at her waist, she pulls away from the kiss as well, his eyes still focused on her like she is something to be consumed. Even that gaze makes her feel like a junkie who wants more, an out of control sensation that she both craves and fears.

"I think I should go, Thomas." she whispers quietly. "Right now, before I regret anything."

"If you insist, Christine." Eddies of desire make the icy color of his eyes shift.

She wavers toward him for a moment, but hesitates, thinking of the many notches he must have on his bedpost. No, he will have to work much harder than pretty words, no matter how delicious his kiss makes her feel.

Whispering a good night on to the sensitive skin under his jaw, she steps away. The need in his eyes is hard to walk away from in the chilling night air, and it eases her heart to see him standing there, watching her leave. Maybe, just maybe, the handsome doctor really is a good man worth loving. Time will tell.

Justine Iarann

Chapter Twelve

Steamy kisses, hand holding during dinner, embraces full of languid heat leave her frustrated and feeling more and more like a junky. They may not have much in common in personality, but the physical feelings between them are escalating rapidly, building to the point that she is afraid for when they will finally erupt.

In fact, she is currently pacing, waiting for him to pick her up, seriously considering calling to cancel their plans. This weekend they are going away together, to a resort in the mountains. Sure, she made sure they have separate rooms, but the chances one of those rooms will be unused is very likely with the current state of tension. Just as she is picking up the phone to beg off the horn of his sports car sounds from the curb, and it is too late.

The drive up in to the Rockies is gorgeous, summer air rolling in the open windows to caress her face, the smell of the pines a heady combination with Thomas's cologne. A flush crawls up her neck line due to the distracting patterns he is drawing against her thigh, barely protected from his fingertips by the thin fabric of her dress. When she can stand it no longer, she grasps his hand in hers, which makes him laugh. He is the picture of suave, nimble fingers controlling the leather wrapped steering wheel with one hand as he navigates the many twists and turns through the gorge. The sun draws golden highlights in his brown hair, making him impossibly handsome.

"You know, Thomas, while I have you as a captive audience, we should talk a little." she says, trying to distract him from any more games along her leg.

His eyebrows shoot up over the edge of his sunglasses, almost as though he is concerned, but he answers readily.

"What would you like to know, baby?"

"We have talked about everything from music to art, travel and food, but I don't think you've told me a single thing about your family."

"Ah, easy enough! Father is an investment banker, Mother is an avid fund raiser for politics. They live right outside D.C., where I grew up and went to prep school. I have a younger sister who ran off to Peru with the Peace Corps after college, and is still there seven years later, married to one of her fellow volunteers and raising alpacas, I think. Much to Mothers complete disappointment."

"How often do you see your parents?"

"Mother comes out several times during ski season, and enjoys patronizing the Denver performing arts community, Father comes once or twice. And Christmas, when I usually fly back home."

"Why did you decide to become a doctor then, and why here? That's a big leap from what you had in D.C."

"Well, I know why I chose to become a doctor. At first, it was the money. Then it turns out I actually am good at it, and

Justine Iarann

I like fixing things. As for why here, well, we had always come out here to ski, so Mother could rub elbows with important people. I knew it was beautiful. Mainly though, it was the job offer. I work among the best in the business here, and the hospital has an amazing track record for growing department heads."

"So, all of this was part of your plan?"

He looks over the top of his sunglasses for a moment, icy blue eyes hot enough to melt the last of her nerves. "All of it is, except you. You are the one fabulously delicious surprise."

Barely able to think past the hum of blood pounding loudly through her veins, Chrissie sits frozen simply from the lust in his eyes.

When they reach the hotel he is very gentlemanly, escorting her up to her room and letting her know what time to expect him for dinner. He kisses her lightly before walking away, and Chrissie feels like it is a stay of execution. She leans against the door after closing it on the view of his sculptured form striding down the hall, and heaves a deep breath.

"What the hell are you thinking, Christine Everett?" she says loudly into the stillness of her room.

After having a quick look at the simple comfort of her space, she sits on the edge of the bed and calls Suzie.

"So, has he had his way with you yet?" are the first words she hears, rather than the hello most people would open with. It startles a laugh out of her, nearly hysterical in her need to blow off tension.

"I take it no." Suzie says. "Why ever not, Saint Chrissie? Live a little, dammit!"

"Well, Suz, I don't think I'll hold out much longer. We are here together all weekend, and the heat is too much to bear."

"About damned time! If you weren't going to sleep with Dr. Perfect soon, I was going to come out there, knock you out cold and do him myself." Suzie says, teasing her mercilessly.

"Why don't I doubt you?" Chrissie says back, laughing again.

"I want details. You call me on Monday, and I want complete, gory details."

"You are so friends with the wrong girl if you think you are getting a play by play!" Chrissie rebuts, still giggling a little.

"Le' sigh. I am doomed to a life with no good men in it, and you won't even share a little bit to help out your best friend! How heartless of you."

"Ah, yes, you know me, so cruel." Chrissie replies sarcastically. "I live to torture you, you irredeemable letch."

"That's me, and don't you forget it. Now, go get ready to scorch the earth with Doctor Perfect, okay? Put on some lingerie for the love of all that's holy, and put your hair up so that he wants to take it down."

"Yes ma'am." A final chuckle lends lightness to her heart. "And thank you for being my best friend, Suzie. You always know just what I need."

"And don't you forget it, Chrissie. I love you. Now get to it."

The call cuts off before Chrissie can reply, and she frowns at the phone. It's a totally Suzie thing to do, to escape when anyone starts talking about feelings. Such a strange tic for a woman who spends her days helping patients with their emotions.

When Thomas knocks on her door she is more than satisfied at the blaze that immediately fills his eyes. She had taken great pains to find the dark emerald green dress, which fits perfectly over her hips and flares fetchingly at the knees. It brings out every highlight in her hair, and turns her eyes a startlingly bright aquamarine color.

"Christine, I don't know if I should let the rest of the

world see you in that dress." His voice is husky with appreciation as he traces her body with his eyes. The blush that climbs up from her décolletage is unstoppable, his words already making her light headed.

"Well, Thomas, I am starving, so regardless, I am going to dinner. Will you join me?" she says, letting a little heat creep in to her voice as she looks over the tailored charcoal wool suit he is wearing.

Again, he steps toward the challenge, and offers his arm. They are not going far, only a few blocks to a restaurant recommended by the front desk. It is a quiet, intimate place, filled with small tables and candle light, ideal for the sensual swirl building between them. The waiter is a tactful man, moving in and out at precisely the right times, bringing them wine, and a meal neither of them really tastes. When the waiter asks about dessert, Chrissie knows Thomas is not thinking of the offerings on the menu, so she shakes her head no. On the walk back to the hotel her steps are slow, unused to the strappy heels she is sporting, and apprehensive about the night ahead. He keeps her hand tucked into the crook of his elbow, stroking a slow whorl over her bare skin, and it is not only arousing, but soothing as well.

When they reach the elevator she angles her lips to his briefly before pointedly drawing away to press the button for his floor, not hers. His eyes pin hers immediately, sharply aware, and then he presses her back into the wall to ravage her mouth, the red wine on his tongue a potent rush. At his door, he lifts one brow in question, offering her a chance to leave, but she doesn't hesitate, walking in front of him into the darkness. He doesn't turn on any lights, but spins her straight into an embrace with one arm, his lips hungry on her neck, moving their way down to her shoulder. Running her hands up his chest, she spreads his jacket back and off his broad shoulders, then moves to his tie, dragging the knot loose. Clothes are hitting the floor quickly as he backs her toward the bed with an inescapable surety.

Her knees hit the bed and she lets him guide her down as he lifts her dress over her head, dropping it negligently on the carpet. The darkness is as drugging as the competence in his hands, and she can't dislike the other women who must have put that confidence in his touch. Her hands undo his belt as he unbuttons his shirt and shrugs it off. She puts her mouth on the navel he has exposed, licking his skin as she works on removing his slacks. The growl in his voice is pure animal as she pushes his pants down along with his briefs, unable to see much in the darkness aside from the shadow of his very obvious erection.

When he pushes her back she goes without a fight, kicking off her shoes while his hands reach for her lace panties. Thomas drags them off her a little roughly, but the friction only serves to raise her excitement, so she reaches back and unsnaps her bra, letting the straps slide down her shoulders. The little light from outside the window shows immeasurable hunger in his eyes when she pulls the scrap of lace off entirely. He climbs on the bed and Chrissie moves toward the pillows, but he stops unexpectedly, and her breath catches when he pulls her toward him by the ankles. His lips follow his soft fingers, and her brain quits functioning as he works his way down to the damp curls where her legs meet. The first touch of his mouth nearly unglues her, a small kiss to her swollen flesh, but then his tongue laps over her wetness, making her bow up with a shuddering breath. He tortures her thoroughly until she is about to boil over, pressing herself up to his mouth. Moments later, he slides one finger inside her, and she orgasms, breath gone, a low gasp all she can offer.

Even before she recovers, Thomas shifts and she hears the crinkle of a condom wrapper. She draws a deep breath, pulling his face to hers and kissing him with all the gratitude she can muster, shuddering as his weight comes over her. One of his hands reaches down and he slides into the heat of her inner embrace. Another shudder rocks her as he moves back out again, his thick chest hair rubbing deliciously over her pebbled nipples. He sets a fast rhythm, beginning the climb back toward ecstasy. Chrissie is ready to weep as she trembles beneath him, growing close to the peak of fulfillment, so close she can taste it in the kiss he angles over her mouth.

Right before she is ready to tip over the edge, he snaps his hips once more, and quivers over her, cutting her adrift. His weight comes to rest on her, and she lays a kiss on his sweaty brow, listening to his breathing slow. Not even a minute later, he withdraws, cleaning up the condom, then pulls her close, cuddling her against his chest. It doesn't take long for the snoring to start, so he doesn't notice that Chrissie lays awake for an hour more, totally conflicted. There is a part of her left hollow and incomplete, yet she feels so very safe and desirable in his arms that she clings to the notion, finally finding sleep.

*****

After waking up several times not sure where she is Chrissie can't take it anymore. Thomas is no longer holding her so it is easy to get up- she looks down at him in the darkness, adorable despite the sounds coming out of his mouth. It really is something between a chain saw and a bulldog with sinus issues.

Far too restless to stay in the room, she quietly pulls her dress on and sneaks out the door with her purse and shoes in hand. The halls of the hotel are empty, thankfully, as she navigates back to her own room. She drops on to the end of the bed without turning on a light and stares into the darkness, wondering what the hell went wrong.

The conflict runs pointless laps in her head and heart,

Better Broken

escalating to the point of making her dizzy, overwhelming any rational thought. So she does the one thing that can stop it- she goes running. She hadn't packed any workout clothes, but she makes do with a t-shirt and hiking shorts, grateful her sneakers can do double duty. The front desk staff give her a good route through town with at least some light, but it is all hills so it doesn't take long to get her heart pounding. An MP3 player is her only company, excepting some startled deer on a street corner, everything else is the concussion coming up from the ground in a steady rhythm.

A mile flies by in no time, so she keeps going until two miles are gone, and it is time to turn around. The route back is more of a climb, all aching muscles and burning lungs that leave no room for fruitless worrying. The clerk manning the check-in desk has a towel waiting for her and a bottle of water, which prompts a heartfelt smile from Chrissie.

Upon reaching her room she heads straight to the shower to ease the muscles already stiffening from the extra activity. As steam boils up, curling her hair, she leans her forehead against the cool tiles and evaluates her feelings. It is hard to escape the disappointment that Thomas hadn't waited for her, had finished without her, but that seems selfish considering that he had made sure of her pleasure before his. It was their first time, so there is still so much to learn about each other, both what works and what doesn't. So this really should be chalked up to a learning experience.

Once she is freshly scrubbed, she steps from the bathroom to find the first light of dawn creeping in the windows. At this point, it is too early to go knock on the door or call, and she really could use a little more sleep. So she sends him a quick text, knowing he usually keeps the phone on silent.

'Sorry Thomas, went out for a run, forgot I didn't have a key to get back in your room. Call when you are up, we can go have breakfast.'

Mind a little more relaxed, and body certainly worn, she slides between the cool cotton sheets to find a bit of undisturbed rest.

*****

Dragging herself up out of the depths of slumber, Chrissie fumbles for the phone, managing to clear her throat before answering.

"Hello, Thomas." she says, swallowing down a yawn. "How are you this fine morning?"

"Well, not as fine as I would have been if I had woken up to find you still in my bed." The hunger in his voice caresses her ego.

"I am so sorry, my mistake. I couldn't sleep, and didn't think about how to get back in when I was done with my run." she replies sheepishly. "I wasn't thinking very clearly."

"Then I will have to get an extra key for you today, so I can wake up with you tomorrow."

"That sounds perfect." She puts a little purr in her voice, warmth gathering in her gut.

"Christine, if you keep talking like that, we may not make it to breakfast."

Her laugh is soft and husky in response. "Breakfast first and then a walk around town. After that, I am open to suggestion."

Thomas concedes and suggests they meet in the lobby in a half hour. It doesn't take terribly long for Chrissie to drag a comb through her now dry curls or to pull on jeans and blouse, so she beats him down. It shouldn't surprise her that he is late again, but she fidgets while she waits, flipping through the tourist pamphlets. When he finally appears, he scoops her up in a big hug, lifting her completely off the ground and sneaking a kiss on the side of her neck. She giggles at the tickling sensation, then grabs him by the hand to drag him off for breakfast.

They both eat a big meal at a local mom and pop joint right around the block, then stroll up and down the streets. He buys her a little horse statuette at a local artists booth, and she convinces him to have ice cream for lunch. They sit down on a park bench to enjoy their treats, him with a cup of rocky road and her with a waffle cone full of cherry cordial. A couple walks by with a young boy in tow, about six years old, and he stops to stare at Chrissie with a shy smile. Chrissie can't help but grin back, which the little guy returns, flashing a set of pearly whites minus one bottom tooth. She giggles and waves hello, then watches him scamper off after his parents. Thomas is watching her intently, with a bemused expression.

"What?" she says, before taking another bite of her ice cream cone.

"You are going to be a great mom someday."

Her cheeks color, not from embarrassment, but because it's something so near to her heart. "I look forward to that day. Kids are amazing, they learn so quickly, are so resilient and brave if they have the freedom to be themselves. I can't help being drawn to them."

"So, basically you described yourself." Thomas says, a bit of tease in his voice.

"Yes, I think you are right." She straightens in her seat, taken aback at the insight. "I try to stay in touch with my inner child. It has helped me through some rough spots, being able to find joy in the little things."

"You know, I think it's one of the things I love best about you."

Stunned to hear the word love, sure she is over thinking things, Chrissie says nothing.

"Is there anything you love about me?" he asks, his eyes now locked deliberately on hers and a bit of panic rolls through her.

"Yes, there are several things, actually," Thinking on her feet, Chrissie answers quickly. "I love how much fun we have together. I love that we expand each other's horizons, and that you are so relaxed outside of work. I really love that you like me just the way I am."

Her smile is genuine and the answer satisfies him, so he returns to his ice cream. Chrissie exhales slowly, anxiety fading, yet she can't help feeling flattered. It's amazing that he is pressing the issue, this quickly, and after she has already slept with him. What a crazy, heady feeling.

That night, dinner is a much more casual affair at the same mom and pop they had breakfast at. Afterward, he leads her back to the hotel and makes sure to present her with a key before he draws her into the room. This time, there is a bedside light on so she can see the greed in his eyes before he pulls her close, his body warm and strong. She welcomes his lips on hers, revels in the feel of his hands on her waist, and allows him to draw her shirt off, their lips breaking apart momentarily. He is so tender, so careful, and it isn't long before she is swaying drunkenly toward him, grateful he is there to hold her up. Clothes come off of them both quickly, but it feels like everything is happening through molasses, all sweet and cloying. As he lowers her to the bed she grasps the prominent erection now at eye level, running her fingers around him in a swirling motion. He growls and she can't help but tease him, eyes locked on his in challenge, high on the thrill of his attentions. That same power is making her wet, raising her pulse as he answers her challenge by pushing her flat on the bed, away from temptation. Chrissie eyes him with appetite as he slowly slides a condom on, then he moves over her. Profuse chest hair across his broad pectorals brushes roughly over her sensitive breasts, gasping as he follows the friction with a finger slid inside her channel. There is no hesitation as he withdraws the finger and replaces

Better Broken

it with his hard length, making her quiver as he presses all the way in.

He manages a series of long, slow strokes, tantalizing her with a cold burn in her veins, until she is clutching at his shoulders, greedy for more. When he picks up speed, increasing the friction, she pulls him to her for a demanding kiss, absolutely intoxicated with the contact. This is what she needed, to be wanted so much. Fighting for breath as his hip bones grind against her pelvis, she hooks her ankles over his powerful buttocks, shifting him even deeper. The devastating sensation makes her buck beneath him, but he does not stop, maintaining a rhythm that shatters her control.

As her core spasms his movements become erratic, until he slams himself in to the hilt one last time, arching over her, emptying himself out. When he lays down on her this time she truly welcomes him, stroking damp hair back off his forehead. It takes a good deal of time, until the sweat is cooling on their skin, before the aftershocks finally pass and he can lift himself off her, kissing her forehead gently.

"Will you stay with me tonight, Christine? Will you be here in the morning?" he asks, voice thick after their efforts.

"Yes, Thomas, I will be here." she whispers back, leaning up to confirm her answer with a tender kiss.

He smiles contentedly, eyes already heavy, post coital sleep tugging at him. When he pulls her close she snuggles against him, hoping against all odds that this man will love her enough to stick around now that he has it all.

Chapter Thirteen

When he asks her to move in a month later it takes every clever word she can muster to tell him no without hurting his feelings. As much as she cares about him, Chrissie isn't ready to give up her personal sanctuary, despite the fact that she spends four nights a week in his bed. The three days that she goes to the barn to ride Smoke, it is much closer to her own apartment to get cleaned up and ready for the next day, not having to worry about Thomas. While she has a toothbrush and a supply of clothes at his place, she is hanging on to her privacy, needing time to recharge.

Tonight, they are going out to dinner, then to a theatre production with his parents. Fidgeting in front of the mirror, double checking her hair for the umpteenth time to be sure the usual curls are properly tamed, she waits. A pair of sapphire teardrop earrings are the only jewelry she wears, a perfect complement to the gorgeous blue gown hugging her body. Thank goodness for mobile phones, so she could try dresses on and get an opinion immediately, knowing Suzie would never steer her wrong. The heels she is sporting are low but appropriately strappy silver grey sling backs. Fussing with her lipstick, the knock at her door comes as a surprise. Thomas is never on time. When she opens the door, he stands on the threshold and stares.

"Thomas, are you coming in?"

"If I come in, we may never leave. I'd rather have you in that dress all to myself." he says, bowing slightly at the waist. "Christine, may I have the privilege of escorting you this evening?"

Chrissie can't stop the full blush that accompanies his pretty compliment, loving how he pulls her to him, placing her hand at his elbow. She pulls the locked door closed, and lets him lead her to the car, grounding herself against the solid feel of his arm.

On the drive, he is uncharacteristically twitchy, easily irritated by traffic and stoplights. "I suppose you are worried about being late to meet your parents?" Chrissie asks, to put him at ease.

"Ah, yes, Father is a stickler and Mother is famous for her guilt trips, which I prefer to prevent whenever possible. It's one of the many things I love about being with you Christine. You never get on my case about things."

If he only knew how much his lateness gets on her nerves; on the other hand she is glad to give him a little peace, if his parents ride him so heavily about it. They reach the restaurant quickly, a high dollar locale in the downtown area, and Chrissie no longer worries that she is overdressed. In fact, it is entirely possible she is underdressed, though she wouldn't be happy attired as opulently as most of the clientele. Thomas moves comfortably among all the linen and cut crystal, perfectly at home, the custom line of his fine wool tuxedo blending in amidst the flash, and she is glad he is there to

Justine Iarann

guide her.

Seated at a small table in the middle of the restaurant, it manages to feel fairly intimate despite its location. The waiter asks for their wine selection, and Chrissie bows to Thomas suggestion for a bottle of chardonnay, her eyebrows raising in surprise. Usually, Thomas orders red to go with his steaks. Following the wine cue, she finds a beautiful array of seafood options on the menu, ordering a simple scallops and risotto. Thomas goes completely out of character and orders fish, which causes her to comment on it. He waves it off, saying he is trying to be healthier, and is saving room for dessert.

They share details about their respective days, Thomas telling her about a car accident victim. The details of the complicated bone reconstruction would likely put their neighbors off their dinner if they overheard. Luckily, Chrissie finds it fascinating, looking forward to seeing the results in person when the patient is ready for therapy.

Excited about the possibility of starting equine based rehabilitative therapy, Chrissie runs on about her ideas for funding a program. Thomas shows genuine interest in her project, encouraging her to discuss the people she has been meeting who run their own therapeutic riding programs. They too have been supportive of her idea, since hers would specialize in wounded veterans, addressing both the emotional and physical challenges.

Conversation is interrupted with the arrival of their food, which turns out to be simply delightful. Her scallops are perfectly seared, and the risotto a gorgeous surprise. Thomas still acts distracted, pushing his flakey trout around to little effect.

"Thomas, is your food alright?" Chrissie asks with concern. "Or are you worried about seeing your parents?"

He startles a little, which is again nothing like him. "Oh, yes, that must be it. The food is great, I am just not very

Better Broken

hungry tonight." he says, delivering his most disarming grin.

Unconvinced, Chrissie chooses to wait until they are alone to push any further. Her confusion compounds when he insists they order dessert, despite his lack of appetite. She allows him to choose a house made cheesecake, watching him fidget to the point of making the neighboring tables look. Trying to ease him somehow, she covers the hand drumming over the linen table cloth, stroking his knuckles soothingly. He meets her eyes with a more genuine smile, placing his other hand over hers and heaving a small sigh. Those deft surgeons' fingers weave between hers, then he looks up at the waiters approach.

"Ah, here is our dessert." he says, and she looks to the plate placed between them. The source of Thomas's nerves becomes apparent, and she forgets to breath. Written in chocolate along the rim of the plate are the scrolling words 'Will you marry me?' A tug at her hand turns her to the man now kneeling beside her, a blue velvet ring box held on an open palm.

"What do you say, Christine? Will you make an honest man out of me?" he asks, voice pitched low and full of anxiety.

The eyes on hers are searching, almost desperate, and for a moment, she fights dismay. The whole restaurant has gone quiet, waiting for an answer while she searches for words. She smiles quaveringly and heaves in a gasp of air, then leans forward to kiss his cheek before whispering, "Yes."

Whooping like a child, he stands and scoops her to his chest, lifting her off her feet. The crowd applauds as she hides her blush in the side of his neck, still in shock. When he sets her back down, her hands are shaking as he opens the ring box to reveal a carat sized diamond set in platinum, with more diamonds along the band. As he slides it on the weight of it hits her, like a tiny shackle of possession- guilt swallows her for even thinking it. Now is for rejoicing in the hope of their future together, not worrying. When the ring is on he lifts her hand to his lips, smiling like she is his north star and she finally, truly smiles back, laughing giddily.

"Christine, you have made me so happy ever since we first met, such unexpected joy. I hope I can give you as great a gift in our future together." he declares, blue eyes flashing.

"Thomas, I can only hope that the joy and love between us grows and grows." Chrissie responds, her words a fervent prayer.

Their kiss is circumspect, considering the audience, but she pours herself in to it, hoping her actions will reassure him. They take the dessert to go, kissing again as they wait for the valet to bring the car. It is not far to the theatre, barely any time to steel herself for meeting his parents, and Thomas spends the whole trip stroking her hand repetitively. She manages her best smile as they walk up the steps to the theatre, beneath a high arched glass ceiling. Once inside, they are directed up some stairs, and she is shocked when they are escorted on to a private box. Inside, a roughhewn man dressed as finely as Thomas is seated beside a devastatingly gorgeous woman of indeterminate age. As they approach, the man stands and holds his thick hand out to Thomas, greeting him with a firm clasp.

"Thomas, good of you to finally join us, your mother was wondering how late you would be."

His voice is much deeper than Thomas's, grey peppering his thick, inky hair. Yet, the eyes are the same piercing blue, and while he is a coarser specimen, she can see Thomas in him.

The lady in question rises, and as she comes close for a brief embrace of her son, she is evaluating Chrissie, judging even as she welcomes them. Her hair is the same nut brown darkness as Thomas, and she is obviously who lent refinement to her son.

"Don't be ridiculous, Walter, I had every faith that my dear boy would not disappoint! And who is this lovely morsel, Thomas?" she asks, her baby blue eyes latching on Chrissie in a very feral manner.

Chrissie is grateful when Thomas pulls her closer to his side, giving her an anchor in such unfamiliar waters. The theatre she is no stranger to, but it is usually in the cheap seats, with a much homier welcome. However, the challenge in the woman's eyes is certainly something she is accustomed to, so she turns up the voltage in her smile and extends her hand.

"Christine Everett, Mrs. Mason, pleasure to meet you."

"Evelyn Mason, my dear. How do you know my darling boy?" Evelyn grasps her hand firmly, still challenging.

"Actually, Mother," Thomas interjects. "Christine is my fiancée."

The gaze piercing her so aggressively falters, showing some tiredness before those eyes snap up to stab Thomas in place like a dead butterfly.

"Is that so, Thomas?" she says, her voice ten degrees colder.

"Yes, Mother. This evening in fact." Thomas affirms, and while he is squirming under that stare, Chrissie is proud of the resolve tightening his jaw, in the hand that closes over hers.

Thankfully, the house lights flicker, signaling the crowd to take their seats, breaking the rising tension. Walter steps between them to escort Evelyn to her seat, though once he has her moving the right way, the older man catches Chrissie's eye and grins. It is enough of an encouragement that she is happy to take her seat and enjoy the show. Thomas spends most of the time holding her hand, caressing over the ring that marks her as his, studying the play of emotions on her face as she watches the actors. The Helen Keller story is book she has read, but it is startlingly more moving to see it acted out. Through the whole thing, Chrissie is torn between tears and joy, exactly as she sometimes is with her own clients' challenges and victories.

At intermission Evelyn is quick to grab Thomas, convincing him to accompany her to the lobby for a glass of wine. Chrissie slumps in her seat with relief, not looking forward to more of the evident hostility, yet she feels badly abandoning him to the task of facing the firing squad alone.

"So, my dear girl, I hear you are to join our merry family now?" Walter asks, moving over to the seat Thomas had vacated.

"Yes sir, it would seem so." Chrissie says with a tense chuckle. "I only hope it doesn't cause a civil war."

"Miss Everett, war with my wife is never civil. But have no fear, Thomas shall charm her around fairly quickly, as will you, I am sure. She is very protective of him, has always been tooth and nail with every woman he brings around, yet you are the first he has been serious about. That carries quite a bit of weight."

"I can only hope so, sir. I couldn't bear to cause conflict in your family." Chrissie bites her lower lip and flicks her gaze toward the entrance of the box.

Mr. Mason reaches across to briefly touch her hand. "Call me Walter, please. I won't have a future daughter calling me sir."

Glad to know someone is on their side, Chrissie offers him a more relaxed smile. "Thank you, Walter. You may call me Chrissie, if you like."

They spend the remainder of the intermission discussing pleasantries until Thomas and his mother return. The frost is still present, but the cutting edge has dulled. Leaning against Thomas's side, the rest of the play is much more enjoyable, rejoicing at the grand victory of the characters without the worry of impending conflict.

After they part ways with his parents, Chrissie asks after Thomas' mother on the way home.

"Christine, darling, it is nothing to worry yourself about. She has protected me from some poor decisions in the past, and I simply have to convince her that you are no mistake. You be your charming self, and I know she will come around quickly."

"Are you sure, Thomas? I don't want to be a cause for strife between you."

"Any strife is hers alone. I am absolutely confident that you will be the perfect wife for me, and she will have to come to terms with that." His tone is so assured that she squeezes the hand resting on her leg, and lets the issue go. When they reach his condo, he immediately draws her in his arms.

"So, future Mrs. Mason, what can I do to make you as happy as you have made me?"

She pulls away a little and wraps his tie around her hand, drawing him toward the bedroom.

"Dr. Mason, I am sure I have a few ideas that will work." Chrissie says with a saucy smile.

He growls and makes a dive for her, but she scampers away with a giggle, running for the bed with Thomas hot on her heels.

*****

Frost is burning off the grassy plains in the late fall sunrise as Chrissie drives out to the airport to pick up Suzie. Blowing on her hands, she scurries into the terminal from the parking garage, excitement at seeing her best friend making her forget her gloves. Her eye is caught on the shine of diamonds gracing her left hand, and she shakes her head, wondering for the hundredth time what had prompted the purchase of such a big ring. Yet it is so obvious how much Thomas enjoys giving her things- like the new SUV she is driving, or the custom saddle he had arranged for. It is hard to be bothered by something that makes him so happy, and Smoke is happy with the new tack as well.

When she sees Suzie's black cap of hair coming up the escalator, almost lost in the taller crowd, Chrissie jumps up and waves. Immediately, a grin splits Suzie's red painted lips, and Chrissie is thrilled when she is finally close enough to hug.

"Good Lord, Chrissie, you'd think we hadn't seen each other in forever." Suzie says, with her normal dry sarcasm as they disengage from a mutual embrace.

"But Suz, we haven't seen each other in forever." Chrissie shoots back as they turn for the baggage claim, grinning madly.

"Okay, point taken, but do you have to be so excited this early in the morning? I've only had two espresso since I left Dulles last night."

"Then aren't you lucky I am taking you out for coffee as soon as we get out of this mess?"

"I take back every rude thing I have ever said about you, Saint Chrissie." Suzie answers, linking her arm through Chrissie's companionably.

After proper caffeination, they check in to the hotel Chrissie has booked in the downtown area so they can be near all the best shopping and clubs. It will be a night out like they used to enjoy, with a slumber party afterwards. Once they drop their bags Chrissie drags Suzie back out to the car, and they set off through the streets.

"Where in God's name are you taking me, crazy woman? I am jet lagged and a mess." Suzie complains half-heartedly.

"Liar. You look fabulous. And it's a surprise." Chrissie says, guiding the compact SUV into a parking spot along the street. She waves an arm out the window. "Surprise!"

When Suzie notices where she is pointing her smile comes big and bright. "You absolute goddess! Tea! All these miles away from Richmond, and you remember tea?"

"I could never forget tea. It is sacred." Chrissie answers, her voice playful, but her eyes serious. "It is an institution meant for the very best of friends."

They make their way into the tea house, engulfed by the buttery scent of fresh baked scones and hints of bergamot, nostalgia washing over them both.

"I swear, every good tea house in the world smells exactly like this." Suzie closes her eyes and breathes deeply. Chrissie can't help but agree with her.

Once they are seated, and their orders placed, Suzie reaches across the table, snagging Chrissie's hand for a closer inspection of the engagement ring.

"Wow, Dr. Feel Good has great taste!"

"Suz, you know I don't care about stuff like this." Chrissie rebukes, resisting the urge to draw her hand back and cover up the glimmering rock.

"Pish posh, Chrissie. You deserve the good stuff, and don't forget it." A negligent wave of Suzie's hand swats away Chrissie's buzzing worries. "He has to be good to you, or I will scratch his pretty eyes out."

"This isn't the good stuff for me, Suz. The good stuff is when he holds me in his arms. When he loves me just the way I am, and doesn't want me to change to suit him. When he talks about our future together and we support each other's dreams." Looking down at the ring again, she fidgets, uncomfortable with the glittering reminder of their commitment to each other. It feels like too much sometimes.

"I'm going to ask you an uncomfortable question, Chrissie, because I notice something important missing." She leans closer and grabs Chrissie's hand so that she will look up. "How about love? Do you love him?"

"Yes, I love him." Chrissie answers defensively, eyes flashing. "I wouldn't have agreed to this if I didn't."

"Sorry, Chrissie," Suzie says, smiling softly to take away the sting. "I noticed that it wasn't the first thing you said when you talked about what was important, and I need to be sure. I'm your best friend, and I have to know you are treated right. I don't want your saintly tendencies to convince you to marry some guy, even if he is gorgeous, just because you think it is the right thing to do."

Heaving a deep sigh, Chrissie is relieved when their tea arrives, taking a moment to gather her thoughts while she pours her cup. The rich color strikes a chord in her heart for a moment, but she squelches it quickly, pouring in cream to muddle the deep brown elixir. After a few moments of simply sipping her tea and mustering the right words, Chrissie looks over to see Suzie's eyes full of concern.

"Okay," Chrissie begins, then takes another fortifying sip. "I will state here and now, that I am marrying Thomas because it is the right thing to do. It is right because I love him and he loves me. We are a great partnership, and bring so much to each other's lives that makes everything better for both of us. I am marrying him because he will make a great father, because he wants me, and it makes me feel good to be so wanted."

"Yeah, but I remember someone else who made you feel that way, and look how that worked out."

An incandescent flame in her heart leaps at the memory, making her feelings now seem pale in comparison, and Chrissie quickly smothers it.

"Yes, there is a risk loving anyone Suzie. But I won't live in fear of the hurt. I refuse. The last hurt is because he was running away, and right now, all I see is Thomas running toward me. I'm going to take that gift without looking too closely at it."

Better Broken

Suzie bites her lip, worrying it over in her therapist brain, so Chrissie waits, sipping serenely at the cloudy sweet contents of her cup.

"Alright, Chrissie. I give. You know I'm on your side, and if it is good enough for you, then it is good enough for me. I want you to be happy." Suzie finally answers earnestly.

Chrissie heaves a sigh of relief. "Well, thank goodness for that! Because frankly, I need you on my side, maid of honor."

Suzie's eyes dampen, but as usual the tears dry up as quickly as they threaten. Chrissie is one of the few people in the world that has ever seen Suzie cry, and Suzie certainly won't spill in a shop full of strangers.

"Thanks for that, Chrissie. Seriously, thanks. Now, any ideas when I am going to need to take time off for your soiree?"

"Ah, I knew you could be counted on for a game face." Chrissie answers with a teasing wink. "And frankly, that is going to be a complete pain in the hinny, because Thomas wants to get married in the early spring. In Hawaii."

"Seriously? Hawaii? Do you know how white my skin is going to be after a Virginia winter?"

"I know, not my perfect plan either, but he doesn't want to waste a day. We would get married now if he could figure out how to make it happen, but it's the soonest we could both get time off. It will keep the guest list small, since it's a destination wedding. We will already be there for the honeymoon, and there are several places that handle this sort of thing all the time. So less craziness for me."

"Whoa, slow down, Strawberry Tall-cake! I know you aren't really a beach girl, so are you at least getting married in a church?"

"Yes, absolutely. Which means our number one goal while you are here is to find a dress!"

"Ah, now you are speaking my language! Shopping, I can

totally do!" Suzie declares.

"I knew I'd have your attention if I said the magic words. So, tomorrow, 10am, I have an appointment. Mom will be meeting us, and we can all get our dresses together. You can pick your own."

"Aw, I haven't seen Catherine in forever! How fun! Girl's day out! Maybe even a little pre-bachelorette party?"

"Somehow, I knew this was going to end with you getting me drunk." Chrissie laughs, rolling her eyes.

"Oh, I know better. This will end with me drunk, and you helping me back to the hotel." Suzie scoffs.

"Anything for you, Suzie." Chrissie says, looking her dear, vivacious friend in the eye.

Suzie reaches over to take Chrissie's hand once more. "Back at you, Chrissie, always."

Chapter Fourteen

The warm breeze coming from the open balcony is not enough to dry the sweat beading on Chrissie's forehead, so she pulls the door shut, hoping to keep her freshly coifed hair from frizzing in the humidity. It's less than two hours until she becomes Mrs. Doctor Thomas Mason, and she is slowly unraveling at the seams. It is too late for panic or cold feet, but sitting alone in her room, waiting for her mother and best friend to join her, gives far too much time to think.

 The last month has been an insane whirl of activity, setting her well-ordered life on its ear. Smoke had felt the lack of her company on far too many occasions, and she had certainly felt that same lack herself, wringing her heart out with no way to soak in the peace that horse time usually provides. Chrissie sips at a tropical smoothie, a delicious concoction that is a resort specialty, hoping to settle her stomach.

 At that very moment, her mother walks in, and Chrissie exhales to dispel some tension. Even better than getting to hug her horse, a mom hug is exactly what she needs, and Catherine sees it in her daughter's eyes before she can say a word. Being enfolded in her mother's arms, surrounded by the distinct lavender and mint scent, huddled in the memories of thousands of such comforting moments, is enough to make Chrissie's eyes water. When the two of them finally pull back from each other the weight on Chrissie's heart is far lighter, and she laughs when her mom uses a tissue to catch the tear threatening to spill.

"I know, wouldn't it be the thing to do, ruining my makeup so close to time?"

Catherine Everett is a beautiful woman, in an artistic, classical way, nothing artificial about her, so it is easy to see the worry and pride chasing across her lovely face. Catherine's red hair is softened by the silver of years, her smile bracketed with the punctuation of a million emotional moments- the green eyes staring so earnestly at her child cannot be anything other than honest.

"Baby girl, I'm going to ask you one more time, then never again. Are you sure about this?"

"Momma, haven't you asked me a hundred times? Do you really think the answer is going to change? I would have thought you would be ecstatic at this point, to see me settling down."

"Ah, there is a dirty word! Settling!" The wrinkle of disgust over her nose is out of place on her flawless face. "I'll have none of that! I raised you to fly, I did everything I could to teach you how to burn with passion. You had better not, now or ever, be settling!"

Chrissie smiles at the flashing fire in her mother's eyes, fierce words at conflict with the soft tremble of her lips. "Momma, it's okay. We are getting married because we help each other soar, not because we want to hold each other back."

"Alright, darling girl, alright." Her tone is much softer as she brushes an errant curl off Chrissie's forehead. "Suzie should be here any moment, and we can head down to the car. Do you need help grabbing anything?"

They gather up what they will need at the church, everything well in hand by the time Suzie breezes in, her silky black cap of hair softened at the edges with a few feathery curls. Like a well-oiled machine, they manage the lobby and load in to the waiting town car for the short jaunt to the beach side chapel.

Once there, time speeds up, fingers begin fumbling buttons and laces, stockings tear under the unaccustomed manicured nails. It feels like a miracle when Chrissie has ten minutes to wait, fully ensconced in her dress, which she stares at in the giant pier glass mirror. Suzie had been completely on point when she picked out the relatively simple gown, dramatic in its fit to her torso, then softened with the long flare of heavy skirt. There is no lace, beading or jewels, just hundreds of tiny gathers and tucks to accent her curves. No veil hides her face, only a glittering hair comb given to her by her mother to compliment an up-do, and her eyes startlingly large with a little soft makeup. She doesn't quite feel herself, but then her mother and best friend step into the mirror with her, each grabbing a hand to anchor her.

"You are so beautiful, Chrissie." Suzie whispers with awe.

That tips Chrissie's lips up as a chance to tease her friend rears its head. "Don't sound so shocked, Suzie Q."

Suzie laughs then, the seriousness lifting from her face.

"And Suzie, so are you." Chrissie says with an answering smile. The cobalt blue dress pays homage to Suzie's perfect alabaster skin, the usually red painted lips made softer in a sheer pink.

"Thanks, Chrissie." Suzie mumbles, looking away from the mirror, hiding from the compliment.

Justine Iarann

A squeeze on her other hand prompts her to meet her mother's green eyes, made almost jade in the steel blue gown. The silver in her hair is shining softly, like a precious metal melting through fire.

"I love you, baby girl." Catherine whispers as she kisses Chrissie softly on the temple, then hugs her tight. Chrissie clings to her for one more moment, until a knock on the door lets them know it is time. Suzie hands her the bouquet, a mostly white affair of lilies, with a few blue orchids thrown in for color. Then she leads the way out of the room, giving one last grin before beginning the march down the aisle. There is only a piano for music and when they hear the tempo change, Chrissie clasps her mother hand before stepping into the door way.

Aside from noticing the smell of tropical flowers, Chrissie can't focus much beyond her first look at Thomas. It isn't the dashing figure he cuts, the breadth of his shoulders carrying the tailored navy blue suit, or how handsome he is in the rays of sunlight illuminating the chapel. It is the absolute naked hunger in his eyes that steals her breath, like he is a dying man receiving his last meal. Some women would shy from it, be afraid of it, but for Chrissie, it is what she needs. That even in this solemn moment, he wants her so very fiercely, is what puts paid to the last of her panic. She smiles as her feet carry her forward, her eyes delivering their own challenge, and when her mother puts their hands together she can feel the sharp lust piercing them both. He holds on gently, but there is possessive pressure in the tips of his fingers. His nostrils flare slightly as she says her vows, gaze sharpening even more, until she is afraid everyone around them will become aware of his claim.

When he returns the vows and they exchange rings, she keeps her eyes on his, trying to soften his demeanor with an easy smile. It isn't until the officiant declares them man and wife that some of the predator fades back, and the kiss they share is soft enough not to alarm the watching family. It still doesn't stop the sour look of distaste on his mother's face, but that is something beyond her control. The heady drug of his want is potent as they walk back down the aisle, her hand fitted into his elbow, but part of her wants to duck away, to blunt the edge that is cutting at them.

Surprisingly, Thomas has read her thoughts, because once beyond the first set of doors he pulls her quickly toward the bride room. The door barely catches behind them before he is lifting her up, completely off her feet, to stake his claim on her lips. There is no tenderness in it, yet Chrissie responds in kind, not only allowing the assault but participating fully in the siege. Just as she begins to feel faint for lack of breath, he sets her down gently, slowly disengaging his mouth from hers, stroking her cheek softly as he steps back.

"Thanks, baby, I needed that." he growls, the tenor of his voice still gravely with pent up desire.

Chrissie stands on her tip toes and kisses his cheek before giving a teasing grin. "I kind of gathered that."

He huffs a chuckle. "I suppose we ought to straighten ourselves out, so we can go do the photos."

Spinning in alarm, Chrissie looks in the mirror, but aside from the flowers she had dropped on the floor, some heightened color in her cheeks and the telltale fullness of well kissed lips, there is no damage to worry about. Thomas, however, requires a bit of lipstick removal, and a quick fix of his hair that she had tangled her fingers in. He pulls her in once more for a brief brush of lips, then tucks her against his side before opening the door to face the waiting crowd. It is all Chrissie can do to not look guilty in front of family and friends, particularly when Suzie flashes her a knowing grin.

Yet, they make it through the hour of photos with aplomb, and if anything, the color on her cheeks truly makes her the very picture of a blushing bride. Thomas is an attentive and dutiful husband, never leaving her side, making Chrissie glad they had kept their wedding so intimate. Otherwise, social obligations would keep them long past the few hours it requires to satisfy their guests.

Suzie has hooked Michael, the best man's attention, a blonde, lean doctor that Thomas was friends with in medical school. Chrissie wants to warn Suzie off, with his womanizing reputation, but two things stop her. One is the fact that Thomas had gone from confirmed ladies' man to committed husband. The other is that Suzie is equally as well known for her love them and leave them relationship style. As things are beginning to wind down, Chrissie's mother pulls her away from Thomas for a few moments alone.

"Oh baby girl, I'm happy for you." Catherine whispers as she wraps Chrissie in a hug, tears threatening.

"Oh Momma, stop, or I'll cry too." she whispers back, knowing it's too late as tears fall off her cheeks. There is a slight tremble of her mother's shoulders as she softly cries, and Chrissie tightens the embrace.

"I want you to be happy." her mother chokes out, echoing Suzie's statement several months before.

"I am, and I will be. We make our own happiness, Momma. You taught me that!"

At Chrissie's words, Catherine steps back with a huge smile. "And here I thought I was talking to a wall all those rebellious teenage years."

Mutual laughter fortifies them both, then Chrissie squeezes her hand and says her farewells. Not much longer after that Thomas hands her in to the town car taking them to the hotel, and they are finally alone. Before he can move Chrissie tugs him to her until his weight is pining her to the seat. His hands span her ribcage as he kisses a hot trail across her décolletage, then he dips one hand beneath her skirt, racing skilled fingers over her stocking until he reaches the garter straps. The growl coming from him vibrates through her whole body, and she is glad she went to the trouble to wear them.

"Wife, I do believe I am looking forward to unwrapping this present when we get to our room." Thomas says, sliding his fingers further up to tangle in her panties.

Gasping, Chrissie drags him in for a kiss, trying to distract him from the lingerie. Luckily, they arrive at the hotel about then and straighten themselves up enough to walk through the lobby. However, rather than leading her to the elevators, he walks down a different hall, then outside through one of the many gardens. The air is heavy with the scent of night blooming flowers, humidity a physical touch compared to the dry air of their home state. As they approach a tiny villa set back behind some vegetation he presents her with the key, much as he had the night she had first stayed with him. She opens the door to find shadows cast by flickering candle light and rose petals scattered on the floor in a heart shape.

Thomas walks up behind her, kissing a damp trail down her neck as she leans in to his solid weight. He pulls at the laces on the back of her dress as they sway their way down the hall, making gradual progress toward what must be the bedroom. She is not disappointed when they turn a corner into a spacious room, dominated by a massive white linen draped platform bed. At that point, she pulls away from his seeking hands, turning to catch his ravenous gaze. Tonight will be about laying claim, and she doubts there will be much sentimentality, a truth made more real as she tugs the dress off her body, allowing it to tangle at her feet.

Like a stallion scenting a mare, his nostrils flare wide and the tension in his muscles ratchets to a new level. To his credit, he does not charge forward, only stalks a circle around her while removing his own clothing, eyes roving over the lacy bra and tiny white panties. His gaze scorches down her hips to the garter straps holding up the sheer white stockings, and his feral expression is almost enough to scare her. Yet, she has stood her ground in the face of much larger and more dangerous animals, so she simply waits, watching as he throws his shirt on the floor. A serene smile dances across her face, appreciating the meaty frame he is uncovering, lingering over the thick muscles. When he pushes his tailored slacks down her attention is immediately drawn to his bobbing arousal, and he growls as he watches her.

"This, my dear wife, has been plaguing me all night." he says, looking down at his erection. "A torture of exquisite proportions, having you so close yet unable to satisfy myself in your wetness. I hope you are ready to welcome me, because I don't know how much patience I have."

Stepping carefully out of the fabric surrounding her, Chrissie slides on to the bed. He follows, but maintains his distance, watching as she pulls the pins from her hair, letting tresses now scarlet in the candlelight spill over her creamy shoulders. Leaning back against the pillows she stretches her arms over her head in mute surrender, offering herself to him with no words at all.

The tiny squeak she utters is completely forgivable as he launches himself at her, normally skilled hands rough with haste. Her welcome is genuine though, reaching for him even as he paws over her breasts, yanking down the flimsy bra in order to lave coarsely over her already tight nipples. As he falls between her thighs in his eagerness, Chrissie is glad anticipation alone has been enough foreplay to make her ready. There is no mercy in the hand that tears her panties, making an easy path for the seeking fingers that find her wet, and he shudders as she wraps her hand around him, guiding him inside her. He does not go slowly, simply drives himself in as far as he can in one motion, leaving her frozen at the shock. There is no time to adjust, just his immediate motion, pressing in and drawing out quickly until the friction is impossible to endure. Her orgasm comes quickly, and while not as fierce as usual, it is enough to make his rhythm grow ragged as he tries to hang on.

When a second wave crashes over her, Chrissie gives a small cry that undoes him, so he slams himself in one last time, bowing down over her for a desperate kiss. As he pours himself out she consciously clenches her inner muscles, drawing a groan from him as his hips ram against her once more. One hand wraps in her hair, as though he is trying to keep her still, while a shudder wracks his frame.

Withdrawing with a grunt, she expects he will fall to the side as usual, and be pulled under by sleep, leaving her surprised when he moves away. When she leans up in concern, he presses her back, the skilled hands he usually employs in their lovemaking tracing her torso. Settling back in to the soft support of the pillows, she watches with fascination as he unsnaps her garter straps, slowly tugging the stockings down. Stroking each bit of revealed skin as he goes, Thomas then tosses the stockings away from the bed, relegated to the floor with the rest of their clothing. Next, he pulls her up with one hand while the other gently unclasps her bra, still kissing every bit of uncovered flesh with tenderness. Lastly, he removes what remains of her panties, planting gentle kisses over her hips. Dumbfounded entirely by the tenderness, she goes willingly when he draws her to his chest as he normally does.

"Thank you, for being my wife, Christine."

"You are quite welcome, husband." she murmurs as sleep quickly draws him under. The snores which once drove her to distraction are now a familiar lullaby that sings her to the rest of a newly married woman.

Justine Iarann

Chapter Fifteen

Their honeymoon is all too brief, a week of unabashed attention to themselves alone, no responsibilities to weigh their time. A breath later finds them back in Colorado, falling in to a familiar rhythm of work and home. Having given up her apartment before the wedding, she also moves Smoke to a barn that sits between the hospital and the condo. They rarely have a moment that isn't filled with activity, but every night they wrap themselves together, desperate to be close.

Having children had come up almost immediately, again not wanting to waste time, so Chrissie throws out her birth control pills, eager to grow their family. Not even a month later, she sits in the grass at Smokes feet in the peaceful safety of the barn. The image of the positive pregnancy test is burned in to her eyes, her heart so full of conflicting emotions. Certainly, they hadn't expected her to get pregnant so quickly, and it is another fast moving change knocking her off balance. Just as her brain is about to start chasing its tail,

Better Broken

Smoke's lips wiggle against her cheek, startling a giggle from her.

"Well, buddy, are you ready to be an uncle?" she whispers, glad her horse at least understands her mood. For several moments, she holds his muzzle in her hands and draws in the warm breaths he blows on her face, centering herself. From that alone she finds peace, so she stands up and brushes the grass off her pants, ready to go share the news with Thomas.

Driving toward town in the gathering dusk, her palms stick to the steering wheel with nervous sweat, so she turns up the radio to sing along with one of her favorite artists. It is easy to get lost in the cheerful lyrics, to let the warm air blowing in the window wash the worry off her face. She isn't concerned about Thomas's reaction, she knows he will be happy, but they had just begun to settle in to married life, and now their lives are about to change again. One hand absently drifts down to touch her stomach, praying fervently that this baby knows how loved it is already.

Pulling up to the diner where she and Thomas eat almost every Wednesday, she parks up front, right next to the his sports car. Sitting in the front seat, he talks animatedly on the phone, offering a big smile when notices her. He holds up his hand to tell her he will be five more minutes, so she goes inside to their regular booth, giving the waitress their usual order. He slides in to the seat across from her as their drinks arrive and asks about her day.

"Well, it was eventful." Chrissie says with a secretive smile, and with no other preamble, she slides a long narrow box across the table to him.

His brows arch up in to his forehead, eyes full of questions, but he says nothing, just lifts the lid. When it reveals the slim stick of the pregnancy test, wonder lights his face.

"Wow!" is all he says, repeating the word several times for

good measure, until she begins to worry. Yet, he reaches across the table for her hand, clasping it gently between both of his. "This is the best present, ever."

"I have an appointment on Friday, to confirm with the doctor. But I didn't want to wait until then to tell you. I'll wait until after the appointment to tell anyone else. So, for now it's our little secret."

"I think we should celebrate! And since you can't have champagne now, I think we should have milkshakes!" Now she can see the excited little boy in him, and Chrissie wonders if he will be able to keep the secret until they have conformation. His obvious enthusiasm makes her smile. "We should start house hunting immediately. The condo simply isn't enough for a family."

Taken aback, and still coming to grips with the overwhelming idea of being a mother, it takes her a moment to process his words.

"Now? Really? We have never discussed it before, I don't even know what kind of house you like!"

He waves a hand dismissively. "Whatever you think is best for a family, Christine. I don't have any experience with this sort of thing and I trust your judgment."

"Neither do I, Thomas. I grew up on my grandfather's ranch, mostly. Not in some suburban neighborhood."

"Then maybe we should look at a little ranch? You could have your horse, and we could get a puppy for the baby."

For a moment, she cannot manage even the smallest reply. Imagining Thomas living on a ranch of any kind a bit of a stretch. She had planned to always straddle the line between his cosmopolitan lifestyle and her outdoor haven.

"Are you serious, Thomas?" she squeaks out. "That won't be easy to come by, and I don't know if we can afford it."

"Anything for our baby, Christine." His indulgent smile is almost patronizing. "I would never wish my childhood on our baby, and I can only imagine how much happier your upbringing was."

Granted, the years on her grandfather's ranch had helped to heal some the hurts left by her father's neglect. Yet, it is a big step to take, financially and emotionally.

"I suppose you will have to stop riding for a while?" he asks as their food arrives. Chrissie stirs her salad thoughtfully, having not considered things that far ahead.

"Well, I have known quite a few women who keep riding most of their pregnancy, but I imagine eventually I will feel too awkward." she answers noncommittally, having not thought through the change in her relationship with Smoke. Perhaps it's time to look into the carriage driving again.

"What about work? Will you keep working?"

"Of course, Thomas!" She wrinkles her nose at the ridiculous question. "I'm not going to be an invalid, only pregnant."

He chuckles, which prickles her feelings. "I am not trying to deprive you, Christine. Simply offering you an option. You know I can afford it."

Nodding her acknowledgement, she knows that he can certainly support them both. Yet her job is not just a means to make money. It is her calling, to heal people, and too much a part of her to give up.

"Thank you Thomas, I do appreciate it, but my job means a great deal to me. Certainly, I will take some maternity time, but I could never leave it."

He smiles, and it eases her pique to have him accept her decision. Certainly she has enough on her mind without having to defend her work.

Conversation falls in to normal patterns as he shares a difficult procedure the surgical team had faced. It is always interesting to hear him talk animatedly about his work, excited to mend what is broken. It is one of the things that echoes most strongly in her. They end their meal with the aforementioned milk shakes, and he lets her steal the cherry off the top of his with an affectionate grin. Likely he is going to spend the next nine months indulging her, and she can't find it in her to dislike it one bit.

*****

Five months in, and Chrissie is already feeling a bit like a whale. House hunting has been an exercise in everything she doesn't want, and her frustration level rises inexorably higher. Yet, as she navigates up the gravel drive toward what must be heaven on earth, all her discomfort is washed away. Mostly a bit of rolling meadow, the acreage has just enough trees to give a sense of privacy and welcoming shade in the noon heat. The house itself has a deep porch with big windows looking down the hill, watching her approach. A little brick accent gives a sense of solidity, with enough wood beams to make it fit the landscape. As if that isn't enough, there is a big barn beyond the main drive that she is looking forward to seeing as much as the house. Running a hand over her now taut belly, round with the growing weight of their daughter, she smiles.

"I think we have found it, baby girl." she whispers in the quiet confines of the car before sliding out to meet the realtor.

The gracious older lady smiles with true sympathy when she sees Chrissie's stomach. "I swear, you have grown a size since I saw you a week ago! What are you feeding that baby?"

Chrissie laughs at Marsha's easy familiarity, having spent so much time in her company the last several months.

"I certainly feel a size bigger! Now, let's look this one over so I can go put my feet up."

The inside is as welcoming as the outside would suggest, everything laid out perfectly, with a big kitchen window that gazes out over the pastures. Her smile grows almost painful when they walk up to the barn. It's easy to imagine Smoke running across the field for his supper at night, to see their little girl with her first pony. Even the shadow of a former dream crosses her mind, remembering the therapeutic equine program she had wanted to start. The property is a half hour commute, which is their maximum range, and on the upper end of the budget. Yet, it has the garage Thomas insisted on, and is on a road that is regularly plowed in winter. She calls him right away.

"You simply must come see it, Thomas! It is perfect! Marsha said she would meet us back here this evening so you could look at it as well."

"Actually, Christine, I am going to run late tonight, but I trust you implicitly. If you love it, we will put in an offer immediately. I don't want this to slip through our fingers."

Gratified to be able to move on it so quickly, she still harbors a bit of regret that he hasn't even seen it. "Are you sure? We could schedule something tomorrow."

"No, no, go ahead. I know you will do what is best for our family. I have to go, baby, time to scrub in for the next surgery."

They trade hasty goodbyes and she turns to begin the discussion that will lead them toward a permanent home. Not only for their family, but for all her hopes and dreams, sure in her heart that this is where they belong.

*****

At seven months, Chrissie is spending half days at the rehab clinic. Co-workers and clients alike are so emotionally invested in her baby's development that it is like having a giant family watching over them. A few people irritate her with their incessant need to touch her belly, but most are unfailingly polite about it.

An older lady working through a hand amputation and learning to use her new prosthetic, had actually presented her with a gift that morning. The darling crocheted blanket is so soft and white it looks to be made of clouds, with a perfect girly frill around its edge. As she drives to the condo to meet the moving company, she lays the blanket over her belly.

"Do you feel all that love, Elizabeth Catherine?" she whispers. "You are so loved."

The squirmy shift under her palm makes her laugh, happy to feel how strong and vital their baby is. Elizabeth had become increasing active, mostly when she is being talked to, though once she had kicked out when Smoke ran his nose over the swelling stomach holding her safe.

Today they are moving, Thomas joining her in the evening for the first night in their new home. It will be an absolute dream to lay together, in the house that Elizabeth will grow up in, while Thomas spends his usual half hour talking to their baby before bed. They hadn't made love for quite some time, leaving Chrissie frustrated beyond words. Yet, the intimacy of him lying in her lap, stroking softly over the skin corralling their unborn child, almost makes up for it.

The movers are young, brawny men, by turns uncomfortable and charmed by her obvious condition. She tries her best to set them at ease, helping fill boxes, but they shuffle her aside kindly, telling her they will take care of it. So she brings them drinks, smiling encouragingly whenever one of them looks at her with concern. Inwardly, she fumes, worrying that before this is all over no one will be letting her do a thing for herself.

In a matter of hours everything important is loaded into their huge truck, the tiny convoy on its way out of town. Unloading at least gives her something useful to do, directing the boxes in to correct rooms, and organizing the placement of furniture. Sleek condo pieces appear very out of place in this warmer, family home, and with the larger space it feels so sterile.

Once the men know where everything goes she begins unpacking some of the kitchen boxes, musing over the right places for everything. As the sun begins to go down, the movers finish up, and Chrissie surprises them with hugs of appreciation. They accept her gratitude with a certain amount of shyness and their hugs back are very cautious.

"Seriously, gentlemen, should any of you ever find yourselves in need of therapy for work related injuries, you call me! I would consider it a privilege to take as good a care of you as you have of me today."

They shuffle out with various degrees of blush on their cheeks at her attention. The oldest offers her best wishes for the baby, and she closes the door as they drive away. Now alone, she walks down the hall to the master suite to make the bed they recently finished reassembling. It takes longer to locate the sheets than it does to actually make it.

She wanders to the room next door that will be Elizabeth's. They hadn't purchased anything except some newborn clothes, waiting until they had space, so she isn't expecting anything when she opens the door. A rocking chair waits for her, right next to where she has imagined the crib will sit, and her eyes fill with tears. Brushing one away, she settles in to the heavy mahogany chair, immediately pleased with its embrace. It has no need for cushioning, curved in all the right places, arms set at the perfect height to support the hands that will soon be cuddling a baby. Those hands drift down again, to caress where she imagines Elizabeth has her head.

"See, baby girl, so very loved." Chrissie whispers in to the hush, grateful for the quiet except the crickets singing outside the open window. She starts the chair rocking, thinking of the hours ahead that she will soothe her little girl to sleep. Her own eyes grow heavy, pulling her in to a peaceful slumber full of tiny curls and blue eyes.

Justine Iarann

Waking up to the sound of Thomas's voice, she rubs the sleep out of her eyes, finding the room twilight dark. Chrissie is about to rise as he comes in the open door, flicking on the light switch. Her smile is radiant even as she blinks against the sudden illumination. Still, she opens her arms and he steps forward to hug her, lifting her to her feet in the process.

"Thank you, this is a beautiful gift Thomas." she murmurs against his ear.

He steps back, smile wry. "Actually, it wasn't my idea, baby. Your Mom found this old thing. I didn't like it when she showed up with it, but she assured me you would love it. I am glad she was right."

Her smile falters a little, but she squeezes him close again. "That's alright, I'm glad you helped her surprise me with it."

He hugs her back, and she stands on her toes to kiss him, wanting to show the depth of her gratitude. Hurt flares brightly when he only pecks her lips and pulls away. Instinctively, she tucks her arms under her breasts, holding herself together; Elizabeth shifts restlessly under the embrace.

Oblivious, Thomas leads the way down the hall to the kitchen, where take out Thai food is waiting on the counter. Immediately, her stomach growls, reminding her it has been long hours since her late breakfast. Digging plates and forks out of a box, she places them on the counter as he pulls up two stools, one of which he hands her on to.

Dishing their food while giving a brief synopsis of his day, the familiar routine soothes her ruffled feathers, aided admirably by satisfying her physical hunger. Later, she lets him rest his head on her thigh as he talks softly to their daughter. The fullness in her heart is enough to satisfy whatever doubt had haunted her earlier.

Chapter Sixteen

Eight and a half months in, and Chrissie is riddled with an impatience that leaves her restless, often easily distracted. Thankfully, she has the month off, because while she is physically capable of most things, mentally, she is afraid to forget something important. It gives her time to nest, painting and arranging the nursery, filling it with all the marvelous gifts they had received at the baby shower.

When the last onesie is placed in the tall white dresser she wipes her sweaty brow, looking out the window at her horse who is standing in the middle of his snow covered field. Sometimes, he moves from place to place like he knows what room she is in, which is ridiculous. Today he is looking at the house, his gaze calling her outside, and she yields to the suggestion.

It takes a few minutes of sweaty effort to lace her winter boots, having to work around her huge belly. Once she is bundled up, stepping outside in to the crisp stillness, it proves worth it. Drawing in a big lung full of the refreshing air, she is gratified to see Smoke heading her way as she carefully navigates the stairs. The path is well walked owing to frequent visits to the barn, but it requires attention in places, icy in the high sun. Still, every few steps she glances up to find Smoke keeping pace with her, just on the other side of the fence.

At the barn, she stops inside the door to catch her breath, every trip winding her a little more than the last. Her lower back is straining under the load, so she takes a moment to stretch, releasing the tension with a sigh. Smoke stands patiently, eyes locked on her until she is close enough to touch, and then he begins a slow, deliberate exploration of her belly. Strangely, Elizabeth remains quiet under his touch, where she would normally shift and dance.

Grabbing a brush to run over Smoke's thick inky coat, she loses herself in the ritual of grooming. As she strokes the last bit of dust off his hip, another cramp rolls through her back. She remains frozen, not for any physical limits, but because it takes her brain that long to comprehend what is happening.

"I'm going in to labor." Chrissie whispers aloud, trying the statement on for size. When it feels right, she looks up, finding Smoke watching her intently. "I'm going in to labor." she repeats, a little surer now. Worry wrinkles the bridge of her nose, knowing she still has two weeks, but it certainly isn't a horrible gap to contend with.

Working on auto pilot, she sends Smoke back outside to his pasture where he has plenty of food and water to keep him. Fingers numb with shock and pleasure, she fumblingly dials Thomas.

"Mason here." he answers professionally.

"Honey, I think I'm going in to labor." she says calmly, smiling at the stunned silence on the line. "I'm going to call Mother and have her meet me, we have plenty of time."

"You're sure?" The vague nature of his question irritates

Better Broken

her, abrading the raw happiness of moments before.

"Am I sure of what? That I am going in to labor, or that we have plenty of time?"

"I mean, are you sure you can drive yourself in, are you okay?" His concern eases the tightening in her chest.

"Yes, we will be fine. It's a rolling back ache at this point. Not even particularly painful."

The next morning, as she moves in to her fifteenth hour of labor, the memory of that statement mocks her. The doctors assure her that Elizabeth is perfectly healthy, if slightly small, and the vital heartbeat on the fetal monitor echoes their sentiment.

Thomas had left to go get something to eat in the cafeteria, where a few of his work friends are waiting for him. Grateful for the respite, Chrissie is exhausted as much from dealing with her high strung husband as from the intensifying waves moving through her body. Catherine is sitting nearby, eyes closed for a moments rest when Chrissie groans feelingly at the acute pain squeezing her abdomen.

"It's okay, baby girl." Chrissie hears, barely feeling her mother's gentle hand brushing the hair back from her forehead. Breathing her way through, she focuses all her energy on slowing her heart rate until the spasm gripping her eases. A nurse walks in to check on them, and after a quick examination she looks up to Chrissie's waiting gaze with a knowing smile.

"Soon, Mrs. Mason. I am going to update your doctor so he is on standby, and you should call your husband back. Things are going to start picking up speed now."

Punctuating the statement, another pang clamps down, leaving her panting as the nurse quits the room. Yet, it proves prophetic, as a half hour later she hears her daughters cry, the surest balm for any hurt in her body. Thomas proudly cuts the cord, his eyes shining at the wonder of their child as they place Elizabeth in her arms for the first time. The baby's cries fade the instant she comes to rest on Chrissie's chest, nestling closer to the familiar heartbeat. Life is so complete, there is a barely audible click of a piece of her heart snapping in to place as she holds her baby girl. Stroking over the tiny wisps of damp, dark auburn hair crowning Elizabeth's head, tears prick her eyes. Thomas is charmed, but hesitant to touch her.

"Thomas, come here and hold your daughter." Chrissie says softly, wanting Elizabeth to know her father.

It takes him a minute to catch the knack of supporting the tiny bundle of brand new person. Once she is settled against his chest, a huge smile overtakes his face.

"Look what we did, Christine." he whispers, trying not to disturb the little girl. "She is so tiny."

The image of her normally so effusive husband in a state of hushed wonder sees Chrissie through the remainder of their hospital stay, warming her heart every time she remembers it.

The first night home is a little rougher, as Thomas is working, leaving mother and daughter to fend for themselves. Chrissie settles into the rocking chair for the sixth time to lull the baby to sleep after another change and feeding. Yet, despite the lack of rest, every moment with Elizabeth is the tenderest of gifts. Though her eyes are gritty and heavy, she stares with rapt attention at the delicate long lashes, fluttering against pink cheeks as she settles in her mother's embrace.

It is the most natural thing in the world, to start singing lullabies about Winney the Pooh and pretty little ponies. In fact, it is the perfect moment, as Chrissie looks out the window to where Smoke lays in the snow. Moonlight reflects blue off his coat as he keeps the nights vigil with her. Quiet, gentle tears well up, all the love in her life wrapping itself around her; mother, husband, friends, her daughter and even her horse.

*****

At six months, Eliza is running the whole house, feedings and changes coming like clockwork. She is perfectly content to go to the barn for chores wrapped snuggly to her mother chest, or to gurgle happily in her carrier. Chrissie returns to work part time, thanks to her mother, who after retiring, insists on playing baby sitter for her granddaughter.

In fact, tonight is her first real date with Thomas since the baby's birth, Eliza staying the night at Catherine's so they can truly enjoy each other's company. Chrissie takes great pains to dress nicely, doing her hair up, and wearing heels since she won't have to worry about carrying the baby. Escorting her to the car, Thomas hands her in like he had at the beginning of their relationship, eyes blazing fiercely at the exposed length of leg she is showing just for him. Dinner is a surprise, as he takes her back to their first date, where she decides to enjoy the duck confit he had suggested back then. When his eyebrows shoot up at her selection, she smiles.

"What can I say, darling? I may be a burger girl, but you have broadened my horizons."

His chuckle is a welcome sound, rumbling over her pleasantly, reminding her of all the times she had made him laugh in their brief relationship. The accompanying frisson of lust that moves down her spine at the sound of his amusement is certainly a lovely side effect.

All night, Chrissie makes sure to touch Thomas at every opportunity, reaching for his hand, brushing her leg against his, steadily building the tension until Thomas pays the check. Her efforts are not in vain, for as soon as they leave the restaurant, he drags her in for a near violent kiss. Desire sweeps through her, erasing all thoughts of responsibility, making her tremble with the impact as it travels down her nerve endings. The drive home is almost unbearable in her haste to rekindle the lost physical relationship with Thomas.

When they finally make it home, Chrissie welcomes him back to her arms, stroking through his hair, clinging to his impossibly broad shoulders like the last drink of water in the middle of a desert. Clothes are flung away, and one breath later he lays her on the bed, covering her completely. Satisfaction is swift for them both, not a surprise considering they last made love over a year ago. As they lie in the panting aftermath, Chrissie reaches to clasp his hand.

"I've missed you, husband." she gasps between breaths.

He makes no reply but to pull her close, tucking her in front of him as is his habit, and kissing her tenderly. As blissful sleep pulls them both under, Chrissie hopes that this, this right here, is enough.

Early the next morning, Chrissie rises before Thomas, no longer able to sleep late since bringing Elizabeth home. Pulling on a robe, she quietly heads to the kitchen to brew a cup of coffee, happy to lean against the counter and watch the sun rise over the field outside. Smoke stands up the hill by the barn, which prompts her to dress and head out to see him. Without thought, she saddles up as dawn fully breaks the horizon of the tree line, swinging on to her partner's broad back. There is no planned route, letting the breeze sift through her hair, baptized anew in the gracious feeling of homecoming she always finds with her horse. They wander down the road awhile, Chrissie waving at neighbors walking dogs, but then Smoke turns onto one of their favorite trails.

Anticipation rises through him, energy lifting her up out of the saddle and closing her legs around his heart. Like an arrow released from a bow, he springs forward, making short work of the hill with his powerfully driving hind legs before slowing at the top so they can enjoy the view. From their vantage Chrissie can see the tip of her chimney and a few of their neighbors' homes - the rest is trees and hills, all lit in golden benevolence from the sun.

Better Broken

Absorbing a few moments of quiet, she stores it away in her heart for future need, stroking a grateful hand over Smoke's thick neck. As she sits amidst tranquility, an old idea rears its head in the back of her consciousness. While she is working part time, now would be ideal to pursue her goal of a therapeutic riding program. This morning drives home that it's as much for the emotional stability it can offer people as the physical side effects. Mind whirling with possibilities, a broad smile stretches her lips, so much to look forward to. Thinking of the husband she left lying in bed, she turns back toward the house, hoping to catch Thomas for a quickie before he heads to the gym.

*****

Four months later, Chrissie wakes in the middle of the night to Elizabeth's cries, tumbling quickly out of bed before the baby can wake Thomas. He never copes well the next day if he is disturbed, leaving Chrissie to exclusively manage night time changes and feedings. Tonight is even more important than usual, as he is leaving at five AM for the airport to attend an orthopedics conference in Washington.

It doesn't take long to get the little girl resettled, just a short nursing session after a diaper check, but Chrissie drops into the rocking chair all the same. Better to be close at hand in case Elizabeth rouses again, than to risk disturbing Thomas. He is so excited about the trip, and Chrissie wants him in a good mood for the next weekend when she will be attending a workshop of her own. Not that he needs to worry about Elizabeth at all, as her mother will take care of the baby, but she hasn't been away from home since their marriage. Leaving him alone makes her nervous, though she can't rightly say why. He never gives a single indication of displeasure at her pursuit of further education, even encouraging her to go to a PT oriented symposium later in the year. Perhaps it is simply unfamiliar territory for them-though he had gone away for several trips of his own, she had always been home.

Her next conscious thought opens on the soft light of dawn as it pinkens the lavender painted walls. Sitting upright to straighten her cramped spine, she finds Elizabeth still curled in sleep. A frown tightens her brow, realizing Thomas must have already left, and she walks back to the bedroom to see for herself. There is no note to mark his departure, only a short text on her phone.

'Didn't want to wake the baby to say goodbye. See you in a few days, have fun.'

'You too. :-)' she texts back, and looking at the clock, figures she ought to catch a shower before Elizabeth wakes. Taking the baby monitor with her, she turns on the water as hot as she can stand it, washing away whatever lingering unease tightens her shoulders. Sometimes, she wishes he would be more affectionate, would kiss her as more than a means to an end. Then again, he is so tender with her, so accepting, it feels like she is being ungrateful to think that way. As she dresses for work, hastily throwing her hair in to a braid, she resolves to be more tolerant, to initiate more touching, and to show him how much she values their marriage. There is so much love in her heart to give, and he deserves more of it.

After feeding and dressing Elizabeth for the short trip to her mothers, her phone rings, an unknown number that she sends to voicemail. It chirps at her a moment later, and she lifts it to her ear to listen to the message.

"Mrs. Mason, this is Abigail Sutton, I was given your number by Mandy Clark, she said you might be interested in a horse I am trying to rehome. Please call me back at your earliest convenience."

Having only recently put the word out to her friends about what she is attempting, the message comes as a surprise.

Better Broken

Perhaps it is a sign that this whole endeavor is the right road to walk. Once she has the baby safely ensconced in her car seat, she sits in the driveway for a moment to return the woman's call, tickled when she answers on the first ring.

"Hello, this is Chrissie Mason, you called me?"

"Oh, thank you for calling me so quickly! I really need to find a new home for my Farley, and Mandy said you were hunting for good, calm horses."

"I am, thank you. We are in the process of developing a riding and driving program for veterans, so I am looking for potential therapy partners for the job. Can you tell me a little about Farley?"

They spend a few minutes more exchanging details before Chrissie hangs up, supremely satisfied with the conversation.

"Baby girl," she says, looking in the rear view mirror at Elizabeth. "Looks like we found horse number two!"

At her mother's happy tone, the little girl squeals and smiles, which makes Chrissie smile even more broadly. By the time she drops off Eliza with Catherine and makes the short drive to the hospital, it's all she can do not to skip in to the clinic, her heart feels so light.

*****

Conflicted emotions have Chrissie pacing circles in the barn aisle. She leaves in an hour to attend a weekend clinic to start her therapeutic riding certification, but her mind is torn in too many directions to focus. Her mother has come to stay at the farm with Elizabeth, able to throw hay and keep the water trough full for the two horses. That alone should be enough to reassure her, but her heart is shredded by worry.

Just that morning, she had tried to initiate lovemaking with Thomas, and for the first time since Lizzy's birth he had turned away. He had been quite reasonable about it, simply very tired after a long shift the night before, kissing her cheek before walking away. None the less, it had left her bereft, thoughts and emotions at war, unable to react as she watched him go. He left for the gym, turning away from a pleasant morning of activity with his wife in favor of the cold company of a treadmill.

On the verge of calling to tell him how upset she feels, she turns to find Smoke staring at her, blowing soft through his nose. In a flash she has him out of the stall, climbing on his broad, bare back with only a halter and lead rope to influence him. They move out the door of the barn to the far pasture, and in moments she is leaning forward over his neck, heels in his sides, urging him to a run. Three strides later, wind is pulling at the tears in her eyes, moisture streaming over her cheeks in a stinging trail as Smoke carries her away from the heart ache.

They round a stand of trees at the far end of the pasture, and Chrissie sits up to slow him. Her soul is more settled and her heart pounding with adrenaline instead of doubts. The sprung steel of his spine is bowing supple under her seat and she asks him to dance, lifting his feet higher with each stride, pushing off the turf like a gymnast on a trampoline. The rhythm steadies her as his neck arches proudly before her. All she can feel is the joy welling through her, grounded in the moment, no past, no future. When they can soar no higher she softens her body, and Smoke settles to a walk, looking back with one eye as she rubs beneath his mane in gratitude.

It is easy to ride the feeling through a quick goodbye to her mother and Elizabeth. In fact, it carries her all the way over the mountain pass to the little town where she meets like-minded people that know what it is to be called to serve. Perhaps they all have different ideas of who and how to help, but one thing is for sure- they are each moved to lift people up until they can lift themselves. It is exhilarating to be surrounded at last by people who truly understand her driving need to help others.

Chapter Seventeen

It takes a year to complete her certifications and build a network, to develop funding and get the word out. In that year, so much has changed, from Lizzy's rapid growth and development to the slow disintegration of her marriage.

Relations with Thomas become more strained, the space between them expanding every day, not only physically, but emotionally as well. Whenever she tries to bridge the gulf Thomas placates her with pretty words, and sometimes a night out that ends with physical intimacy. It is enough to keep her trying, just enough to let her think that this is what happens to married couples. Things simply get stale, right?

Talking to Suzie leads her to believe a lot of couples face the same thing, and her friend had suggested they visit a relationship counselor. When she mentions it to Thomas, he actually grows angry at her for the first time. Insulted that she feels he isn't good enough, and that she would talk about them with anyone, even her best friend. In turn, Chrissie tries to see things from his perspective, tries to be a more understanding wife, since he provides their family with so much and asks for so little in return.

The result is losing herself in work, escaping their marriage by the same route Thomas is. To the benefit of the riding program and even her work day clients, her immersion is fierce and complete. The only exception to this is Lizzy, dear darling Lizzy. When Chrissie picks up her little girl at the end of the day, they spend every moment together until the next morning, and all day together on Sundays once the horses are taken care of.

This morning, Chrissie sneaks in to Lizzy's room after taking a shower, pausing at the foot of the bed. It is amazing to contemplate all the transformations her little girl has made in the last year. Lizzy went from walking to running with hardly a breath of time to mark the transition, which keeps everyone on their toes. Chrissie is now taking her jogging in a stroller, to satisfy the child's growing curiosity to see everything. And honestly, partly to have her strapped down long enough to get some exercise without having to chase her.

Eliza's hair grows like a cultivated weed, giving her the most adorable auburn curls, a darker shade of chestnut than Chrissie's own flaming hair. The daily struggle of brushing it out often results in frustrated tears from mother and daughter. Catherine teases that she is a miniature of Chrissie herself, outside and in, giving Chrissie occasion to thank her mother profusely. After all, as fun as her walking, talking, in to everything copy may be, she still tests Chrissie's patience and fortitude on a daily basis. Regardless, memories stretch a broad smile over Chrissie's face, loving every moment of chaos. They are balanced by the quiet moments like these, where her baby's angel face is still, and the miracle of her is so prevalent.

Better Broken

Unable to resist the lure of her softly sleeping child, Chrissie scoops her up and breathes in the strawberry scent of soap still lingering on Lizzy's skin. Her mother will be arriving soon, having volunteered to watch Lizzy while Chrissie gives her very first solo lesson to a soldier recently returned from Afghanistan. Right now, though, she simply slows her breathing to match Lizzy's, watching the turquoise blue pajama top rise and fall with every breath, living absolutely in the moment.

Early afternoon is coating the world in sunshine when a minivan pulls up the drive, the steady crunch of gravel bringing Chrissie out of the tack room. Climbing out of the passenger side is a man who looks two seconds away from throwing his hands in the air and leaving, shoulders hunched defensively over a ram rod straight spine. His wife says something that takes the wind out of him, and he turns toward Chrissie as she approaches.

"Good afternoon, Staff Sergeant Collins, nice to see you again." she offers with a smile. "Mrs. Collins is welcome to stay if you like."

"No," he bites off abruptly, "Cindy has some errands to run, and will be back in an hour or so. And please, call me Jim."

He follows in her wake, Chrissie keeping quiet so the soft light of the barn can do its work. After his evaluation last week she knows he is still coping with a muscle strain to his back, but the deepest wounds are on the inside. In light of that, she had chosen Smoke for this first lesson, as he had proven most responsive to emotional damage. He has a gift for grounding out the worst of it, and calling bullshit when needed. While completely intolerant of jerks, genuine hurts bring out a deep seated kindness that people respond to without understanding why.

The soldier reacts viscerally to Smoke as they approach his

stall, body growing rigid enough that the very air around them thickens. "That's a hell of a big animal. I thought we'd be working with smaller horses."

"Actually, Smoke here is the quietest of my partners." she explains with a careful smile. "Larger horses usually feel less threatened by things around them, less likely to react to outside stimuli."

"I guess that makes sense." The man accepts grudgingly, stepping closer.

Understanding that his normal forward approach won't be appropriate, Smoke stands with his head low and eyes half closed in a sleepy manner. When Chrissie demonstrates how to halter the horse Jim is still hesitant to touch the animal, completing the task correctly, but without so much as a pat, or a how do you do. When she asks him to lead the horse in to the aisle he yanks on the halter with impatience, causing Smoke to plant his feet in flat refusal.

"Sergeant, that was the equivalent of yelling at him when he hasn't done anything wrong, which I'm sure in your leadership experience is not the best way to get people to want to work for you." Chrissie explains patiently. "We believe in partnership here, and the horses expect to be treated fairly when it is within our control to do so."

"Sorry," he bites off. "I thought I was supposed to be the boss."

"Well, there are bosses, and there are bosses." Offering a wry grin to the man, she pets Smoke apologetically. "As I'm sure you've seen in your career, if your heart is in something, you're going to give more than asked for, above and beyond the call of duty. If not, then you go through the motions, and do your best to endure."

"True." he says, relaxing marginally.

"So, you said you work with helicopters? Think of it like yanking back hard on the stick. You either get a violent reaction or a stall out. Luckily, Smoke only stalled a little. You can still adjust things, and get where you need to go, only now you know you need a little more finesse."

The next try, she shows him how to put a feel on the lead, and Smoke follows his charge with a gusty sigh of relief. They spend awhile grooming until tension leaves the man's shoulders completely, taking the time to tack up while explaining what all the equipment is for. Every bit of knowledge she offers puts him more at ease, until he finally runs his hand over the horses shoulder in an unthinking gesture of appreciation. Yet, the harshness plaguing Sgt. Collins features returns as they walk toward the arena, increasing until Chrissie fears he will snap under the strain.

"Okay, now for the pre-flight check." A crack appears in his defensive shell, confusion coloring his expression. "Much like with your birds, we have to kick the tires before you leave the ground."

Demonstrating each task at the walk on a long lead, she sends Smoke around her, checking the brakes and steering while Collins focuses fiercely on every motion. Military personnel find comfort in ritual, indoctrinated in it from their first moments as raw recruits, drilled in to them until they feel lost without it. Even without injuries or PTSD to shadow their return to the civilian world, it is often difficult for them to cope with the lack of structure the rest of the world functions in. The man repeats her actions to good effect, though it is going to take some time to develop tact, to learn to give softly when he receives what he asks for.

When they approach the mounting block stiffness returns, though not nearly as strong as before, hinting that they are on the right track. She has him climb up an extra step to accommodate the tightness in his torso from his injury. This way he doesn't have to lift his leg as high to clear Smokes back, allowing him to mount with minimal discomfort. His disciplined body is easily positioned, but like all new riders the instant Smoke moves everything falls apart. Luckily for the Sergeant, Smoke knows to stop immediately at his rider's tension, Chrissie still at his side to assist as she looks up in to his now white face. His hands clutch the horn of the saddle so hard that the blood has left his knuckles.

"Okay, Sergeant, let us cover proper halting procedure before we start marching." Chrissie says, gratified when he looks to her for help. After a few minutes of sitting still, learning how to stop his mount with voice and hand, he regains a bit of color. When she suggests they try moving again the horror is clear on his face.

"It's a damn long way to the ground, Miss. What if I can't stop him?"

"Well, Sergeant, there are no guarantees in life. But as this is my personal horse, I can vouch for the quality of his training, and the sheer level of smarts he has. Whoa is his second favorite word in all the English language, carrots the only thing he likes better." she replies with humor, relieved when the man unbends enough to answer her grin. "I'll be right here to provide an emergency brake if you need me, but you are going to do fine after a few laps."

They begin again, Chrissie keeping Smoke moving despite the Sergeants absolute inflexibility, using her words to give him something to think about besides his fear. Likely, he wouldn't thank her for noticing, his pride as much a part of him as what color his eyes are, but it is there all the same. A few laps of slow walk later she releases her hold on Smokes halter, reaching back to adjust the Sergeants leg, helping him find a comfortable position as his spine slowly begins to move with the motion of his mount.

"Think of it like flying. If you sit like a board, not only is it exhausting in the long run, if your aircraft slips sideways or moves unexpectedly, you end up jarred. Let the horse's motion move you. You'll be more comfortable, so will he, and it will help loosen up your back."

A couple laps later, they successfully practice the halt. After a few changes of direction Chrissie feels safe challenging him, encouraging him to ask Smoke for a more cadenced walk.

"You wouldn't let him get away with that on the drill field. Get that horse marching like you have somewhere to go."

The lesson doesn't last much longer as she doesn't want him too sore from the unaccustomed work. Yet, by the time he dismounts the perpetual frown lines have disappeared. When they return to the barn to care for Smoke, the Sergeant yields at last to the horse's good grace, offering the big black a few genuine strokes of gratitude. No, this will be no instant miracle, but today is the seed of one- Chrissie looks forward to watching him grow back in to the man he had been, and then beyond even what he thinks is possible.

*****

In Elizabeth's second year of life Chrissie settles in to a blistering routine, losing herself entirely in the people she cares so much for. She still shares a bed with Thomas, but no amount of affection or seduction can bridge the widening gap. During the day it is easy to pretend all is well, to apply the façade of a happy marriage when they are in public. But, home alone usually finds her occupied in the barn or with Lizzy. Thomas often volunteers for extra surgery, attending every seminar he can manage, and spends evenings in his study whenever he isn't required.

During a family vacation to D.C. to visit his parents, Chrissie steals away for some much needed time with Suzie. The only down side is her dear friends ability to see through the charade, and strike right at the heart of the matter.

As Chrissie walks back in to the living room after putting

Lizzy down for the night, she falls gratefully in to the deep sofa and closes her eyes. No matter how long her days are at home, the previous week of playing Stepford wife in front of Thomas's parents has worn her down to a nub. When Suzie comes back from the kitchen with a bottle of wine to share Chrissie almost weeps with relief. They spend a while in silence, slowly savoring their first glass of buttery chardonnay. A cool evening breeze coming in the window makes the curtains dance, Oscar swatting half-heartedly at them. It isn't until they pour their second glass that Suzie makes her move.

"I never ever, ever, should have encouraged you into that man's arms." she grumbles as if to herself, but Chrissie knows her friend never says anything without a purpose.

"How were you to know I was going to set my cap on him?" With a drawn out sigh she rubs her stinging eyes. "If it had been you, you'd have used him for a little while, then ditched him before your heart got involved."

"True enough, my dear friend." Suzie acknowledges with a nod. "Though I know you never open your legs for someone you aren't willing to give your heart to."

If it were anyone else Chrissie might be put off by the turn of phrase, but Suzie is known for the unvarnished truth, a trait both endearing and exasperating. She reaches for Suzie's hand, grateful when her friend grabs on to her fingers in understanding.

"I'm guessing it's much worse than you are letting on." Suzie continues after another sip of wine, her dark blue eyes deep wells of concern.

"It's horrible, actually." Chrissie answers, finally tearing up in the face of her friends regard. "I mean, he isn't abusing me or anything, you know I wouldn't stand for that. Yet, at the same time, it's like slow torture, being so close to him yet so far away. We don't touch except for the rare occasions when he pecks my cheek or takes my hand in public. It's a wretched

Better Broken

way to live when I thrive on physical contact. If I didn't have Lizzy to hug and cuddle, I'd have gone crazy already."

Silent for a moment, Suzie mulls over whatever she has to say, as if it is something she doesn't want to give voice to.

"Do you think he is cheating on you? I know you said he comes home every night he isn't working, but what about when he goes off to seminars?"

Stunned, Chrissie nearly loses her grip on her wine glass as she processes, then sets it on the table to give herself time to think. It is possible, and maybe even likely, considering his ravenous appetite when they first got together. Yet, for some reason other than not wanting it to be true, she doesn't think that is the case.

"I don't think so. I mean, I couldn't swear to it, but my gut says no. I think he is just too busy with his career at this point to even bother."

Suzie relaxes minutely, as if she agrees at a cellular level, which lets Chrissie breathe easier.

"I don't know what to do to fix this, Suzie. I don't think we are so far gone that we can't rebuild."

"Chrissie, I hate to say this, but you can't make it better on your own. He has already proven uninterested in patching things together, so the real question is what are you going to do if it continues down the same road?"

"I don't know, Suz." Chrissie chokes off, her throat closing on the emotions rising in her chest. "I just don't know."

*****

When they return home Thomas repacks his bags immediately for a conference in Atlanta. Chrissie breathes a sigh of relief at the break from the false front they have maintained. Four quiet days without him, only she and Lizzy to do for, and work a welcome routine to slide back in to. There are now six horses to care for, plus a growing cadre of volunteers to assist with therapy sessions and barn work. Her client list is full to the brim, giving her an outlet for the overabundance of affection in her heart. The day Thomas returns from his travels, however, is like dropping a fox in an otherwise peaceful hen house.

"Christine?" His bag thuds heavily when he drops it by the front door, breaking the tranquil silence. "Where are you?"

"In here, Thomas." she answers from her perch at the dining table, looking up from a stack of paperwork for the therapy program. "How was your trip?"

"Fine, actually." he replies with a warmer smile than usual. "Made some great contacts, and I will be visiting a few colleagues over the next year to do some interesting case studies."

"That's wonderful, truly." Her voice is full of sincere warmth, happy to see him so very pleased. But when she reaches out to touch, he reflexively withdraws.

"So, what I really wanted to talk to you about is an offer I received from a hospital in Denver." he begins, her heart dropping in to her stomach with a sickening lurch. "It's an opportunity to get some experience under one of the best surgical heads in the U.S., but it would mean a big commute from here in the foothills."

"If that's what you need to do, Thomas, I will support you. It will take a lot to get everything moved, but I want you to be happy." she chokes out, managing a fake smile even as conflicting emotions crash against each other. When he smiles back with his old charm, she prays against all odds that perhaps this will bring them closer together. The next sentence mercilessly snuffs out her hopes.

"Actually, Christine, I am thinking you should stay here with Elizabeth, to be near your mother, and to continue your own work. I'll get an apartment near the hospital to stay in during my work week, and then come back up here on my days off to spend time as a family."

It feels like a car wreck in her chest, as relief and despair collide, leaving her heart as bruised as a hit and run victim. Clearly, he really thinks this is the best answer, yet it is obvious that their relationship is never going to be as it once was. If it was even real to begin with.

"If you are sure, Thomas." With a sigh of defeat, she rises from her chair. "Go tuck Lizzy in, she has been waiting up for you. I'm going to go up to the barn to throw some more hay, I'll be back shortly."

Managing to remain calm, she pulls on her boots and quietly goes out the back door. Yet, halfway up the hill, the tears break free, running down her face uncontrollably as she walks toward her only sanctuary. Smoke is out in the pasture for the night so she sinks down on the shavings in his stall to sob out her heartbreak.

All she has ever wanted is to love, to be loved in return. Now, she is repeating her parents mistakes, stuck in a one sided marriage. She can't even lay the blame at Thomas's feet, remembering all the times her own mother had asked her if she was sure about him. Even Suzie, a proclaimed cynic of love, had questioned her feelings for Thomas, and if that isn't telling, nothing else is.

Still, for Lizzy's sake, she will endure, not wanting her child to grow up without her father- an innocent in all of this, she doesn't deserve to be punished for her parent's misjudgment. As she gains control of her leaking eyes, hoof falls sound from outside, then Smoke walks through the door. When he stops in front of her and lowers his nose into her lap she finds the tears welling up again. Only now they are more of a cleansing rain than the previous wash of acid.

Justine Iarann

Chapter Eighteen

Thomas quickly suits word to action, finding a tidy apartment two blocks from the new hospital in an upscale complex catering to the well to do. He sets up housekeeping in short order, and Chrissie can hardly contain her guilt ridden relief when he leaves for the first week. It makes sense, from a time perspective, and certainly in the winter Thomas will have an easier commute to work. Truthfully though, she is glad to not have to work around him, quietly enjoying the peace it brings to her life even as she feels horrible for it.

Lizzy doesn't take it much amiss, though she is confused the first few weeks when she can't find her Dada, letting herself in to the study to hunt for him when he doesn't answer her calls. There are no temper tantrums over it, only a puckered brow, and a need to carry her favorite stuffed unicorn everywhere. Chrissie's mother proves a God send, gently and tactfully uncovering the growing distance between Chrissie and Thomas. It provides her daughter with a completely non-judgmental shoulder to lean on when needed. After all, if anyone in the world knows what it is like to have an absentee husband, Catherine understands.

When he comes home on weekends, usually Saturday morning, he takes Lizzy for a breakfast out, leaving Chrissie time to get ready for her morning sessions. In the evening, they have dinner together as a family, though the cold between husband and wife keeps expanding, eventually resulting in Chrissie sleeping in Lizzy's room. Sundays are a slower day, still with the ritual of morning cartoons in their PJ's, though Thomas typically adjourns to his study after a while. He makes no complaints about how Chrissie runs the house while he is gone, leaving the bills and chores in her capable hands. That extra work is a small price to pay for the tranquility of his absence, though she berates herself for thinking so poorly of the father of her child.

Sometime after Elizabeth turns three, Thomas sets himself up in the guest bedroom on the weekends, and Chrissie reconciles herself to their eventual separation. Refusing to be the one to discuss divorce, she is determined to make the peace last as long as possible on Lizzy's behalf.

After a run in with a nurse at the hospital who inferred an intimate relationship with Thomas, Chrissie makes it her mission to find a new clinic to work out of. Whether it is true or not, she can't find it in her heart to care, but she is tired of the pitying looks as she walks the halls.

Gratefully, it doesn't take long to land a job at an independent rehabilitation facility that caters to ambulatory issues. They make her feel at home immediately, open to her ideas for integrating yoga in to their practice, as well as expanding her own horizons. Several of the staff are practicing body work, one is even involved in Chinese medicine, but all are fascinated by her work in equine assisted therapy. Chrissie quickly develops an idea to bring her two work spheres together, arranging a social event at the farm so her co-workers and her military family can meet.

It is a gorgeous Sunday in early summer when she finally manages it, even Thomas in attendance at the potluck picnic in the backyard. Catherine had appointed herself the head cook, providing an unending supply of fried chicken to the hungry crowd, and Chrissie manages to rent a hay wagon and horses for the afternoon. Everyone enjoys a trip down the quiet country road to the steady clip clop of the giant horse's hooves, Lizzy especially begging to go on every circuit they make.

"Chrissie, this is amazing." says Darla, one of her new co-workers at the rehab. "How do you manage to find time and energy for all of this? I mean, you have a three year old, which is almost a full time job as it is."

Just as she is about to reply, Cindy Collins beats her to it. "Frankly, we all have been contemplating whether she secretly has super human powers that no one will discuss."

Chrissie laughs and denies the accusation. It sparks Cindy's husband Jim to speculate her energy has alien origins, making Chrissie laugh even harder. Thomas, sitting right across from her with Lizzy on his lap, remains silent as she banters with her friends.

Later that night, after everyone has left, Thomas stops on his way out to congratulate her on the success of her event.

"Well done, Christine, truly. I can appreciate what you have been doing on an even deeper level after today."

His tone feels condescending, which scrapes a raw spot on her otherwise mellow mood, but she decides not to let it bother her.

"Thank you, Thomas. These people truly mean a lot to me, and I am glad you finally got to meet them all."

"I do wonder though," he continues in a musing fashion, tilting his head to the side in faux concern. "Maybe you are

Better Broken

enabling some of your equine therapy students."

"Enabling?" she queries carefully, stomach clenching tight at his tone.

"Yes, some of those soldiers are recovered enough to return to their units. Surely, they don't need their hands held anymore."

"Hands held? Seriously?" she bites off, incredulous at his willful disparagement. "Jesus, Thomas, I feel like I don't even know you right now. You sure as hell don't know me if that's what you think of my work here."

He back pedals in the face of her anger, something she has tried so long to keep from welling up between them. Yet, while she can endure a hundred barbs and stings herself, she refuses to allow one more ignorant stab to be directed at her friends.

"These men and women have given up so much, physically and mentally, certainly emotionally, so that you can sit there in judgment of them. They have sacrificed time with their families, and while I can see how that wouldn't mean much to you, their families as well have accepted that sacrifice. The least you can do to enjoy the freedom these soldiers have secured for you is to broaden your mind, or keep your mouth shut on such petty thoughts."

He stands like a man before a firing squad at her barrage, silent in the wake of her vehement outburst. Down the hall, Lizzy begins to fuss from the disturbance, so Chrissie rises abruptly from her seat, pleased when Thomas steps back.

"I'm going to see to our daughter, Thomas. I'll see you next Saturday, and I pray you have occasion to reconsider your egotism by then."

With that, Chrissie leaves him flatfooted for the first time in years, feeling strangely peaceful after allowing her temper to finally boil over. The front door closes softly a few moments later, and she can't find even a modicum of guilt over the outburst she had delivered. Lizzy is agitated enough that Chrissie scoops her up and carries her into the master bedroom, settling them both in to the king size bed. She cuddles close for as long as it takes Lizzy to relax in to slumber, then tugs the old quilt up over both of them after flicking off the lights. For the first time in years, Chrissie falls asleep with a peaceful heart, praying that somehow, some way, everything will all come out right in the end.

*****

In a way, Chrissie gets what she prayed for. Three months later, Thomas presents her with divorce papers, which stings even after their long term estrangement. Yet, what is truly unexpected are the terms- he offers full ownership of the house and land with a maintenance allowance, as well as complete custody of Lizzy. It feels like a wordless apology for everything he couldn't give her. He expects visitation rights, but since Chrissie would sooner sever a limb than deprive her daughter of a father, it is easy to settle.

Shortly after the divorce is finalized he accepts a department head position at the hospital in Atlanta he had been visiting regularly. Voicing concern that their child will miss him chases Thomas away even faster, severing the last bit of real affection Chrissie harbored for him.

Understandably upset, Lizzy resorts to uncharacteristic temper tantrums over the smallest things, screaming for her Dada until she falls asleep from sheer exhaustion. Despite that, Chrissie hopes things will stabilize soon.

One night, as they sit in the living room enjoying an animated fairy tale, Lizzy crawls in to her lap for a cuddle. Chrissie strokes over the long curls on her daughters head, tears springing up in her eyes, catching her off guard. Not because she is sad- she has mourned the loss of her husband for too many years to linger on it now. They are simply an outlet for her very full heart as she focuses on the many

Better Broken

blessings in her life. Family, friends, home and horses surround her with a love that warms the deepest shadows of her heart. Yes, this, right here, is truly enough.

Justine Iarann

Part Three

Chapter Nineteen

Late afternoon sun stretches the shadows long as Chrissie stands up from under the belly of one of the Clydesdales, having spent the last hour working over an abscess in his hoof. It will be the work of a few more moments to finish bandaging the foot, but her back needs a break first. A vertebrae pops into alignment when she stretches, leaning against the big horses side with a groan of relief.

It had been a heck of a morning, two mini horses escaping their pen, the resulting chase and subsequent fence repairs only the beginning. After that, it had been a full day of therapy clients, some working through significant challenges, but all of them making progress. However gratifying these days are, it always leaves Chrissie a little wrung out at by the end, riding the emotional rollercoaster with people she considers a second family. Her mother had dropped off Elizabeth an hour ago, once the last client had left. As the sun migrates toward the horizon, she wants nothing more than to

Better Broken

scoop up her daughter and go up to the house. Tomorrow, aside from feeding horses in her pajamas, she has no plans except to sleep in and watch cartoons with her little girl. First, she has responsibilities left to tend to, just as Eliza is currently doing her own chore of filling water troughs. With a heavy sigh, she picks up the big feathered foot once more.

Five minutes later, as she places the last bit of duct tape holding the bandage on the dinner plate sized hoof, a white pickup turns up the driveway, dust creating a nimbus around the vehicle. Chrissie can't remember expecting anyone, but isn't terribly concerned. Sometimes people drop in, needing a few moments with a favorite horse or having forgotten something earlier in the day. She unclips Dusty from the cross ties to take him back to his stall as the truck engine shuts off. Her view is momentarily obscured by the large girth of the Clydesdale, but the distinct sound of cowboy boots stops right inside the main door. When she can see again, a dark silhouette covers the length of the aisle. Shoving disheveled hair back under her ball cap, she adjusts the hat to block out more of the sun, hoping to get a better glimpse of her visitor.

"I'm sorry, sir, but we are all closed up for the day."

"I'm looking for Christine Everett." the faceless stranger says, voice tight and clipped. A strange flutter starts in the tired depths of her heart at the timber of his voice.

"Actually, it's Christine Everett-Mason, but I answer just fine to Chrissie." Allowing a welcoming smile to stretch her cheeks she walks toward him with hand outstretched. So many come in the door of this barn a little lost, and she is hoping the smile will disarm this fellow like it does most folk.

He moves into the shadows of the barn, and her steps falter as she runs smack in to a pair of brown eyes she never thought to see again, outside of a few fitful fantasies. In shock, she stands frozen as he clasps the open palm she still holds out, wrapping it in both his hands.

"It's good to see you again, Chrissie." James Fletcher says, voice now more deeply colored with the bourbon and vanilla warmth she remembers, his eyes just as rich as she had dreamed them.

Caught in an emotional whirlwind of disbelief, raw attraction and old sadness, Chrissie cannot speak. In self-defense, she pulls away from the delicious warmth of his clasp, shivering as his calluses slide over her skin. Right then, as though summoned by the spirit of chaos, Lizzy comes stomping in to the barn with one of the miniature horses in tow, pique painting her features. Dark chestnut curls that have escaped her braid bounce fitfully around her face, sharp blue eyes searching the dim aisle for her mother.

"Momma, Jelly took a bite out of PB again!"

It gives Chrissie a moment to move away as James looks toward her little girl, letting her plaster on a lopsided grin of pride.

"Mr. Fletcher, I'd like you to meet my daughter, Elizabeth."

Elizabeth drops the little horses lead rope and confidently approaches, her hand held out and a bright smile welcoming this new stranger. The mini doesn't bat an eye, turning aside to shove his fat head in to a nearby bale of hay.

"Hello, Mr. Fletcher. Are you going to come learn about horses with my Momma and her other friends?"

James acts not at all discomfited as he reaches for Elizabeth's hand and shakes it vigorously, mirroring her daughter's energy level with a humorous glint in his eye.

"I don't know if your Momma will let me, Miss Elizabeth, but I sure would like to." He ends the sentence by turning his gaze to Chrissie, which makes Lizzy look up at her mother in inquiry.

"Eliza Kate, I need to talk to Mr. Fletcher before I know if our program is a good fit for him." Chrissie answers, lifting her chin in challenge, old hurt frosting her words. If he thinks he is going to walk back in like nothing ever happened, he is about to be sorely disappointed.

Giving a barely perceptible nod of acknowledgement James turns back toward Elizabeth, an exaggerated cowboy drawl in his next words. "Miss Elizabeth, I'm guessin' you're the boss of this here outfit, and I'd be honored if you'd show me around."

"Momma, can I?" Elizabeth asks, her aspect the very picture of a pathetic waif, eyes limpid and round. Heaven help her, but Lizzy could sell firewood in hell.

"We can show Mr. Fletcher around while we feed, baby girl. But after that, it's time to go to the house." Chrissie concedes, voice firm even in the face of her daughter's monumental adorableness.

Elizabeth drags James from the barn, leaving Chrissie to turn back, putting the mini in an empty stall. It gives her a moment's peace to press a hand to her chest where her heart is leaping around like a rabbit in a snare. To have the object of her most private dreams and anguished tears suddenly appear before her is almost more than she can handle. Almost.

Grabbing up the feed cart, Chrissie squares her shoulders and heads after her precocious daughter. James is allowing himself to be led around, petting noses and stroking necks momentarily before Eliza drags him off to another of her favorites. There are twelve horses on the place now, each of them Lizzy's favorites for one reason or another, all of them equally loved. Every size, shape and color decorates their program, as varied in personality as they are in looks- some shy, some a little emotionally distant, some downright dog friendly. Each are the priceless combination of intelligence and heart that Chrissie cherishes, able to read people with an ease most actual people can't comprehend. They are her partners in this massive endeavor of healing hearts and minds, while challenging bodies damaged by war. Tossing hay as she walks the fence line, she is taken aback to find James has hold of the cart, following in her wake. His thoughtfulness shocks an unbidden smile to her lips, but she tamps it down and breaks eye contact, unwilling to provide encouragement. Thinking it best to ignore him, she spins on her heel to head off toward the next paddock.

With his and Eliza's help, feeding outside is done in a matter of minutes, the herd peacefully chewing in the lowering light, so she turns toward the barn with a hurried step. Upon entering, Smoke hangs his head into the aisle, staring intently. Moving forward to cup his muzzle in both hands, she presses a kiss to the soft spot between his mouth and nostril. The warm breath that the big horse expels soothes her like nothing else on earth.

"This is Mommas special horse- she says they are all special, but he is her special-est." Eliza says with a dramatically lowered voice.

"I see that." James replies softly, prompting Chrissie to look up, so much feeling in his eyes that the chocolate brown color shifts erratically.

It also triggers a response from Smoke, who lifts his head to stare fixedly at this stranger. He leans over Chrissie's shoulder in a gesture that leaves no doubt that he is staking a claim. The moment is stretching tense until Eliza steps closer, touching Smokes shoulder. Then the big horse abruptly turns his attention to the little girl, mussing her hair as she giggles at his long whiskers tickling her neck. The smile her giggle prompts is soft on Chrissie's face as she gazes fondly at the two biggest loves of her life, so different and so important in their own ways. Turning to James, she is a bit swayed to catch him staring at the girl, his smile mellow and his gaze fuzzy at the edges. Elizabeth just does that to people.

"Eliza Kate, how about you run up to the house, and get washed up for supper while I finish talking to Mr. Fletcher."

After a moment of whining complaint Elizabeth obediently drags her feet all the way to the back porch, leaving Chrissie alone with James. Quickly, she turns to him, a barely hidden glint of hurt flashing behind the questions plaguing her. She starts with the most obvious.

"What are you doing here, James?"

He coughs and looks away then, grinding the heel of his boot in the gravel of the drive before answering, taking time to formulate a reply. It irritates Chrissie that she finds the self-conscious gesture charming, so the frown on her face is no reassurance when he looks back up.

"Well, I'm traveling around, between jobs. I was looking for a job in this area, and the feed store I stopped at said I should come here, once they heard I'm a veteran."

"I don't need help." she replies shortly, arms crossing over her rib cage defensively, covering her pang of concern with a terse manner. As much as he had hurt her, she had never stopped wishing him well, and now it is within her grasp to assist in that prospect.

"No, I can see that now. It felt like fate when they told me your name. I'll be going then, I'm sorry to have bothered you." he finishes, a world of apology in his tone that speaks of far more than today.

Watching him walk away, Chrissie unconsciously evaluates his gait even as she drinks in the sight of him. He has a barely perceptible deviation to his walk, just enough to draw the eye. The therapist in her wonders what model artificial limb allows him to travel so easily, and how much work it has taken to get him this far. It lightens the years of worried curiosity that had sprung up whenever he crossed her mind. James Fletcher is a danger to her focus, a reminder of too many nights crying on a pillow, but even with all that, part of her is still drawn toward him. Between that, and her natural compassion for anyone in need, her feet follow him of their own accord.

"Wait, James." she calls, as she steps out in to the bright pink and gold wash of the sunset. When her eyes adjust, he is half way in his truck, pushing back a big spotted hound even as he looks up, a glimmer of hope in his expression. "Does your dog need to get out and run around?"

The half-smile that had always charmed her appears as he steps back out of the truck. "Shove him down if he gets too friendly. His name is Shane."

The galumphing animal spills out of the cab, a slight limp showing as he heads straight for the grass, intent on a place to relieve himself. Chrissie remembers the silly dog that had gotten injured all those years ago, and she smiles at James's soft heart, to know he still has the animal after all this time. Her musings are interrupted by the excited squeal of her daughter, who shoots out the back door like a cannon ball at the sight of the dog. For a moment, Chrissie is afraid she will bodily fling herself on the oblivious critter, but years of being raised with animals comes to the fore as she slows twenty feet away and looks to James.

"Mr. Fletcher, can I pet your dog? Please?" Elizabeth asks, polite, but quivering with barely contained eagerness.

James is opening his mouth to answer when Shane turns from his thorough investigation of the fence and notices the little girl. In two galloping steps he is shoving his head carefully under Elizabeth's arm, sniffing her like he had never smelled anything better.

A small bark of a laugh escapes James, surprised by the dog's enthusiasm. "Shane says yes, you should certainly pet him."

Elizabeth strokes the hound's large ears, then scratches enthusiastically behind his collar, the dog's eyes rolling back in ecstasy. Satisfied that they are okay with each other, Chrissie turns back to James.

"I'll tell you what, I may not need help, but I'd sure appreciate some. I can offer part time, if you are interested."

A weight visibly lifts off of James at her offer, his shoulders lightening, which leaves her unaccountably satisfied. His smile is genuine and full, even with the edge of sadness still in his eyes, an emotion she hates to see in anyone, even James. Maybe even especially James. Damn him.

"I'd be happy to be of use, ma'am. When should I report for duty?"

"Monday, 0700 sharp, Sgt. Fletcher." An edge in her voice dares him to be late. "I have a day off work, and can show you what needs doing. It's not much, but if you are still interested after that, then we can talk about hours. Bring your dog."

Her abrupt tone softens as she watches Elizabeth getting her cheek swabbed by the liver spotted hound. Which means she misses the look of longing and regret that briefly appears on James face. It is gone by the time she turns back to shake his hand, relieved to see him still smiling.

"You can count on me, ma'am. That's a sleep in compared to things at my Dad's ranch."

When he lets go of her hand it takes considerable self-control to not react to the loss of contact. She manages an answering smile, even as her traitorous heart clamors after him. He turns and whistles up the hound who moves slowly away from Elizabeth, eyes mournful. A minute later, dog on board, James fires up his truck and pulls away, leaving Chrissie to gather up her daughter and her scattered emotions before heading up to the house for supper.

*****

James makes it back to the hotel parking lot before his

Justine Iarann

emotions finally boil over, a few tears leaking out as he leans his head back against the truck seat. Not necessarily from sadness, but as a pressure release from all the feelings stampeding around his heart. Well, maybe a little from sadness too. Clearly, he has some serious fence mending to do, and that is just so she will tolerate his friendship. Any midnight dreaming he had entertained about sweeping her off her feet and right back into his arms are unrealistic at best. He can't blame her, since the fault all lay with him.

Today was supposed to be about him stopping by to apologize, to try to make amends, but she had looked so tired, so very worn, despite her well-deserved pride. He doesn't really need the money with his inheritance waiting patiently in the bank, but he does need something to do with his days. What better thing to do than to spend time making it up to the only woman who has ever really mattered?

*****

Monday morning, James arrives at five minutes before seven, slightly smoothing Chrissie's already ruffled feathers. The nights had not been kind, fitful sleep interspersed with vivid dreams of brown eyes and hot skin that leave her flushed and breathless when she wakes. She manages a welcoming enough smile as he pours himself slowly out of the truck, big dog eagerly dancing behind him.

Today, Shane manages to focus enough to say hello to Chrissie, and as she runs her hands over him, he leans against her legs with unexpected weight. Barely moments later, Eliza comes running in from the far end of the barn, and Shane leaves Chrissie in the dust in his haste to reach the child. As she watches the unlikely pair fawn over each other, James appears beside her with a rueful smile as he jams a sweat marked cowboy hat on his head.

"Silly creature. You know, he has never much liked kids, tolerated them, been kind of course. But he sure likes your darling."

Chrissie has no problem returning the smile after his compliment about her daughter. "She is a special girl, that's for sure."

"I'm betting she gets that from her momma." he replies, still watching Shane rub up against Elizabeth's side.

Chrissie coughs and turns away to hide the betraying flush of her skin. She gestures abruptly for him to follow, grateful that he makes no further comment. It's amazing that after all this time, and how jaded she is after life with Thomas, somehow James still has an effect on her. She pokes tentatively at the thought as she shows him where to let the horses out on their pasture. James may not have told her what had happened all those years ago to make him walk away, but he had also never lied to her. His charm, his compliments, all come straight off the cuff, completely, honestly natural. He had always said what he felt when they had been with each other, however brief that time had been, and she has no reason to think that has changed.

However, as she hands him a manure rake, it is clear that she is going to have to guard her heart very carefully. Chrissie has no desire to revisit the hurt, can't afford to be so vulnerable again. Not only Elizabeth counts on her to be emotionally healthy, so do all the people she helps, both at work and here at the ranch.

After pointing him to the first stall she turns back to the tack room to turn up the radio. Music washes over her, freeing her from the serious thoughts bogging her down. Grabbing her own equipment, Chrissie makes short work of a few stalls, but then her phone goes off, signaling her find her daughter. Surprisingly, she discovers Elizabeth already waiting in the aisle way door, backpack beside her, arm draped over the hounds back.

"Time to go meet the bus, baby girl." Chrissie says, taking

hold of the purple princess back pack for the walk down the drive. "Say goodbye to Shane."

Lizzy plants a noisy kiss on the top of the dogs spotted head and strokes him one last time before reaching for her mother's hand. It almost breaks Chrissie's heart to lead her away.

"It's okay, sweet heart. School will be over in a couple weeks, and then you have all summer to have fun."

"I know, Momma, but I don't want Shane to be lonely." Elizabeth replies, looking back over her shoulder mournfully. Chrissie looks back as well, finding Shane watching them, James gripping the big dog's collar. Though it's hard to tell at a distance, Chrissie could swear both hound and man look a little forlorn.

"It's okay, he can stay with Mr. Fletcher all day. You'll see him again tomorrow." she consoles with a squeeze of Lizzy's fingers.

"They won't be here when I get home?" The pleading in Elizabeth's eyes needs no words at all.

"Probably not, baby. I don't have much for Mr. Fletcher to do around here. But you know the stalls will need cleaning again tomorrow."

"I wish they could stay longer."

"I know baby, me too." Chrissie is surprised to hear truth in the statement meant to reassure her daughter. Surprised, and more than a little afraid. Right then, the big yellow bus pulls around the corner and she is hugging her little girl goodbye, promising to be there to meet her in the afternoon. Then it's time to walk back up the hill and face her past head on.

*****

James is surprised with how quiet the day is, expecting her to have clients, but this is the dark day for the barn, time to catch up on chores not done during the week. It gives plentiful opportunities to think while his body keeps busy, filling hay feeders, cleaning cobwebs, stripping stalls. The best part, however, is working beside Chrissie, few words between them, the quiet harmony of mutual effort uniting them. He catches himself several times, staring at the way her hands stroke over a horses face, entranced by the peaceful glow she radiates without even trying. The only real change over the years is how much deeper that peace lives in her.

Sure, her waist isn't quite as slim, but neither is his, and there are faint smile lines bracketing her mouth. The freckles on her cheeks are a bit more populated from the time she spends in the sun. Yet, she is the same natural beauty she had always been, unaware of her charm, content in her own skin. The only change in his feelings for her are that they had grown stronger, something he hadn't realized over years of keeping that part of himself in the dark. He may not need her in order to get through life, but the level of want gripping him has an unshakeable hold. No longer content to simply survive, he wants to live to the fullest, and part of that is loving Chrissie.

As he sits back on the seat of his truck to catch a few gulps of water before the next task, his eyes are immediately drawn to her as she leans down to scrub a bucket in the heat of the day. The view of her shapely hips encased in worn denim warms his libido in rapid fashion, making him turn away quickly before she can notice. When his thoughts are more orderly, he walks inside to find her moving things around in the feed room, her back to him as she lifts some bins on to a shelf.

"So, what else can I do, boss lady?"

Chrissie jumps at his voice, lost in her own thoughts, then turns to face him with what appears to be a genuinely regretful smile.

"Actually, that's all I really need. Stalls cleaned, water tanks scrubbed, everything tidied. The only thing left today is a delivery from the feed store, but you don't need to stick around for that."

Leaning against the edge of the counter, in no hurry to leave, James watches her tuck loose hair back under her cap in what he is beginning to guess is a nervous gesture. Not wanting her to feel uncomfortable, he takes a slight step back from the door so she doesn't feel stuck in the close quarters.

"Well, I don't have plans for the rest of the day. I could stay out here awhile, find a shady spot to read after I have my lunch. That will give you time to do something for yourself before your girl gets home."

It's interesting to watch her eyes, as thoughts and emotions flutter openly in them, many discarded before she is fully aware of them. He can see her settle on saying no before the words appear on her lips, though he has one more ace in the hole if he talks fast.

"You could go for a ride."

The no screeches to a halt and he watches her swallow the idea, relishing the thought, but hesitant to accept his help. After all, she has done so much on her own, but he has a strong suspicion it has been at her own expense. Chrissie, always thoughtlessly giving everything of herself. James sets it in his mind right then to try and stop that from happening as long as she lets him.

"Please, let me help. Otherwise, I'll have to go back to the hotel and watch infomercials." James says with a self-depreciating grin. "And this way, Shane will get to see Miss Elizabeth again."

"Well, when you put it that way, I suppose it is up to me to save you from afternoon TV programming." A ghost of her old smile nearly knocks him off his feet with its potency. "Once you eat lunch, this room needs swept out before the delivery, and the boys from the store usually off load. So you should have plenty of time to read."

"Sounds good, I've got an old Louie L'amour in the truck waiting for a visit, and you've got plenty of shade here for me to relax in. I'll see you after a bit."

With that, he tips his hat at her and saunters out the door, in no rush. Out of the corner of his eye, he can see her standing where he left her, hand pressed to her chest and a trembling smile crossing her face. While he knows he still has a long way to go, he is grateful to know he can bring her a measure of happiness again.

Chapter Twenty

The following weeks are the calmest and easiest in any recent memory for Chrissie. It's not to say there are not hiccups, because life with a six year old and a dozen horses is nothing if not surprising. Yet every time her anxiety level rises James is there, tool in hand, half grin on his face, making Elizabeth laugh and lightening the load.

The days she works at the rehab they met in the morning to go over what needs doing, and when she gets home it is all finished as if she had done it herself. Half the time, he is gone before she returns from work, but the evening feeding is always set out and organized, making short work of her chores. The days that she is home they split the load, and it leaves her with a little time for Smoke, a little more energy for Elizabeth after school. On weekends, when he doesn't come, she misses his steadying presence, his energy a perfect fit in the peaceful solitude of the barn. It completely floors her that in such a short time she has become so dependent on him, and it also frightens her. That is the only fly in her soup, really.

Today, he arrives on time as usual, and as she walks up from the house she is still shaking off the dream that had woken her- indistinct images of being held as she slept, sated and safe.

James is dressed in a worn grey Army t-shirt, bringing up old memories, leaving her momentarily distracted as her mouth goes dry. So distracted, in fact, that her feet forget their job and trip over a spot of loose gravel, shoving her right up against the muscular chest she has been trying to ignore. His 'oof' of surprise at the impact makes her eyes fly up to his, but what truly knocks the air from her are his hands as they grab hold, not letting her tumble back on to the driveway. The dreams haunting her every night hadn't quite captured the impact his touch has always had on her. Limber, yet strong fingers, masterful in everything they do, including now, as they grasp her upper arms. It takes a supreme effort of will to not lean into him, so she goes one better and steps back, arms wrapped around her waist to keep them from clinging of their own volition. The concern in his eyes is colored with another emotion she doesn't want to look to closely at.

"You alright, Chrissie?" he asks, voice rumbling deliciously over her now sensitized skin.

"Ahem. Yes, thank you, I didn't watch my feet. But I'm glad I found that soft spot in the gravel before the weekend. We can't have anyone tripping." she manages to stammer, cheeks coloring faintly in embarrassment. "Not everyone will have someone to keep them from a fall like I did."

"Glad I can be of service." he chuckles, and she shakes her head, thoughts going a little haywire again at the sound.

Grasping at any kind of solid thought, she brushes past him into the barn to find a little solace in the morning routine. It's a relief to hear him grab the feed cart, doling out hay to the few horses that stay in stalls, and she grabs a stack of buckets to begin dishing out the mornings grain rations. After the horses are turned out for the day and stalls are cleaned they meet up in front of the barn by habit to go over the rest of the days plans. Chrissie fiddles aimlessly with her gloves as she works up the gumption to speak.

"So, tomorrow is Elizabeth's last day of school, and we are having a barbeque on Sunday to celebrate the start of summer vacation, kind of a yearly tradition. Everyone from the program will be invited, along with their families. Lizzy and I would very much like for you to come. And truthfully, some of the fellas who come out here for the horses have been asking when they will get to meet you."

"Well," he starts off, and she leans forward on her toes nervously, a little afraid won't accept the invitation. She isn't sure what to make of it, as he stares down at his boots in contemplation and runs a hand through the hair brushing his collar. "I'd love to come spend time with y'all, but I don't want to be an inconvenience either. You'll have enough on your plate without having me around."

"James, you are, by far, the least inconvenient of my acquaintances." she replies with a warm smile. "Mom is cooking, a few of the guys will probably take over the grill, and some of the other folks will be bringing dishes. There will be plenty of food, even some of the neighbors are coming. And we are going to have hay wagon rides in the evening too. Please, come, relax."

"Alright, Chrissie, you drive a hard bargain. But I have some conditions. You have to let me help with chores, so you have a little time for yourself."

It crosses her mind to deny him, because she doesn't want him to think she only wants him around for his help. The realization actually leaves her speechless. All she can do is nod an agreement to his terms, pleased when he grins his acceptance. They move on to the next task in comfortable companionship as she demonstrates how to clean the draft harness the Clydesdales will need to pull the wagon. Fascinated by all the straps, he pays careful attention to his work, polishing the brass with an ease she envies.

After lunch she heads off to take Smoke for a ride, working in the arena on some old, familiar dressage movements. Her thoughts begin to order themselves to the steady rhythm of hoof beats, drawing figures in the blank canvas of the dirt footing. Smoke's inky black coat reflects the high noon sun, making them both sweaty in short order, so Chrissie decides to head down the road for a little ways to cool off in the trees. They skirt the verge of the road, Smoke grabbing mouthfuls of the belly high grass, chewing methodically as they walk along. He automatically turns down a side road that leads to their favorite hill, and she lets him pick his own path from there, rising up in her stirrups as he tackles the slope.

It occurs to her that next time she ought to invite James, another echo from the past sneaking up on her. Resolving to call Suzie later, she hopes her sensible friend can help sort through the conflict between her old hurts and new hopes. How can it be possible for him to have broken her heart, and after all this time, he is now mending it, fixing places she didn't even know had been cracked? Is it okay to now be a little happy that Thomas had asked for a divorce, had left her and Elizabeth behind? She has come to terms with the failed marriage, has rebuilt her life, and is doing just fine. Yet now, light is shining on everything she has hidden in the recesses of her heart, which is not nearly as painful as expected. All of it brought about because James has walked back in to her life.

Thoughts whirl as she lets Smoke decide their direction, trusting his better sense to keep them safe, but then the alarm on her phone goes off. Elizabeth's bus will be arriving shortly so she turns Smoke and sends him back toward the barn, taking the shorter route past the back of the neighbor's property lines. Smoke reads her intent, increasing speed, trotting on a loose rein all the way to the side gate of their own farm.

As they approach the barn James is propped against a tree, dozing in the afternoon heat. It provides the rare opportunity to study him without fear of discovery. The cords of his throat are stretched tight, his head tipped back to rest on the tree, and the lines at the corners of his eyes relaxed in sleep. Damned if she doesn't have an overwhelming desire to simply watch him. At the sound of hooves on the gravel drive, he comes awake pretty quickly, using the broad trunk behind him to rise to his feet. It's a treat to watch the muscles of his arms ripple with the effort, his thighs taut under the denim covering them, but she looks back to his face before he can notice her regard.

"James, could you grab Elizabeth's purple riding helmet out of the tack room? I want to go meet her at the bus stop." Chrissie says, smiling at the faint drowsiness still riding his features. Without a word he steps inside the dark aisle way of the barn, returning quickly with the requested helmet, and an accompanying smile.

"You know, my momma used to come meet us at the bus stop with our ponies when we were little. Thank you for refreshing that memory for me."

Chrissie pictures James as a little boy, a cowboy hat bigger than he is balanced on his head, skinny legs wrapped around a fat pony. The image instantly triggers a warmth in her heart that spills out on to her face, a broad smile spreading from her lips to her eyes.

"Wow, now that is one bright ray of sun shine." he rumbles, his own grin stretching a little bigger in response.

Her heart softens, but before she can tell him what she is thinking of, she hears the school bus bumping over the washboard at the head of the road. So she throws him an apologetic glance and turns to trot Smoke down the hill, eager to see Elizabeth's face when she finds them waiting.

*****

Watching her ride away, long flame colored braid swaying with her horse's movement, James wonders how it is possible to fall more in love with her every day. Every moment. To find more to admire, more to be charmed by, more warmth filling his heart simply being near her. It worries him to feel so deeply, knowing that at any time she can send him away. There are moments where it feels like he is seeing a reflection of feeling in her eyes. Yet he can't risk exposing his own affections, worried it will scare her away for good. This, what they have right now, will have to be enough.

With a brisk whistle he calls Shane to his side, petting the whiskered muzzle that the dog rubs against his thigh. Leaning against the barn wall, they wait for the two girls who have stolen his heart to return. It doesn't take long until the precise, marching hoof beats of Chrissie's horse grow louder. He is rewarded a moment later with a clear view of the black horse carrying mother and daughter on his broad back. Elizabeth is perched in the saddle with her hands on the reins, Chrissie sitting behind her whispering in the little girl's ear. A peal of laughter breaks the quiet and James finds the grin that had faded spreading once more over his face. It is easy in that moment to be content with basking in the reflection of love between a mother and her child. Yes, for now, this is enough.

Justine Iarann

Chapter Twenty One

Saturday is busy, back to back lessons for the therapeutic riders and drivers. Chrissie barely manages to drag herself to bed at a decent hour, grateful her mom had come out to spend the day with Elizabeth to begin preparing for Sundays barbeque. Luckily, the exhaustion of the day is enough to make for a full night's sleep, dropping her in to a dreamless rest. When the alarm goes off at six AM Chrissie wakes with an overwhelming need for a shower and a giant cup of coffee. Elizabeth is already bouncing around the kitchen when Chrissie emerges from her room, helping Catherine with a batch of blueberry muffins just coming out of the oven. It's downright miraculous to sit down and enjoy one still piping hot with her morning dose of caffeine.

"Mom, thank you, these are divine." Chrissie mumbles around a mouthful of fluffy decadence.

Catherine chuckles and dodges around Elizabeth before answering. "Good, I'm glad you like them baby girl. Maybe you should take a couple up to James, since he just pulled in. I'd say the man has earned a treat for volunteering to come help this morning."

Chrissie jerks in her seat to hear he has beat her to the barn, spilling scalding coffee on her jeans. It nearly results in swearing in front of Elizabeth, but she manages to keep it behind her teeth. Her mother's twinkling eyes are all amusement as she approaches with a dish towel to mop up the mess.

"Thanks Mom. I'll take him a cup of coffee too."

"You do that, Chrissie. He is a good man, deserving of a little kindness." At that point, Catherine's gaze is quite serious, her words loaded for maximum impact. To escape the knowing watch of her mother, she quickly loads herself down with a fresh cup of coffee and a basket of muffins. When she walks in the barn aisle all the horses are already busy consuming their own breakfast.

"James?" she queries, unable to hear him moving around over the sound of chewing coming from the stalls. When there is no answer she walks out the other end of the barn to find him leaning against the wall, eyes closed and soaking in the warm rays of the sun. It brings out some highlights in his black hair, trimmed away from his collar since Friday and sharpening his tan to a cappuccino shade that makes her want to taste his skin. "James." she tries again, voice husky with the need flashing through her like a brush fire.

When he looks over faint shadows smudge the underside of his eyes, and she steps closer by reflex. Only her hands being full stops her from reaching toward him. He flinches away, which stays her forward progress.

"Are you sure you are alright to be here? You look like you had a tough night."

"Didn't sleep well." he says with sigh, voice rough with exhaustion. "Went for a run yesterday and the blade on my prosthetic broke on the way back so I took a tumble. Managed to limp myself back to the truck with Shane and got changed back in to my regular limb. Then last night I had new neighbors at the hotel, who apparently came here to party. I already have a problem sleeping, so yeah..."

"Do you want to go back and sleep it off? You don't have to stay. I can manage." she offers with a soft smile, trying to reassure him.

He barks a laugh, some of his good humor returning. "Lord no! The neighbors are still there! I'm only waiting for the pain killers to kick in and I will be fine."

"Would it help if I said I brought you coffee?"

His eyes sharpen at that, so she hands him the heavy pottery mug, still steaming even in the rising temperatures. When he takes it his hands close over hers and the gentle strength in his grasp brings back old memories that widen her pupils. It feels a crime to pull away, but she manages it, covering her hesitation by lifting up the napkin covering the golden colored muffins and waving the scent toward him with a teasing smile.

"I have officially died and gone to heaven." he rumbles as he snatches a muffin from the basket, chewing thoughtfully for a moment then gulping from the mug to wash it down. Pressing his back against the sun warmed siding of the barn, he carefully folds his good leg to sit on the ground, and Chrissie decides right then that the rest of the chores can wait. So she lowers herself down within arm's reach, but not close enough to be a bother, prompting him to crack an eye open.

"You know, I forgot how pretty your hair is in the sunshine. It's like looking at flames through a glass of whiskey." he says, startling them both with his candor. Immediately, he takes another large bite of muffin and looks away, which lets Chrissie turn to hide the flush on her cheeks.

He clears his throat after a minute, and changes the subject. "So, what is on the agenda today?"

Trying to focus on business, Chrissie outlines the day's tasks. "Once we get stalls cleaned we need to run a brush over the Clyde's and then it's to the shed to dust off the big wagon. After that, we are at Mom's beck and call, filling ice chests, putting out enough chairs and tables for everyone to be comfortable in the back yard. The next door neighbors will show up right before lunch to put out sandwiches, and people will start arriving around one. If we crack to, you might have a few minutes to catch a cat nap before they all descend on us."

He makes motions toward getting up so she reaches out with the basket of muffins again. "Mom said you had to eat three at least. Or she would be very offended."

Smile widening at her challenge, he settles back down to eat the remaining muffins and empty his coffee cup. The silence is companionable, and Chrissie's skin warms as much from his nearness as from the sun they are both basking in. Chores are quickly knocked out and once they arrange furniture to Catherine's satisfaction, Chrissie chivies James to the porch into a deeply padded chair. After making sure he is situated with an ice cold glass of tea and a fresh round of ibuprofen, she leaves him alone. Hopefully, if he has any sense at all, he will take the aforementioned nap.

*****

Heart awhirl at her concern for him, and his hip aching abominably, James is sure there is no way he can doze. Staring off in to the blooming haze of summer heat, he watches the horses graze, slowly moving from shady spot to shady spot in the front pasture as he thinks on Chrissie. How attentive and worried she acts, but not feeling sorry for him either. How her blue eyes had widened deliciously when he wrapped his hands around hers to take the coffee. What a miracle she is to his heart, even after all this time.

Exhaustion and the ache have another agenda for him, weighting his limbs and his eyelids as he daydreams. It comes as a surprise when his next aware moment is the sound of a car on the gravel drive. Rubbing the sleep from his eyes, he scrubs his cheeks to get the blood moving and ruffles a hand through his freshly shorn hair for good measure. When the front door opens he turns to behold the vision of Chrissie in a fresh pair of jeans and soft looking baby blue cotton blouse. The scoop neck is wide, giving a glimpse of her collarbones, all peaches and cream in the shadowed light of the porch.

"You're awake, good." A broad smile graces her full lips and James returns the expression with an edge of hunger. She tucks a loose curl back behind her ear, letting him know he is having an effect on her, that she is aware of him. Standing abruptly, James stretches, lengthening his whole body until his finger tips are brushing the exposed beams above him, watching her out of the corner of his eye. Her arms wrap around her waist defensively, but she doesn't look away, studying his physique. The best part is when she actually licks her lips as he groans when his spine pops noisily. Yet, skittishness still shadows her eyes, so he tones it down, casually hooking his thumbs in his pockets.

"So, boss lady, when is lunch?"

Her laughter at the expense of his appetite assures he has effectively dispelled any tension. Still smiling, she motions him to follow her in to the house. His first steps in to the living room are as revealing to him as reading a book. There are no pictures of her ex-husband decorating the mantle of the large fireplace, no fussy furniture or decorations. Everything is comfortable and durable, leather furniture, comfy pillows, quilts and Afghans draped over the backs of the couch and recliner, warm colors mixed with cool blues. It is a home for living, a sanctuary to rest in.

Better Broken

Evidence of Elizabeth is everywhere, from art projects on display to a small shoe poking from under a table, as Chrissie leads him through to the kitchen where Catherine is holding court. The rich scent of the apple pies cooling on the counter makes his stomach growl noisily, but no one seems to notice. Elizabeth immediately bounces from a high backed chair at the heavy wood dining table, coming toward them.

"Mr. Fletcher, where is Shane?"

"Ah, Miss Elizabeth, what did we talk about? I'd rather you called me James." he rejoinders with a smile to soften the chastisement. A blush pops out on her cheeks, reminding him so strongly of Chrissie it causes a physical ache as his heart expands to encompass the little girl even more.

"Okay, Mr. James. I'll try." she answers with a shy smile of her own.

"See, much better. Now, Shane is up in the barn and we can go see him later, but I didn't want him down here where people would trip over him."

"Or where he can snatch at food." Catherine mutters darkly from her position at the kitchen island. James laughs in acknowledgement.

"Yes, for that reason too. But we can go see him after lunch."

Elizabeth's answering squeal of happiness blooms warmly in his chest, but then she launches toward him, wrapping her arms around his hips and squeezing. He freezes like a deer in the headlights, and looks up at Chrissie who is covering a soft smile with her hand, eyes suspiciously moist.

"Thanks, Mr. James." the little girl mumbles against his side. Then she turns away with the same speed she had arrived, running out the front of the house to greet the neighbors.

The rest of the day is spent functioning in a state of fuzzy feelings. Overwhelmed with the welcome of not only

Justine Iarann

Chrissie's neighbors, co-workers, but also the men and women involved in her riding program. There are soldiers of every variety, some with lost limbs like him, others with nerve damage, disfigurement, or other impairment. What truly binds them together is the dark shadow that had followed them all home from the wars. As he stands with a few of the guys minding the grill that afternoon, he wonders why he ever thought Chrissie couldn't accept him damaged- clearly, her heart is so much larger than he had ever known, to welcome each of these people in to her life. What a fool he had been, a terribly blind idiot. Shaking his head to clear away the colors of their past, he is brought in to the moment when one of the guys says his name.

"What was that? Sorry, I got a little lost."

Alan, a short young cowboy who had lost functional use of his right hand after a building had exploded during a routine patrol, nods sympathetically. "Yeah, that happens to me sometimes too. Luckily, no one here thinks any less of us for it."

"What I was saying is that we are all so damned glad Christine has help now. I've been here since the beginning of her program, and it was rough watching her go through her divorce. She wore herself awful thin for a long time." Jim says, an aviation crew chief who battled with PTSD long after his physical injuries had healed. "If not for this program, my own marriage would have bit the dust, and it was hard to watch her lose her own husband. Hell, Cindy and I still wonder what would make a guy walk away from such a great woman. Even before the divorce the man was barely around."

Wondering that himself, James only nods, trying not to wince at the stinging realization that he had done the same thing to her. It isn't in him to fish for information, anything Chrissie wants him to know is up to her. So he redirects the conversation to something safer. Like the war.

Later, after burgers are consumed and the flock of children belonging to all the families present begins to wind down, Chrissie pulls him away to help with the Clydesdales. Or rather, she harnesses while he throws hay for the rest of the herd, which he is grateful for; impressive as the harnesses are, that is a confusingly large amount of buckles and straps. She does trust him to hold the horses while she hitches them to the wagon. It's a task he feels equal to considering the generally sleepy nature of the two huge animals. When she mounts the wagon he is surprised when she asks him to join her, but it is an invitation he is eager to accept. All afternoon long he had barely spoken five words to her, so it is a relief to park himself beside her on the driver's bench.

"Do you think I could get you to play conductor? It's best to have someone help load and unload with all the kids, and in case anyone needs a hand getting on or off." she asks, sharing a smile with him as she directs the big horses down toward the rear of the house. "I've got just enough time to get in a few rides before the sun is totally gone, and it will go more quickly if you can help."

"It's my pleasure to help, Chrissie. You tell me what you need."

An intriguing flash lights her eyes, but with typical interrupted timing they stop in front of the gathering crowd before he can decipher its meaning. Walking briskly to the rear of the wagon despite the stiffening of his sore hip, he steps down to hand in a long line of kids accompanied by a motley assortment of parents. The neighbors, Craig and Deb, with their two grand babies, are among the first. Elizabeth is somewhere in the middle, Jim and Cindy bring up the rear with their little boys of three and seven. It is no surprise when he saunters back up to the driver bench to find Elizabeth perched beside her mother. Sitting close to the little girl, he leans in, pretending to squish her, which makes her squeal and squirm. Chrissie shoots him a look of fond irritation, and he grins back unrepentantly even as he moves over to give Elizabeth a little room.

"Alright, ladies and gentlemen, seats and tray tables in an upright position, all electronic devices turned off, your nearest exits are over the wings and to the rear. Please remember your seat cushion functions as a flotation device in case of a water landing." Chrissie calls back over her shoulder.

"What seat cushions?" Craig rejoinders, making the whole group laugh as Chrissie asks the big horses to walk on. James marvels at the strength of the quiet creatures, as they start the full load without a problem.

"Wow." he mutters under his breath, thinking no one would hear him. Chrissie's sharp ears, however, catch the quiet word.

"Yeah, they are pretty impressive. Each of them weighs a little over a ton, and they can pull nearly four times their own weight in a pinch. Luckily, this load doesn't really tip the scales for them, so they won't have a problem repeating this a few times. And they love all the pettings the little ones give them."

"They sure are magnificent. And they work perfectly together."

"Well, they rely on each other. Dusty is blind in his left eye and Rock came to us with a bum leg that took some time to heal. Dusty kept the rest of the herd from picking on him, and Rock works on Dusty's blind side, so that he feels safe. That's what makes them a good team- they cover for each other's weaknesses, are stronger together."

"So you don't just take in people whose lives are a mess, you take in animals too?"

"Mommy likes to save things. Granma says she has a soft

Better Broken

heart." Elizabeth interjects, which earns her a quick squeeze from Chrissie's free arm.

"Damaged doesn't mean useless. Sometimes, it means learning how to do things differently. That's the whole point of this program, really. I enjoy the clinical side of therapy, but there is only so much we can accomplish in that environment. Here, there are challenges, but no one faces them alone. In learning to accomplish great tasks, it heals you inside as well. It gives you hope, shows you are capable of more than you imagined. After all, if you can control a thousand pound or larger animal, what is to stop you from doing anything else you set your heart on?"

The passion flaming in Chrissie's eyes is an awe inspiring thing to behold, and it leaves him humbled to be a small part of her mission. Certainly, her strength of heart is a force to be reckoned with, and so many of the people present have her patient faith to thank for their ongoing journey toward wellness. Including him, because without her encouragement all those years ago he would not have tried as hard. What in heaven's name makes him think she could possibly have room in her life for anything more?

Eyes focused down the road, her hands quiet and sure on the reins, the slow setting sun burnishes her peach skin to a golden glow. Her beauty stirs him mightily still, yet the depth of her soul is what he truly loves - with that knowledge comes the realization that once before he hadn't had faith in her ability to love him. As wrong as he was then, he is more than probably wrong now. She catches his intense gaze and rather than looking away, she smiles softly, refueling his hope.

"So, we really need to work on getting you out of that hotel, if your neighbors are going to be disturbing you so much. I can't have my right hand man being kept up nights." Chrissie says, breaking the quiet between them.

Behind them, the masculine clearing of a throat catches

their attention, Craig moving to his feet. James welcomes him up beside the bench with a steadying hand as the wagon drops in to a small dip, jostling everyone. The kids squeal with excitement before settling back in to the quiet mood brought on by the steady clop of the horse's hooves on the dirt road.

"What's this I hear you need a place to stay, James?" Craig inquires, with a smug smile that defies interpretation.

"Well, sir, the hotel has been alright. It doesn't cost much and they don't mind the dog. But I have some new neighbors that act like party folk, so last night wasn't my best rest."

"Hmmm, we might be able to help each other out then. Deb and I have been talking about letting out our guest cabin, but I won't have any old stranger on our property. You'd save me the trouble of sorting through all sorts of riffraff if you would take it."

"Sir, I sure appreciate the offer. If it's not too much more than the hotel, we should be able to come to an arrangement." James answers, a little nonplussed at the kindness of people he has just met.

"Well, Chrissie told us what a good job you have been doing, and we know how stringent her standards are. If you would be willing to do some occasional handy work with me, and watch the place when we go on our trips, I think I can beat the hotel price." The offer is punctuated by a puckish wink.

"And it's right down this driveway, so close you could walk if you wanted." Deb pipes in from her seat, snuggling her chubby grandson close as she waves at a mailbox on the side of the road. "Save me the trouble of listening to him complain about interviewing people, please?"

The wink she throws echoes her husbands, and James chuckles, looking over at Chrissie. Her warm smile is all the blessing he needs, though he is pleased to hear her add "I think that would be lovely, guys! Much closer, much quieter, and if Craig has anything to say about it, maybe cheaper."

"Oh, Mr. James, then maybe I would get to see Shane more too!" Elizabeth wiggles on her perch beside him, delight sparkling in her eyes.

"Why do I have the feeling that I will have to worry about you dognapping my hound, Miss Elizabeth?" James teases, enjoying the blush creeping up the little girls cheeks. He turns his attention back to Craig then. "Sir, I would love to discuss this further. When should I come have a look, and see if we can come to an agreement?"

Craig rubs his stubbled jaw. "If you aren't too tuckered out after today you could come by tonight. Or Deb will be home in the morning, if that would be better. The place is stocked with linens and dishes, though it will need a dusting. You'll need some fire wood chopped before winter, but there is plenty of time until that becomes an issue."

James extends his hand then, to shake on it, agreeing to come by that evening after chores are finished. The next ride is a rag tag crew of singles, either from the program or old clients and employees from the rehab center Chrissie works at during the week. One guy with a set of crutches needs a little steadying getting on, but most are able to manage the wide steps of the wagon with no assistance. Folks are generally quiet, absorbing the peace found on a country road.

Part way through, Chrissie invites up anyone who wants to take a turn at the reins, and James clears his seat so they have enough room. It is a marvelous thing to watch her work, offering guidance, but giving them every opportunity to discover things on their own. They only come across one car, a blessing considering a few of the novice drivers have the big horses veering sharply before they catch the knack. Alan, the cowboy from earlier, needs a little extra instruction due to working one handed. But even he catches on quickly, executing the U-turn back toward the farm with a smooth feel.

When they have almost reached the driveway Chrissie motions him to rejoin her- she hands the lines to him without a word, a twinkle of challenge in her eyes. James nearly drops them in his nervousness, but manages to grasp the leather straps cleanly enough.

"I figure if you are my right hand man I should be showing you the ropes with the horses, so you can help out in a pinch." Chrissie says softly, so her words won't carry to their passengers. "Right now, there is too much slack in the lines, which will make the turn in the driveway difficult. You will need to gather them up a little more."

He spools them up like so much tangled spaghetti, but apparently a little too much as the big bays start slowing down.

"Keep your hands closed, but loosen your elbows so your feel follows their motion. In fact, you can soften your death grip a little too." Chrissie encourages and teases with comforting familiarity, setting him at ease as he follows her directions. The horses relax back in to a smooth walk, particularly when she clucks to them. "First, look in to your turn- they can feel it. Now, it's like driving a truck, with your hands on nine and three. One hand comes back, the other goes forward, slow and subtle, even tension on both reins or they will veer hard."

Surprisingly, the turn up the drive is clean, and she leans closer with a pleased smile. "I knew you would have a knack for this. When you turn toward the back yard ask them to come left with your voice, and repeat the same maneuver. When they are in place, squeeze like you are gripping a rubber ball and say whoa. We use as much voice as possible when they know their jobs, so we don't have to pull on their mouths."

Better Broken

She remains close as he pulls in, ready to assist if needed, her warmth a comfort and distraction. Yet, her manner is more reassuring than one of doubt, so he takes a dose of her confidence and drawls out a soft whoa. Dusty and Rock become statues before he finishes the word, cocking hind legs in matching expressions of relaxation.

"Well done, Sgt. Fletcher." Chrissie's hand strokes over his shoulder blade in approval. If she would touch him again he would walk through fire for the privilege. "Think you can hold these wild beasts while I turn on the lanterns and get the last load on board?"

Mute with emotion, he nods, grateful that it is getting too dim for her to see his expression of naked hope.

*****

The last ride of the evening fills with couples, leaving Chrissie shifting from foot to foot. As if the fire building between her and James needed more fuel, now she has to deal with romantically minded passengers. Not that she begrudges them the time- giving these families already stretched tight with challenges a chance to recharge is one of her greatest joys. Her mother and neighbors will watch the children that are all piled on blankets under the gathering stars.

Once everyone is settled she moves back up to the driver's seat to take the lines from James. The warmth of his skin against hers leaves her a little lightheaded, making her fumble the transition. Covering the awkward moment with a cough, she gets the horses walking slowly down the drive and turns to address her passengers.

"If I knew the Love Boat theme, I feel like I should hum a few bars." she quips, earning a few soft chuckles in the twilight. "In any case, sit back, relax, and leave your troubles at my house for a while. You can pick them back up when we return if you like."

A deep baritone from the back of the wagon teases, "Are you trying to say our kids are trouble, Ms. Christine?"

"David, if she wasn't saying it, then I am." answers a gentle alto. "Now shut up and kiss me, you dork".

"Yes ma'am." the baritone acquiesces, over the sound of more chuckles.

All is quiet as the last bit of residual light fades from the horizon, except for the occasional giggle or the muffled sound of lips brushing over each other. Propping her feet on the dash of the wagon, Chrissie pointedly doesn't look in James direction, desperate to ignore the warmth gathering under her skin. Each shifting sound raises her temperature another degree until she is squirming in her seat. James slides a little closer, and she stifles a squeak of panic, her traitorous heart yearning for him like a caged bird trembles for the sky. At the first brush of his fingers along her spine she freezes with indecision, motionless except for a slight turn of her head. His eyes, while hard to see in the lantern light, are soft and sympathetic.

"Well, this is ten shades of awkward." he whispers, which startles the breath she is holding out of her chest in the form of a laugh.

"I would like to disagree with you, but I've never lied to you before, and I don't plan to start a trend now." Chrissie whispers back, leaning closer. "My ex-husband only came with us once, and was so uncomfortable he didn't even stick around to say goodbye to our guests. It was shortly after that he moved out entirely."

"His loss, I think. I can't imagine any man worth his salt wouldn't want to sit next to a beautiful woman on a starry night." he answers, and Chrissie can't resist dropping a gentle kiss on his cheek, relishing the slight friction of his five o'clock shadow against her lips.

"Flatterer." she teases as she sits back, away from the

temptation of him. "But thank you just the same."

His hand touches the spot she had kissed, like it means something special to him, and it takes a good deal of willpower not to kiss him again. Once again, she is in danger of falling prey to a sweet talking man's charms. Rationally, her brain argues that sweet words cannot be trusted. However, it would be ungenerous to clump him in the same category as Thomas, who had said all the right things when it gained him something. James is as genuine and constant as the mountains she lives in the shadow of, showing how important she is to him every day with little gestures of caring. Soon, they need to clear the air, if there is to be any hope for a future together.

They pull back up the drive to the sound of clothing being straightened and she smiles, pleased with another successful picnic. Elizabeth's holiday is a good excuse, but days like this are what truly knits together a community. Stopping the big horses by the back yard, she asks James to hold the lines so she can meet her mother. At Catherine's heels is a jostling pack of children, all eager to feed the horses from the giant bucket of carrots. The treats are quickly reduced to a pile of orange slobber by the careful lips of the Clydesdales, and parents are gathering up children and dishes, saying their farewells. Many of them, particularly the men, stop to say goodbye to James, shaking his hand despite his seat in the wagon. It warms her heart to see so many people accepting him, gathering him in. Jim invites him over for a poker game, and James accepts with good grace, laughingly disparaging his card playing skills. Soon, the last person is meandering toward the front drive, and Chrissie turns to thank her mother.

"Momma, you truly are a treasure. Well done, once again." Chrissie says, hugging Catherine tightly. As she pulls away, she looks about for Elizabeth.

"I sent her to bed, she was about asleep on her feet while you were on the last ride. You get those big boys put away,

I'll go check on her." Catherine reassures, waving her away, so Chrissie climbs back in the wagon.

"Alright, cowboy, let's take this rig to the barn, and make sure these giants are well rewarded for their work. You drive." Chrissie challenges.

Taking up the reins a little more smoothly than before, James asks them to step right, sending them up the slight hill. The horses go eagerly, knowing their work is done, pulling straight into the barn aisle without qualm. James's soft whoa is hardly needed to stop them, and Chrissie climbs down to unhitch, leaving James at the reins.

"Stay up there until they are undone, then you can come help me."

It takes a few moments to unclip traces and get the pole unshackled from their collars before she motions for James to come down. He joins her quickly, despite the stiffness in his gait.

"I'll start unharnessing, you go straight to the tack room and get some more ibuprofen." Stubborn rebellion boils up in his eyes, so she decides to short circuit it. "Please, James, I can't bear seeing you hurting if you don't have to be. At least it will kick in before we are done, and you'll sleep better."

Shaking his head, he turns toward the tack room, and Chrissie begins the lengthy process of unbuckling the harness. When he returns, she drags the first set off Dusty and hands it to him to go hang it up. His arms tangle with hers in the middle of the myriad straps, eyes searching hers before he moves away. Clipping a tie to each horse, she catches up a moment later with the second harness, brushing against his back as she squeezes past him to the other rack. They go back out to the waiting horses and he follows her lead to the wash rack to hose the sweat marks off of their bright red bodies. Then it's out to their pen with buckets of cool mash as a thank you for their work.

Better Broken

James turns to let Shane out of the stall he had been left in and doesn't appear terribly surprised to find the dog is gone, smiling ruefully. As they leave the barn and flick off the lights, the waning crescent of the moon is rising, giving just enough light to see their way to the house. A pleasant thrill hums through her body when he bumps his shoulder against hers in playful companionship.

"I have to say, Chrissie, I am impressed with what you have built here. I mean, I was already impressed, but now that I can see the results of your work, I am amazed."

"I'm glad you can see it. Flaws in people made Thomas uncomfortable. Like once he had fixed the physical damage people could simply get over it and move on. You, of all people, can appreciate the road these people are walking to get back to themselves."

"Walking? Sometimes crawling. Often lost. It is no picnic. I'm glad these folks have you in their corner to fight beside them, to love them through it."

"I wish you had let me love you through yours, James." she whispers, the darkness giving her courage. Rather than rebuffing her, he runs a hand around the back of his neck, rubbing absently before answering.

"Yeah, me too, Chrissie. Me too."

The words settle in to her as they walk, sad to think how many years had been lost, but grateful for this chance to make things right. She hopes. When they arrive at the back porch he follows her in without a word. They find Catherine waiting up, going over a crossword at the kitchen table.

"She is asleep, go see for yourself." A twinkle of humor in her eyes raises Chrissie's curiosity level a notch.

With James at her heels she heads toward Elizabeth's room, stopping right inside the open door at what she finds. Eliza is sprawled artlessly across the bed, big dog stretched the length of her body, his back pressed to her side. The hound is totally out of place in the purple and silver fairy decorating scheme and yet, somehow completely at home.

"Yup, I knew it. Dognapped." James whispers, close enough that she can feel the vibration of his words against her ear, goosebumps raising on her neck.

"I hate to disturb them. Do you mind if he stays?" Chrissie murmurs as she backs slowly out of the room and closes the door behind her. The generosity of his heart couldn't be more obvious as he agrees, a fond smile on his face.

"I should have taken a picture. My Dad, if he were still alive, would be busting up to see that big goofy dog wrapped around a little girl's finger."

Chrissie chuckles softly, then turns away to lead him back outside, partially out of self-defense. Having him two steps from her bedroom door had been straining her better judgement. "You'd better get over to Craig and Deb's before they hit the hay. If things work out like I think they will, tomorrow you will be able to move in. Pack your stuff up in the morning and bring it with you, then you can go straight there after chores are done. We'll make it a short day."

"Yes ma'am." he answers with a two fingered salute, then taking her hand and squeezing it gently, he rubs his thumb over her knuckles. Waves of electricity move up her arm, but she doesn't pull away, letting the moment swirl and eddy between them. When he lets go regret batters her, but the adult part of her knows they have bridges to repair before they go a step further. "Thank you, Chrissie. For everything. See you in the morning." With that, he saunters up the hill toward the barn, his stride a little less stiff, and her heart much more light.

Better Broken

Chapter Twenty Two

Infinitely pleased with the little cabin Craig shows him, James is tempted to fall right in to the comfy queen sized bed with his clothes still on. However, good manners rule the day, and once they agree on a fair price he drives back to the hotel for the last time. Luckily, the neighbors are partying elsewhere, and without the snores of the dog to contend with he is asleep in short order. It is one of the longest sleeps he has enjoyed in quite some time, restful and deep, only one dream intruding. Not that he minded, since it was all about Chrissie, her body bowed up under his, hands grasping at his sweat slick skin. He can't even begrudge the erection he wakes up with at five AM, which is quickly remedied with a cold shower. She is burning him alive, and he is happy to stand in the flames.

Owing to years of practice his duffel is quickly packed, and it is hardly any trouble to toss Shane's crate in the back of the pickup- he even catches himself whistling as he heads to the lobby to check out. The lady at the front desk sends him on his way with her blessings for good things in his future, and he can't help but think that it really is going to come true. When he arrives at the farm the abrupt sound of erratic banging in the feed room makes him rush inside.

In high dudgeon, Chrissie is slamming buckets down on the counter top, and noisily sloshing feed in to them. She nearly jumps out of her skin when he clears his throat, and he resists the urge to reach out to steady her. In her current mood she might not appreciate it, and he could end up dodging buckets.

"Chrissie, what is wrong?"

"I can't even talk about it right now." The answer is forced through gritted teeth. "Let's get chores done, and if you are still willing to listen to me vent, I'll tell you."

"Okay, we can do that. But do you want me to mix feed? You are as likely to mix concrete as a meal at the rate you are going." he asks, smiling to show he is teasing. Luckily, she laughs, and some of the tension goes out of her shoulders.

"No, no, I have it. You start hay, I'll go a little softer."

Leaving her to it, he is delighted to find her spending a little extra time with Smoke when he returns from throwing hay to the pasture horses. The inside horses are already munching their supplements, so he goes back out with the rest of the buckets to tend the outside critters, happy to let the sun bake away the last of his stiffness from the day before. When the final bucket has been dropped he leans against the fence to wait for Chrissie to join him. She doesn't take long, coming out to prop her arms on the top rail of the fence, resting her chin on them as she stares off toward the tree line.

"So, penny for your thoughts?" he asks, turning slightly to face her.

"Ugh." Chrissie groans, thumping her forehead on to the

wood rail in a gesture of frustration. "I hate to dump my problems on you, but I need to get my complaining out before I go up to the house to talk to Elizabeth. I left Shane with her so she would be sufficiently distracted until I could be an adult about this. Her father called me this morning."

"I take it the call wasn't a welcome one?"

"Understatement of the century." she grumbles. "Thomas and I have had an amicable relationship, once I got over his abandonment. But this morning he called to tell me he isn't going to be able to come visit Elizabeth next week, which is going to break her heart. They were supposed to rent a car and he was going to drive them out to Disneyland. Luckily, she didn't know about that part, or she would be even more devastated. Now, he has a conference in Brussels to attend."

A growl builds in his chest at the thought that this man would neglect his child so thoughtlessly, but he manages to choke it back. Chrissie doesn't need his anger on top of hers. "So, his job is more important than his daughter?"

"His job. Always his job. His damned career goals. He was married to them before he ever met me, and I was too blind to see it. It's just like what happened with my father, and I hoped it wouldn't happen to Elizabeth."

This time, when she drops her forehead on to her arms, her shoulders shake silently. James steps closer, risking putting an arm around her. She initially stiffens at the contact, but then she leans in, relaxing, so he pulls her against him. The sides of their bodies meet from thigh to shoulder, and while the warmth between them is present, it does not flare. It melts like cotton candy, spreading a grounding comfort through his veins, and he prays she is feeling the same thing. He would be content to have her lean against him for hours, to lend her a little strength, offer her some stability when her world is shaking.

When she starts sobbing, he isn't sure what more he can

do, but he knows for himself that sometimes you have to cry. Better to empty it all out into the light than to hold it in where it can grow dark. His free hand strokes gently over her arm as it rests on the fence, and when the hiccups start, he rubs circles on her back. When the crying slows he pulls a bandana from his pocket, luckily still fresh from the wash, and presses it in to her hands. Her laughter is light when she notices what he has handed her, a counterpoint to her now swollen eyes, red and damp with tears.

"You know, I'm beginning to suspect you've done nothing but take care of me since you showed up here." she says, voice thick from crying. Yet, she doesn't hide her face, doesn't try to cover up her humanity, and James can't help admiring her even more.

"Well, you are dead set on taking care of everyone else. I figured someone ought to look out for you." he replies, letting his grin spread. "You're strong, Chrissie. I know you don't need me around here, but it really has been my pleasure to lighten your burden a little."

"Thanks, James, really. You have been an unlooked for gift."

"Funny, I recall thinking the same thing about you, back then. And now too." he intones seriously, letting his eyes linger on hers as he tucks a strand of hair behind her ear, tempted to let it slide through his fingers. Her expression is a mixture of surprise and a flitting glimmer of hope. Yet, he doesn't give her time to respond, putting his hands on her shoulders, and leaning close to her ear. "Now, let me give you another gift. Go talk to your daughter. Let me do chores this morning." Then he gives her a tiny shove to get her moving, watching warring emotions cross her face before her mother's heart wins. The flickering smile she offers warms his heart as she keeps walking all the way out of the barn.

*****

"Baby girl?" Chrissie calls as she walks in the back door, following the sound of the TV to the living room. Lizzy, still in her PJ's, is sprawled on the sofa using Shane as a pillow. It amuses her to no end that not only has James answered her unspoken wish for love to come back in to her life, he has also answered Eliza's often vocalized begging for a dog. What is truly heart softening is that he doesn't mind his dog being stolen at all. "Eliza Kate, that dog doesn't need to be on the sofa!" Chrissie chastises, trying not to giggle as girl and hound shoot upright in a tangle of limbs and almost fall off the furniture.

"But Momma, he's clean!" Lizzy pleads. "And he is being very good. He didn't even try to steal my muffins when I ate breakfast."

"What about the dog hair on the upholstery? No but's Elizabeth. Get him off."

Eliza pulls half-heartedly at the big dog's collar until the animal slides off the couch, flopping dramatically at the little girl's feet with a long suffering groan. Assuming the spot the dog had vacated, Chrissie opens her arms toward Elizabeth, inviting her close, smiling as her little girl climbs in her lap.

"Is Mr. James mad that I dog napped Shane?" she mumbles in to her mother's neck, Chrissie's arms tightening as if to protect her from the news she has to deliver.

"No, baby girl, he knew Shane was safe with you. Though I think if he sleeps over again, we will have to put down a different blanket- the quilt Grandma made you is covered in hair."

Sitting back to check her mother's face for the truth, Lizzy smiles broadly. "Thank you, Momma!"

"You make sure to tell Mr. James thank you too, when you see him later, alright? I think the fine for dog napping is some extra chores." At her teasing smile Lizzy flops in her arms in mock outrage. "Now, before I send you to get showered and dressed, I have something to talk about with you."

At the serious tone Elizabeth straightens up and looks back in her mother's eyes. "What's wrong Momma?"

"Your Dad called me this morning to say he can't make it out here next week. He wants you to call later so he can apologize, and talk about doing something later this summer."

To Chrissie's utter surprise, while she can see the glimmer of tears in Eliza's eyes, her frown is quite serious. "I don't think he is a very good daddy, Momma." The words break Chrissie's heart, and tear the scab off the still fresh anger that Thomas could be so unworthy of his little girls love. She tries to mend the hurt as best she can.

"Lizzy, he really wants to be, and you know he loves you."

"I know he does, Momma, and I love him too. But he doesn't love me as good as you do, and I don't love him as good back either." Elizabeth answers thoughtfully, before flinging her arms back around Chrissie's neck for another hug. Chrissie gathers her close, pressing her hand in Elizabeth's wild curls as the threatening tears finally spill over. It takes a while before the crying stops, then the hiccups so like her own finally settle and Chrissie loosens her hold. She fishes in her pocket for a tissue and smiles as she comes up with the bandana James had offered her earlier, pressing it to the damp cheeks of her big hearted child. Some apples really didn't fall far from the tree.

"Momma, is it okay if I don't call Dad later? Can I call him tomorrow? I think I'm angry."

"Yes, baby, it's okay. I will let him know you will call tomorrow, so he doesn't worry. Now, since Mr. James is here helping today, and I am too tired to go riding, how about you go get ready? Then we can go to town and get pizza buffet at Woody's?"

Elizabeth's eyes light up greedily at the offer and she

shoots from her mother's lap, disappearing down the hall before Shane can get up to follow her. Chrissie laughs as she grabs the dog's collar, then rises up off the couch to holler down the hallway.

"I'm sending Shane back to the barn, Eliza Kate. Don't take too long."

The slamming of the bathroom door is her answer, along with the sound of running water in the shower. Chrissie isn't looking forward to untangling Eliza's wild chestnut mane, but since the genetics responsible are her fault she has no business complaining.

Once out the back door Chrissie is able to convince the dog to follow, though the glances he throws toward the house are pretty pathetic. It isn't until Shane hears James distinctive whistle that he gives up trying to turn back and lumbers up the hill. As she walks in the barn aisle James is bent over the forlorn animal, patting his ribs with affection.

"Ya' big traitor. Throwing me over for a tiny bit of a girl." he rumbles kindly at the ridiculous creature.

Chrissie's laugh makes him look up quickly, and she can't help a tease at his expense. "I thank you to remember that is my tiny bit of a girl you are referring to, Mr. Fletcher."

He grins back, smile lines deepening around his eyes, and tips his head in acknowledgement. "And she is a fine little bit indeed. I'm almost as taken with her as this big idiot is."

"I don't know, the fact that he adores her smacks of some kind of higher intelligence, don't you think?" Chrissie asks, leaning against the doorway and crossing her arms. James matches her posture and grins even wider before answering.

"No ma'am. Poor dumb creatures like he and I, we can't help but turn our faces to the sunshine. It's a built in survival mechanism, or we would be lost in the darkness."

At the end, the weight of his regard speaks of their history together and she shifts uncomfortably. Yet, being made of braver stuff than most, she keeps her eyes on his.

"Sadly, even sunshine is at risk of being snuffed out." Chrissie answers, letting her old broken heart show.

"Well, more the idiot us, who have walked away from the light of the sun. It's a terribly lonely place to be." His heart blazes in his eyes, all warm with sincerity, lightening the dark brown with golden highlights. Chrissie is a half second away from asking him why he ever left, but then the back screen door slams, Elizabeth calling for her.

"I'd love to stay here and listen to you tell me why you did, but duty calls." She softens her words with a gentle smile. "I'll be back after I manage the herculean task of taming Elizabeth's hair."

With that, she walks away, hoping against hope that they can clear the air soon. It is hanging over their heads like a storm cloud, and at this point she would rather it rained than continuing to linger.

Immediately, she focuses on her child waiting on the porch. Sporting her favorite unicorn t-shirt and a pair of shorts on over her cowgirl boots, Lizzy shifts from foot to foot with nervous energy.

"What's going on, baby?" she asks as she climbs the steps and accepts the comb from Elizabeth. Sitting in a big wicker chair, she waits for Lizzy to sit on the matching foot stool before taking up the first hank of damp tangles.

"Um, Momma?" Lizzy starts anxiously. "I was wondering if maybe, um, I could invite Mr. James to lunch with us."

"Hmmm, good question, Eliza Kate." Chrissie ponders aloud. "I think he meant to move in to his new little house today, and might have other plans. But you could certainly ask him."

"I hope he can." Lizzy says apprehensively. "I want to make up for dog napping, and I can pay for his lunch with my allowance."

Touched by her daughter's sweet heart, Chrissie longs to gather her close, but keeps her hands moving through the heavy strands of curls. "Baby, I think for all his help I'd be happy to buy him lunch. As soon as I'm done with your hair you can go ask, okay?"

"Okay Momma." Lizzy voice clearly conveys her impatience, Chrissie guesses partly because she wants to go, but mostly because she hates getting her hair brushed out. Chrissie can't blame her, remembering years of her own mother brushing out her wild curls.

It is the work of several tedious minutes to twist the uncooperative locks in to a French braid. Then she follows as Eliza shoots up the path to the barn like a wild deer. James is outside scrubbing feed buckets in the usual Monday routine, straightening up to greet them as they come, grinning widely at Elizabeth's dancing excitement.

"What's up, Princess?"

"Well, um, Mr. James, me and Momma would like you to come have pizza with us." she stammers, first looking him in the eye, then down at her toes, then back up. His whole posture softens as he bends at the waist to get closer to Elizabeth's level, and Chrissie's own heart softens too.

"I'd be honored to go have pizza with two of the prettiest girls in the world." he answers, immediately rewarded with a brightly blazing smile from the little girl. "But we have to finish chores first. Do you think you could go fill the water troughs like you usually do on the weekends?"

"Sure, Mr. James!" Elizabeth agrees. "I can do them every day now that school is out!"

"You are going to be my helper? All summer? That's great!" His enthusiasm is completely genuine as he extends his hand to her. "I'm sure Shane would like to go with you, if you want."

He wraps her tiny hand in his strong fingers and they

shake on it solemnly. Then Elizabeth is off again, all forward motion as she calls to the big dog that is already on her heels. Chrissie watches them go with a half-smile, joy filling her up in the face of so much love.

"You really are very good with her." Chrissie tells James as she turns to help him gather up the freshly scrubbed buckets.

"Kids are the most real people on the planet. Kinda hard not to love them. I always hoped I'd get to be a father, someday."

Chrissie's pulse stutters at the longing in his voice, her throat abominably tight, a picture of him holding a baby in his arms forming behind her blinking eyes. Hope that they are headed toward sharing that dream steals her concentration, and she trips over the threshold of the feed room, catching herself against the counter.

"Sorry, didn't mean to get so serious." Regret darkens his voice as he moves past her to deposit his stack on a shelf. His whole body freezes as she lays her hand on his bare arm, cautious eyes seeking hers in the low light. Her voice is raw when she finally speaks.

"James Fletcher, don't you *ever* apologize to me for being honest. I want to know what you are thinking, to share what you are feeling. The only mistake you ever made was shutting me out."

The shutters in his gaze are flung open then, so many unspoken words clamoring to get out, wild need and soft yearning at the forefront. Knowing Elizabeth is right outside, she can only respond with a touch to his cheek, nearly moved to tears when he closes his eyes and leans in to her palm, the warmth of him filling her. Oh how she wishes to forget the past and move in for the kiss she desperately wants.

Just then, the sound of Shane's claws ticking against the concrete aisle intrudes and Chrissie starts to pull back. Before she moves too far James silently takes the hand that had rested on his cheek. Placing a tender kiss on her knuckles, his eyes are full of a thousand promises she wishes she had time to hear. He nods his understanding and lets her go, following her back out into the barn aisle where Lizzy is skipping toward them.

"Alright, Princess, let's get Shane put in a stall so he can be comfortable while we are gone, and we can go get that pizza you promised." James says, holding his hand out for Elizabeth to take. She grasps on to him, trust shining in her eyes as they move down the aisle, the dog on their heels. Feeling like her whole heart is walking out the door ahead of her, Chrissie follows, her next steps moving confidently toward her future.

Justine Iarann

Chapter Twenty Three

The following days are far busier than normal with Chrissie pulling extra hours at the clinic. James is busy getting his broken running prosthetic fixed, and setting up housekeeping at the neighbors. Elizabeth glories in the freedom of school vacation, out in the barn with them if she isn't with her grandmother, helping with chores or riding one of the ponies. There is barely enough time in the day to breathe, let alone find a few minutes of quiet to clear their past out of the air.

It is Thursday, Chrissie finally headed home from work after stopping to pick up Elizabeth from her grandmothers. Only a quick trip to the feed store for fly spray stands between them and the road home. Maybe tonight she will be able to invite James in for their overdue chat. Yet, as she stands at the counter waiting to be rung up she is approached by Mr. Murphy, the elderly owner of the store. There is a pinch of concern between his eyes, bringing an answering alertness to her posture as she holds out her hand to him.

Better Broken

"Ms. Christine, it's been a dogs age since last I saw you! How are you doing?" he asks, pumping her hand vigorously.

"I am doing great, Mr. Murphy, thank you. Elizabeth will be thrilled to see you when she gets done looking at the new model horses."

"Did that young man we pointed your way prove to be of any use?" he inquires, bushy eyebrows beetling over his sharp green eyes. "I thought he looked to be a good sort, and I knew if anyone could help him, it would be you."

"Mr. Fletcher has proved to be indispensable, actually." she answers, trying to ignore the warmth creeping over her cheeks. If his shrewd eyes detect anything, he is polite enough not to mention it. "I'm sure the feed delivery guys gave you a thorough report after their last visit to the farm."

"Yes, Adam and Aaron said the place is looking even better than ever. I could hardly believe it, since I know the care you put in to your horses and barn. I'm glad it is working out for you both." he says with a smile, but then his mouth tightens in to a line before continuing. "Now we come to the real purpose of my bending your ear; I think I have a horse that needs you to save him."

Chrissie frowns inwardly, not sure she can manage another horse, but he keeps talking.

"He's an old duffer like me, got a hitch in his get along, but one of the trying-est horses I've ever met. His owner is having to relocate to Florida for family reasons, has already sold off most of the herd, only him and few old mares left. The mares are proving easy enough to place, but the kicker for the fella is that he's a stud. Nobody wants to take on an old man with a bum leg, and Mary isn't too sure he can make the trip to Florida with the couple horses she is taking with her." He tips his Vietnam vet cap back off his head enough to run a work roughened hand through his thinning white hair.

"Mr. Murphy, I don't exactly have a good set up for a

Justine Iarann

stallion." she begins, working up the gumption to turn him down. But the man steamrolls her, not letting her say no.

"Christine, I know it in my heart you are his only hope. He's a little thing, compared to most of your lot, but he is a pure bred, died in the wool, traditional Morgan, with more heart than four of my own horses put together. Handsome as the devil too. First off, I know you don't mind someone having a bum leg if they are intent on still living. Secondly, I think you could use him for some of your driving. But lastly, it's because his name is Warrior." His hand grabs hers, leathery callus and knotted joints combined with fierce determination. "And I know exactly what sort of soft spot you have for old Warriors. Like me, like that James, like all those other soldiers you help."

Chrissie sighs deeply and the gentleman grins, seeing his victory in her posture. "I can't swear I will take him, Mr. Murphy, so don't you go making promises to this lady. I will have to make a few changes to have a stallion, as he's likely too old to geld. And you know I won't suffer him just because he is a pretty face. However, if he has half the heart you say, I think I can make room for him."

Shaking her hand heartily, he promises not to say a word, and ambles crookedly back toward his office to retrieve the contact information. Chrissie gets her items rung up by Mrs. Murphy, who's eyes twinkle as she watches her husband go, her beautiful face stretched by a gentle smile. The smile broadens when Elizabeth appears from around a saddle rack, automatically reaching beneath the counter for the basket of candy she keeps for children. "Miss Lizzy! How about a treat for you, sweet heart?"

There is a lengthy discussion of the options available- which lollipops tasted best, or should she take the tart candies, or perhaps the golden wrapped chocolate drops. Chrissie takes the information from Mr. Murphy who has reappeared at her elbow, handing her the slip of paper with a confident air. Then he steps forward to try snatching a candy from the basket and earns himself a swat from Mrs. Murphy, which makes Elizabeth giggle just like always. As they climb back inside the car Chrissie wonders what new trouble she has gotten herself into? The kind that she will be forever changed by, certainly, but will it be for good or for ill?

*****

Starting from his nap at the sound of Chrissie's car, James sits up in the deeply padded chair he had dozed off in on the back porch. Shane leaps up from his spot in the shade to launch himself toward the garage, which must mean Elizabeth is home as well. Not wanting to appear over eager, James leans back in to the welcoming comfort of his seat and lifts up the Zane Grey novel that had fallen from his tired fingers earlier. Best to give her a little time to wind down from her day anyway. After all, he has waited years for her, an hour or two will be easy in comparison.

Footsteps move through the house, grocery bags landing on the kitchen counter with a thunk before the back door swings open. Chrissie walks purposefully toward the steps, obviously heading toward the barn, when he coughs lightly to draw her attention. As she pivots toward him, he's drawn immediately to her smile, full and welcoming. Yet, there is something else, and he wants to ease the tension he can feel as much as he can see, so he rises before she can ask him to join her. Her smile widens as she turns back toward the barn, her steps slower to allow him to catch up.

"So, how was your day?" James asks, now firmly intent on ridding her of whatever has her stressed.

"It was great actually. All the way through. Just became a little more complicated toward the end." The tightness of her shoulders slowly releases as they walk. "I am considering bringing in a new horse, and I need to work out how to manage it."

"What can I do to help?" he questions as they enter the barn, the last of the emotional pressure washing away from her at his words. Leaning against the front of Smokes stall, her hands run unthinkingly over the horses midnight dark coat as she shares everything she knows. With every word a sense of rightness spreads through him, both a sense of calm about the additional horse, and a genuine contentment to be here with Chrissie. Like sitting by a fire on a cool night, warmth spreads through him until every cell is infused with peacefulness. It leaves his mind free to focus on the problem she is spreading before him, his brain working double time to solve any issues with adding a stallion.

In short order they have things sufficiently decided, moving a few horses around so the stallion can have an end stall and an empty stall between until they evaluate his temperament. Shutting the door on the last horse they move, he freezes when Chrissie steps in behind him to wrap her arms around his chest, her cheek pressed along the inside of his shoulder blade. At her sigh of happiness he relaxes into the weight of her, bringing his hands up to cover hers. When she steps away he hangs on, pulling her around in front of him. "What was that for?"

Shuffling a foot slightly, she doesn't quite meet his eyes as a flush builds on her cheeks. "For trusting my judgment, backing my play, being on my side. For having good questions and great answers. For being you."

"Aw, dammit, Chrissie." he rumbles softly, tugging her toward him for a real hug. She folds in to his embrace with a softness he cherishes, fitting against him body and heart, kindling the warmth that always moves between them. The fire now is a soft, constant ember, but with a little encouragement, it will flare readily. Not now, not today, but soon. Now is about comfort, acceptance and encouragement.

Better Broken

"Don't ever change. Not for me, not for anyone, unless it's for yourself. Your heart is in the right place, and you don't let it go haring off without your common sense. I'll back your play because I know I can trust you to back mine."

Her arms tighten around him and a tremor moves through her when he returns the embrace, risking running a hand over her long braid. God, how he has missed even the simplest touches and textures of her. The face she tips up to him is a picture of wonderment, smile tremulous, eyes slightly damp with what he hopes are tears of happiness.

"I wish we had time, right now, to just spend together, but we have this crew to feed as well as a starving six year old who is likely to start making dinner herself if I don't hurry. That is not a mess I want to deal with. Help me get the horses fed and stay for supper?"

He accepts, a growing sense of joy blossoming in his chest, and they make short work of the chores. When they walk back toward the house Chrissie reaches for his hand, and James feels what has been missing from his life since losing his leg- a sense of wholeness.

*****

A rare humid mist spreads over the foothills as Chrissie pilots her truck toward Denver on Saturday morning, and she mutters a prayer of gratitude for the scarcity of traffic. It is one thing to drive her little commuter car into the belly of the beast for work purposes, and another thing entirely to pull a trailer through the outskirts of the city. The return trip would likely be the bad one, if she has a live load on board, particularly considering the horse in question has bum leg.

Luckily, Sam and Colleen had volunteered to cover the therapy sessions today, or this trip would have been on a Monday. She shudders at the thought of muddling through rush hour with a loaded rig. The lady had been eager for them to come see Warrior as quickly as possible, and Chrissie herself feels a pressing sense of urgency about the matter. With everything else on her plate she doesn't need worry for a horse she doesn't even know rattling around in the back of her mind. In less than an hour she will be able to decide and move forward. It is hard enough getting through the days and nights, her unresolved past with James playing merry havoc with her heart. Maybe, if she is very lucky, they can clear that bit of unsettled business from the air too.

Speaking of which, James is trying very hard to stay awake, eyelashes fluttering heavily in the overcast light. Heavens, he is still pretty to look at, even sleepy. Hiding her smile in the fragrant cup of Irish Breakfast tea she lifts to her lips, she draws in a large swallow of the caffeinated elixir. The sigh of satisfaction it brings on as it slides down her throat focuses his attention, making him sit up straight.

"James, it's okay, you can sleep. I've got this. You didn't even have to come, you know."

Grinning sheepishly, he rubs listlessly at his residual limb right above the socket of his prosthetic. "Sorry, Chrissie, had a rough night. Couldn't sleep for a hill of beans, and when that happens I sometimes have to deal with phantom pains. It's getting better, the meds are kicking in, but the lack of sleep is going to take a while to resolve."

"Good to know. Does ice help the pain? Or heat? I have both kinds of packs in the trailer first aid kit."

"Oh no, the pain itself is under control. I kept having dreams that woke me up, so really I just need to sleep. It will be fine."

Wincing sympathetically, she thinks of the dreams of him that have peppered her own rest, hoping he won't notice her blush. He chugs several gulps of his lukewarm coffee in a futile effort to stay awake.

"Seriously, James, sleep. I know it's not the same as a bed, but I'm just glad for the company. I don't need you to keep me entertained." Not to mention how entertaining watching him sleep will be.

"Alright, if you're sure."

"Trust me. I've watched Elizabeth try vainly to stay awake in this state, and it is a losing battle. Better to give in now, then you'll be fresh when we arrive."

A few sips of her tea later, one hand smooth on the steering wheel and her attention on the road, a soft snore signals that the battle for wakefulness has been lost. His chin is tucked to his chest, baseball cap pulled low to shade his eyes with the side of his head pressed to the window, and she smiles tenderly. Truly, there is nothing so sweet in the world to her as watching him at rest, trusting her enough to be vulnerable. Right then, just as she had the first moment she held Elizabeth's tiny form in her arms, she feels the audible click of a piece of her heart sliding into place.

*****

As the truck slows down James gradually wakes, blinking his eyes open as the exit sign for Larkspur flashes by. There is traffic on the off ramp, a big surprise for such a tiny town. Passing through the single stop sign in town is slow going, which makes little sense until he sees the sign for the renaissance festival. He rolls his eyes to clear the last cloudy bits of sleep, remembering something similar in Texas that had bogged down traffic every weekend for a month or more. When he sits up Chrissie looks over with a smile.

"Welcome back, sleepy head."

"I'm sorry, I didn't mean to fall quite that hard. Did I snore too badly?" he asks, reflexively running both hands through his short hair.

"Only a few mild kerfuffles, nothing terribly frightening." she teases, which makes him grin back at her. "Here's our first turn, help me keep an eye out for the farm. It's on your side."

Dutifully, he turns his attention to the road side, scanning automatically for addresses on mailboxes, which means Chrissie stomping on the brakes catches him completely unaware. His heart immediately leaps into his throat going a hundred miles an hour as his eyes search for the incoming threat, ready to jump in to action. Chrissie, as if sensing his hyper response, reaches for him once the vehicle comes to stop, brushing her fingers over his leg and leaning down a little to draw his attention to her. When his eyes flicker to hers she points to the side of the road so he can see what had prompted the stop. A deer and her fawn are half way across the asphalt, stopped and staring at the big vehicle in apprehension.

"Silly deer." Offering him a hint of a smile, she drives onward once sure they aren't going to move in front of the truck.

Sucking in slow, even breaths, James attempts to ratchet his reaction down to reasonable levels, trying to keep Chrissie from seeing how distressed the incident has made him. A few minutes later he realizes the futility of his efforts. When she pulls in the driveway of the farm, a quarter mile of dirt road in front of them before it disappears in to the tree line, she puts the truck in park, and he hears her seatbelt unclick.

"Can I help? Or is it best to let you ride it out on your own terms?" Her voice is compassionate, and soothing inside his pounding head. James opens eyes he didn't even realize he had closed to find her turned toward him, giving him space if he needs it.

"I don't know. I'm usually alone, so I've learned to work through it that way." he answers, voice rough with the adrenaline still flooding through him, words clipped around the deep breaths he is sucking in.

"Can I touch you?"

The sweet voice, and sweeter words, cause his pounding

heart to trip over itself momentarily, the rhythm slowing as if in surprise. His eyes squeeze shut at the relief, and rather than using words he lifts an open hand toward her in invitation. Strangely, she doesn't take his hand to move closer, but uses her agile fingers to find a tender spot at his wrist, applying light pressure. When he looks up she smiles gently and scoots closer.

"I've learned some interesting things, Sergeant Fletcher. Adding some acupressure to my bag of tricks is pretty handy when dealing with PTSD. We will start here, and I'll move on in a minute. Meanwhile, do you remember that night I gave you a massage and we synced our breathing? Close your eyes and focus on following my breathing."

Giving himself over to her touch, he closes his eyes on a world too bright, too exposed, too raw to deal with. Listening, he matches her breath for breath, a sliver of sanity slowly creeping in past the adrenaline high. He hears her shift closer, her hands lifting up where she deftly massages the tops of his ears between her thumb and forefinger. The release is nearly immediate, and he blows out a gusty sigh as the tension between his eyes eases considerably.

"Better?" Her voice so close he can almost feel it on his skin, so he risks opening his eyes. The aquamarine concern focused on him has no pity in it, for which he is grateful, and it comes to him again how much he had underestimated her strength. She had never doubted his strength, and it isn't her fault his own self-doubt had eaten him alive. Pulling her hands away from his head, he draws them down into his lap. Turning them over and back again, he studies the lines and calluses, all showing her strength, then the soft spots in between that could give tender comfort when needed. The sensitive finger tips that find the hurt and ease it, the fluttering pulse that carries her heart in to her hands. What a gift. A gift she has shared with him again. A man has to be stupid to walk away from that sort of gift, and he prays he is no longer the idiot he had been.

"Yes, thank you, much better." he rumbles, words colored with the love he wants to share with her, no longer taut with anxiety. "Sorry I made you late."

She lifts one of her hands away from his grasp, brushing over his cheek briefly before moving back to her seat. "It is my privilege. I'm grateful you trust me enough to let me help." The edge of the past shades her words, and he holds back a wince.

"Chrissie, it wasn't you I didn't trust, it was me. I promise, I will tell you all about it later, you have my word."

A flicker of doubt crosses her face as she puts the truck in gear to start up the driveway, and he hates the fact that he put it there.

There isn't much time to stew on it, as once they reach the tree line he can see the barn flashing through gaps in the forest. Pulling up in front of a large green and white barn with pastures stretching out behind it, Chrissie kills the engine, leaving it eerily quiet. There is a pickup parked out front so they head inside, pushing the large doors further open. Immediately, the stillness is broken by a stallions cry, demanding to know who is invading his territory. At the sound a petite woman steps from the tack room, the concern in her eyes and a smile of welcome at war with each other.

"Mary?" Chrissie asks, stepping forward with a warm smile and an outstretched hand. "I'm Christine Everett-Mason, we spoke on the phone about Warrior. This is James Fletcher, my barn manager."

Relief eases across the woman's face as soon as she takes Chrissie's hand, and James settles back to watch Chrissie masterfully charm her like she does everyone else. It would be irritating if it were fake, but she exudes a sense of peace everyone is affected by. Trailing behind the women as Mary leads them down the aisle, he takes in the brass name plates shining on empty stall fronts. How hard must it be for this woman to let go of something she so clearly cherishes?

"I apologize, he has gotten increasingly distressed as more of the horses left. Now that we only have the three mares on the other end of the barn, he is quite upset. Not the picture I was hoping to present." Mary says, her voice quavering with concern.

"It's alright, Mary. I'd rather see him at his worst and make sure we can get along all the same. Mr. Murphy said he is a sweetie, but everyone has bad days. I can't really blame him for being upset that his herd is shrinking."

"I wish I could explain it to him in a way he could understand. It breaks my heart to see him this way." Mary's shoulder hunch over in obvious discomfort.

They reach the stall then, and James is arrested by the sight of a dark mahogany horse pressing against the bars, desperate for a glimpse of his visitors, skin quivering eagerly. The air being displaced through the horse's nostrils has a force to it, vibrating the area before him with surprising intensity. When Mary swings open the top of his stall door he leans in to the opening, drawing in their scents greedily, and then staring down the aisle in search of something. Chrissie shows no fear, stepping forward to rub along the crest of his neck, her deliberate movements not enough to put pressure on the animal, but enough to draw his attention. She is rewarded shortly as his neck curves around as if to embrace her, the stallion's upper lip wiggling madly in response. When he tries to groom her back Chrissie gently nudges his nose with an elbow, reminding him of his manners.

"Oh my! He likes you!" Mary exclaims, eyes wide with wonder. "You cannot imagine how difficult it is to let go of my babies, but Warrior deserves better than being shuffled off to some huge farm to be a pensioner."

Justine Iarann

"I like you too." Chrissie whispers directly to the little horse, caressing over the huge dark eye watching her so intently. "You must be so worried, all your ladies going away. If you are mannerly, I have an older girl you will enjoy the company of. Or at the very least, I have a good gelding who can be your friend."

"So you think you will take him?" Mary inquires, her hands gripped apprehensively around the stall bars. "I can send you with his things. He has his own harness, and blankets and such."

"Do you have a cart I can hitch him to? I'd really like to see him work before I agree. I don't have time to work with a problem horse, he will already have enough of a learning curve with the physical challenges my clients face."

"He hasn't been out in a while, but I think you will manage him just fine. Let me show you were everything is."

Thirty minutes later, James holds the little horse by the bridle while Chrissie makes small adjustments to the harness. When they had first come out to the arena the stallion had been dancing and twitching with nervous energy, eyes rolling with anxiety. After a little ground work, Chrissie seemed pretty satisfied, her confidence steadying the stallion considerably. Each light touch along the muscled frame presses another measure of calm through the horse's skin until he is practically a rock, only his ears flickering to follow every movement Chrissie makes. He ignores the hand on his bridle as though James is a hitching post.

At last, Chrissie steps into the little exercise cart, reins gathered softly in her hands, and nods to James to step back. There is a moment of stillness so profound that it could spell a disaster or a miracle, but then Chrissie's voice breathes out "Warrior," so softly James hardly hears it. Yet, the little stallion hears, both tiny ears seeking out her words like radar locking on a target. "Walk on." she asks, and is gifted with an instant response.

Not three strides go by before a beatific smile spreads over Chrissie's face, and he knows that they will be taking the little stallion home with them. They do a few laps at the walk, bending and changing directions, halting and backing before Chrissie asks for more speed. Her expression goes from peaceful contentment to hedonistic pleasure as the horse becomes a live wire in front of her. James can hear her murmuring almost incessantly as they move around the ring, he can see the horse making changes in his speed and direction, but aside from that the communication appears magical. When she slows him to a soft jog, bringing him back to the middle of the ring, she utters a quiet whoa, her hands barely moving before the little creature once again becomes solid rock. His breath is barely elevated, though his nostrils are stretched wide, and James notices how soft the creatures eyes appear, as if all he needed was purpose to make him feel at home in his own skin.

Chrissie has that effect on everyone. Calming, soothing, then invigorating and challenging in the next breath. Yes, James well knows what a heady brew the stallion has running through his veins, making him sober and drunk at the same time. Reaching up to take the bridle so Chrissie can dismount, James offers the stallion a pat of sympathy and congratulations along the sinewy neck. She is an addiction there is no escape from, a love so deep you want to drown in it.

When she walks to the stallions head her hand brushes over James arm, whispering a quiet thank you before she reaches for the horse. The words of endearment she murmurs to the intent little creature are a mystery, but the giant sigh the horse blows out leaves no doubt that he appreciates her gratitude, enjoys her touch. Mary approaches from her spot near the gate, her smile a beacon of joy.

"Chrissie, you have to take him. No one else has come close to working him so beautifully. And he loved it."

"Mary, I don't think I could leave without him." Chrissie answers with a smile of her own, motioning James to take the horses head again as she begins unhitching. "He is exactly perfect the way he is. I have plenty of quiet, slow moving horses to start folks on, but Warrior is the next step up. Willing, for sure, but not wild. You can hardly tell he has the twist in his hind leg when he is working. I have perfectly sound horses that don't move that well."

Mary's sigh of relief is palpable, tension draining out of her shoulders that James hadn't even noticed until its absence. "Thank you, so much. So very much. I can tell he will be family for you, as he has been here. At twenty years old most folks assume he is washed up, and don't even bother to come discover otherwise."

"Oh, no one will ever think that at my farm, Mary. I can promise you that. He has a valuable lesson to share with people, and I intend for him to have a chance to teach it."

Pulling the cart away from the horse, Chrissie steps up to the horses head. James relinquishes his hold and Chrissie walks away, the stallion quiet under her hand. Jealousy and sympathy flood him for a horse she has just met. Mary shadows them, talking of arrangements. Shaking his head at the mystery of it all, he smiles before grabbing the cart to follow them all back in to the barn.

*****

They go to town for lunch with Mary, filling out paperwork over sandwiches, and discussing the stallion in detail so that his transition will be as smooth as possible. When they return to the farm it doesn't take long to pack up the horses belongings in the tack room of the trailer. Warrior loads in to the spacious trailer like a seasoned pro, though he does trumpet a last few farewells to the mares left on the farm. He accepts a couple cookies from Mary through the window, even though most of his focus is bent toward the barn, letting her stroke his sculpted muzzle as a few tears leak from her eyes. Chrissie can't let the tears go unnoticed, and embraces her with one arm, squeezing the woman's shoulder soothingly.

"Mary, please remember, when you come out here to visit you are welcome to come see him. I post picture updates on our website all the time, so you can always follow him there. You aren't losing a family member, you are gaining more family."

Sniffing back her tears, dabbing with a tissue to catch whatever moisture lingers, Mary's smile is one of happiness. "Thank you again, Christine. I truly think this is the very best thing for him, and I can move back east without worrying now. That is a huge relief. But I will certainly miss seeing his face every morning."

"I can't blame you in the least. I promise to give him kisses from you all the time."

With one last hug, Chrissie closes the feed door at the stallions head, and walks around the trailer to double check all her doors and latches. Everything secure, she waves at the petite woman, hoping the tears will dry quickly for her. It is a shame to have met such a beautiful hearted person, and to not be able to get to know her better. As the truck rumbles to life she vows to make sure they stay in communication, with lots of photos to keep Mary from feeling too far away from her little Warrior. Ah, Warrior, such a fitting name, so strong, yet so soft, so intense, yet still capable of quietness. Not unlike the warrior sitting across from her, she thinks, finding James watching her, eyes piercing straight in to her soul.

"What?" she asks, puzzled by the half grin riding his mouth.

"Nothing. Just wondering if I had the same docile, pole

axed expression on my face as the stallion did the first time you touched me." he says teasingly, the lines around his eyes deepening with humor.

It shocks a laugh from her, and she responds in kind. "No, not the first time. But the second, for sure."

He laughs outright at her rejoinder. "Still quick witted, I see. Glad to hear it. Hope to hear it more often."

As they move down the drive the trailer rocks a little as the stallion voices his wordless objection to leaving the farm.

"Poor guy, wish I could do more to ease his worry." Chrissie musses aloud.

"He's a survivor, that one. I think he will settle in pretty fast once you get him back to the farm."

"Ah, but there is a difference between surviving and thriving. I want him to find his place and be happy. Just like I want for all my guys and gals." A grin spreads over her lips, showing a fair bit of teeth. "You too." she adds for good measure.

"Oh, I have found my place in this world." he assures her, voice gruff with emotion. "And I'm very happy here."

The trailer rocks again, distracting Chrissie from the serious turn in conversation as they pull out on to the paved road, concentrating on keeping the rig straight despite her displeased passenger. Once they get back on the highway the horse finally settles. For a while the atmosphere in the truck is one of quiet companionship, but then Chrissie begins to fidget, tension creeping over her skin. When they make it over the big freeway interchange, and traffic begins to slow, Chrissie succumbs to her own angst.

"James, I have to know what happened. Did I do something that made you doubt me? Did I not love you enough?"

She looks away from the road long enough to see him run a hand over his face, as if trying to wipe away something he doesn't like.

"Chrissie, I don't think we should talk about this right now. I want to share everything with you, but now is definitely not the time."

Her breath hitches, and color rises in her cheeks along with her temper. "Don't you dare think you could possibly know what is good for me, James Fletcher! Don't you dare take my choice away from me. Thomas assumed he knew what was best for me too, and I refuse to let anyone ever decide for me again."

Her anger is totally stilled when his hand closes over her shoulder. She can't look away from the road in the busy traffic, and she wants so badly to see his eyes, to read what they say.

"That is the one thing I regret more than anything else, Chrissie. I had no right to take that away from you." he says, voice soft and infinitely tender. "I do want to talk to you about it, more than anything. But not right now. We have to get this guy safely back to the farm, and then we can talk. I promise."

Squeezing her shoulder once, he retreats to his side of the truck, and she misses the feel of him, every small touch a bit of a homecoming. That touch, and the peace it brings, is enough to see them safely back to the farm, where Chrissie settles the stallion in his new stall. The farm is quiet, all the clients gone for the day, and she is thrilled to notice that her fellow instructors have already fed the herd, freeing what remains of her afternoon. The small horse investigates his surroundings, trotting out to his run and calling to the horses in the field. Tomorrow, she will introduce him to Smoke, which will give her a better idea of this brave little horse's place in their world.

James walks down the aisle, his distinctive gait as familiar as her heartbeat, and she turns to watch him approach, arms laden with hay. Another crack appears in her heart, just having him there, always walking in when needed, always lifting his eyes to hers and giving his half smile. She slides the stall door open so he can leave the stallions evening meal, then closes it once he steps back in to the aisle free of his burden, the click of the latch abrupt in the thick silence.

Fear colors the eyes that meet hers, compelling her to soothe the worry from him as she once had. Yet, she refuses to give up her own need to understand, to fill in the years of doubt that have plagued her, so she holds his gaze expectantly.

"How about a walk, Ms. Everett?" he says, his voice so much softer than the tension riding his shoulders.

"Tell you what, Mr. Fletcher, how about we walk up to the house. I'll pour us some tea and we can talk on the porch. Mom will be dropping Eliza off in an hour so we have the place to ourselves for a while."

"That suits me fine." A wave of his hand indicates that he will follow her lead.

It's a gorgeous afternoon, the sun sinking toward the horizon like molten metal, but his eyes follow her as she strides out of the barn. Pulled toward her like a magnet, toward the fire and the peace she represents to his heart, he can't stop watching her. She catches his gaze, her smile softer than he expects, then drops back to walk beside him. Some of the fear eases, seeing no anger in her, only expectation.

She leaves him on the porch after waving him toward the seats arranged to look out over the meadow in front of the house. Sitting in the chair he had used the day of the picnic, the familiarity comforts him. He focuses on a black horse grazing in the softening sunlight, blue flaring briefly over the dark coat. As soon as he realizes it is Chrissie's horse, Smoke, the big animal raises his head from the grass and stares fixedly toward the porch. James can't explain why, but he is sure the horse is watching him with disconcerting interest, which makes him shift nervously. The intense scrutiny is broken at the sound of the screen door, both man and horse lifting their eyes to the woman walking on to the porch. Chrissie sets two glasses of tea on the table between them, carefully not touching him, which James cannot blame her for. Yet he wishes for the old familiarity, aches with missing it. These few weeks working alongside her, so close, yet so far from each other, has been a blessing and a torture. She watches him unwaveringly as his thoughts jumble, but offers him no easy way out, simply waiting. He runs an impatient hand through his hair and takes a drink of the sweet tea before settling back to pay his dues in earnest.

"I am going to start and finish this with a heartfelt apology, Chrissie. I am so sorry. You deserve so much more than a weak soul like mine could give." He can see the words she wants to offer to refute his statement, but stops her with a wave of his hand. "No, no, I'm not going to let you let me off the hook here. You should have had the truth a long time ago."

Curling her legs up in to the chair, she pulls herself further away, waiting patiently for him to continue.

"When we met, I was broken. Beyond repair, or so I thought, not only physically, but mentally, emotionally. I had left some part of my soul behind in that war, along with fallen friends and the missing limb. I was living in the dark, and I felt like I deserved it. Then, like a miracle, there you were, shedding light on all the darkness, which hurt even as it healed. When things with my dad drew me away, it left me back in the dark, seeing the bad in myself at every turn. I had a few awful spells, torn up with panic and despair. Even as I got stronger physically, I felt like you didn't deserve to be saddled with my PTSD. You were so bright, like a shooting star, and I didn't want to hold you back. I didn't want you to know about my weakness, how the night after I said goodbye I woke up dreaming something happened to you, and I was too weak to help, too crippled by my memories to save you."

Looking up from the boards of the porch when he hears her shift in her seat, he relishes the miracle of her fingers resting lightly on his forearm. There is no pity in her eyes, only acceptance, which encourages him to continue his confession.

"My dad was on my case for months, calling me a damn fool, trying to find a way to contact you himself so he could save me from my own idiocy. When I wouldn't yield he managed to get my sister on the bandwagon. One of the most memorable moments was when she accused me of drowning myself in work like Dad always had in the booze. It took months of nearly sleepless nights before I realized she was right, and that no amount of work would make me tired enough to sleep without nightmares. One night, I found one of my Dads old bottles of whiskey in the barn, and as I stood there about to open it, I realized exactly how bad it had gotten. The next day I called the VA, to find out when the local support groups met, and thankfully some good people helped me start the climb out of the hole I had dug for myself. It was spring again when I felt stable enough to contact you. Your old cell number was a dud, so I tried the hospital. The only name I recognized from the website was Suzie's. I called her once a week, for two months, before I caught her at her desk. She hung up on me as soon as she knew who I was, but I called back and left a message, asking her to just tell me how you were doing. She called me back that night, left a message on my phone, telling me I was an idiot. Everyone else had figured it out well before I did."

A shift in her fingers causes him to look up, her pained smile showing a shadow of humor. James can only shrug his shoulders in acknowledgement, clinging to her soft gaze as he continues the narrative.

"I called her back the next day, agreeing with her. She told me you were doing great, I didn't deserve you, and you had someone in your life. I can't say it didn't hurt, but it was more the pain because I had done this to myself. You always deserved the best, even if it was with someone else. I sunk myself back in to work, lost myself in training the dogs. Dad would get a little sicker every time work slowed down. But then the seasons would begin, and he would pull himself together, so we kept going. I taught myself to ride again, with my old mare. I went on a few dates with old high school friends, but every one of them was so forced, so awkward when I compared it to you."

Her eyes look a little moist at that, but he could be imagining it, so he plows onward.

"I called Suzie the next spring, and she told me you were engaged, going to get married. That was a rough night- we put up hay that day, and I felt as beat up on the outside as I did inside. But I kept on going, kept working, got far enough in therapy that I was starting to help other soldiers returning from the sand box. I started running again, and it helped with the sleeping. The year after that she told me about your little girl, and I told her I wished nothing but the best for you."

Rubbing at his burning eyes, the memory of that night and the present knowledge of that little girl wrap around his chest like a vise.

"At that point, life turned in to one long, exhausting day after long, exhausting night, on repeat. The next year she told me you were starting an equine therapy program. I was so proud of you, and I wished there was something similar in Texas, to help those cowboys who had come back from war needing to get back in the saddle. I didn't hear from Suzie for a couple years and, dammit, I tried to be a good man to a few different women, always falling short. The next spring, Dad died in his sleep, resting in the armchair he always occupied, with a hound at his feet. It was for the best, considering how he hated the doctors."

He sucks in a deep, cleansing breath, feeling the weight lifting as he shares the story with Chrissie. She hadn't moved an inch as he spoke, her eyes steady and reassuring.

"He left the ranch to my sister and I. Jenn and her husband turned the home place into a lodge for hunters, and I stayed on to help. A while later, as I was cleaning one of his old rifles, I came across a note from my dad. All it said was that he had lost the light in his life through illness, and that shouldn't lose mine because I was an idiot. That sort of light is one of a kind, and unless I opened my heart and tried to let it in, I would live in darkness forever. So I tried Suzie- when she told me you were divorced I wasn't sure what to do. I found your website for the equine therapy program, even followed the fan page, got the newsletters, but wasn't brave enough to write. Just because I didn't want to be alone with my own darkness didn't mean you would want to share your sunshine with me again."

Her hand tightens on his arm, the heat of her touch grounding him in the moment.

"Then one day, my sister was telling me I needed to take a vacation; that I needed to go recharge my batteries. If I didn't go, she was going to kick me out." A rueful smile splits his face as he remembers her standing in the doorway of his tiny loft, hands on her hips and fire in her eyes. Chrissie answers his smile with a larger one of her own. "I swear, before I could stop myself, I started driving north, half way to Colorado before I noticed. Then I figured if I was going to make an ass of myself I ought to do it in person. But the day I arrived, you looked so tired, so overwhelmed, I thought maybe I should wait. Maybe you could use some help. Maybe some of your light would shine on me being your friend."

Better Broken

The tears in her eyes are a little more pronounced than before. "And frankly, Eliza charmed my socks right off that first day. I was so stunned by her, I couldn't hardly manage a straight thought." One tear leaks down her cheek then, before she wipes it away with her sleeve, and he swallows hard around the emotions boiling in his chest. "So really, I am sorry. I don't know if there is any way you can forgive me for hurting you. For taking the choice from you, for rubbing salt in the wound now. You are so strong, in the family you have created, in the people you are helping. You welcomed me in to this safe place you have made for so many people and animals. I am so grateful, so lucky to have been loved, even for a little while, by you, and those remain the best memories of my life."

The tears are traveling steadily down her cheeks now, but the moment is broken with the sound of tires on the driveway. Her eyes dart up to the headlights coming in the thickening darkness, then back to his face.

"James, I have so much to say, but first I have to be a mom. You are welcome to join us for dinner, if you like, and we can talk more afterward."

When she lifts her arm to mop up the evidence of her tears James reaches up before she can and brushes the droplets away with a knuckle. A breath catches in her throat, then he stands and moves out of her path so she can meet the car pulling up to the steps.

Eliza spills out of the vehicle with an enthusiasm only a six year old can manage and throws herself in to Chrissie's arms, a sight which squeezes James heart almost painfully. It nearly bursts when the little girl then turns and holds her arms out to him for a hug.

"Hey, Peanut." he says gruffly as he lifts her up, ignoring the ache in his leg that the extra weight creates when she wraps her arms around his neck to squeeze him.

"Hi, Mr. James." she replies with a thousand watt smile. "Did you and Mommy bring home the new horse today? Is he pretty? Can we go see him?"

He sets Lizzy down, then turns toward Chrissie who is now standing with her mother, and asks the question with his eyes. Both of them cast puppy dog looks in her direction, so she rolls her eyes and waves them away.

"Eliza Kate, you remember he is a stallion, so no going in the stall without an adult with you. And both of you had best be back here in thirty minutes to wash up for supper."

As her little girl takes James by the hand to drag him toward the barn Chrissie knows her heart is his- it has always been his, even in the midst of breaking. Judging by the heavy gaze her mother is laying on her, it is showing, so she turns and heads inside with her Mom in her wake.

"I don't think I need to ask if you are sure about this one." Catherine says drolly, the upturn of her lips prodding Chrissie to smile.

*****

After supper Catherine volunteers to tuck Eliza in to bed. Chrissie mouths a silent thank you over her daughters head, blushing when her mother winks knowingly in response.

"James, can I walk you out to your truck?" she asks after they watch the pair disappear down the hall.

Opening the door, he gestures for her to go first. The full moon illuminates everything so brightly it is casting shadows, making it easy to see their footing, and letting her look over at him repeatedly. Sparks skitter between them, even though they aren't touching, bringing an ache Chrissie thought to never feel again. By mutual consent, they stop beside his truck and turn in toward each other.

Drawing a deep breath, she anchors herself in the moment and reaches for his hand, his eyes snapping up to hers.

"James, it might be hard for you to believe, but you had

my forgiveness even as you broke my heart. I loved you so much, I couldn't stay angry with you long. The damage it did do fractured my confidence, which is what drove me so quickly to my ex-husband. I can't bring myself to regret the marriage, it was a lesson I apparently needed, and it gave me an amazing gift in Eliza. But I mistook his want for love, his need for a placeholder wife as the future I wanted for myself. It was hollow, most of the time, and I am glad you came back to me after I had figured that out. He broke me down pretty well, because he did not give me a choice, because he didn't have enough faith in us. I didn't forgive him for his own sake, but I loved me enough to forgive him so I could rebuild, just Eliza and me."

"Your ex is as much an idiot as I ever was." James says with a smile and a squeeze of her hand, which prompts her to step a little closer.

"No, not an idiot. A selfish man, perhaps, but he is good to Eliza the few times a year he sees her. I would have hung in there, tried to keep our marriage together because I didn't think it was beyond redemption. I am glad he saw how empty it would have been. I am beyond glad now, because it made room for you."

Her heart stutters eagerly at the old familiar flash in his eyes, and he lifts a hand half way to her face before pulling back. Stepping in to him, now having to look up a little to meet his eyes, her body brushes softly against his.

"No more taking choices away from me, James. Don't doubt me. That's all I ask. I'll go as slowly as you need, wait until the end of time if I have to. But you can't run away anymore."

Bowing his head, he shudders against her, overwhelmed at her declaration, swimming in the need that swamps him. She wraps her arms around his chest, pressing kisses to his heart like she once had, tearing an involuntary sob from him as he finally pulls her close. As she squeezes him even harder the darkness that he has spent so long mastering softens to her touch, like a wild thing gentling to her hand, exactly like the stallion had that morning. It feels like coming home- everything he had ever hoped for but hadn't felt he deserved.

"Chrissie, I can't promise I won't do something wrong in the future, but I can promise that I couldn't run away from you again." he whispers in to the soft curls near her ear. "If I look like I will do something stupid you have my permission to steal my leg, my truck keys, or my pants, whatever."

Delighted laughter spills from her, chasing away at least some of the lingering self-doubt. The rest of it disappears when she tips her lips up to his, starting a rapidly growing fire with every brush of her mouth. Just when he is afraid he will lose his hold on the desire roaring through him, she breaks the contact to meet his eyes.

She pitches her voice low and tugs playfully at a belt loop on his jeans, watching quicksilver moving in his eyes. "I think the pants stealing may happen sooner than you expect."

He answers by pressing closer, pivoting to put her between him and the solidity of the truck. The kiss he delivers scalds her all the way to her toes, his hands wound in her hair, his tongue exploring her mouth, bringing her arching up into the contact with his body.

Oh how he had missed the flavor of her, the taste of her hunger satisfying a need so long unfulfilled. When he finally breaks the kiss they are both panting, quivering in the face of their mutual desire.

"I'm going to go now, Chrissie, before I just hand you my pants." he breathes in to the small space between their lips. "I'd rather not make a total ass of myself with your Mom in the house with Eliza."

Growling, she lays a quick kiss on the pulse at his neck, then unwinds her arms from his torso. He leans away slightly, gratified when she steps right back into his space, her eyes searching his in the darkness.

"James, I'm glad you came to make an ass of yourself in person," she teases, sliding her hands in to the back pockets of his jeans. That claiming touch alone leaves him unbearably hard. "And I look forward to seeing more of that ass in the future."

"Woman, you keep that up, and we will end up making a mess of ourselves in the barn." James teases back, warming himself with the fire in her eyes.

"On that note, I am going to go spend a sleepless night alone in my bed, with fantasies of a roll in the hay to keep me company." she says, backing away slowly.

His thoughts go feral at the images crossing his mind, but he lets her go, afraid if he pulls her back he won't be able to let her go again.

"Well, sleepless nights are normal for me. At least tonight I won't be alone in my thoughts."

The seriousness in his eyes belies the humor he is trying to put in his voice, so she only answers him with a small smile.

"See you in my dreams, James. And tomorrow morning as well, 0700 sharp."

"Yes ma'am" he answers with a crisp salute, before turning to climb in his truck. "See you in my dreams."

It's all Chrissie can do not to chase after the tail lights of his truck, remembering the last time she kissed him and he drove away. But she turns toward the warm lights of the house instead, eager to tell her baby girl good night, and to call Suzie who had helped orchestrate this miracle without breathing a word to her best friend. After that, Chrissie hopes she really does see him when she closes her eyes to sleep.

Justine Iarann

Chapter Twenty Four

A few days of stolen kisses and nights of fevered dreams have Chrissie so wound up she can't stand herself. Just this morning, they had tangled behind the closed door of the feed room while Lizzy was doing her chores, Chrissie's legs wrapped around his waist from her perch on the counter top as they kissed each other insensible. It had taken every ounce of her self-control not to drag him up to the house where they could indulge in each other better, particularly at the feeling of his erection trapped between them.

When Elizabeth had skipped back down the barn aisle and they pulled apart, it appeared to bother James not at all, which only served to add to Chrissie's frustration. Now, at the end of the day, she is stomping around so energetically it wakes up Lizzy. Once she tucks her baby girl back in to bed, she retreats to her own room more quietly, grabbing her cell phone before clambering under the sheet. Swearing softly under her breath, Chrissie texts James.

'Are you awake? May I call you?'

It isn't long before her phone chirps and he has replied to the affirmative, so she punches his speed dial before her nerve fails.

"What is up, Sunshine? Everything okay?" James answers, his voice rough in her ear.

Swallowing the tears that threaten at the use of his old nickname for her, she chokes out a short "No."

"What's wrong, Chrissie?" he asks, words now sharp with concern.

She laughs with little real humor. "Me, I am a mess. I'd blame you, but I set myself up, volunteered for this torture."

"What did I do wrong, Sunshine? How can I fix it?"

"I don't know that we can fix it, right this minute, much as I wish otherwise. James, I am slowly burning alive, wanting you, trying to wait for you, trying to let you set your own pace."

He barks a short, strangled laugh that raises her hackles, until his words smooth things over in the next breath.

"Hell, Sunshine, I've been moving slowly to give you time. I have missed you so much, all these years, I didn't want to assume anything."

Her insides quiver as she answers. "My God, I don't know what I did to deserve you. I didn't wait for you, I tried to move on with my life. I can't believe you could even want me after that."

His voice is soft and so sweet with his reply. "Chrissie, I love your strength, the depth of your heart, the will you have to make the most of your life. I couldn't hate you for trying to rebuild after I pushed you away. I can't begin to tell you how weak I felt, not being able to love anyone. That took a long time to come to, to be at peace with the monster that lives in me. Whatever we build now will be so much stronger than what was broken before. I didn't want to rush things."

Justine Iarann

"Would it be too much to ask you to come over tonight?" she asks, voice trembling. "I can't promise you the screaming passion I'd prefer, but I think we would both sleep better together, if history is any indication."

"I'll be there in twenty minutes." he answers, the sheets rustling as he begins to move, then the line goes dead.

True to his word, she opens the door to find him clad in workout shorts and a worn t-shirt, arms open without prompting. Chrissie steps in to the invitation gladly, letting her leg bump against his artificial limb with the same enthusiasm she embraces the rest of him with. There is no part of him she doesn't love. After a minute of simply being held, she withdraws just enough to lead him inside the dimness of the living room.

"I thought maybe we should stick to the couch. Getting you in my bed would be more than my willpower can handle tonight." she whispers as he follows her to the overstuffed sectional where she has pillows and blankets waiting.

James smiles with very male satisfaction at her statement, but he doesn't argue the logic of it, lowering himself on to the welcoming depth of the furniture, pivoting his legs up on to the length of the sofa. When he opens his arms to her again he is confused when she shakes her head, but then she touches his prosthesis.

"We should take this off, so you can be more comfortable. I don't want you a mess in the morning."

Finding the catch that affixes the limb with practiced ease, she draws it off and sets it within easy reach. He beats her to removing the sleeve, but that doesn't stop her from kneeling down to run her hands over the residual limb. The touch is not sexual at all, wholly professional, but that doesn't prevent the frisson of fire that shoots through his body. None of the women he had tried to be with had ever done anything other than ignore the missing limb, like an elephant in the room that no one talked about. Chrissie walks the fine line between acknowledgement of the sacrifice and never making him feel less for it, or assuming he can't do things because of it. It is a heady draught, knowing she is as willing to touch the parts of him that are damaged as those that are not. When she notices his burning stare her touch changes, finger tips softly grazing over the puckered skin, teasing the nerve endings and tracing the scars with love.

Gulping loudly, James swallows down the wave of desire threatening to overtake him before he drags her up for a kiss, capturing her skilled hands before she can cause more trouble. She comes to him eagerly, mouth open against his in blatant invitation, so he explores her thoroughly until she is moaning softly. He breaks away, sharing breaths with her for a few moments while his thoughts settle into coherency.

"Sunshine, as much as I am enjoying this, I thought we were going to sleep." he says against the warmth of her lips, rewarded with a gusty sigh.

"I know, James. My intentions were honorable, I promise. You just are too much temptation sometimes."

"Back at you, lady." he answers, drawing her up on to the couch. She settles beside him without argument and starts to fit herself against his side when he stops her. "Hold on, darlin'. I have a better idea for both of us."

Propping a few pillows in the corner he scoots himself back into them, spreading his thighs open and holding an arm out in invitation. Bringing a blanket with her, she slides against him, her hip fitting in to the juncture of his legs. One arm wraps around his body as she pillows her head on his chest, just over his heart. Originally, she worried that so much body contact would circumvent any attempts at sleep, but once he sets his arms around her, one hand tangled gently in her hair, sleep sneaks up on them both. The beat of his heart is a steady metronome, hypnotic as it lulls her toward slumber. In her half asleep state, at home in his embrace, she isn't sure if the whispered "I love you." she hears is real or dream, but it doesn't stop the mumbled "Love you too." that falls from her lips.

*****

The next morning Chrissie doesn't wake until her alarm goes off, a miracle of immense proportions in and of itself. It takes a few moments to disentangle herself from the blanket and a still groggy James to get to the cell phone chirping annoyingly on the side table, but she is glad to be aware of the growing erection pressing against her side. Turning her body fully against James, she lays the softness of her abdomen over him, reaching up to run her fingers over his jaw as he blinks his eyes free of sleep. When he is finally aware enough to meet her gaze, he smiles slowly.

"You know, soldier, one morning, we are going to have to do something about this." she teases, sliding her body up his enticingly.

"Seriously, Chrissie, you keep that up and we are going to make quite the scene for Lizzy to discover." he half groans, tugging her in for a quick kiss.

"We have fifteen minutes until her alarm goes off. We could get in lots of trouble between now and then." she pleads against his lips.

His gaze sharpens then, locking on to hers. "Oh no, Chrissie, I plan on taking far more time than that for our first go around. I've waited too long to rush things." His hands travel down to the curve of her ass, lifting her further up his body so he can reach her breasts with his mouth; even with the t-shirt between them, Chrissie sobs softly at the moist heat on her nipple.

"James, are you trying to break me?" she whimpers even as she pulls him closer with the hand that settles in his dark hair.

He grows quiet under her, so she leans back to look at

Better Broken

him, his eyes now serious. "I remember someone telling me some things are better broken."

Tears well up to hear him remembering that long ago conversation, tears she can't stop, that spill over until they drop on to his chest.

"Oh no, lady, this won't do at all." he whispers, the echo of the past in word and gesture as he draws her down, kissing her so softly she can feel her soul catching fire. Yet that isn't the only echo, the moment shortened by an alarm clock sounding down the hall.

An unladylike epitaph falls from her lips at the interruption, and she pulls away, her eyes apologizing.

"It is okay, Sunshine. We will find time, I promise." His smile soothes her ragged heart as he lets her go. "I'll go out to the barn and get dressed, start getting critters fed."

"Oh no, my dear. If this is going to work, it has to work for us all. Time to face the morning monster that is Elizabeth." Chrissie says, backing away with mischief in her eyes. "I'll be back with the beast in a few minutes."

The sassy sway in her hips as she walks down the hall makes James rub his hand over his face, then reach down to adjust his shorts. Voice muffled by the walls, Chrissie cajoles her daughter out from under the covers. After a minute of low talking there is a sharp squeal, and the sound of small feet pounding down the hall. Elizabeth erupts into the room and spotting him, skids to a halt, her mother on her heels.

"Good morning, Mr. James." Eliza says quietly, uncharacteristically shy.

"Good morning, Miss Elizabeth" he answers gently, smiling at the similarities between mother and child, both of them sporting a wild case of bed head. "How are you this morning?"

"I'm good, I think. Momma says you had a sleep over. Next time, I want to have a sleep over too."

"Sorry we didn't invite you, peanut." he answers seriously. "Your Momma couldn't sleep, so I came over to keep her company. We didn't want to wake you up."

"Momma can't sleep very well by herself. I used to sleep with her, sometimes, but she says I steal the covers, so I have to sleep in my own bed now." The little girl moves a bit closer, sitting on the edge of the ottoman, careful not to knock over his prosthetic limb.

"We have lots of blankets out here. So next time, I will ask your Mommy if you can come too."

Forty or so pounds of squealing little girl throws herself in his lap, landing elbows and knees first on all the softest parts of his body. Restraining himself from a very unmanly cry of distress, he manages to wrap her up in the blanket still covering him and starts tickling the exposed feet peaking from beneath the edge. The resulting screeches and gasps have him laughing in moments, and he looks up to see Chrissie laughing as well. Their eyes meet over the top of the bundle of giggling little person, and as she steps closer to extricate her daughter she mouths I love you, the words sincere even if they are silent.

Chapter Twenty Five

A much calmer week of sweet kisses and evenings curled on the couch with Chrissie and Eliza fill James with peace. Now, it is Saturday night, the horses are fed and James rushes home to shower and change while Chrissie does the same. They are finally going to spend time alone, with no obligations to tear them away from each other, nothing to interrupt the fire demanding their attention.

    Fiddling one more time with the button down collar of his shirt, he walks up the front steps of Chrissie's home. Breathing deeply of the twilight air, he knocks on the heavy wooden door and hears the sound of Eliza's feet running toward the entry. When she drags the door open to let him in he bends down to offer her a small bouquet of daisy flowers, hugging tightly when she wraps her arms around his neck. She smells like a child should, one part rich dirt, the other part soap. As he lets her go and stands up Eliza looks him over with a critical eye.

"Mr. James, you sure are handsome."

"You sound surprised, peanut." he teases as he walks inside. "Where is your Momma?"

"She's doing her hair, I think." Eliza says, answering him honestly. "I want her to leave it down, it's so pretty, but she doesn't want it to get tangles. Which is kind of smart, because tangles are no fun." Her freckled nose wrinkles in disgust, he imagines because she remembers getting the tangles brushed out of her own hair.

"Thank you for letting me borrow her tonight, kiddo."

"I like it when Momma smiles, and you make her smile lots Mr. James."

"She makes me smile lots too, Lizzy."

"Did you bring Shane with you for the sleep over with Grandma?" she demands, hands on her hips in a very distinct echo of her mother.

"I did," he answers, smiling broadly. "Did you ask Grandma if it was okay? Otherwise, he has to go back to the cabin."

"Yes, she did ask Grandma," he hears behind him, turning as Catherine walks out of the hallway with the unassuming grace she had passed on to her daughter. "And Grandma said yes, because honestly, who can say no to this face?" Catherine finishes, sitting down on a chair arm and dragging her granddaughter in for a big kiss on the cheek. Sending Eliza to the kitchen to put her flowers in the sink she turns to face James, her expression very serious. The weight of her regard is heavy with expectation, measuring him.

"James, you are a good man. A man worth loving. But I love my daughter too much to see her hurt again. I pray you can love her as well as she deserves."

"Yes ma'am," he answers with a nod of respect, in complete agreement. "I pray I can too."

Apparently satisfied, she turns to the kitchen to see what

trouble Eliza has gotten up to, leaving him alone to wait. Soft footsteps encourage him to turn, and he drinks the sight of Chrissie in. A paisley skirt swirls fetchingly around her knees, making his mouth water as much as the peach colored blouse clinging to her curves. Thank God she had listened to Eliza, leaving her hair down where it can catch the light and he can wrap his fingers in it.

He would have put the idea to immediate action if not for the return of scampering feet. Lizzy skids back in the room at high speed, barely missing the corner of the sofa as she shoots toward her mother.

"Momma, you are beautiful!" she crows, leaping for Chrissie's arms, confident in her landing, folded safely to her mother's chest. Joy brims over the edges of his heart, just watching them together.

"Thank you, baby girl. You are beautiful too."

"Grandma says we are going to do each other's hair and paint our nails, so I will be even more beautiful when I see you in the morning." Eliza says with solemn conviction.

Stepping close, James wraps his arms around both of them. "Miss Elizabeth, if you get any prettier, I'll have to fall in love with you." he says, looking the little girl square in her lovely blue eyes that are only a few shades lighter than her mothers. As quickly as the words fall from his lips, she transfers her grasp from her mother to him, supported between them.

"Good, Mr. James, because I already love you." she answers earnestly, planting a noisy kiss on his cheek, not noticing his sudden stillness or the moisture in his eyes. She drops out of their arms, shimmying down the length of her mother's leg and shoots off toward the kitchen, waving her goodbye.

Not one to waste time, Chrissie grabs her small overnight bag and leads him out on to the porch before James can manage a complete thought. Closing the door behind them, she wraps her arms around him while he gathers his scattered wits.

"My God, Chrissie! How do you even have room for me in your life with that little girl blowing holes in your heart every day?" he mumbles as they lean against each other, needing her to anchor him.

Her laughter clears some of the fog swirling around in his head. "James, the only thing I am worried about is when she figures out that you are my Prince Charming, not hers."

The haze in his eyes is gone with her declaration, and he tips her chin up so he can kiss her lightly. "Well, I do call her Princess. But I am definitely in love with the Queen."

They make their getaway once James takes Shane up to the house where the dog greets Lizzy with sloppy kisses, following her toward her room without a backward glance at his master. James tells Chrissie how even his big dumb dog is thoroughly in love with her daughter as they drive away, and they laugh together as she winds her fingers in his.

"So, where are we off to, my dashing prince?" she asks as the warm summer breeze blows in the open windows of the truck.

"Would it be entirely too cheesy to say I packed a picnic that we are going to eat in the moon light?" His eyes dart away from the road long enough to watch a smile curve across her lips.

"That sounds absolutely perfect." she answers, gently squeezing the hand entwined with hers.

The meadow isn't far away and before she knows it, he is spreading a blanket over the grass under the slow blossom of stars. They settle close together by mutual design, brushing against each other casually while he unpacks the basket. Though she has no appetite for food Chrissie says nothing, so touched by the thoughtfulness he has put in to planning the night. It isn't until he offers her a half sandwich and she notices it is her mother's chicken salad that she realizes exactly how thoughtful he has been. The tears that erupt blur her vision as she reaches for the plate with a trembling hand, and she nearly drops the sandwich.

"Chrissie, are you okay?" he asks, voice low.

"Isn't that my line?" A soft laugh colors her words as she dashes away tears. "I'm guessing you have managed to charm my mother as well as my daughter, judging from this picnic."

It's hard to tell in the low light, but a flush seems to darken his cheeks, so she strokes over the warmer skin to be sure.

"Sgt. Fletcher, are you blushing?" she teases gently.

Barking an uncomfortable chuckle in response, his eyes dart away from hers briefly. Chrissie covers his discomfort by leaning forward to kiss his cheek, feathering her lips along his jaw. His hands run their way up to her shoulders, one reaching even further to tangle in her hair, which encourages her to drift back to the base of his ear. Licking a soft trail of moisture along its curve, she slides down to pull the tender lobe into the heat of her mouth, grateful for the chance to taste his skin.

James jumps at the sensation, a lance of need rushing from her mouth straight to his groin, and he is torn between the panic of his past and the pleasure of the moment. When he freezes she doesn't move much, only enough to be sure he can hear her whisper.

"It's always more than okay, James. Always."

The words break through his fear like nothing else could have, echoing across the years and washing him clean with the fire that follows. The hand caught in her hair tugs just enough that he can find her lips, and he kisses her with all the pent up need that had accumulated over time. It rocks him to his core when she answers his possession of her mouth with softness, letting him control the kiss. He starts to lean back, pulling her with him, but she resists, confusion muddling his senses.

Reaching down between them to grab their sandwich plates, she holds them up in answer to the unspoken question.

"I have idea," she offers, quickly packing the food back in the basket. "How about we save this for breakfast?"

Struck dumb at the thought of sharing the picnic with her in the morning, fixated on everything that he wants to do between now and then, he can only nod.

Her eyes stay on his as she slides the basket away, letting all the hunger she is feeling flood through her until she sees a glimpse of the same fire in him. Leaning close to fit her mouth to his once more, he offers her a softer kiss, but she pushes him back instead, now staking her claim.

Letting the fierce heat crash over him, clearing away whatever darkness remains, he gladly falls back. Pulling her flush against his chest, wrapping her in his arms, he offers himself up to the flames, sacrificing not only his fear, his terror and worry, but his very soul to her. Not his heart- his heart has always been hers. When the kisses slow and her hands begin to reach for the buttons of his shirt he brings her fingers to his mouth for a damp kiss.

"Sunshine, I think we had best take this back to my place." he whispers over the hammering of both their hearts. With a groan she drops her head to his shoulder in acceptance.

Packing goes quickly, and she scoots closer to him once they climb in the truck for the short drive, running her hand over his thigh. As soon as she clears the threshold of his tiny cabin, she kicks off her shoes. Before he can flick on a light she lifts her shirt up, exposing her back where it meets the swell of her ass as she walks away. Mouth suddenly dry, he bumps the front door shut, dropping his keys on the floor in his haste to reach her, stilling her movements with his hands around her waist. Pressing her back along the front of him, he keeps her from turning around, silencing her with his mouth against the column of her neck. God, the heat of her skin begs to be lingered over, tasted like a fine wine. She clasps him closer, one hand tangled at his nape and the other guiding his palm flat along the softness of her stomach.

"James, please." she pleads softly, pressing closer.

"Wait a second, Sunshine. Just wait. We have waited this long, a few minutes more won't kill either of us, no matter how much it burns." He pulls her hand from his hair and turns her in his arms. "I have to make a confession first."

Quieting in his embrace, her expression is infinitely patient, a surer sign of her love than a million grand gestures could have been.

"I didn't tell you the whole truth, before." he starts raggedly, looking away from the kindness in her eyes. "I said I dated other women before. And I did. But what I didn't tell you was I never had sex with any of them."

"You mean to tell me those stupid women couldn't see how very hot you are?" Her affronted frown startles a laugh out of him.

"I mean, I tried, a couple times. But I couldn't find enough of a spark to follow."

"Oh James," she whispers before drawing him in for a brief brush of lips. "What we have isn't a spark. It's a damned bonfire. I think we can find our way together."

"No, seriously Chrissie, listen." He sets her back enough that she is hurt at the degree of separation. "What this really means is I haven't done this since I lost my leg."

Her regard sharpens, the wheels turning in her head before she tamps her inner therapist back in to hiding, which makes him grin a little. The hand on his neck travels down to land over his heart as her lips follow suit, so he pulls her close again, happy to hold her. But she doesn't stop there, reaching toward the buttons on his shirt, nimbly managing them even as she looks him in the eye.

"Do you trust me, James?" she asks, gravity in her heavy lidded gaze.

"Yes." he breathes out as she pulls his shirt from his pants, the buttons now undone.

"I trust you." Leaning in to push the shirt back off his shoulders, she plants a heart kiss on the now bare skin that sets him ablaze. "I trust you to tell me if something isn't working for you. I trust you to listen to me if I need something from you."

She walks behind him to slide the sleeves off his arms, leaving kisses along his shoulders as she goes. "I trust you enough to say that if this first time is difficult that we will learn from each other, because I want making love with you to get better with time. We will adapt, together, because we trust each other."

Chrissie stands before him again, eyes piercing even in the low light. "Nothing has stopped you, not years, not fear, not pain or regret." she says, sliding knowing fingers over the scar tissue texturing his hip. "I think it's safe to say that if you can endure that, mere mechanics are going to be an easy obstacle to overcome."

The conviction in her voice is sincere and the challenge in her eyes is clear, so he steps closer, answering her with a fervent kiss. She backs toward the darkness of his bedroom door, and he maintains the contact of their lips, following her lead. Their progress is stopped by the edge of the bed, but he doesn't push her back on to it, instead pulling her shirt off, thumbs skimming her ribcage as she lifts her arms to help. Even before it disappears in to the inky blackness surrounding the bed, his hands are stroking lazy rivers of fire over her hips, sliding the silky skirt down as his palms cup over her generous buttocks. Her breasts tempt him as he leans down to push the skirt the rest of the way off, and he cannot resist a quick taste of her cleavage, his efforts making her tremble.

When he straightens she quickly finds his lips, her tongue sliding inside his mouth, eager to be close to him. Muscles tighten involuntarily as her fingers trace over his stomach, his lungs freezing as she finds his belt, then the button of his jeans. With a deft touch, his pants are loose, but she leaves them at his hips, palming the length of his cock through his boxers. James bucks forward into her touch, startled by the intensity of his reaction, his already hard member stiffening even more, blood pounding in his ears.

Roughly, he grabs Chrissie's upper arms, kissing her hard, as much to distract her as to show the depths of his desire. Her response is immediate, leaning confidently in to his grasp, pressing her heated flesh against his, so close that he rocks against the contact. Breaking away with panting breaths, he turns so the bed is behind him, pushing the jeans and shorts down over his thighs, pulling her toward him abruptly as he sits. His mouth makes contact with her sternum first, kissing a wet trail along the edge of her ribcage while his fingers find the clasp of her bra, fumbling briefly with the hooks. Keeping an arm around her waist so she cannot move, the other hand peels the silky garment from her, exposing her breasts to his gaze. In the dim light he studies the changes being a mother has wrought, and while he wouldn't have imagined it possible, the thought of her with a child to her breast only stokes the fire higher. Drawing one puckered nipple in his mouth, he feels her knees quiver, and he lets her lean back against the strength of his arm, immensely satisfied to hold her this way.

Chrissie soughs a breath out of aching lungs at the sensation of his tongue moving over her sensitive flesh, the wet friction compelling a new wave of ache to move through her body. When he lifts his hand to cup the other breast, his thumb moving over the tender nipple, she can't help the shudder that rocks her, her knees giving way even more. She smiles at the very masculine chuckle that vibrates against her, opening her eyes to catch him staring, satisfaction blatant in his gaze. Even as her muscles quiver his hands urge her to step away from him, and she complies despite the neglect of her breasts.

He kisses hotly across the delicate skin of her stomach then whispers against the pulsing under her skin. "Stay there. Don't move."

It takes every bit of will power she possesses to do as he asks, particularly when he begins removing his prosthesis, but she waits all the same, trying to show him with her actions that he can trust her. The hasty sound of his pants hitting the floor makes her smile, negligence with his things demonstrating the level of his desire. When he lifts his hands on to her hips, drawing her toward him, she steps eagerly into his embrace. Looking down in to his eyes, dark pools gone swirling black, she is hypnotized, watching him lean down to kiss her hip bone, hooking his fingers in the lace of her panties, drawing them down slowly. Every inch he exposes, he kisses until he reaches the edge of the curls concealing her womanhood- the lick he bestows there nearly makes her come on the spot, moisture building to welcome him.

Voice husky, she tangles her fingers in his short hair, tipping his face back up. "James, remember, together or not at all."

"Oh, I remember, Sunshine. I never could forget."

Guiding her panties lower, his fingers trail down her thighs, palms turning to caress the back of her knees until he lets them drop around her feet. Caressing her with his gaze, his knee coaxes her to spread her legs and she complies, staring steadily into his eyes. The hand running up the inside

Better Broken

of her thigh sends a shiver through her body, shortly followed by a wave of need when he reaches her cleft, cupping her wetness.

"So hot, so wet, Sunshine." he says with reverence.

Impatience bites at her a little when she replies. "James Fletcher, I've been wet for you since the day you cast your shadow on my barn aisle."

His stunned stillness at the rough confession gives her the opening she needs, pressing him back on to the bed with a hand on his shoulder. Following him down without hesitation, she places a knee on the bed beside his hip and lifts the other leg to straddle him. The intimate contact freezes them both, her hands braced on his abdomen for balance, their eyes locked together. The silky feel of her thighs against him, her moist center hovering perilously close to his eager member, even the look on her face, one part concern warring with two parts desire, it is all more fuel for fire raging under his skin.

"Do you think this will work for you?" she asks after drawing a stuttering breath, searching his face for any indication of discomfort.

Before he can even formulate a reply James has to gather his scattered brain cells. Even then, a hoarsely choked "Perfect." is all he can manage, his voice like gravel in the heat of the moment, frozen underneath her. When she shifts forward one last rational thought causes him to blurt out, "Condom."

Settling back on his thighs, Chrissie leans down, trapping his throbbing cock between their bodies for a moment. Her hair cascades around them, creating a private sanctuary for the intimate kiss she presses to his mouth. When she lifts up just enough to meet his eyes, her lips almost brushing his, her words spear through the haze.

"I'd rather not. If we are both clean, I'm on the pill."

Unable to resist her a moment longer, a growl rumbles from his chest as he ravages her lips, pressing into the weight laying so deliciously against him. Even as their tongues dance together, thrusting greedily into each other's mouths, Chrissie rises up on her knees, arching her body away from his enough to reach between them. There is a sharp leap of ache when her fingers find him, but it is eclipsed in the next instant when she slides down. Slowly, her molten core eases over his hardness, leaving him mute with the terrible intimacy of being inside her with nothing between them. He catches the choking sob that spills from her with a gentle kiss, then a groan tears free from his throat when she has him fully sheathed. The shiver that moves over her skin travels through her body as well, a tiny tremor wrapping around his cock that sets fireworks off in his skull.

"Are we okay?"

Those whispered words touch his heart, so he replies "Always more than okay."

Then he escalates things, rocking his hips underneath her, pressing a mewling cry from her that makes his heartbeat trip, stopping his movements until his pulse can level. But she doesn't give him time to recover, pushing herself up above him, eyes closing as she fully seats herself on his shaft. James would happily die this way, never moving from this moment with her claiming him like a pagan goddess, her liquid heat wrapped around him, her eyes gone as pale as the moon outside.

The next moment breaks him against the jagged rocks of desire when she snaps her hips forward, then back, starting a rhythmic friction. He cannot look away from her riding him to her own satisfaction, but the lightning going off behind his eyes leaves him nearly blind, so he reaches out. Finding her breasts, he gently latches on to her nipples, swirling over the peaked flesh, desperate to bring her to the edge with him.

Lost in the feeling of moving him inside her, Chrissie moans, the nub of her clitoris rubbing between them where they are locked so tightly together. His hands create a flash fire against her breasts and she arches her back even further to offer them up for his touch. The movement shifts him to a whole other angle within her, touching her elusive g-spot, a pleasure that is nearly painful, forcing a sharp cry from her as she continues to surge against him.

Unable to lay still any longer, he presses his foot against the floor, lifting to meet her every roll until they are crashing together. Hands on her hips, he helps her snap down even stronger, setting a rhythm soon accompanied by her whimpering cries, which drive him to an erratic pace.

Wrapping her hands around his forearms, Chrissie clings to him like an anchor in the firestorm engulfing them, and with one last downward stroke she erupts with a keening sob. As the force of her orgasm tightens around him, James follows her over the edge of the abyss with a lift of his hips, spilling himself body and soul in to her, every muscle clenched in a rictus of passion. She collapses on his chest like a puppet whose strings have been cut, panting desperately for air even as she continues to throb around him. Those aftershocks draw every drop from him, his balls aching even as he lays in smoldering bliss.

When their hearts finally stop thundering furiously against each other she begins to push away, but James draws her back up to his lips. As he pours his gratitude and awe in to the kiss, his softening member slowly withdraws, the friction enough to steal another breath from him. Tangled hair half covering her damp face she kisses away whatever breath that remains, her smile an unmistakable indication of satisfaction.

Lifting her with the strength of his arms alone, he makes her squeal in surprise, bringing her beside him and indicating with his eyes that they should move up to the head of the bed. Every ounce of remaining energy is depleted in the move, sliding beneath the sheets, still brushing against each other at every opportunity, intimacy a welcome side effect of their love making. With her back flush against his stomach they start to settle, her head pillowed on his bicep, his other arm wrapped just below her breasts. Chrissie kisses the curve of muscle beneath her cheek, and an unseen smile crosses her face as his lips deliver an echoing kiss on her shoulder. Then, for the first time in her life, she falls asleep completely sated, every fiber of her being knowing she is safe in his arms.

*****

Sunlight is slanting across Chrissie's face when she wakes, and she turns immediately to reach for James. Finding herself alone she stretches out in the empty bed, any worry soothed by the sounds of James moving around in the next room. Muscles scream in protest at being so well used the night before, but each twinge widens her smile. She climbs out of the bed, reaching for a t-shirt draped over a chair back, sliding it on as she walks toward the door. The vision that greets her is welcome indeed, James setting the picnic items out on the table next to a pot of coffee, clad in nothing but a pair of running shorts.

She leans against the doorway before announcing herself. "Well, between the two of us, we have a complete outfit."

He turns with a start, almost overbalancing, but recovers with a hand on the back of the chair. Hunger immediately flames in his eyes as he looks her over, but it is shadowed with what looks like insecurity.

"It's okay though, I don't suspect we will be dressed much longer than it takes to eat." With a saucy flip of her hair, she walks toward him, stepping close enough to cup her hand around his rapidly growing erection. "No, definitely not going to be in clothes long at all."

The doubt goes up in smoke, and he leans in to kiss her,

swatting her gently on the ass to shoo her into a chair. He tastes of coffee and sweat, a heady brew that makes her lick her lips, darkening his eyes even further. They sit beside each other civilly enough, as she pours their coffee and he pushes the plate of sandwiches toward her, even as his eyes travel the length of her bare legs. Lifting a sandwich for a quick bite, her eyes run over him in answer, enjoying the rare treat of bare skin he presents. The purpose built muscles she had admired all those years ago are still there, if slightly less defined around the edges, giving him a sense of solidity that she cherishes. Heaven only knows what he will think of her post motherhood body in the light of day, but the years have given him a more finished appearance that she wants desperately to explore.

Watching her eat over the edge of his own sandwich, ravenous after the previous night's exploits, James is certain he had best recharge his batteries quickly if the look she is scalding him with is any indication. Thankfully, he now knows they have all day to themselves.

"So, your mom called." he says casually over the rim of his coffee cup.

Chrissie straightens in her seat. "Is everything okay at the house?"

"Yes. Apparently, we are to take our time. She is taking Lizzy and Shane to the farmers market to pick out something special for dinner. Which I had better be there for if I know what is good for me."

The raised eyebrow accompanying his statement lifts a grin to her face, imagining the fumblingly good natured dog dragging her mother all over the market on the heels of a very precocious six year old.

"Heaven help us, even my mother is conspiring to get us together." Her musing is silenced by the intense look he levels on her. Wrapping his fingers around hers where they lay on the table, he leans forward earnestly.

"Chrissie, I love Eliza. I'm pretty sure I love Catherine. Heck, even your horse and I have reached an agreement." He hesitates briefly, then grins. "I think. But none of that matters to me. All that matters is that I love you, have loved you all these years, and will love you all the years ahead of me."

Throat gone dry with the influx of emotion, Chrissie swallows audibly. Turning his hand over to run a soft caress over his palm, she speaks straight from the heart, no second thoughts.

"James Fletcher, with all the years between us all I ever wanted was to love you, and be loved by you. That never changed, even when I was trying to make my life without you. I see you in my heart every time I close my eyes, I feel the peace of you in my bones, and I cannot imagine a day in my life without you."

He stands up, and pulls her toward the bedroom, sitting her down on the edge of the mattress before turning away to rifle through a dresser drawer. When he sits down next to her, angling sideways to take her hand, there is a ghost of threatening tears in his eyes.

"A wise woman once told me sometimes things are better broken." James begins, smiling at the gentle grin tugging at Chrissie's lips. "I didn't know what that meant, then. But one day, a friend at the VA was talking about something called kintsugi, where the Japanese people take broken pottery and repair it with gold, seeing the value of its history and making it more beautiful in turn. In that same vein, I'm hoping gold will knit our love together, stronger and more beautiful than it was before."

With that, he lifts their joined hands, flipping her palm up to place a small gold band there, a tiny diamond winking in the sunlight.

"This was my mothers. My father kept it with him every

day of his life after she passed, clinging to the love he had found with her. I found it wrapped in that note my father left me, and I am praying you will wear it now so it can be part of our story too. Would you do me the incredibly privilege of being my wife?"

The tears pooling in her eyes are now running freely down her cheeks, a very unattractive hiccup coming on, yet she doesn't hesitate to close her fingers around the ring, his fingers still tangled with hers.

"The privilege would be mine, you idiot." Chrissie whispers.

Kissing her tears away as his heart threatens to give out, he reaches for the ring she holds, lifting it toward her finger. "May I?" A fine tremor moves her hands at his words, the lips he loves to kiss parting on a sigh as she nods. The thin filigree band slides on as though meant for her, and he sends up a silent prayer, hoping the love his parents shared will shine down on them. Laying a kiss on the hand now wearing his ring, he tugs her closer, their lips meeting naturally as they tip over on to the bed together.

Moving up the length of the mattress they reach the jumble of pillows at the headboard to lay face to face, their eyes locked together. Wetness gathers between her thighs from the intimacy of their gaze alone. This blatant honesty is a heady thing that had been missing from her previous life, where the words had been planned, everything by rote instead of by feel. What she shares with James is the most real and genuine love, the kind she shares only with her family. Perhaps that is it- James is family, the real home her heart has always craved.

As he guides her back, she goes willingly, eager to feel the raw freedom of his touch. He pulls up the t-shirt concealing her body, exposing the softer places, the stretch marks and thickness that are hallmarks of motherhood. A small part of her wants to cover them, but she is proud of her child, so she arches her body under his reverent touch. His expression bears only the passionate fire she longs to bathe in again, so she surrenders herself to feeling as he strokes over her stomach, tracing her waistline. When he moves up to her breasts, gently letting each of them fill his hand, her womanhood throbs. Never in her life has she been as damp and ready as he makes her, and she presses her thighs together to create some pressure on the swelling flesh. He chuckles softly at her reaction.

"Ah, lady, this won't do at all." he whispers over her lips before pressing her down for the tenderest of kisses.

The kiss distracts her slightly from the touch traveling lower on her body, catching her waist to tug her hip right up against his very firm erection, and she moans into his mouth. He does not stop there, sliding down to the thighs she has pressed together, urging them apart.

Anticipation alone starts a quiver that feels like a brand when his fingers slide inside her heat. It bows her spine up off the bed as he traces her swollen tissues, exploring her slit with a thorough determination. His lips leave hers, dipping to her aching nipple, and she watches him engulf her, urgent need rolling through her at the reverent stroke of his tongue. It collides with the possessive slide of his fingers into her channel, a quick thrust that short circuits the inherent need to breath. They withdraw, even as she clenches around them, sliding to the aching bundle of nerves directly above, his timing exquisite as he sucks hard at her breast. A moan tears from her, rocked in a tumult of sensation, yet he does not stop, touch gentled slightly as he rubs her clitoris, a rhythm that rocks her back and forth between his mouth and his hand. The tears that have only just dried return then, stunned and entranced to be so achingly close to breaking, as he keeps her at the edge of the precipice.

"James," The cracking in her voice lifts his head from her breast. He is torn at the sight of her tears, between stopping and continuing, but she prompts him with a whispered "Please. I need….." that trails off as he slides inside her again. The friction begins slowly, driving her inevitably back toward the edge of orgasm, picking up speed. When he turns his hand, thumb rubbing over her clitoris as he pushes into her, her breathing changes dramatically into short desperate pants. Chrissie bites her lip to quiet the building moans.

"Sunshine, let me hear you. I need to hear you burn."

Like his words have opened the floodgates, she cannot stop the whimpering cries as the strokes come faster and faster. When she is sure she can endure no more, her toes curling in to the sheets as she pushes herself against his hand, he drags the stubble on his jaw across her nipple, flinging her abruptly into a climax that explodes beneath her skin. Spine drawn taut as a scream escapes her, with fireflies dancing behind her closed eyes, every muscle in her body clenches around his fingers. Tremors are still riding her when she opens her eyes to find him watching.

"James, James, James." she says, husky with satisfaction, parting her lips in invitation for his kiss, grateful beyond measure when he obliges her immediately. As he leans away again, she offers him a smile. "I am hoping you aren't very attached to this cabin."

He raises an eyebrow in question which serves to broaden her smile.

"I don't think I could stand even one night without you. So, would you be willing to stay with me? To come home?"

A tender expression softens his visage, but rather than answer, he moves away, asking her to stay still with a raised finger. She is perplexed until he reaches to remove his artificial limb, dropping it on the floor along with his shorts. Taking advantage of the moment, she draws off the t-shirt still bunched under her arms and settles back to wait. As he turns back her eyes travel slowly over the glory of him, lingering on his erect penis with particular relish. When she manages to look back up in to his eyes, Chrissie lifts her chin defiantly at the teasing expression he levels on her.

"So help me Chrissie, you are going to break me all over again, looking at me that way."

"Seems fair, considering the justice just done to me." she answers saucily.

"Ah, but I have my reasons." he says, lifting himself up over her, his arms holding most of his weight, intent made clear as he settles between the legs she hasn't managed to close yet. "I'll probably be okay, but I wanted you satisfied first in case this doesn't work out well."

"Oh." is all she can choke out, tenderly stroking his face, the vulnerability in his eyes starting an ache in her chest. It gives her enough energy to wrap her legs around his waist, supporting more of his weight. The strain in his shoulders eases so she leans up kiss him, his erection jerking in response. A seeking hand finds him hard and ready, and she tips her hips to angle him inside. Wet and still sensitive, the quick slide of his flesh parting her, she whines as the tip of him comes achingly close to the end of her.

"Chrissie, I need you to look at me, darlin." His accent runs thick and syrupy in the heat of the moment, bringing her blue eyes up to his chocolate gaze. "I'm not going to last long."

He punctuates the statement with a careful slide out, arms quivering with effort, rewarded when she clutches at his shoulders.

"Me either, my love." she rasps out, consciously tightening her inner muscles, making his hips buck until he drives back inside her. By a supreme force of will she keeps her eyes open and locked on his, heightening every sensation, watching passion light his eyes. "I'm so close already. You don't have to be slow or gentle."

"What I need to tell you, before I finish us both off, is that I am home, right here. Anywhere you are, that is home." he says, leaning down for a kiss, then moving back so he can see the emotion swirling through her eyes. Whatever reply she would have given he silences with a backward slide of his hips and a rapid drive forward, her mouth flying open in delight. The animal need to claim her completely erases any muscle fatigue bothering him as he plunges inside her. Just like when he runs, he loses himself in the rhythm, but Chrissie urges him a little faster, hands grabbing urgently at his waist as she nears her own pinnacle. The little touches spur him on as much as the soft cries falling from her mouth. As he wishes he could lean down for a kiss she braces herself on an elbow to lean up and draw on his mouth. The instant their tongues wrap around each other it is like completing an electrical circuit, the passion driving them growing stronger as it races circles through them.

Undone against him, Chrissie comes softly this time, giving her enough thought to breath an "I love you." into his mouth, wracked with slow but fierce shudders. The first wave throws off his rhythm, but the combination of the second and her declaration of love fuels him just long enough to slam himself home. Spilling himself in to her, looking down in to her bright eyes, soft and shining with love, breaks him apart all over again. He collapses on her despite his intent to move away, and her arms embrace him as he pillows his head at her breast.

"I love you, Sunshine." he whispers over her sweat damp skin, watching with fascination as her skin shivers again, lulled into a moments rest by the slowing beat of her heart under his ear.

When he can master himself, he moves, charmed when

she reaches for him as he goes. Settling on his back, she slides in beside him, her arm and leg casually tangled around him. They doze off bathed in sunlight and satisfaction.

Chapter Twenty Six

Waking from a brief nap, Chrissie takes in the afternoon angle of the sun now coming in the window. He hardly moves when she shifts away, making a break for the bathroom to clean up. It is going to take an effort to untangle the mane of hair James has so thoroughly mussed, a thought that makes her smile, and carefully count the aching muscles protesting her progress. Twenty minutes of wrestling with a hair brush later she has her tresses moderately tamed into a braid.

    James is still out, stretched in glorious fashion across the bed, sleep easing his typically guarded body. A thing of rugged beauty, washed in the golden light coming in the window, old scars add character to the skin she loves to touch. Twenty years from now, watching him sleep will remain among her greatest memories, his face relaxed in rest. In years past, she thought her life had been enough, but looking at him now, she knows she will never get enough.

Justine Iarann

After locating her blouse and skirt that he had thoughtfully hung in the closet, she sneaks out to the truck for the overnight bag that never made it inside. Dressing in a fresh pair of jeans and a thin sweater, she returns to the bed to wake James, leaning down to kiss him. Slow but sure, his mouth angles open under hers as he pulls her down on to his chest. When his hands encounter her sweater his eyes blink open, but she maintains the kiss, letting him draw her in. They break apart naturally, and she sits back up, immediately noticing his now hard member.

"I really am going to have to do something about that someday." she muses aloud, slyly offering him a smile. "But not right now, sadly. We have dinner in an hour, and hell hath no fury like a momma who expects her children to be on time."

He groans dramatically, throwing a forearm over his eyes in mock despair, tempting her to lean down, quickly swiping over the head of him with her tongue. It incites a rapid inhale of breath from him, and he props himself up on his elbows, staring like a hungry wolf.

"Something to remember me by." she quips, then runs for the door, giggling at the pillow that smacks her on the backside.

Dressing and quickly packing a small bag, James gets them back to the farm in good time, stopping at the barn first to feed their waiting charges. Her horse Smoke is staring at him fixedly as he walks down the aisle and it slows his strides. It is a look he is used to seeing directed at Chrissie, sometimes Eliza, never at anyone else. That fact alone draws him up in front of the horses stall. Ears up, the big animal forcefully blows a huge breath on him, freezing James on the spot, leaving him vulnerable to the whiskered lips that reach up to wiggle around his collar.

A giggle of delight erupts from down the aisle, and he

looks over at Chrissie, her hand pressed to her mouth. "What the hell is he doing?" James asks, confusion warring with an echo of her laugh.

"I think he is saying he likes you." Stepping up behind him, she wraps her arms around his waist, cheek pressed to his shoulder. "Such a gift, considering he has never, ever liked a guy except for my grandfather. So I'd say he is an excellent judge of character."

Smoke's lips migrate down to her hands which James has tangled with his own, where the black horse blows softly out. It feels like a blessing, if he believed horses were capable of that sort of thing. Then just like that, the horse turns back to his food, like the moment never happened.

Hand in hand, they walk toward the house, brushing peacefully against each other until the back door bursts open. A small blur of humanity hurtles toward them with a hound hot on her trail. There is time to share a quick smile before Lizzy is on them, but James is rocked when she bowls deliberately in to him instead of her mother, clutching his pant leg for support.

"Mr. James, Mr. James, look at Shane, isn't he pretty?" she crows, James looking quickly at his dog. The besotted animal staring raptly at Lizzy is as far removed from his hunting roots as a bird dog as he possibly can be, unless you count the feathers of the purple boa wrapped around his neck. James eyes grow even wider at the glitter nail polish winking from the tips of each of the dog's toes.

Panicked, he looks to Chrissie for support, but she is one sniggering giggle away from exploding into laughter, covering her mouth with her hand, hoping to contain herself. She slants her gaze toward her daughter though, and he turns back to the expectant child.

"He looks great." he manages to choke out. "You really did a good job."

Justine Iarann

The beaming smile Lizzy levels on him eases the alarm in his body, replacing it with a love so pure it aches to drink it in. Carefully, he kneels down on the gravel so he can look her in the eye, pleased to have her slim arms wrap around his neck as he draws her closer.

"Hey Princess, I've got a question to ask you before we go in to supper, if that's okay?" he asks, reaching his other hand up toward Chrissie. He is reassured by not just her hand, but also her hip bumping softly against his shoulder as she stands with him.

"Sure thing! But we better hurry, Grandma said we better not let the food get cold, or she won't let us have pie." the girl answers, her eyebrows shooting up at the thought of missing out on dessert.

"You know how we had a sleep over a couple weeks ago, and you said you wanted me to sleep over more? How about if I stay over forever?"

"Really?" Eliza questions breathlessly, her eyes growing impossibly wide. "Forever?"

"Yes, forever. I love your Mommy, and I love you too. Will you be my family?" James asks seriously.

Lizzy leans in close to his ear, simultaneously breaking and mending his heart with the quaver in her whispered words.

"Can you be my Daddy?"

Chrissie's fingers clench his shoulder at hearing that heartfelt plea, and he gives the only answer in his heart as he hugs Eliza tight.

"Forever."

Kneeling to join them, Chrissie wraps her arms around them both, glimmering tears on her cheeks as she meets his eyes. Lizzy turns in their arms to kiss her mother, but then clutches at Chrissie's neck when she notices the tears.

"Mommy, don't cry! I love you, don't cry!"

"Oh no, baby girl, these are happy tears! It's okay."

Better Broken

Chrissie soothes, squeezing her darling child more tightly. Then she sets her down, giving a great big smile to reassure her. "Why don't you run and tell Grandma we will be right there?"

Tossing them a blazing grin, Lizzy dashes back down the drive, Shane a galumphing shadow in her wake. Catherine stands in the open doorway, smiling a blessing on them before she waves her granddaughter back inside. Turning to James with smile on her lips and concern in her eyes, she offers him a hand.

"Do you need help up? This gravel is rough on the knees even with all original parts."

It startles a laugh from him, and he balances against her arm as he straightens out his artificial limb, making an otherwise awkward transition much easier. Kind of like everything else in his life, she simply smooth's out the rough edges. He gathers her close once he is standing, breathing in the scent of her, the peace of her.

"Chrissie, I can't promise I won't still have problems. The panic attacks will come sometimes, the insomnia could be an issue. Physical limits could crop up in the future. I will promise to love you every single day of my life."

She squeezes him tightly for a moment before catching his eyes, letting him see the truth of her next words.

"My darling, I would rather hold your hand to walk through hell than stroll through heaven without you."

Crushing her to him, his kiss is a soft, sweet counterpoint to the fierceness of his arms, which she returns with every ounce of her being. They stand together after the kiss ends, dragging out the quiet intimacy.

After a rowdy dinner full of laughter, and much playful scolding from Catherine, they put Lizzy to bed. She begs James to read her a story and he yields gladly, giving silly voices to her favorite characters. Moved by the gentle heart he shows her daughter, Chrissie wonders if her eyes will ever stop filling with tears. Despite the evening's excitement, the long day finally catches up with Eliza, her eyes succumbing to the gravity of sleep. When they exit the room, Shane flopped at the foot of the bed, Catherine is gone, only a short note to mark her departure.

"For the first night of your forever I wish you joy. Don't waste a day, love each other as you both deserve."

Beside the note is a bottle of Pinot Noir, left open to breathe, and two goblets. Before Chrissie can even ask him if he drinks, he is pouring them each a glass, the wine a swirling deep burgundy.

"I'm not much of a connoisseur, but your Mom has good taste, so for the occasion, I'll risk it." The corner of her mouth tips up at the answer to her unspoken question, even as she lifts her glass to touch it against his. "It's been a long time coming, Sunshine, but I can't wait to be your husband. To be your partner, your help meet, and hopefully, father to our children."

Lost in the honesty of his gaze, the thick reassurance of his words, she struggles to form a reply around the old doubts left by her previous marriage. Before she can manage a word, he takes her glass from her nerveless fingers, setting it back on the table beside his own.

"Tell me what you need, Chrissie." Those words come on a breath against her neck as he surrounds her with the strength of his arms, and she yields to the weakness gripping her heart.

"It's not you, James. It's not you." Sobs make the words come out broken, shame filling her to ruin such a beautiful moment, her hands clutching his shirt. "I'm scared."

"Tell me why."

The soft plea is edged with a strangely reassuring command, allowing the bitter truth to spill from her lips.

Better Broken

"I want to have children with you, I really do. And you don't deserve to be lumped in with my ex, not in the least." Every word comes rushed, trying to get it all out before she loses her nerve or her throat closes up. "But he never wanted me the same once I was pregnant. His rejection hurt, but if the same thing happened to us, I couldn't bear it. I can't do without you, James, I just can't."

For a moment, she can't breathe as his arms tighten around her, his full strength brought to bear around her ribcage. The sheer force startles her, halting her tears, then he softens his touch, a careful hand stroking her cheek.

"I take it back. Your ex is not as big an idiot as me. In fact, calling him an idiot is a step up. He's a cretin of monumental proportions."

The sober delivery is belied by a discreet twinkle in his eyes, waking laughter in her. Relief makes her bones watery, but he supports her, shifting to his good leg a little more.

"But there is more, Chrissie."

Straightening, she steels her heart against the seriousness of his tone, worry tightening her face.

"I've wanted you to be the mother of my children since the first night we spent together, watching Andy and Opie walking down the road." he confesses, exposing his heart completely. "And the mere thought of you pregnant has me so turned on it is almost painful." Pressing his hips closer, he watches her eyes lighten at the feel of his hard length between them. "I didn't believe I was enough for you, didn't think I could be whole enough physically or emotionally to be a good dad. You never doubted my strength, Chrissie, even when I doubted myself. Cling to that now, please?"

Silence is the first answer she offers as the tears dry on her face, and his chest tightens with each passing second. Then she shakes herself, giving a half smile that dispels the tension.

"Thank you." Two words, dripping with so much emotion

his own eyes water.

"For what, Sunshine?"

"For being you, my love. For letting me share my darkness. For loving me."

Pressing a kiss against her temple, he feels her lips on his chest. "Thank you for loving me right back, Chrissie."

So much of their past is echoing in to their future in the best way possible, letting her release all the leftover pain of her failed marriage. Everything with him is so much better, so different, there really is nothing to compare it to anyway. She reaches for her glass of wine and he echoes her movement, the goblets touching together between their bodies.

"Marrying you will be one of the greatest joys of my life, but it will be pale in comparison to the day you came back to me, James." A bit of moisture pools in the corners of his eyes and she lifts up on her toes to kiss it away. "I'm yours, for always and in all ways."

They drink down their wine quickly, eyes never breaking contact, and she takes his hand to lead him to bed. Grinning, he tugs her back, kissing her playfully as he puts the cork back in the bottle.

"We'll save this for another night." he says, nipping her bottom lip, eyes darkening when she growls impatiently. "Right now, I'd rather get a better taste of you."

Chrissie flicks on the lights as they enter the bedroom, needing to see, to remember every moment of their coming together. As much as she cherishes the night before, now is even more important. All the furniture that reminded her of Thomas is gone, replaced with a light pine bedstead and dressers that fit the warmth of the room. There are no shadows to dim the memories they will make in this room.

Turning in place, James studies what will become their sanctuary. Thin curtains stir in the faint summer breeze coming in the open French door, and if he isn't mistaken, the bed is covered in the same quilt that had sheltered them in Virginia. A huge painting of the mountains dominates the space over the king sized bed, acting as another kind of window. The comfort of the rest of the house is reflected here as well, everything solid and livable.

"Do you mind if I take the side closest to the bathroom?" he asks, cautiously exploring this new portion of their relationship. Excited as he is, he has never shared space with someone since his injuries, and his missing limb is going to be playing awkward third wheel. "It'll make getting up in the middle of the night easier if I don't have to go as far."

Striding forward, she plucks her phone charger from the bedside table and moves it to the other side before coming back to him.

"Whatever you need to be comfortable, just tell me. Elizabeth necessitated putting no slip footing in the shower, so you'll be good to go there. Do you want to take the bathroom first?"

Hurriedly, he cleans up, shedding his clothes in to the hamper where they mingle with hers. That small thing is representative of their lives coming together, a little messy, but absolutely right.

They trade places, and he settles on the edge of the bed, grateful that it is so tall, making the removal of his prosthetic much simpler. It props in the space beside the nightstand perfectly. Minutes tick by and he fidgets with the hem of his boxers, eager to touch her again. Tonight, he means to prove his devotion to her, fully and completely. It had been difficult to remain calm in the face of her fears, the urge to throttle her ex even now making his fist clench. All that had stopped him from outright anger was the knowledge they wouldn't be together if the man hadn't been a selfish prick. Nor would Elizabeth be around to bless him with her sunny smiles.

When Chrissie walks out of the bathroom, his mouth falls

open at her undeniable beauty. Even in a simple cotton shift her elegant strength affects him. Without hesitation, she comes to his side of the bed, moving between his open thighs to embrace him.

"You look like you belong here, James."

"I do, Sunshine. I belong in your arms." He reinforces the statement by leaning against her chest and sliding his arms around her waist. Kisses press against his scalp, her fingernails scraping gently through his hair, raising goosebumps all over his skin. Her soft skin tastes like salted caramel where he licks across the low neckline of her pajamas.

"Do you still have Mickey Mouse pj's?" he asks conversationally, hands drifting lower to trace her round buttocks, his cock hardening when he finds her without underwear.

Laughter vibrates against his lips as he explores her chest, then stops when he finds her nipple through the thin fabric.

"No, they have been gone a long time." she finally whispers, pulling the tiny straps of her nightgown off her shoulders, then peeling it down.

He leaves it resting below her breasts, looking his fill at her, fingertips tracing the faint stretch marks with reverence. "We'll get you some new ones when we take Lizzy to Disneyland."

"Oh, James." That soft murmur beckons him closer, along with the hand she slides around the back of his neck.

She'll never tire of the way her body thrills to his touch, the gentle suckling at her nipple drawing her to her toes with a hiss. Impassioned strokes travel from her ass to the back of her thighs, dipping between to find her soaking wet.

Looking up at her, a quiver of need moves through every muscle in his body. "I want to taste you so badly, Sunshine. Will you help me?"

The hunger and vulnerability in his eyes pushes away the self-consciousness that threatens her confidence. "Tell me what you need, James."

That simple echo travels along every path to his heart until it sounds like a thousand birds taking wing at once. He tugs her shift off, bending to press kisses against the gentle swell of her belly, lingering on the faded spidery marks left by motherhood. When he straightens her cheeks are pink with discomfort, and he tugs her hand down to touch the largest of his battle wounds.

"You love my scars, Chrissie. Let me love yours."

Palm flattening against his side, sliding around to trace the peppering of rough skin, she kisses him, swallowing his moan when her nails curl along the smoother skin at his spine. He pulls away from the allure of her mouth, still hungry to taste her fully, and lays back on the bed.

"Up here, Chrissie, on your knees." Those clever eyes recognize his intent in less than a second, and she bites her lip, hesitating as a blush starts on her chest.

"I've… never. Like that."

"Well, lucky me." he grins, patting the bed beside his head in challenge. One raised eyebrow is all she allows before breaking eye contact and climbing up his body, deliberately sliding along his rigid shaft with her hand.

Still unwilling to meet his eyes as she moves in to position, she struggles against years of inadequacy before forcing herself to straddle his face. Her ankles hook easily over his shoulders as she opens herself to him, and his hands wrap around her thighs, anchoring her in place. Unsure of what to do next, she fights the urge to squirm, so wet she's afraid she will drip on him.

Knowing the sort of trust she is placing in him, he only takes a moment to study the dark pink of her slit, rubbing his nose in the curls keeping her concealed. A startled gasp greets the simple touch, and he inhales the scent of her arousal, powerful in the knowledge that he makes her so ready. Before she can change her mind he pulls her down, plowing his tongue inside for the first taste, greedy for the sweet evidence of her desire.

The hot contact startles a yelp from Chrissie, and she slaps a hand over her mouth, freezing. James, thankfully, goes still as well, and she looks down her body, finding his eyebrows drawn together in confusion.

"Lizzy." she says, looking over her shoulder toward the door, listening for any stirring from the next room. When everything stays quiet she giggles in embarrassment. "Hand me a pillow?"

He reaches to the side, latching on to a pillow case with two outstretched fingers before tugging it closer so she can grasp it.

"As you were, soldier."

The return of her playfulness wakes a fast response in him, and he applies himself with alacrity, pleased by her stifled whimpers as he licks at her folds. She tastes like heaven, each response to his strokes making his erection leap with the urgent need to be buried in her. Slowly, he shifts his attentions higher, tugging at her thighs so that she settles down against his mouth. The more he savors her, the wetter she becomes, rocking her hips restlessly as he pleasures her. Reaching her clit, he lays his tongue flat against the nub, feeling her throb against him, rolling circles around it. Her cries become sharper, needier, hips rolling forward to press closer, and her thighs begin to tremble with strain. Lifting the pillow from her face momentarily, she begs him for release, unintelligible words mixed around the breathy sound of his name.

Willingly, he shifts again, tightening his arms around her thighs, digging his fingers in to the soft skin as he suckles at her clit with enthusiasm. Her scream is instantaneous, the pillow barely muffling the sound as she bucks over him before falling on to her elbows with a keening sob. Bringing her down slow, he softens his touch, stroking every bit of skin he can reach, marveling at the miracle of her. So responsive, his pleasure is linked directly to hers, and she gives him everything she has every time. Even when he was whole sex was never so satisfying, and she makes it easy to forget that part of him is missing.

Collapsing to the side, Chrissie gasps desperately for air, tossing the pillow away so she can breathe. Pleasure still coasts through her veins as she considers the unlikely possibility of sound proofing their room. Having a lover as focused on giving as getting, enjoying her pleasure as much as she enjoys his is the thrill of a lifetime. Amazingly, he is also hers, for the rest of their lives, firming her resolve to move Lizzy further down the hall. The pillow was only a temporary stop gap in a much longer timeline.

"How do you feel, Sunshine?"

His voice is close and she opens her eyes, smiling at the loving gaze he lays on her. Reaching across the short space between them she touches the waist of his boxers, hooking a finger along his hip.

"I feel like I should return the favor."

The sultry tone of her voice makes his cock sit up and beg, but her heavy eyes tell him exactly how spent she is.

"No, not tonight darlin'. You're done in."

When he leans in for a kiss she licks across his mouth, tasting herself on his lips, the fire he was trying to fight engulfing him completely. Eyelashes alluringly low, her palm slides beneath his shorts, friction against his shaft tightening his back with anticipation.

"I'm not done 'til you are, James."

Going to his back at her soft push, he fondles her breast as

Justine Iarann

she rises up on one arm. Eyes rich with womanly power she tugs his shorts off, guiding them down until he can kick them from his foot. It won't take much to finish him, as hard as he is, but he wants desperately to end this inside her channel, not her mouth. Neither can he deny her what she wants, steeling himself as she leans down, lips soft against his sensitive shaft. Even her breath narrows his focus until all he can do is watch, fists clenched so he doesn't grab her. When the tip of her tongue ventures out he chokes back a growl at the wet tease, but she changes the game, instantly swallowing him to the root, forcing a harsh expletive from his throat. He laughs when a pillow smacks him in the face, which has the added bonus of knocking him back from the precipice, and he breathes deeper for it.

Relief doesn't last, her renewed attentions stoking the pressure building at the base of his spine. Plump lips combined with her hungry tongue unravels his control a stroke at a time, stopping his breath until his lungs ache. She nearly pushes him over the edge, but he scrabbles for supremacy, blindly pushing her on to her back.

As he slides up her body she pulls her knees toward her chest so he can rest on her thighs, leaving herself open to his intrusion. The instant the tip of him clears her entrance he slams himself in to the hilt, balls slapping against her with the force of it. He takes her hard and she arches her back, glorying in being claimed by him. In fact, she fights for it equally as hard, answering his thrusts with fierce abandon, biting her lips against the building cries pressing against her teeth. Endurance stretched to its limits, she capitulates, yielding to bliss with an unhampered wail. Sweat drops from his forehead to slide down her chest and he fixates on it, fisting his hands in the blankets for a few more thrusts. Then he follows her, struggling to stay upright as his release shoots into her hot embrace.

Better Broken

Shaking with a combination of fatigue and satisfaction, they slowly part to rearrange themselves under the covers, boneless limbs tangled together. Before sleep takes them her lips press against his heart. The last thing he hears is her voice, telling him what his heart already knows.

"Welcome home, my love. Welcome home."

Justine Iarann

Epilogue

This time, Suzie walks the aisle ahead of Chrissie with a much lighter heart. It is a short trip down between hay bales lining the barn corridor, but the abundance of smiling faces makes the stroll a happy one. Looking at James, she finds him grinning, the happiness in his eyes warming the whole space. He cuts a handsome figure in deeply creased blue jeans, starched white shirt and a long black wool coat, relaxed but with an edge of anticipation.

When she reaches her spot and turns to face the crowd, her own smile widens at the sight of Elizabeth carefully scattering petals. The concentration wrinkling her brow is a stark contrast to her sunny smile each time she looks up and meets someone's eyes. Each forward step shows a flash of pink cowboy boots under the flouncing hem of her full skirt, adding charm to an already cherubic picture.

They had done little to decorate, just some flowers tied to stall fronts and a draped tulle arch at the front. Chrissie had insisted they spend as little as possible, so they had done much of it themselves, early that morning. Now, the late afternoon sun shines in the entrance, and the fall air is warm, giving everything a pleasant cast.

Better Broken

As Lizzy takes her place beside Suzie, the guitarist, James's brother in law, changes the tune to a gentle country love song. The chords signal Chrissie's entrance perfectly, her shadow stretching the length of the barn. To say she is radiant would do her an injustice, but it is the closest word Suzie can think of. Unlike the past in every way, her hair is down around her shoulders, and the flush on her cheeks accents a ready smile rather than anxiety. The dress is a simple confection, comfortable to move in with a full skirt that almost reaches the ground, but still fitted enough to trace her curves in lace. She walks the aisle alone, her eyes fixed on James as her smile grows, and it prods Suzie to look toward the groom. He stares at Chrissie with a softness that brings up an unfamiliar feeling in Suzie's heart- if she had to give it a name, she would call it jealousy. Yet, for her best friend, she can be nothing but joyful that years of heartache have ended. Now, there is only love glowing brightly in their eyes, coloring everything perfectly.

James steps forward to meet Chrissie, escorting her the last few steps toward the preacher, an older cowboy with thinning white hair and twinkling eyes. Suzie finds herself grinning even more when Chrissie leans into James slightly, tipping her head on to his shoulder with comfortable familiarity. The preacher is a mere technicality, taking them through the simplest vows, saying a blessing over their union, presiding over the exchange of rings. Here, the script changes as Chrissie holds out her hand for Lizzy, and the little girl steps forward to join them. James kneels down, carefully balancing himself with Chrissie's help, and takes Lizzy's other hand.

"Elizabeth Katherine Mason, will you take me as part of your family?" he asks her seriously, the glistening in his eyes hinting at tears.

"I will." Lizzy replies, equally seriously, but then she spontaneously flings herself around his neck, hugging him tightly. "I love you, Daddy James." she whispers, just loud enough for everyone to hear.

The whole gathering sighs a soft "aww" before she lets go, a furious blush on her cheeks. James distracts her, lifting a necklace from his pocket, a silver heart with veins of gold running through it. Her mouth rounds in to an O of surprise, but she tips her head readily so he can slip it on. When James stands back up they all three move together, Chrissie and James leaning in to each other with Lizzy before them.

"It gives me great pleasure to announce you are now not only husband and wife, but also a family in the eyes of God and this assembly." the preacher announces with a broad smile. "You may now kiss your bride, Mr. Fletcher."

He turns to her slowly, lifting a hand to her chin where his thumb strokes her cheek, both of them smiling so hard it's a wonder they manage to touch lips. The instant they do, everything softens, and Chrissie melts against him for a moment, a gentle kiss to treasure for years to come.

They part and move back down the aisle with Lizzy in tow, but the subdued music of the guitar and the well-wishing of friends is broken by a pounding against one of the stall doors. Chrissie's laughter rings out as she opens the door to reveal her big black horse Smoke, who immediately puts his chin over her shoulder to tug her closer. When her arms lift around his neck James and Lizzy step closer to pet the horse as well, so Suzie pulls out her phone to snap a quick photo. For this is the family that Chrissie has always deserved, and Suzie wants to keep this memory close at hand when she heads back home.

Eventually, they all migrate down to the tent erected in the back yard for the reception. The fading sun adds a crisp chill to the air, so Suzie brings up a fur trimmed shrug for Chrissie to pull on, having donned her own moments ago. Chrissie smiles her thanks, but before Suzie can slip away again

Better Broken

Chrissie pulls her closer, tugging on James's elbow to get his attention.

"I know public displays aren't really your thing Suz, but both of us wanted to say thank you together." Chrissie says as James turns toward them. "Without you, we might not have found each other again."

"I'm pretty sure he would have found you eventually anyway." Suzie demurs, blushing and averting her eyes. "He's too crazy about you to not have shown back up eventually."

James takes Chrissie's hand and lifts it to his lips before answering. "Maybe so, but you saved us a lot of fumbling years. For that, and for recognizing how much I love Chrissie, I thank you."

Suzie's cheeks feel like they are on fire in the face of so much praise, but she accepts as graciously as she can.

"You are both welcome, though I did it for you, Chrissie. I have gone most of my life without real, unconditional love until I met you. I couldn't see my dearest friend going without."

"You deserve this kind of love too, Suzie." Chrissie answers with a hug to reinforce her words. "One of these days, it's going to hit you out of the blue."

Catherine appears then, letting Suzie make her escape, heading outside to cool her heated cheeks. As much as she wishes for their kind of love she doesn't know if she can ever trust anyone enough to give her closely guarded heart to them. Too many years of love denied have built walls too hard to tear down.

Hours later, after barbeque has been consumed and the cake is cut, one last surprise remains to be sprung. James and Chrissie are swaying quietly on the tiny dance floor when the DJ calls them out front where a horse and carriage await. It is the perfect ending for the perfect day as the small crowd blows bubbles under the glow of thousands of twinkling lights in the trees. Chrissie turns, and all the single ladies lean forward with anticipation, but she denies them with a shake of her head.

"Suzie?" she calls and Suzie moves forward reluctantly from her position in the back of the crowd, surprised when Lizzy grabs her hand to hurry her along. Chrissie leans down and places her bouquet in Suzie's hands, deliberately making sure her fingers close around the gathered stems.

"I wish you love, Suzie. Wild, sweet, gentle, crazy love." she murmurs between them, tears in her eyes as she turns to take another bunch of flowers from James. She tosses the blooms high in the air where they scatter among the suddenly outstretched hands, gathered up quickly despite the surprise. "I wish you all love." she cries out as the carriage begins to roll, tipping her off her feet and on to James's lap with a giggle.

Suzie watches them leave with a smile on her lips, but when she leans down to press her nose in to the roses in her hands it is so she can hide her tears.

Read Suzie's story in

Softly Shattered

Coming soon!

About the Author:

Justine has spent most of her life catering to the needs of show horses and a large assortment of dogs. Throughout that time, she filled notebooks with hundreds of stories she never finished. These days, she's found cuddling with foals, discussing manners with stallions, and arranging beauty treatments for broodmares. Evenings are devoted to writing happy endings for her imaginary friends, and now that she has started there's no stopping! Most commonly found in the company of her supportive husband. Blessed with several incredible girlfriends who know the value of good tea and great company. While she loves to travel Colorado fills her heart to the overflowing, and will always be her home.

And yes, Smoke is a real horse. So was Warrior.

Want to learn more?

www.JustineIarann.com

https://www.facebook.com/Justineiarann

On Twitter: @Justine_Iarann

Printed in Great Britain
by Amazon